MOTHER LEGS

by

Ty Greenwood

A HellBound Books Publishing LLC Book
Houston TX

A HellBound Books LLC
Publication

Printed in the United States of America

ACKNOWLEDGEMENTS

For my parents, who never stopped believing in me.

For Elsa and Cory, who took time out of their own busy
lives to read my work.

For Jessica and Baylie, who always had a word of
encouragement when I needed it most.

And for Jim Koons, who introduced me to the joys of a
good book.

MOTHER LEGS

Prologue

1992
British Columbia
Canada

She waited until the scientist's family visited to escape. The man was always a little absent minded when they came, taking longer with feeding and forgetting simple routines such as properly latching cages. He was extra inattentive today, his thoughts so overrun with making up for something called *Valentine's Day* to his sweet wife.

The jittery little man remained unaware she could hear his thoughts, each morning feeding her grasshoppers while she perused his mind with leisure. She took pains to hide her talent, keenly aware of how often the word *dissect* flared up whenever any of her brothers or sisters exhibited signs of higher intelligence.

"Ah, you're here," he called as a red-faced woman strode between the two soldiers guarding the entrance. The visitor card dangling from her neck was partially covered by a child's body. Another child trailing behind her with had ruddy blond hair and piercing eyes.

"So glad you could come, took me forever to convince them it was safe for you to visit again."

The woman sniffled. "They raised such a fuss last time."

The man reached out and took the smaller child from the woman, rocking him in his arms. "Well, what do you think?"

The woman shuddered. "You know I don't like it, far too many of the little beasties here."

The man laughed, playfully dipping the child in his arms. "Beasties? Pfft, you're looking at the future of cognitive science."

The other child walked slowly through the room, pressing his face against each of the glass cages to examine the creature's within. *I'd like to pull that one's legs off,* he thought, a smile tugging his lips.

"See," said the man, "our son likes them."

The boy nodded, eyes remaining fixated on the cage's inhabitants.

The woman pursed her lips. "He takes after his father too much."

The man walked over to his son, placing a hand on his shoulder. "Do you want to be like Daddy when you grow up?"

"Of course, Papa," chimed the child. *I want to cut up insects for fun too.*

"There's a good lad," said the man, love for his family washing away what little remaining thoughts he had of his daily duties.

She used this moment to escape, silently crawling to the roof of her cage and squeezing through the tiny slit left open by the scientist's negligence. She'd planned on scampering to the air duct hanging a few meters away, but the cool voice of the child's mind held her in place.

I wish I could weave webs.

She wavered in place, a new potential course of action springing into her mind. Her eight eyes flickered between the air vent and pale skinned boy.

I'd wrap up everyone I didn't like. Starting with my brother.

The tubby woman joined her sons and husband in front of the glass cage. "Just remember to look after mommy when you're rich and famous."

The scientist smoothed the collar of his white lab coat before plucking a kiss on his wife's cheeks. "He won't have to, I will."

Mommy is an idiot, I'd dangle her over a fire.

"Oh stop," giggled the woman, her thick cheeks blooming red. "Why don't we go to the cafeteria for lunch and then you can tell us all about your research?"

"Fantastic plan, what do you say, son?"

I'd make Daddy watch as Mommy burned.

"That sounds great, Daddy."

The family turned towards the door, leaving her with an agonizing choice between freedom or potentially pursuing something more. She stretched out her mind, again digging deeper into the small child's consciousness as he made his way to the door.

After Mommy I'd burn my brother. Only slower.

She blinked twice before scurrying across the floor, leaping for the woman's swinging purse as they reached the doorway. The leather was slippery under her feet but she managed to crawl inside an open pocket before they'd passed the room's guard.

For the first time in her life, she found herself outside the four walls of the lab. Nestled between tampons and lipstick, she curled into a ball, content to listen to the family as they paraded towards the cafeteria.

"Honey," said the woman, "I wish we did this more often."

"Me too, dear, me too."

I wish you were all dead.

Part 1: The Missing Villagers

I want to turn the clock back to when people lived in small villages and took care of each other.
-Pete Seeger
American folk singer and optimist.

Laura

An ugly town situated in one of the most enchanting parts of western Canada, Hope was filled in equal parts with rednecks, nature enthusiasts, and junkies. Most other Canadians ignored the little municipality, deeming it only useful as a place to stop for gas or beer before beginning the treacherous journey along the Coquihalla.

As a rule, there were only two reasons a person lives in Hope: One, they hit rock bottom, or two, they were born there. Laura's mother had been the prior, she'd been the latter. Laura didn't mind though, she enjoyed the beautiful surroundings, and junkies were only a problem if you had things worth stealing.

Besides, rent was cheap.

It had come as a shock to both her friends and mother when she'd moved back home upon finishing university. She chose to settle as a forest ranger, a job nearing volunteer work for how little it paid. Some of the townsfolk gossiped she'd started smoking too much pot or gotten pregnant, but in truth Laura simply enjoyed being outside.

She'd spent her youth driving Hope's gravel roads, climbing the surrounding mountains, spelunking in abandoned mines, and (one time at her then boyfriend's request) hunting. There was peace in the rainy forests surrounding her home she couldn't find elsewhere. Or at least there had been.

Recently, Laura had grown to believe, or at least feel in her gut, something sour brewing in their country town. She felt it, her coworker felt it, even the townsfolk, in their own odd ways, felt it.

It had started with hikers. Normally a few went missing a month, usually tourists who misread the trail markings or old timers who overclocked their tickers while doing their weekly trail walk. Most times they were found within days by the local search and rescue volunteers, a group Laura was a proud member of, but once or twice a year a person vanished without their body being recovered by the impressive search efforts of SAR and its affiliates.

This year there'd been twenty such vanishings, and it was only April.

Laura thought the number might actually be twenty-one, but poor June McCormack was adamant her daughter had run off to live with her Dad and just hadn't bothered to call. At least this is what she said when a needle wasn't jutting from her arm.

Gossip abounded on the subject. Many were fearful of a serial killer while the more drug fueled residents talked of alien abductions. The mayor said it was simply proof wilderness survival needed to be a mandatory class in public school, an opinion in no way influenced by the fact he owned the only outdoor wares store in Hope.

The minister (for lack of a better word) of the Flint Street Church believed the rapture had begun, with God only taking those willing to return to him in nature. One infamous sermon ended with the thirty-person congregation marching naked through town and into the surrounding wilderness with the singular goal of ascending to heaven.

Finding them dehydrated and starving three days later had been a particularly satisfying rescue for Laura, who distinctly remembered the minister calling her a whore as he sauntered past her wearing nothing but a silver crucifix. She'd only been on her way to the store to buy some milk and found the insult quite unnecessary.

As to the disappearances, Laura was of the opinion a serial killer was active. B.C. held the dubious honour of being the home of a statistically high number of serial killers. Pickton, Clifford, The Smiley-Face killer, all lived here. Even Highway of Tears ran through the province, though Laura doubted it was something the tourist office would be quick to brag about.

She remembered when they'd caught Pickton, his ruddy face pressed against the dim screen of their tiny television and making her and her mother recoil in disgust. The news station had done a fine job of honoring his victims, holding a minute of silence followed immediately by a segment on why pigs were the perfect way to dispose of bodies.

Her mother, usually too full of gin to care about the decline of quality journalism, had bothered to turn it off. "Such a shame no one noticed they were *hic* missing." Her definitive statement on the subject immediately followed by some light snoring interrupted by the occasional burp.

Laura thought of this memory as she stepped out of her truck or, more specifically, as she pulled her gun from the backseat. The hunting rifle was old, faded handle bearing the scars of many long years of use. It had been handed down from one Hope forest ranger to another over the last thirty years, seeing its fair share of use in the process. Dennis Lam, the weathered little man Laura replaced, swore it was the only thing that kept him from being mauled by a cougar last winter. Hal told her it was the man's gleaming bald head and poor hygiene deterred the beast and not the three shots he'd fired at it.

The gun wouldn't be the first choice of any professional hunter, but it was enough to comfort Laura during her deeper hikes into the woods. Besides, it still shot mostly straight.

Slinging the old rifle over her back, she clicked her radio to life as her feet started pacing the overgrown trail before her. "Hal, I'm going up Baker's Ridge now, only be an hour or two."

Over the crash of static came a lazy reply, "gotcha, let me know if you need anything."

Harold Jones was her partner. Middle aged, currently undergoing divorce, with one child he hadn't seen in three weeks. Laura loved him, but she wouldn't say he was the heart and soul of their ranger outpost. Hal spent most mornings nursing a hangover and most afternoons stoned. The only time he showed any initiative was when he helped with search and rescue, a task he occasionally performed without complaining.

"I will." She took a deep breath of the crisp mountain air, a contented smile covering her lips. "See you soon."

"Excellent, I want to burn one." A true gentleman, waiting until Laura finished exploring the wilderness to smoke a joint. Well, maybe a true gentleman would have come with her, but this was Hope, Laura would take what she could get.

"Will do partner."

The radio cracked static twice, their cordial way of saying "OK" without having to burn the half calorie it took to speak. She reciprocated the gesture before replacing the radio on her belt.

It was sunny out and warm for April. They'd been spared usual torrential rains, but it hadn't affected plant growth any. Baker's Ridge's path was nearly overgrown with tall green grass, some of it had been visibly parted, likely by Joe Santos yesterday, but to a nonlocal it would be hard to tell a path existed here at all.

As she slunk deeper into the forest she found relief from the sun but not the heat. Even in the shade it was a scorcher, a fact evidenced by the sweat now dripping from her arms and face.

Baker's Ridge was a short but winding hike, it ended at a small lake (pond really) that some of the old timers were adamant still harboured a healthy supply of fish. Laura had never seen a fish there, but she liked the hike.

She found herself so entranced by the gentle lull of swaying trees and tapping melody of her own footsteps that she nearly forgot the reason she'd came. Already over a kilometer from the entrance she shook her head and called out for the first time.

"Hello?"

Her words hummed through the forest. She waited for a minute, scratched her head and began walking again.

She could have turned back after not receiving an answer, they had already searched the place twice, but the deciduous trees already had most of their leaves and the greenery was inviting. Laura never could turn down a good hike.

She hummed as she went, a catchy pop song about bad boyfriends that had been overrunning the radio waves the past week.

Laura had no doubt Joe Santos had heard voices at Baker's while fishing the other day, only it was unlikely to have been one of Hope's missing citizens. It's common for forest rangers to attribute unexplained noises in the woods to teenagers smoking pot, in Hope they simply removed the teenagers part.

Hal had said as much when Joe had come in during their morning coffee, "don't bother, Laura, we all know it's just some local getting some *fresh air*," this was accompanied by an over the top smoking motion that was, frankly, insulting to Laura's intelligence.

She was halfway through the hike. Sweat now poured from her brow. It really was hot.

The trees were taller here, their towering bodies casting shade so deep it was only pinpricked by the most determined of sunbeams. It wasn't even three o'clock, but Laura figured night would fall soon. Far off, a bird sang, its sweet song catching in Laura's ear and causing her to stop humming and listen. When the bird song died it was followed by something else.

"Hello?" A soft voice called out, distant and echoing.

Laura stopped abruptly. Unable to tell where the voice came from, she cupped her hands to her mouth and shouted to the sky. "Hello? Who's there?"

"Hello?" The voice was closer now. Laura craned her head intently as it continued in a soft whisper of which she only made out a few words. "I'm… me."

Laura walked calmly from the path towards the voice, careful to note her surroundings as she went. "Where are you? Do you need help?"

"Yes… Hello?" Laura had walked nearly ten meters before it came again, remaining surprisingly distant despite her pace, "I want… mommy?"

"What's wrong? How do you need help? Are you hurt?" The surrounding foliage grew thicker as she walked, she found herself having to squeeze between two trees simply to keep going.

"I'm. Me. Help?"

Laura unhooked her radio and called out. "Hal, I have a possible injured party up here, can you dispatch?"

Hal's response was immediate. "Shit. Really? I mean yeah, I'll get Andy on the phone right away."

Andy was the town's ambulance dispatcher, a fat old man with a heart (in Laura's opinion) the size of a fucking planet.

"Help? Me. I'm…" the voice called again, its sound being quickly engulfed by the surrounding mass of bark and leaves.

Laura raised her walkie, "sounds like shock, maybe drugs."

"Roger, I'll let Andy know. Keep me posted."

She clicked her walkie twice and began to look slowly around. Shades of green and brown struck out from every direction, even the warm blue of the sky eclipsed by the towering trees.

"Where are you? I'm here to help."

This time the whispering was in her ear. "Can't you see I'm…?" She whirled around, finding only tree trunks and moss behind her.

A chill crept down her spine. "I need you to keep talking so I can find you, who are you?"

"I'm.. me. Can't you see… me? I'm."

A tight unease knitted Laura's stomach, she'd helped more than her fair share of tripping junkies in her life and not one of them had sounded as strange as this voice. "I can't see you, can you describe what's around you?"

"I'm. Me. You… front."

This time the words were clear enough for Laura to note her familiarity with the speaker. With a gasp she spoke out, "Jenna, is that you? It's alright, dear, I've come to help you."

"I'm. Me. Jenna." The young girl's voice, her words growing clearer as they ran sweetly through Laura's ears. "I'm Jenna."

"Jenna, we've all been so worried. Where are you?" Sweat now ran profusely down Laura's arms and face, her hand running slippery across the radio as she pulled it from her belt.

From far to her right she heard a response. "I'm Jenna. Where are. Me?" A tinkling of child's laughter followed the words, ringing out through the thicket and into the sky.

Laura rushed towards the sound. "I'm coming, Jenna," she called before clicking on her radio. "Hal, I hear Jenna McCormack. I think she's hurt."

Hal's breathless response was barely audible over the beating of her own heart. "Jesus Christ."

"Where are you, Jenna?" she called again. "Hal, I need you to get SAR out here, I can't find her."

"On it," Hal's voice cracked over the radio, bringing Laura slight relief which quickly dissipated when Hal's voice called out again, this time not from her walkie-talkie but from a huddle of trees far to her left. "On it."

Laura froze, unsure if her mind was playing tricks on her in this dark patch of forest. Hal's voice called out again, as scratchy as if it had rung through the radio in her hand but this time from her far right.

"On it."

She spun around, scouring the tree line for a sign of Hal. The radio remained quiet on her hip. "Who's there?" She unslung the gun. "If this is a prank I guarantee you're getting a fine."

For an intolerably long moment, silence filled the air. No birds chirped, or animals cried. Even the gently swaying trees seemed uninterested in breaking the suffocating silence. When the voice finally did return it was with a garbled crash, making Laura flinch slightly as the gun bounced in her hand.

"On it. On it."

This time the source of the voice was clear. Laura marched boldly forward through the thicket, branches and vines lashing at her face and arms as she struggled to push herself forward. With a curse she barreled through the foliage until a mighty crash of twigs and dirt brought her breathlessly into a small clearing.

Blood dripped unnoticed from Laura's forehead, her attention overcome by the looming face of a little girl. The girl's dress was torn and dirty, mud caked her shins and arms. Her head turned down as she stood like a bored marionette.

"Jesus Christ, Jenna? Oh my god I almost shot you." Laura said as she lowered the gun.

The girl pulled her head back in an awkward fashion, staring up at the sky in an angle that made it seem as if she might tip over backwards. Her arms dangled limply from her shoulders.

"What's wrong, Jenna? Oh god, you're hurt." Laura could see the outline of a cut along part of the girl's neck, the blood around it was rust coloured and caked to her skin.

"I'm me. Hurt." The girl continued staring at the sky as she spoke, her body lurching backwards if she was doing some sick limbo. "I'm Jenna."

From somewhere in the trees behind them, Hal's voice rang out again. "On it."

Laura flinched, her heart beat so fast it physically hurt. She coughed a garbled cry, noticing Jenna's feet for the first time.

The cute little feet Laura used to pull and tickle when she babysat for Karen, the feet that squirmed and kicked as when they were forced into shoes for school, the feet that spent their days getting wet and muddy in the school's pond after every rainfall, weren't touching the ground.

They were dangling, bouncing lazily through the air as the girl's body jerked and flailed about.

Laura sucked in her breath, biting her tongue so hard warm blood leaked into her gums.

Jenna spoke again, for the first time Laura saw her lips weren't moving. "I'm me. Help? Me."

Jenna's tiny body gave another jerk, her shoulders jumped up and her head snapped forward. On its downward arc Laura saw Jenna's whole face for the first time.

Laura's scream was pitched, it carried for miles and sent a nearby flock of birds into the air. "Jesus Christ, Jesus Christ." Her fingers clenched so tight around the gun that the old wood frame began splintering.

"On it," came Hal's scratchy voice again.

Jenna's whole body tilted diagonally, her arms reaching loosely towards Laura while her legs bent and her feet pushed into the dirt. Her top shoulder pulled back, forcing a side of her face to look up at Laura. "Help? Hurt."

One dead eye looked out at Laura, shrouded in tangles of dirty blonde hair. The girls mouth hung open, unable to fight the downward pull of gravity from this angle. Her teeth were covered in dirt and grime.

Laura jumped backwards, landing heavily on her tailbone. The gun went off, an angry crack which didn't elicit even the slightest flinch from Jenna. Over the ringing in her ears Laura heard Hal's voice again, "on it."

Laura began to crawl backwards, scraping the bottom of her thighs painfully across an upturned root as she did. "Jesus Christ. Jesus Christ. Jesus Christ."

Jenna began to glide towards her. Legs bouncing up and down exaggeratedly each time, while her torso drooped forward. "Hurt. Me. Hurt. Me," chanted the girl as she approached.

Laura tried to get up, but her own limbs were fighting her, even her tongue felt sluggish in her mouth. "H-h-how?" Soon the dead girl was dangling over her, arms and legs drifting languidly in the breeze while her jaw hung open to allow a stream of blood and other liquids to dribble onto Laura's face and chest.

"Hurt. Me. Hurt. Me. Hurt," continued the chanting. The voice appeared to be emanating from Jenna, despite her dead eyes and drooping jaw.

Hurt me. Hurt me. Hurt me.

A snapping sound hissed through the trees as the girl's stinking body fell on Laura. She pushed her away, terror flooding her body as her fingers sunk into rotten flesh while the horrid stench of death burned her nostrils. With a cry she shoved the girl from her body, revolted as some of the child's putrefied skin clung to her own fingers like a bloodied paste.

She could still hear the girl's voice, now drifting down from above. "Hurt me. Hurt me." The girl's laugh came again, this time surrounding Laura from all directions. "Hurt you."

With terror choking her lungs and mind, Laura looked up to see what had dropped the child's corpse, the scream rising to her throat never escaping her lips.

Interlude
1992

The house was large. Six bedrooms, three bathrooms, a spacious basement, and a kitchen rivalling most restaurants. Only four humans lived in it. The spider passed her days watching them.

It kept its web small, hidden in a corner of the kitchen unreachable by the woman. She had a particular dislike of eight legged beings. More than once she had watched the fat woman extinguish the life of one of her less intelligent brethren, muttering as she brought a thick newspaper down on their spines. "Disgusting little creatures, lord knows how many are hiding in this house."

The children spent most of their time outside, playing in the yard and surrounding woods. The mother only bothering to check on them every few hours, while the spider kept constant watch.

She could sense the child's presence farther away than any other being, only losing track of him on the occasions the woman or man bundled him into their automobile and drove off into the nearby town.

The child's interests were of constant amusement to the spider. Each day the boy would invent a new form of torture for his smaller brother, taking special care to ensure the little one couldn't prove his brother's guilt. Yesterday he'd put two dead bees in the small boy's shoes, laughing when one of the bug's stingers got stuck in the child's tiny foot. Today he'd tied some spare twine between trees and made his brother trip while running to catch a Frisbee he'd "accidentally" thrown past the yard.

These tricks inevitably lead to the smaller boy running inside to be held by his mother. The woman would pretend to care, waiting until the boy calmed so she could sit him in front of their television and open a bottle of wine. Most days the woman would drink until the spider had trouble following her thoughts, only stopping on the odd occasion the father phoned to inform her he'd be home in time for dinner.

When his little brother had left him for the false care of their mother, the boy would be free to play alone. Most days he would romp the yard, imagining himself a king or president set to rule over the land. His subjects were the rodents and insects populating the vast yard, they were unruly citizens and the boy often found them deserving of punishments such as limb removal or burning via magnifying glass.

The spider noted how carefully the boy stopped his activities when his mother or father came out to see him, his thoughts flickering to something called a "shrink." The spider understood humans, in their baser stupidity, frowned upon the boy's exceptional disposition. This made her love the boy even more.

If one flaw marred the boy's perfect mind, it was that he lacked spider's gift of hearing. Night after night the spider tried to say hello to the boy, blasting him with every ounce of her mental strength while the boy lay sleeping in his bed. So far he hadn't responded, but she'd noticed he'd begun dreaming of webs more frequently.

One night he'd murmured about arachnids in his sleep, this made her quiver with joy. The boy would learn to listen to her, they would be friends. All it would take was time.

Blake

Blake slammed the trailer door, the noise waking Ms. Brightly from her afternoon siesta. She waved a middle finger from across the way, screaming something about manners as she did.

Blake ignored her, setting a quick pace into town.

He hadn't cried since he'd been nine and found what little the coyotes had left of his pet cat Ruffles. He hadn't cried a year later when his father left for a fishing trip with a suitcase and no rod, or the year after that when a drunk driver ran down his older sister Linda as she walked home from her minimum wage job at Dairy Queen.

Blake became a master at repression, just like adults.

When his mother started using again and money grew scarce, he didn't complain, instead choosing to spend more time at the same Dairy Queen that employed his sister and less time at school. His grades suffered but it kept them afloat.

When his mother disappeared altogether he suppressed every juvenile impulse he could, dropping out entirely to provide for his little sister like an adult.

And his reward for being a productive member of society? The government forced his aunt on him.

His aunt who hadn't called once in the last ten years, his aunt who hadn't shown up to Linda's funeral, his aunt who spent most of her government allotted childcare benefits on beer and cigarettes. His aunt whose only qualification to care for his sister was being twenty-nine while Blake was seventeen.

Blake's blood still simmered as he arrived at the hotel. He stopped across the road from it, placing his wallet and cellphone in the gnarled branches of a large elm before continuing.

The building was tallest in Hope. Although the sun hadn't set, its red neon letters were already bright in the sky. AINSFIELD HOTEL was what they read now, when the sun descended from its lofty perch the sign would transform into A FIELD HOT, it had been two years since the N and S had burnt out and six since the I, E, and L.

Outsiders wondered how a hotel could turn a profit by only charging thirty dollars a month per room, locals only wondered why the police hadn't bothered to close it down. Blake wondered why junkies would pay to live here when there were so many abandoned cabins at the edge of town. The cabins were certainly cleaner.

Blake pushed cautiously through the dingy front door, greeted by the smell of cigarettes, pot, and what was most definitely feces. Last time he'd come he'd asked the concierge if his mom had been in, today the same man was passed out with an unlit cigarette in his mouth. Blake didn't bother waking him.

An out of order sign clung to the elevator's metal exterior, forcing Blake to brave the smoke-filled stairwell to reach the second floor. The hallways were drab. Stained grey carpet met walls of equally dirty linoleum. Most doors were open. Inside the room, bodies littered floors and couches in equal measures.

A few of the soberer individuals eyed Blake warily, hands reaching clumsily to cover wallets, needles, or exposed flesh as he passed by. Most simply ignored him.

His search was methodical. Room by room, making sure to look in each closet and bathroom no matter how wretched the sight or smell. When he was occasionally accosted by a junkie he pushed them away with a surprising gentleness, thankful he'd bothered to put his wallet in a tree before walking in.

Searching the second and third floor left him with nothing but unpleasant memories, the fourth floor was worse.

Blake had seen three dead bodies in his life. His sister at her funeral, his grandfather at his, and a tourist pulled from the river while Blake had been taking his sister for a walk. He'd found the corpses unsettling, leading to the occasional nightmare and sleepless night. It didn't bring him comfort to know people could look worse alive than dead.

The woman was strapped to a gurney, writhing against her restraints like a wild animal. Foam dripped from her mouth, her eyes bulging so wide it was hard to spot the pupil in the sea of white. Her face was skull-like, hollow looking with most of its hair gone.

Even now strands were slipping from her scalp, drifting away with each wild thrash of her head.

Two men were with her, one forcefully holding her down while the other knelt on the floor to rifle madly through a large case of vials and syringes.

The woman shrieked, it was high pitched like a banshee and accompanied by a large spray of spittle. "Don't you touch me, I want my daughter."

The man holding her had bright blonde hair and healthy supply of muscle, his voice was calm as he spoke. "It's ok, Mrs. McCormack, we're here to help."

The woman turned to look at the man, her body becoming still for a moment. She tilted her head to gaze at him, pausing for a moment before violently snapping her head towards him. She snarled like a dog, teeth gnashing as she tried to bite him. The blonde man sighed as he moved his arms away from her twisting head.

The other man rose from his bag. He was large in weight and height, he held a needle proudly in the air. He walked towards the gurney, his low voice pouring out like honey. "It's alright, Mrs. McCormack, I've got something to help you sleep."

The woman snarled before articulating her thoughts, "Don't let that dirty goat fucker touch me."

If the man was offended, he didn't show it. He continued forward, bending over to slip the needle into her skin. When the man removed the needle, the woman looked up helplessly, her skinny arms ceasing their struggle and drooping towards the floor while her wide eyes begin to dim. She uttered a final soft sentence. "I want my daughter."

The blond man slouched forward, using the rails on the gurney for support. "Jesus Christ."

The other man stood still, looking over the skeletal body before them. "Yep."

The blond man wiped his brow, sweat had stained through his white collared shirt. "She made such good progress this last year too."

"Yep."

Eventually the blond man stood up straight, his breath no longer long and ragged. He turned the gurney around, catching his full frame in the dim hotel light. To Blake the man appeared angelic, hovering protectively over the frail body of one of God's creations. It was an illusion quickly shattered when the man spotted him. "Fuck, Blake, what are you doing here?"

Realizing he'd been lurking in a fashion more akin to the hotel's inhabitants than himself, Blake walked towards the two men and breathing corpse. "Sorry, Glen, didn't mean to scare you."

The blonde man frowned. "Blake, you know it's not safe here."

Blake shrugged, turning his gaze to his feet. The other man appeared even larger now that he was no longer examining the patient, he turned to meet Blake with bright eyes. "You must be Mr. Turner."

Glen began to twist the gurney towards the stairs, he nodded his head to his colleague. "Blake, this is Dr. Nand. He volunteers with the first responders on his days off."

Blake stuck out a hand awkwardly, Dr. Nand shook it with a warm but slightly sweaty grip. "I'm afraid your mother isn't here, Mr. Turner." Blake tilted his head up to look at the man, a frown forming on his lips.

Glen's friendly voice echoed from near the stairwell. "It's alright, Blake, I told him about her. We've been keeping an eye out."

Blake kept his eyes on the Doctor, having the decency to mumble. "Oh... thanks."

The Doctor gave a wide smile, his teeth stark white against his brown skin. "Brave young man coming into a place like this." His smile continued as a large hand rose to wipe sweat from his brow. "Why don't you help Glen wheel Ms. McCormack down the stairs?" He scratched his balding head vigorously, "I'm sorry to say I'm not the physical specimen I was at your age."

Blake still had two more floors to search, he started to stutter out an apology but was stopped midsentence by the warm look from Dr. Nand. "I guess I could help."

The doctor slapped his hands together, turning with good humor much at odds with his surroundings. "Atta boy." Glen, for his part only gave a tired smile.

The gurney and its occupant were light, but the stairs were narrow and twisting. Blake, a fit young man, still tired from carefully hauling the body down.

At first, he was disgusted by looking at the woman with her missing teeth and a wretched supply of hair, but soon his revulsion was overcome by pity. He knew who she was, everyone in the town did. He wondered if it might have been kinder for Glen and Dr. Nand to simply let her die.

When they emerged into the hotel lobby the concierge was now awake and smoking his cigarette. He gave them one slight look of interest before returning his gaze to a small portable television blaring before him.

Dr. Nand, walking slowly behind them, gave a sad shrug. "Guess he hasn't heard the news about indoor smoking yet."

Glen let out a weak laugh as he pushed through the front door. "It's only been illegal for eight years."

Dr. Nand moved forward to help hold the door. "Oh my, your backups arrived."

In the fading light of the dusty street were parked two ambulances, their lights off and two paramedics huddled before them smoking. The paramedics gave a cursory head nod as Glen and Blake rolled Ms. McCormack onto the street.

Glen let go of the gurney, pulling a crumpled pack of cigarettes from his pocket as he walked over to join the two smokers. Blake stood awkwardly beside Ms. McCormack, unsure of what he should do.

Dr. Nand joined him, smirking at the three paramedics chattering in the haze of smoke. "I keep telling them, they should quit the darts, but do they listen?"

Blake's eyes remained focused on Ms. McCormack, she had started to snore.

"Do you smoke, Mr. Turner?"

A trickle of drool escaped the woman's lips, Blake wiped it with a napkin from his pocket. "Not cigarettes."

Dr. Nand sighed and sat down on the sidewalk curb. The skin around his eyes was stretched, thick cracks forming in his otherwise smooth skin. "I guess that's half the answer I wanted." Blake suppressed a laugh as the man raised an e-cigarette in his mouth. The metal tip glowed bright red when the doctor inhaled.

"Trying to quit?"

Dr. Nand shrugged, more to the floor than Blake adding, "My son's four."

Glen returned from his coworkers, the thick smell of tobacco clinging to him. "You know smoking ruins your choirboy image," said Dr. Nand as he put away his own cigarette.

Glen let out a sparkling grin, "Good, I want the ladies to know what a bad boy I am."

"More the pity, why were they so late?"

Glen flicked his head back towards the paramedics who were climbing back into their ambulance. "Another overdose at the same time, up near Ladner."

A note of exhaustion crept into Dr. Nand's voice. "Jesus, they save them?" Blake's heart started to race, he hadn't bothered to check up Ladner when his mom went missing.

Glen shook his head. "Dead on arrival, their guess is Fentanyl but who knows." He noticed the look on Blake's face. "It wasn't anyone from town, they think it was a camper. Probably looking to make their weekend a little more relaxing."

Dr. Nand chuckled. "Guess they're pretty relaxed now."

Blake frowned but Glen laughed. "Dead to the world, man."

Ms. McCormack's snores were interrupted by a dry groan.

Glen sighed. "Guess we shouldn't underestimate her ability to metabolize sedatives." He opened the doors to his own ambulance, Blake helped him lift the small woman into the back. "I'm going to get her to the hospital and sick her on some poor RN." A mischievous grin played across his face, "I don't want to have to listen to her bitch about us killing her high when she wakes."

Dr. Nand nodded. "Ah yes, our just reward for saving a life."

Glen slammed the ambulance doors and walked around to the driver's side. "Thanks for your help Blake, believe me when I say we're keeping an eye out for your mom."

Blake waved as the man drove off, leaving only a spluttering cloud of smoke in his tracks.

"Jesus, they need a new ambulance," sighed Dr. Nand, turning to Blake "You want a ride home? I'm calling it a night." He let out a yawn. "Been up since five."

Blake looked through the thinning cloud of smoke at the hazy orange sky, if he left now he could make it up Ladner a half hour before the sun set. It would give him plenty of time to see if his mother, or at least her corpse, was around.

"No thanks, Dr. Nand. I think I'd rather walk."

Dr. Nand laughed, it was deep and warm. "At least someone exercises in this town. Here, take my card, call if you need me," he said before disappearing behind the faded brick of the hotel towards its parking lot while Blake stood holding his plain white business card.

He stared for a minute, wondering what would make a man spend his free time putting up with the citizens of Hope, when the minute ended he began the walk to Ladner. It was slow and uphill.

Interlude
1995

The spider was three years old when the boy started going to school. She was the size of a football and lived in the boy's closet. Once the little brother had found her, but the mother had only laughed when he told her, scolding him for making up stories.

The spider didn't mind when the boy went to school. Their bond was now so strong the miles between the house and school were irrelevant. The spider could hear the boy's thoughts, feel what he felt. If they both concentrated, they could see through each other's eyes. At school the boy learnt about the human world and the spider learnt with him.

He was a quick learner, faster than his peers in acquiring the knowledge of letters and numbers. The spider, who struggled to understand the humans' strange rules and customs, was proud of him. She was even prouder when the boy showed the same aptitude in learning about her world.

In the beginning it was simple hunting, catching frogs and squirrels for the spider to eat. The boy couldn't spin a web or stick to walls, but he could tie a rope as intricate as any trap devised by insects and his reflexes were sharp. The spider remembered how the boy had once slapped a delicious hummingbird out of the air, striking out a skinny arm in the breadth of a second as the tiny bird flew by them in the woods.

The boy was also adept at lying. In the spider's world lying meant feints of movements, crawling left when the prey expected right. In the boy's world it was different, he had to pretend he was a human, a normal boy, not the exceptional creature he was.

At this, the boy excelled too. His teacher loved him, his mother was always talking about how smart he was, and even his brother (who was routinely tormented by the boy) constantly thought of playing with him, all while the boy hid his thoughts of murdering them all.

There were other lessons; patience, agility, how to hear with the mind as well as the ears, and the boy learned them all.

There was only one problem in the early years; the boy's father.

Where the boy's teacher and mother saw genius, the father saw secrets. Where the boy's brother saw playground accidents the father saw malicious intent. Sometimes in the deep of night when all the others were sleeping, the spider found the father thinking of the boy, wondering if he was truly the perfect child his peers touted him to be.

The spider was troubled, but time was on her side. The father was a slow man to act, burdened by worries far exceeding that of most other humans. His thoughts about his son's behavior were brief and his thoughts of acting on it were briefer yet.

Still, he would eventually act, taking time off work to be with the boy more or paying the money to send him to the strange thing he called a "psychiatrist."

The spider would stop this. It was necessary.

Laura

The first thing she noticed was the tips of her hair were wet. Long strands skimming a puddle on the floor, sending shivers up her spine. The second thing she noticed was the smell, wet stone and wood, unmistakable to a lifelong hiker.

A cave.

Or something like.

Narrow and dark. She tried to scream but was only able to push out a groggy murmur. She felt like too much blood had filled her head. The fact she was dangling from the ceiling didn't help.

Her extremities were distant, she could wiggle her toes with great effort but little more.

At first the world around her was pitch black, an engulfing dark that seemed to have swallowed every little speck of matter in the world. After an hour her eyes adjusted, allowing her to make out the faintest outlines of her surroundings. Somewhere far away, light trickled in.

It was quiet, no wind, no dripping water, only Laura's groggy cries and the calm breathing of her neighbour.

She wasn't sure how close they were, a meter, a mile, it was impossible to tell how well sound traveled wherever she was. Regardless, she could hear them. Not speaking, not crying, only breathing calmly. In and out, in and out, the same way Laura's yoga instructor would have them do at the end of every class.

Laura was scared. A few tears rolled up her forehead, beginning to wet her hair from the other end. "Please… please…"

Her tongue rebelled against her, lapping sluggishly in her mouth as she tried to croak out a prayer.

"Please God... please God…"

The dark places only other occupant's breathing continued peacefully, unchanging in the face of Laura's tiny break of silence.

"Oh God. Help God."

Laura's own breathing was getting faster. She could weakly wiggle her arms now, her tongue slowly escaping its paralysis.

"Oh God, oh God, oh God."

She tried kicking her feet, lamely pushing against whatever rope or net she was wrapped in.

"Why me? Why me?"

Her voice was gaining in volume, she'd managed to start swinging her body. She pushed in rebellion against whatever substance had cocooned her from the ceiling. Soon all her muscles were alive and screaming, sweat dripped over her face and into the puddle below. She found a voice, finally able to raise it above a whisper.

"Help. Anyone. Help."

After the echoes of her cry died down, the only sound was her ragged breathing and the soft, calm breaths of whoever she shared the dark enclosure with.

"Help. Please, anyone."

She wriggled and screamed, swaying in her upside-down prison but getting no nearer to freedom. The darkness' other occupant's breathing continued calmly. Laura was reduced to tears. "I can hear you breathing, asshole, say something." She let out a choked sob. "Anything."

The soft sound of exhalation continued, her plea unanswered.

Blake

Blake thought about buying a water bottle from the tiny convenience store near the trail head entrance, painfully remembering he'd left his wallet hidden outside the Ainsfield hotel. Shaking his head, he started up the dirt path. Every year some asshole died because they got lost on this trail and forgot to bring water, but Blake was past the point of caring.

It hadn't rained in a week but mud still filled the trail. He could make out the tracks of the paramedic's stretchers in it, thin ruts in the dark goop. Within minutes of walking in it his sneakers were ruined.

"Always be prepared," he muttered, thinking of his singular year as a boy scout. His words causing him to do something he hadn't done in months: laugh. It was a sorrowful little thing that died in his throat but not his eyes.

It was a briefly happy moment, only ruined when a similar laugh echoed out of the woods around him.

At least he thought it had, he couldn't quite discern the direction it had come from. With his smile fading he continued forward. Night was coming and he'd need to be quick if he wanted to get a decent search in.

Hal

Hal was having a bad year. His wife was gone, which he didn't mind, and she'd taken his child with her, which he did. Last month he'd been passed up for transfer to a desk job he desperately wanted and a week ago his partner had gone from investigating missing persons to being one.

His only respite was alcohol and pot (consumed in amounts his doctor found abhorrent) and the occasional nature walk.

Today's hike was the first one made in a month solely for pleasure. He'd spent nearly every waking moment of the last seven days scouring the local wilderness, calling out Laura's name and praying he would stumble over her unconscious body as opposed to her dead corpse. He was exhausted.

He wanted to sleep but he couldn't at home. A tiny apartment surrounded by too many neighbours was no place for relaxation and the ranger cabin was only good for a nap in the afternoon to alleviate a hangover. So he'd packed up his backpack, grabbed his tiny tent, and sputtered his truck up to the Ladner trail entrance.

The hike from the trail head was an hour long, difficult only in its slight elevation. His knees burned when he reached the summit, but they were the only part of his body to do so.

Near the top was a little clearing, enclosed from the rest of the world but open to the sky. When the sun set he'd be able to see the stars and it looked like the night would be warm enough to sleep without worrying of a chill. He'd already set up the tent and lit his first joint when he noticed the body.

It was slumped against a log, fat head drooped forward at an uncomfortable angle. Initially, Hal thought they'd fallen asleep. It gave him a fright when he called out and didn't wake them.

It wasn't the first body he'd found, it wouldn't be the last, but it certainly put a damper on his weekend getaway.

The paramedics joked about it when they arrived, fucking assholes, telling Hal the only useful things he did were off the clock.

They were quick to call DOA and even quicker to brush off the need for police. The cornucopia of drugs in the deceased's backpack gave them a sporting chance on guessing the cause of death. With all the fentanyl being pumped through the province it was miracle it was the only body they'd found that day.

One of the paramedics offered to help Hal bring his stuff down but Hal declined. "If finding a corpse stopped me from camping somewhere there'd be nowhere left in Hope to go." It was an exaggeration but not a large one.

The paramedic had only laughed and lit a cigarette. "Ah well, if you find another one can you dump it? It's tough work pulling the stretchers up here." They were a dark lot, Paramedics.

They wheeled the corpse away while Hal returned to his lawn chair to smoke an incredibly thick jazz cigarette and drift off to some rock music that wasn't even popular in the decade it was released in. He managed to regain some of the calm the body had blasted away, closing his eyes and drifting under the gentle kiss of the sun.

It lasted a whole hour before the screaming ruined it.

At first he thought it was part of the song, then he thought it was birds. By the time his ash stained brain managed to comprehend what was happening it had been going on for five minutes. "Oh fuck."

He rose unsteadily, looking around. The sun was fading from the sky, casting a soft orange glow over the sea of green and brown around him.

"Oh fuck."

He'd brought a first aid kit, if you could call thirteen band aids, some gauze, and a bottle of ethanol a first aid kit, but he didn't want to use it. Laura had been the better medic, always quick to take over when he hauled in some hiker with a broken arm or twisted ankle.

"Hello?"

The screaming continued. It was hoarse and causing birds to erupt angrily from the thicket. Hal moved to the edge of his clearing, he was sure of the direction it was coming from but he hesitated a while.

Rumours of a serial killer in the woods had abounded since Hal had been a boy. It was something people talked about to make camping with boring relatives more bearable. He'd never really believed it, even after the disappearances started. Still, when he stepped to the edge of his quaint little campsite he wondered what had happened to Laura, if it was safe to run towards the screaming without a gun or some bear mace.

With a shrug, he proceeded anyways.

Laura

Her voice grew coarse as the cruel daggers of dehydration began to dig into her mind. She didn't know how long she'd been screaming for. No one had come, the infernal breathing had continued, and she wasn't even capable of shedding tears anymore.

Things were bleak. So bleak Laura, a lifelong optimist, found herself descending into the realm of utter depression. Alone in the dark she gave up hope of rescue and accepted a philosophy Hal had always cynically spouted; life was complete bullshit.

In the oppressive dark she closed her eyes and waited for her life to end, unwilling to believe things could get worse.

It seemed her futility could not increase when, far away, she heard the soft patter of footsteps.

It couldn't be true. They were getting closer. Echoing down the cavern to her prison.

Her spirit rose, soaring out of the depths of despair and into the clouds of happiness and faith in humanity Hal refused to believe existed. She was being saved.

She screamed out in pleasure. "Help, I'm in here." The footsteps sped up. She wondered who it was, maybe it was Andy from the ambulance or Ricky from search and rescue. Christ, it might even be Hal if she was lucky, the man did a lot to numb his brain but no one could deny he was a competent forester.

"I'm tied up, can you come quick?"

A voice called out, "Be right there." It reverberated through the tunnel. Laura felt a wave of relief, it was familiar.

"Oh thank God. I don't know how long I've been stuck here." Light sprung from down the hall, the brightness of it blinding her eyes. Behind it was the outline of a person.

"Well look who's awake." The person walked over. To Laura's sweet relief they put their flashlight down, liberating her from the burning of her eyes.

Laura whimpered, the tears she thought she'd exhausted began to flow again. "I've been in the dark for so long. I thought I was going to die here."

She felt a hand on her stomach, pressing against the mesh encapsulating her body. "Yes, she'll do nicely I think."

"Please, can you cut me down? I want to go home, I want to see my mom." The hand gave her a gentle nudge and she began to spin, not fast but enough to make her brain swim. "I want to see my mom."

"I know her from town. Strong and smart, perfect."

A hand reached out of the darkness and grabbed her waist, stopping her spin. Fighting the vertigo, her eyes struggled to focus. The light was at her back now, casting dimly across the surrounding area.

She could make out bending stone walls and wooden rafters. In the distance something was moving towards her. Creeping at the edge of the shadows with steps making only the softest of patters on the stone floor.

Laura began to cry harder. "Oh please, I just want to go home." Her voice cracked, "I miss my mom."

"Shush girl, forget your mother," rattled the stern voice.

Laura heard a faint clatter on the stone. Something rustled imperceptibly in the thick black before her. Her breath stopped as her eyes tried to pierce the twisting shadows. "What's there…?" she whimpered, struggling against her binds.

A cold laugh rang out. "Let me introduce you two."

Suddenly it was in front of her, snapping out of the darkness so one massive eye glared in her face. She could feel the creature's calm breath against her body, it was causing her to swing gently.

A chill slid down her spine as her heart skipped a beat, her whole world was darkness and the eye peeking out at her from it. In her mind she heard a voice, it was primal and cold.

Don't worry child. I'm your mother now.

Blake

Blake had seen corpses before. He'd just never seen them hanging from trees, drifting in the wind like kites struggling lamely to untangle themselves from a snare in the branches.

He screamed. A lot. It didn't seem to bother the corpses.

He'd only stopped when a man had crashed through the bushes and tried to calm him down. It worked until the man, curious as to what had startled Blake, looked up at the tree line, the sight causing him to squeal like a small child himself.

All in all, it took them nearly a quarter of an hour to come to their senses.

The man pulled out a hand radio and began directing a long stream of curses into it, ending with a joke about the difficulty of pulling stretchers up a mountain Blake didn't quite understand.

By now only the last strand of sunlight was stretching across the sky, making the bodies' shadows stretch out across the land and reach for surrounding dark hungrily. A soft gust of wind blew by, warm and shifting, it caused the bodies to swing loosely. Blake was reminded of something he'd seen as a child.

He'd been six and his sister had taken him to a traveling fair the city over. They'd eaten cotton candy and ridden the merry-go-round, he'd even coerced his sister into taking him through the haunted house. There had only been one thing he hadn't liked. It was a puppet show run by a stooped old man.

The dolls were gaudy with big mouths and wide eyes that never seemed to completely shut when they blinked. Blake disliked the way they danced. Their movements weren't their own, how the cruel old man swung and dropped them for cheap laughs of the audience. Blake easily imagined himself on one of the strings, forced to flip and smile for the amusement of drunk tourists. It had stuck with him.

He wondered where the puppet master was here, and how large their stage was.

Part 2: Journalism

Ken

Ken wasn't his real name, it was only the one they gave him. When he'd first heard it he'd thought it ridiculous, like his assignment. Deep cover in Hope British Columbia? He'd thought he'd been on the fast track to upper management.

He'd requested reassignment twice, he'd even consider another stint in the Iraq if it meant getting out of Hope. He'd been denied both times, told he was in a key position and reassignment would risk loss of valuable operation resources. Given the nature of the op, he grudgingly agreed with their assessment.

Officially he'd trained as a soldier and police officer, he had the credentials and war medals to prove it, less officially (in the eyes of the United Nations, at least) he'd trained in espionage. He'd been prepped for wet work, quick and nasty jobs that rid the world of undesirables. He was good at it.

Without being modest, a character flaw he'd never developed, he could state he was destined for great things. He'd had the highest kill count in his unit when he was twenty-five and the highest in his section when he was twenty-seven. Unsurprisingly, he felt like a wasted asset pretending to be a police officer in a town whose only exports appeared to be racism and depression.

He spent his days pulling over drunk drivers and scaring kids about the dangers of marijuana. It was unfulfilling but that appeared to be changing quickly.

"Do we have anything to go on?" It was a constable speaking, fat and suffering from asthma he'd clearly lied about in the interview process. Ken didn't approve of him.

"Just what we can see," he gave a curt nod towards the witnesses (if you could even call them that) seated on a nearby log, "And these two saw *nothing*."

One was a teenager. He had a serious expression and hazel eyes that were currently digging into Ken with annoyance. The other was a local park ranger, unshaven and already bearing firm crow's feet despite barely being thirty. The boy had asked if he could leave, twice, while the park ranger had taken three smoke breaks in the last hour, Ken may not have been a real cop but he still easily deduced the cigarettes hadn't contained tobacco.

Both were getting on his nerves.

"Like I said, I wanted to get some camping in."

"Is it a crime to go hiking?"

Ken wasn't sure who's response was more disrespectful. He took a deep breath and imagined how it would feel to slash their throats and leave the incompetent constable crying over their dead bodies. It was a satisfying image.

"Just two campers lost in the woods, who happen to come across a mass murder?"

The dullard of a constable spoke up. "Why would they phone it in if they were the killers?" He was the kind of man who couldn't hold his tongue in public, it caused Ken no end of inconvenience on patrol.

Often when he left a posting it required him to clean house, scrub every speck of evidence that he had been there, including individuals who had known him personally. He sincerely hoped Command would classify the constable as such an individual upon the operation's completion.

"Regardless, they're coming in for questioning. I'll phone it in while you book them."

The constable mumbled a reply but Ken was already walking towards his car. It was an official RCMP squad car, outfitted to their specifics and ready for every aspect of police work, the radio on his belt was not. He placed an earpiece in his ear and clicked it to a secure frequency.

"Command, we have suspicious activity. Seven casualties. Two civilians and one member of law enforcement on sight, please advise."

His earpiece screamed to life immediately after he'd finished speaking. A cool voice spoke in his ear. "Roger, Agent Dawson. Maintain operational cover."

Ken raised the radio to his lips again, his eyes scouring around him as he did. "Command, I expect heavy media activity on location, please advise."

"Understood, Agent, please await further commands." Ken sucked in his breath, praying for relief from the monotony. When the voice returned, it maintained its cool tone. "Agent Dawson?"

"Yes?"

"Be advised orders regarding the subject have changed from surveillance to capture, expect additional agents tomorrow. Command has opted to keep you as operation leader."

"Understood, Command."

Ken smiled for the first time in months. His index finger began to twitch. It appeared Command expected to start utilizing his talents.

Hal

"Come on, Jeb, you know we didn't do this." Hal looked over at the teenager beside him, now that the panic had worn off, his face had settled into a surprisingly intimidating scowl. "Well, you know I didn't do this."

The word to describe Jeb was flabby. A pasty skinned man child that looked more like a pizza shop employee than a law enforcement professional. Not to say he wasn't a brave and honourable man, only that he didn't fit the authoritative and serious look the RCMP prided itself on cultivating in its members.

"Sorry, Hal, you know we have to take this seriously," Jeb murmured as his gaze was lost in the tree line, no doubt wondering how someone had managed to climb so high to hang the bodies. The sun had set, causing him to shiver. "I'll make sure you're treated fairly."

Hal spit, he highly doubted Jeb would influence his treatment at the hands of the law. It didn't take a detective to notice who was in charge. Ken Dawson, policeman extraordinaire. He wrote more tickets in a week than Hope's three other officers combined, only without the stupid jokes.

Locals said Ken was a war veteran, turned to police work after a few stints in the middle east. Hal's personal theory was the man was actually a robot built by the government in a failed attempt at creating the perfect asshole.

If Jeb's fault was looking nothing like a police officer, then Ken's was looking too much like one. His uniform was always meticulous, his posture straight, and his brow furrowed. It was like they'd cut him out of a recruitment ad, only forgetting the famous Canadian politeness.

The teenager spoke, his voice low with exasperation. "Can we hurry up at least, I need to get home to my sister."

A spark of sympathy spread across Jeb's face, his pasty skin sinking into a sorry wince. "I know Blake, we'll get this sorted out as quick as we can."

Blake. Blake. Blake. Hope was small, but Hal had to strain to his considerably drug addled brain to remember who the boy was. He was coming up short. With a sigh he resorted to what he considered the lowest form of human interaction, small talk.

"So, are you from around here?"

The forced casual tone made the boy's lip curl. "Live down on Crescent."

Hal nodded slowly. "I see, I see." Crescent was a small road surrounded by a large trailer park. As far as trailer parks went it was nice. It had drunks and addicts, sure, but not much violence. A place for the wealthiest poor people.

"You, uh, like hiking?"

The boy laughed. It was sharp and cold but brought a grin to Hal's face. Maybe he was in shock. "I like hiking. I don't like sitting in the cold under a bunch of dead bodies." The last part of his sentence was raised, his brown eyes darting towards Jeb who was still gazing into the forest.

Jeb shrugged. "You think I want to be here? This place gives me the heebie-jeebies."

Hal lit up another joint. "A credit to law enforcement you are, Jeb."

In the distance, they could hear sirens, the slamming of brakes and calling of voices. The second wave of inquiry was arriving.

Branches rustled as Ken walked back into the clearing. His serious face somehow looking more smug than usual. His voice calm and almost, almost, warm as he spoke. "Alright, the backups arrived. We're going to take you back to the station to get your statements while forensics move in."

"Oh, a police interrogation, just like on TV," said Hal halfheartedly. "Better hope you're innocent kid," he added as the teenager cast a sour look.

They were led back to the police cars, thankfully, without handcuffs. They passed people as they went, coroners in white body suits, policemen with waving flashlights and serious faces, and two reporters being held back at the trail entrance by an officer Hal didn't recognize.

"Must be help from out of city, huh?"

Jeb looked around, his bewildered eyes shining in the glow of the flashlights. "Must be."

The teenager spoke, he was walking behind them in the dark, the only one without a flashlight. "Quick response time."

Jeb nodded dimly. "Sure is."

Ken, who led the party, didn't speak, only stared straight forward as they marched while his thin lips curled into a smile.

Blake

The police detachment was cozier than he'd expected. In his imagination it was a place of thick cement walls and iron bars, the reality being it was a little more than a glorified office.

He was drinking hot chocolate while Officer Benz, a regular at his work, typed out his statement. She paused every few minutes to ask if he was feeling alright and fuss about the station not having enough blankets.

He wanted to go home to his sister, but it could have been worse. Hal, as he'd learnt the other hiker was called, was giving his statement to Officer Dawson. Officer Benz might fuss and talk to him like a baby, but he much preferred it to Dawson's icy gaze and condescending tone.

"Alright, Mr. Turner. Just sign here and we can get you home, I made sure to phone your aunt before we started."

Blake grunted a reply, his aunt was the last person he wanted to think about.

"Very good, now why don't you go lie down on the couch until she gets here? It's been a long day and I'm sure you- oh, Sargent Dawson, what can I do for you?"

Dawson was standing in the doorway to the small breakroom they'd been working in, the edges of his muscular arms pushing against the frame. His chilly blue eyes were squinting down at Blake and Officer Benz.

"I came for the boy's statement." His voice was flat and terse.

Blake saw Officer Benz roll her eyes as she picked up her notes from the table. "Of course, I have the signed copy right here and I already emailed you."

Ken Dawson's icy features folded into a scowl, Blake felt the urge to shrink away from the man's gaze but forced himself to sit still. "I am aware, I will be conducting my own interview," he said drily.

Blake sighed, he wanted to go home.

"Officer, I can assure you I have interviewed the witness according to the circumstance."

Dawson's jaw clenched. When he spoke again it was with measured restraint. "I am sure you did a commendable job, but I will nonetheless conduct my own interview."

Officer Benz shrugged and gave Blake a sympathetic smile. "Suit yourself. Please follow Mr. Dawson, Blake."

The interview room was bigger than the break room, it had a long table and what Blake assumed was a two-way mirror. "Can someone let my aunt know I'll be late?"

Dawson grunted what might have been a response as he pushed Blake into a chair. Beside him sat Hal, face buried into folded arms atop the metal table. At the sound of the chairs scraping, Hal raised his head from its resting place, his brown hair standing wild.

"Hey, could I get some food?" He scratched his beard as he spoke. Blake guessed he'd been in here for about four hours.

Dawson sat across from them in his own chair, there were blank papers in front him, but he didn't bother to pull out a pen. "Gentleman. As you are aware, you've witnessed a tragedy."

Blake squinted at the man, this didn't sound like an interview.

"We have recovered six bodies so far and have not had time to identify and notify their families." Dawson leaned back in his chair, the relaxed posture unfitting of his demeanor. "As such, I hope you understand you cannot talk to anyone about this."

Hal let out a derisive snort. "There go my TV aspirations."

Blake crossed his arms. "And why aren't we allowed to talk about it?"

Hal leaned back in his own chair, he did a much better job of looking relaxed than Officer Dawson, despite his tired face. "Yeah, why can't we talk about it? I might need counseling." He paused to rub his eyes. "I definitely need counseling."

Behind them a door opened, two more policemen walked in. They were broad shouldered with impassive faces, they nodded curtly to Dawson who raised one hand in salute.

"You will keep this to yourself so that myself and the special task force formed to investigate the murders aren't forced to waste our incredibly valuable time prosecuting you."

Hal got up, brushing his pants as he did. "Well your voice said prosecute but the two surly sergeants behind me give me other ideas." He reached out a hand to Dawson. "I, for one promise not to tell a soul."

Dawson ignored the outstretched hand, instead turning his gaze to Blake. Hal waited for a moment before lowering his arm with a sigh.

"Yeah, I won't tell anyone."

Dawson smiled. Blake wished he hadn't, it made him think of a crocodile he'd seen on Discovery channel. "Good, now your aunt is waiting in the lobby. These gentlemen will escort you."

Hal

The large officers weren't rough in taking Hal and Blake to the lobby, only intimidating, looming silently during the walk down the stone stairwell. When they left, Hal called out a cheerful "goodbye," but it went unreciprocated.

The lobby was warm and clean. Mocha coloured tile clashed with bright fluorescent lights. Its only other occupants were a bored receptionist and Blake's aunt.

A high-pitched scream greeted them. "Blakey, you're out, oh my god." A slim woman ran over to hug the kid, her platinum hair sweeping across his glowering eyes as a frown tugged at his lips. "I was so worried."

The woman began rummaging in her purse. "They say you found a body, that's so frightening. This is why you need to stop going on those silly walks, I tell you." She pulled out a pack of cigarettes. "Let's go outside, I want to get one of these in me before I get back to parenting."

Blake put an arm on her shoulder. "Where is Sarah?" he growled.

Ignoring the boy's tone, the woman continued fitting a cigarette between bright pink lips. "She's in the car."

Blake didn't run, exactly, but he moved quickly to the door. Long strides pushing him through the thick doors in a matter of seconds. His Aunt was left fumbling in her purse for a lighter, dropping it when she looked up to see Blake's companion.

Hal grinned, rubbing a hand through his mousy hair. "Charming kid."

"Tell me about it."

Hal walked past her and onto the street. An old Honda accord was parked in front of the building, Blake was hugging a small girl through its unwound window. It was a tender moment, Hal looked back into the lobby to see if the aunt had caught it. She might have if she wasn't currently being scolded by the receptionist for smoking inside.

With drooping eyelids and a growling stomach, he reached into his pockets for his truck keys, realizing, not for the first time, life was an unfair game comprised of endless torrents of bullshit.

Blake's aunt emerged onto the sidewalk beside him, smoke curling from her mouth. Blake himself was currently talking excitedly to the small girl whose pitched giggles were floating out of the car.

"Hey, uh, don't suppose I could get a ride? My truck is, uh," he waved his hands in the air helplessly, "You know."

He'd directed the question at Blake, his alleged partner in crime for the day, but it was the aunt who answered. "Of course, sweetie, do you mind if we stop at Dairy Queen first? I haven't made the kids dinner yet."

Blake's brow furrowed at the statement, his expression contrasting with that of the smiling child peeking her head out of the car behind him.

Hal rubbed his stomach, he'd take an awkward car ride over trying to get ahold of the only taxi in Hope any day. "I don't mind at all."

Blake

It was nearly midnight and his sister should already have been in bed, he couldn't blame her for not sleeping but he could blame his aunt for not feeding her. The restaurant was ready to close but the cook was a friend, turning the fryer back on when he saw Blake walk in.

Their orders were taken by a teenage girl, black hair with a single strip of neon pink and an extravagant nose ring. "Two salads and a burger, god you're lame," she said, punching their order into the tiny computer screen before her.

"Sarah and I are on a diet."

The girl's smile reached out from behind the counter. "Such a good brother. By the way, do you think you could take my shift on Friday? I want to go to the river."

The beginning of Blake's sentence was cut off as his aunt reached for her burger. "Sorry hun, he has to babysit that night."

Blake's fingers dug into the tray he was holding. "I'll let you know, Michelle."

Speaking with a mouthful of cheeseburger, his aunt continued. "No, he won't." Blake's glare caught her eye. She swallowed and continued, "What? I have a shift at the bar that night." She reached out a manicured hand and roused his hair. "Sorry, sport, but you know I make way more serving drinks than you do blizzards."

Blake's aunt made more working at the bar than he did at Dairy Queen, but she also spent most of her profits in her own workplace, getting drunk after shift and playing scratchers. It was only the smiling face of his sister that stopped Blake from pointing this out.

The girl behind the counter seemed unfazed by the firm rejection. "Well if anything changes let me know." She looked past Blake to a salivating Hal, "Do you want me to give your friend the employee discount? He looks like he needs it."

Behind them, Hal's patch work beard quivered with delight as he gazed upon the menu, his face taking on the appearance of a castaway on a deserted island who'd stumbled upon a hidden cache of chocolate bars and rum.

"Please."

"Will do, Blake, here are some cups for the soda machine." The girl brushed back a loose pink bang. "What? I know you let Sarah drink pop."

"Thank you, Michelle."

Blake wasn't a health nut, he ate too much ice cream for that, he just considered himself responsible for his sister's health. His mother had problems and money was always tight growing up. Often, supper had been Kraft Dinner and a bottle of Coke. Blake had been fine with the processed food, his stringy metabolism made it hard to gain weight, his sister was less lucky.

The last time he'd taken her to the doctor the man talked about childhood obesity and diabetes. Sarah wasn't "fat" or "big boned," she wasn't made fun of at school or insulin dependent, but if she kept eating the way she was, she'd be saddled with a lifetime of problems before she was even ten.

The doctor, a portly fellow himself, was clear in his explanation. Excess weight was more dangerous in childhood than adulthood. A child's heart was weaker than an adult's, less capable of handling the strains of obesity. Furthermore, overweight children often never shed their weight in adulthood which resulted in much shorter lives.

This didn't scare Sarah, who, at the time, could barely pronounce diabetes, little alone understand it, but it scared Blake.

For the past three years he'd made sure she'd had at least one healthy meal a day. Even after his mother left, when he spent most of his time at Dairy Queen working, he made sure to make her a healthy breakfast and equally nutritious lunch to take with her to the babysitter or school.

He brought the tray of food to their table and sat across from his sister. She eyed the half-finished burger in his aunt's hands with envy but didn't say a word about it. They'd agreed in the beginning she'd eat any healthy meal as long as her big brother ate the same.

Sarah nudged her salad with a plastic fork. Blake began to eat his own, pretending the lettuce had a different taste than the cutlery he used to eat it.

After a minute, Hal joined them, cradling two burgers, four crispy chicken wraps, and a milkshake in his hands. His eyes were bright and Blake half expected a pool of drool to begin dripping from his lips.

They ate quickly and quietly, the only sounds in the restaurant coming from the three remaining workers cleaning.

When Sarah finished her plastic flavoured salad, Blake went to the soda machine and filled her a small glass of coke. She slurped it greedily. For a minute Blake forgot about the swaying trees and dangling bodies, about his missing mother. Even his aunt was quiet for once.

The moment didn't last long.

"Harold, I've been looking everywhere for you."

Hal's mouth was full with his second wrap but he tried to push out a response. "MmmMm."

Sarah giggled. "He's silly, Blake."

Hal gave the girl a look of indignation which was only slightly diminished by a mouth clogged of crispy chicken and dripping ranch sauce.

"Seriously, Harold, what's going on? The cops won't tell me anything and I know you were up there. I saw your truck."

The new speaker was a tall woman, mid-twenties with short blonde hair in a bowl cut to make Velma from Scooby-Doo jealous. She had a white cotton sweater on and a notepad in one hand.

"Urm," Hal swallowed the last of his wrap, "God dammit, Bobbi, can't a man eat in peace?"

Blake snapped, "Language."

Hal turned sheepishly to the teenager. "Apologies to the little lady," he said before snapping back to the woman. "Bobbi, whatever the police told you is what I know."

The woman let out a snort and began digging in a cloth bag draped over her shoulder. Blake's attention was caught by the many buttons adorning it, *I'm With Her, MADD, PETA, UFV, GREEN PARTY.*

Hal smiled apologetically at Blake and his aunt. "My cousin, the hippy, everyone."

"That's rich coming from the man who spends his days smoking pot in a woodshed." She ripped something from her cloth bag. "I found this just off the trail, when I was trying to sneak in." She placed a dirty doll on the table, it was missing an eye and only had a few strands of red hair remaining.

Hal let out a long groan. "Jesus, Bobbi, sorry Blake, that's how people get lost in the woods, leaving it up to me to find them."

Bobbi let out a huff and continued. "They found me though, even in the thickest parts, cops were standing guard. What the hell happened, Harold?" She rolled her eyes at Blake's frown. "Oh, blow off kid, the little girl grows up in Hope she's going to hear a lot worse than this."

Blake had to concede she'd made a fair point there.

Hal's words were tired and sagged, as were his eyelids. "Look, Bobbi, I'll tell you about it later. Not," he tilted his head towards the restaurant counter where a neon haired girl was eyeing them with wry amusement, "in the middle of a fucking Dairy Queen, oh shut up, Blake."

Blake's aunt was busy with her phone, oblivious to what was a rather typical conversation in Hope.

"Well," said the woman, tilting her head to the door, "let's go."

"Only if you give me a ride home."

"Oh, I see how it is, beg the dirty hippy for a ride," replied the woman with a smirk.

Sarah's light laughter filled the restaurant. "They're funny, Blake."

Hal rolled his eyes and stood up from the booth, snatching the doll from the table with a tanned hand. "Come on, just be a good cousin and get me home." He rolled his eyes and added lowly, "Please."

Bobbi squealed. "I knew we were related." A business card slammed onto the table before Blake. "Here, in case you guys ever have something to share."

"Cool," Blake said dully as his sister reached towards the card with curiosity.

Bobbi moved to the door, waving at Hal to follow. Blake grabbed the man's arm as he rose from his seat. "Are you really going to tell her?"

Hal shrugged as the coy smile vanished. Blake wondered if the dark patches under his eyes were only from today. The man blinked a few times before the halfcocked smile reemerged on his face. "Fuck no, I just want a ride home."

Blake shook his head, "Well, goodnight at least."

"You too, kid, I hope we never meet again."

Sarah waved. "Bye mister." Blake's aunt glanced up from her phone, "Later."

Hal tipped an imaginary hat and joined his cousin at the doorway. Blake watched them go through the window, slipping into a battered Subaru Outback and then into the night.

"He was hot," said Blake's aunt, fingers absentmindedly twirling a strand of hair.

"Jesus Christ, aunty."

Sarah giggled, chastising Blake in her singsong voice, "Language, Blakey."

Bobbi

She didn't drive him to his house, she didn't even know if he'd been back since the wife and kid left. She took him to his work cabin, a tiny little shack that was older than the both of them combined. It was cramped, filled with one chair and one bed.

Hal's desk was covered in maps and empty beer bottles. The maps were heavily marked, vast areas shaded in black marker. Occasionally she came across a hole where Hal, drunk or angry, had pushed the pen tip through the thin paper.

Bobbi sunk into the room's only seat, a leather office chair far too elegant for Hal's shack. "Still haven't found her?"

Hal had slumped into his tiny cot, staring dead eyed at the ceiling. "No. Don't think I will now."

Bobbie swiveled around in the chair to reach for the office's minifridge. It was a relic from Hal's college days, covered in faded band stickers and humming so loud Bobbi wondered how Hal could sleep with it in the room. She pulled a beer out and tossed it to Hal before reaching for one of her own.

Bobbi wasn't stupid. She knew Hal didn't plan on telling her everything. She also knew he was more than susceptible to the simplest methods of persuasion.

She took a sip of cheap beer, nose wrinkling at the taste. "That bad?"

Hal sighed. "That bad."

Bobbi picked at one of the stickers on the fridge, flaking tiny white bits onto the dust laden floor. When she heard the sound of Hal dropping an empty can she opened the fridge and threw him another one.

"Look, Bobbi, I don't want you getting mixed up in this."

"I think you mean, I don't want myself getting mixed up in this."

Hal shrugged, Bobbi straightened up. It must be bad if Hal didn't have energy to joke about it.

"Come on, Hal, I need a good story. There's only so many articles about heroin addiction and school sports you can write before you go crazy." She pulled her notebook out of her bag. "I want to write about something that matters for once, and judging by what I can only assume is a small militia stationed up the road, something is happening."

"I told the police, and that kid now that I think about, that I wouldn't talk about it."

"Oh, my big brave cousin, afraid of a few cops and a teenager?"

Hal leaned forward and cupped his head with his hands. He massaged his temples hard, messing up the few strands of hair that had been left in place by the day. "Fuck, fine."

Bobbi smiled sweetly, tossing him a third beer from the fridge before opening a second one for herself. She brushed away some of the maps on the table, noting the words Hal had carved into the desk beneath them.

I hate my life.

She wriggled her nose and covered the scratches with her notepad. Looking at Hal expectantly, she uncapped the lid of her pen, savouring the last sip of beer in her mouth as she did so.

"Bobbi, it's a serial killer, it's got to be."

Bobbie tried not to roll her eyes. "I know, Hal, half the town knows, the police can deny it all they want but we have too many missing people, even for Hope."

"I know, I know."

"And?"

"It's just, you didn't see."

Bobbi leaned forward over her notebook, her blood had started pumping so fast she half expected it to spray out over her notes like ink from a burst pen.

"What didn't I see, tell me?"

Hal took another gulp of beer and let the can drop to the floor, shaking his head when she propped open the fridge door to replace his fallen comrade.

"You can't print this."

This time Bobbi did roll her eyes. "Don't get my cousin arrested, got it."

Hal shook his head, his eyes were getting bloodshot. "Seriously, the cops today, they're not playing around." He looked past Bobbi to the cabin's only window, eyes raking across the night sky. "If they even were cops."

Bobbi knit her brow, maybe Hal was drunk already. "You don't think they were cops?"

"I don't think they were normal cops."

"Jesus, Harold, stop being so mysterious and tell me what happened." Bobbi's words were accompanied by the exasperated look her cousin had become well acquainted with over the last twenty years.

Hal giggled, sobriety slipping from his eyes. "You sound like the cops, maybe your true calling was as a Mountie."

"The mounties won't beat you for wasting their time, Harold."

"These ones might, Bobbi."

■■

She spent the night in Hal's cabin. Partly because she'd gotten too drunk to drive and partly because she wasn't sure if she felt safe sleeping alone with what was certainly a crazed killer on the loose.

Hal had graciously given her the bed and decided to rough it on the floor, at least that's what she told herself as she pushed his limp body out of the single cot.

Sleep didn't come quickly. She churned Hal's story in her mind, trying to picture how the killer had managed to scale the trees and hang the bodies. It was an impressive, if morbid, feat. Thoughts of the swinging corpses kept her awake into the early morning.

When she finally did start to drift from consciousness it was with a tired acceptance, sighing as the loud hum of the minifridge grew more and more distant. In the last moments of her wakefulness, in the faded edge between reality and dreams, she thought she heard a voice.

A sweet and soft voice calling out to her from far away, a caring voice that urged her into the land of dreams with a smile on her face, a voice of longing that was fitting of only a mother.

Perfect... family...

Ken

Ken watched Officer Benz from the window of his office. She was walking to her car in the parking lot three stories below. It was well past midnight and her feet dragged as she walked, sleep written in her posture. Beside him was a colleague, a large black suited man with a video camera pressed against the window pane.

They'd spotted it, whatever it was, at nine P.M. A surveillance van caught it shambling out of the woods, quickly discerning it was more than a drunk camper coming into town to replenish a dwindling stock of beer and chips.

Dripping in blood, incapable of walking straight, and with a third arm sporting from its back, the team was quick to radio it in. The team had offered to abduct the thing right there, but Ken was content to watch for a little while. The night was dark and the streets mostly empty now, the intel they gathered from observing its uninhibited movements could prove valuable.

At least that's what he'd say when questioned on it, the truth was his own morbid curiosity led him to allow the strange creature to wander Hope's streets.

They'd followed the thing closely. It stumbled through town, pinwheeling from street to street with obnoxious jerky movements. It was late in the night and the few people awake were too drunk or stoned to comment on the meandering route the creature took if they even noticed it at all.

They were unsure about the thing's final destination, but the surveillance van surmised that if it kept up its general direction it would pass the police station. This had made Ken smile, he'd asked for an ETA and then walked from his office to Benz's.

"It's getting late, why don't you go get some rest?"

She'd been poring over the day's reports, no doubt getting ready to help with the upcoming investigation. When she looked up it was with slight surprise which was quickly followed by a yawn. "I just want to make sure I'm ready for tomorrow."

"I understand, Officer, but really, you can go."

Benz squinted at him. "Well, aren't you all sweet at night."

Ken smiled, his bone white teeth glinting in the fluorescent light. "I want you well rested for tomorrow." Benz looked at him blankly. "It's not a request," he added awkwardly.

The woman shrugged and stifled another yawn. "If you say so, boss." She grabbed her purse and walked to the office door, as an afterthought she paused to look back at Ken. "You know, you've never told us much about yourself. You should get a drink with me and Jeb someday."

Ken nodded. "I would love to." He'd tried to look friendly, but his expression made Benz's lip curl. She tilted her head stiffly and walked out into the hallway. Ken let the false smile drop from his face, pausing to reflect for a moment before returning to his own office and increasingly uneasy colleague.

Below them, Benz was fiddling with her keys. Her personal vehicle was an old Pontiac Sunfire that would have looked more in place at a dump than a police officer's parking spot. The creature had finally lurched onto the concrete a few meters behind her.

Ken pushed his face against the glass, eager to see what would happen. Beside him, his colleague, a man who could easily be mistaken for a grizzly bear in a suit, let out a shiver.

Officer Benz

A late night and a strange night. Benz longed for her bed. Working in Hope was routinely exhausting but today took the cake.

Her pace was glacial through the parking lot, her steps and mood sinking into the pavement as she went. At forty-three she expected to be past the point of having to pull double shifts, maybe even have a desk job. She'd majored in accounting and would have made an excellent addition to the budget committee. She promised herself after this case finished she'd reapply.

She dropped her keys while trying to push them into her car door. The car itself was a dilapidated thing she drove so she could cut costs and put more money into her niece and nephew's college fund. When she rose from picking them up she caught her reflection in the tinted window.

It was warped and made her tired eyes seem to sag down to below her teeth. She gave a weak smile, shuddering when the caricature reflecting back reminded her of her boss. It was bad enough he was ten years younger than her, it was even worse that he was a total creep.

She finally managed to prop the door open. She sunk her weary rear into the ragged nylon covered seat. Maybe she would reapply to accounting tomorrow. After all, they had all those new officers arriving to help with the investigation, it wasn't like Dawson needed her. Ken had even ignored the only beneficial thing she'd done today when he'd conducted his own interview with poor Blake Turner.

She had to jiggle the key a bit to start the car up, she was rewarded with the scratchy blasting of Hope's only pop station. The music was vapid trash, but her car's cd player was broken, and she preferred it to Hope's only other radio station, Christian ministry that preached a very old testament message of fire and brimstone.

She leaned back and cracked her shoulders. In another year she'd have saved enough to send Lucy and Vernon to college for four years each, then she would buy a new car. Or maybe she would do it earlier, they could pay for a year on their own, it would build character.

She chuckled. She must be getting old if she used building character to justify hardship. From the distant end of the parking lot a matching laugh echoed out.

Startled, she looked over. "Is that you, Jeb? Crazy day, eh?"

"Crazy day. Eh. Eh."

Benz squinted into the darkness surrounding the brightly lit parking lot. She could see a figure hobbling towards her. It was taking wild, shaking steps, and swaying from side to side.

Benz sighed, she'd always felt it wasn't her place to criticize drug users, but she did get tired of dealing with them. "Sir, are you alright?"

"Are you alright, Jeb? Sir."

Benz's heartbeat rose. "Sir? I repeat, are you alright?"

The figure lurched forward, arms pinwheeling as it nearly collapsed on the pavement. Illuminated by the street lamps above, Benz finally saw the figure clearly. He was tall, wearing a dirty white shirt with equally dirty jeans. The balding brown hair on his crown was in stark contrast to his corpse white skin.

Benz gasped as her eyes scanned the man's wild face. "Jesus Christ, Tony."

The man continued to stumble forward. Benz unbuckled her seatbelt and climbed out of the car, her engine continuing to idle behind her.

"Christ, Tony?"

The man's face tilted forward, darkening in the poor light of the parking lot. Benz could spot more than a bit of blood caking his head.

"Tony, are you alright?"

Tony leaned back, swaying on the spot while his dazed eyes flickered across Benz's face. "Alright?" he slurred as Benz reached out to steady his tilting body.

He looked up at her and smiled. His teeth were black and yellow, the stench made Benz blanch. "Jesus, Tony, what happened to you?" She kept her hand on his shoulder, trying to stifle her sudden urge to run.

Tony's eyes drifted from Benz's face and to the sky. His head tilted back, and Benz was sure he would have fallen over backwards had she not reached out a second arm to steady him. Stilling slightly in her grasp, his head snapped forward as a small giggle croaked from his cracked lips.

"Mother likes you."

"Mother who? What are you talking about?" She reached for the radio attached to her belt. "This is Officer Benz. I have a confirmed sighting of a missing person, require assistance in headquarters parking lot."

The reply on the radio was instant. Ken Dawson's voice crackled out to her. "Confirmed, Officer Benz. Be right there."

She replaced the radio and turned her attention back to Tony. His body grew still as his pale eyes fixed firmly on her face, mercifully he'd closed his putrid mouth.

"Mother doesn't want you, though."

Benz shuddered and tried to gently nudge Tony to the ground. "Why don't you have a seat, Tony? We'll get you some help." His body stood rigid as she increased the pressure of her palm.

"Why don't you have seat. Mother doesn't want." His eyes muddled as his face dissolved into confusion. "Seat. Tony. Mother. Says."

"It's alright, Tony, just sit down please."

Tony stood looking confused, his glossy eyes unfocused as they twisted in odd directions inside his skull. "Mother says. Mother says."

Benz let go of Tony, reaching for the taser she reserved for the users on violent trips. "Tony, who is mother? Where have you been the last month?"

"Mother says, Mother says."

"Mother says what?" Benz had readied the taser, slowly backing away from the now foaming man. She noticed something was sticking from his back, but she was unable to make it out fully in the poor light.

For a minute Tony didn't speak. Benz had pushed herself back against her car, taser raised and pointed at the rigid figure. Tony's voice rose as his eyes widened. "Mother says…" His blistered lips cracked to reveal a wolfish smile of rotting teeth.

"Mother says… too old."

He giggled as he started to walk again. Benz screamed, firing the taser in reflex to his hungry look. It shot out and bit into Tony's chest, the barbs sinking through his ragged shirt and into flesh.

Benz could hear the hum of the electricity. Tony hopped a few times, the smell of burnt flesh wafting from him. She pulled the trigger to send more volts through the man but was petrified to find it did little to dissuade him from continuing forward.

Fumbling for her pistol, Benz tried to force authority into her voice. "Tony, I need you to stop approaching me." It was the second time she'd pulled her service firearm in twenty years, a fact evidenced by her shaking hands.

"Too old. Too old," screamed the man as he bent forward slightly. With disbelief, Benz caught sight of what appeared to be a third arm sprouting from between his shoulder blades.

Finally managing to unclip her pistol, Benz dropped the taser and leveled her gun at Tony. "Tony, please, don't come closer."

His giggles continued. Benz screamed as two teeth fell out of his mouth and tinkled onto the pavement. She fired her pistol twice, striking him square in the chest. Blood pumping, she shrieked into her radio. "Officer in need of assistance, parking lot, parking lot."

The radio cracked to life, but she didn't catch the response, her attention focused on Tony who was still shambling forward. Now, less than three feet away, he stopped and stared. Benz raised the pistol again, her ears still ringing from the first shots.

"Tony. Tony, please."

Tony tilted his head and eyed her, the hunger in his eyes flickering to one of mixed curiosity. "Tony, please. No. Mother says."

Benz kept the gun level, her back pressed against her still running car. "Stay away, stay away."

Tony shook his head, his eyes flicking back to an expression of greedy want. Blood was seeping out of his chest, wetting his shirt and pants. Benz shuddered as she noticed the blood wasn't red.

Tony licked his lips. "Mother says… eat."

He let out a childlike giggle as he sprung forward, spit and blood spewing from his wild smile as he did. Benz managed to sink another bullet into his chest before he landed on her, but it did little to stop the man. His decaying teeth sunk into her neck and she felt the warm spray of blood erupt from her body.

He chewed on her ravenously, ripping the skin and muscle from her neck like a malnourished dog.

The world started to fade, her terror ebbed into mild confusion. Darkness filled her vision as the sounds of the surrounding world were replaced by a warm hum. In the last distant thoughts of her conscious mind a few muddled questions persisted. Why hadn't Officer Ken come? Why was she dying? What would happen to her niece and nephew?

Soon the questions began to fade, it was hard to think. At last there was only darkness and a sweet hum. The hum reminded Benz of her mother, cradling her and singing as a child, it grew more and more distant until only the black remained.

Ken

Ken stood tall in front of the window, his hands now gripping the video camera. In the corner of the room his bulky colleague was making liberal use of a trashcan to empty his stomach. The colleague was a large man but even Ken was impressed with how much he evacuated from his body.

He lowered the camera and spoke into his earpiece. "Alright, bring it in. Alive."

The flashlight beams flared to life, crisscrossing the parking lot as four black suited agents surrounded the creature. The glass was too thick for the screaming to reach his ears but he caught the hollow pop of gunfire.

"God dammit, I said try to take it alive."

Ragged breathing pushed through the device. "Sorry, Agent Dawson, target is secure, still alive but heavily injured." Below, three figures dragged the thing that had once been a man away from the nearly unidentifiable remains of Officer Benz and the fresh corpse of a fellow agent.

"Put it in the holding cell and have a medic look at it."

"Rog- fuck. Shit." Ken winced as screaming filled his right ear, accompanied by further cracks of gunfire. The men had been tightly packed together, shrouding his vision of what was attacking them. He frowned as they began to fall.

Eventually the screaming subsided. "Report."

The colleague behind him had finished with the trashcan and lurched forward to press his face against the window, his voice shaking as he spoke. "What have they got us tracking here?"

Ken ground his perfect teeth. "I said report."

A wheezing voice filled his ears. "Sir. Sir."

Ken cracked his knuckle. What kind of pussies were the agency sending these days?

"Report, soldier."

Ken chose to ignore the curse words proceeding the update. "It…. It changed, sir. Sprouted a mouth from its stomach. Christ, it got Leonard." Ken stared stone-faced at the carnage below. One man was clutching a stump of a leg and rocking back and forth, a companion comforting him while the other agent dragged the limp body of the creature away.

"Orders stand, take it to the cells."

The agent dragging the creature put a shaky hand to his head in salute to the window, his shaking voice continuing in Ken's ear. "Under… understood, sir."

Ken shook his head, he'd been promised ex marines for this assignment. "And clean the mess up when you're finished," he said as he clicked off his earpiece.

He turned to face his colleague. The man had a fatty throat and a deep black beard that seemed to crawl down his face to his chest.

"You can report to the secretary for reassignment."

The man's jaw began to shake violently. "Please, sir, I just had a bad lunch. I swear. Did three tours in Syria, I don't need to be reopped."

Ken glared. "You trust the food in this town? You're stupider than I thought."

The agent bent his head forward, Ken wondered if he'd try kneeling. "Sir, I got a little girl, it's why I do it. Pays more than we could ever hope for."

"Oh, your pay won't change." Ken glanced back at the parking lot, eyes darting over the bodies being quickly hauled away by a team of white hazmat suit wearing medics. "Life expectancy might."

He left the man standing in the dark vomit-smelling room and made his way to his own office. He lifted his laptop screen and opened a private line. There were things his employers would want to hear about.

Part 3: Surveillance

Blake

It was five-thirty, the sun already falling from its perch. The sky was a blaze of pinks and oranges marred by only a few clouds. Three weeks had passed since Blake had stumbled upon a site of mass murder. He'd done a great job of forgetting it.

Through the classroom window he could see his sister playing on the school's swings. Her face alive as she swung back and forth, pumping her tiny little legs to bring her closer and closer to the birds flying above.

"I think that's enough for today, Blake."

Blake turned his head from the window towards his teacher. "Sorry, Mrs. Notley, I can keep going."

The woman rose from her desk. She was thirty with quickly greying hair and an easy smile. "You can keep going, I can't." She let out a gentle sigh as she cracked her bony back. "You're doing great, at this rate you'll have no problem graduating."

Blake shuffled his homework into an overflowing binder, stealing another glance at his sister playing happily. "You think so?"

He walked with Mrs. Notley to the classroom door, waiting for her to lock it. "I know so. Have any plans for after school?"

Blake nodded firmly. "Trades, probably plumbing or electrical work."

She gave him a warm smile. "That's a good boy, thinking of the money."

Blake shrugged, "Money and my sister."

"Of course, I should have remembered." They paced through the silent hallways. Somewhere in the building Mr. Rutgers, Hope Secondary's only janitor, would be mopping away, a lonely prisoner stuck between walls of pep rally posters and forgotten trophies.

"Be nice if they could leave some lights on." If the sun had already set, they would have been walking in total darkness.

"Principle's orders, only Jerry- sorry, Mr. Rutgers, can turn on lights." She booed like a TV ghost. "Budget cuts… scarrrryyyyy."

Blake groaned and held open the door to the parking lot for her. "Better the lights go than the teachers, right?"

"There's a good lad Blake… Ms. Stone, what have I told you about smoking on school property?"

A skinny girl in jeans and a black t-shirt sat on a concrete barrier in the near empty lot. Her hair matched her shirt save for a single strand of hot pink. "Sorry Mrs. Notley. Just waiting for Blake."

"You can wait without a cigarette."

With a roll of her eyes the girl crushed her smoke beneath a large black boot.

"Thank you."

Mrs. Notley walked to her red sedan while the girl ran over to Blake. "Hey, I managed to get off Friday, Jerry said he'd take it."

Blake shuffled his feet, finding it hard to meet the girl's bright gaze. "I know."

"I was wondering if you wanted to hang out? We could go to the river. Your sister could come of course."

Blake wished Mrs. Notley had parked farther away. She made a good job of pretending to busy herself with her keys as she opened the sedan's door.

"I can't."

"What?"

"I, uh, took the shift from Jerry."

The girl's smile slid from her face. Behind them, a car door slammed and an engine started. "You what?"

"He was bitching about it in math today and I need the money so…"

"What about your sister?"

"I'll let her hang out in the store, she still has an unfinished colouring book, plus Dusty lets her pick the TV station when the rush dies down."

"It's ok. I understand." The icy look she gave him did not convey understanding. Blake started to speak, interrupted by Michelle's thick voice. "I said I understand, look I have to go."

Blake stared in disbelief as she rushed off into the adjacent soccer field. Mrs. Notley pulled out from her parking stall, stopping beside Blake with an unrolled window. She found it hard to speak through her laughter. "You know, Blake, just because you look after you sister doesn't mean you have to be celibate." She waved a hand at Michelle's slowly shrinking back. "You're breaking the poor girl's heart."

Blake gave her an affronted look. "How is this my fault?" he asked as the laughing woman drove away.

Frowning, he started to walk around the school towards his sister, purposely going in the opposite direction Michelle had taken. Most of the windows were dark, classrooms lit only by the occasional glowing computer screen.

At one point he passed the janitor, Mr. Rutgers. He was mopping one of the biology labs, or at least trying to with arms flailing and water spraying in every direction but to the floor.

Blake looked away and continued faster. "Well, if there was ever a profession you needed drugs to enjoy."

When he finally reached his sister, she'd moved on from the swing set to the jungle gym, his blood pressure skyrocketing in the brief moment it took for his eyes to find her.

He was wondering if he might be too overprotective when Sarah ran up and hugged him. She'd drawn a picture for him in school today and wanted to know if they could put it on the fridge. As they walked hand in hand back towards their trailer, Blake decided it was impossible to ever be overprotective with the girl.

They took a snaking path along the school's side, Sarah running ahead to scare crows and pick up clovers, her gleeful cries bouncing off the brick schoolhouse and disappearing into the fields surrounding it. She stopped only once, stone faced and staring into one of the school's classrooms.

Mr. Rutgers had managed to make his way from the biology lab, now dancing manically in a drab English classroom. Thankfully, for the book shelf nearby, his mop bucket had long ago spilled over, leaving him only able to flick dust about the room.

"Is he sick?"

Blake took his sister and pulled her gently away. "He's sick like Mommy."

Sarah nodded before returning to her play. Skipping ahead of Blake and chanting broken children's songs to the wind.

There was a trail connecting the school to the trailer park. It thread itself through a light patch of woods. Most days it was mercifully free of mud. A well-known haven for stoners and deer—Blake saw neither as they walked through it.

If he'd glimpsed back he might have seen a janitor watching them, mouth open and eyes wide as he muttered incoherently about mothers and children, but he didn't.

Hal

Hal's eyes itched. He'd put Visine in them twice in the last ten minutes. It had done little to alleviate the painful burning accompanying each blink. He checked his watch—seven thirty—he'd officially been hungover for twelve hours.

He wanted his bed. Or even the floor—it had felt soft enough last night. And yet here he was, sitting with his hippy cousin in a cabin somehow more derelict than his own.

The cabin didn't have lights, but Hal had brought a lamp. He sat it on the scratched wooden table, turning it on with a lazy click

Beside him Bobbi fidgeted with her phone. It didn't have bars but that didn't stop her trying to reach the outside world.

"Jesus, Bobbi, would you give it a rest?"

She flung a battered iPhone on the table. "When I bought this, they promised me it would work anywhere in Hope."

"Was that before or after they gave you the worlds dirtiest cell phone?"

"Lay off, Hal, I've had a busy day."

Hal leaned his head against the wall. The lawn chair he sat on was missing an arm and one of the front legs. He doubted he'd be able to get up if it collapsed.

Bobbi straightened her back and let out a deep breath. The agitation left her face, replaced by a gentle smile. "You spend all day looking for her?"

Hal reached into his pockets for more Visine—he would overdose on the stuff if he had to. "Yes, went up near Linderman.

Nothing." His clothes were dirty enough to prove it too. It was thick country, only rednecks and drug dealers bothered to brave it.

"You know she's probably dead right?" said Bobbi flatly.

Hal squeezed the last drops of the solution into this eye, the relief it provided fleeting. "I know."

Bobbi squeezed his shoulder, careful not to tip his balance on the lawn chair. "You're a sweetheart, cousin. Thanks for coming with me."

Hal grunted. "Don't know why I bothered. No one's coming."

Bobbi flashed him a wicked grin and pulled a cigarette pack from her purse. "Ye of little faith."

Hal helped himself to the pack, to his delight it wasn't filled with cigarettes. "My reward for being a fearless protector?"

"Your reward for being my cousin."

He put the joint in his chest pocket, smoothing the fabric over it with a soft caress. "I like it," he said as he put his head against the wall to indulge in—despite his chair only having three legs and his pillow being composed of rotting cedar—a nap.

When he woke night had fallen. The lamp he'd put out earlier hummed on the table, its tiny batteries working furiously to push away the encroaching darkness.

Across from him sat a woman. Late forties, early fifties at Hal's best guess. It was warm inside, despite the sun setting, but her head was wrapped in a pale blue scarf. She wore round glasses which didn't quite cover the deep wrinkles in the pudgy face behind them.

Bobbi's arm gripped him. She'd been shaking him. "Sorry, my cousin is a heavy sleeper."

"Huh." He took a deep breath, coughing as his nostrils met the overpowering scent of peppermint and vodka. "Hello."

He rubbed his eyes while the woman stared at him, hers buggy and magnified behind her wide lenses. Her lips curved into a trite frown. "Do you trust him?"

"Oh yes," said Bobbi with a mild hand wave. "You can ignore him if you like. He won't mind."

The stranger's eyes stayed on Hal as she heaved her purse onto the table. Reaching in, she produced a grey spray bottle. The label had been removed but Hal could see copper tinted liquid shifting inside it. She gave two curt spritz before returning it to her bag.

Hal sniffed. "Is that hazel?"

The woman nodded, her straw hair shaking as she did. "Oh yes, mixed with insecticide, keeps the spiders away."

Hal nodded slowly. "I see." He glanced over at Bobbi, she was staring intently at the woman with a notepad gripped in her slender fingers. "So, uh, who is this?"

The woman readjusted her glasses. Hal caught a glimpse of the skin covered by the frames. It was worn and drooping like her cheeks and neck. With her spectacles firmly in place she began, "You can call me Jane. Now let's get on with it."

Hal leaned back in his chair, nearly tipping it in his loss for words. Bobbi let out a small cough before speaking. "So, Jane, you know something about the disappearances in Hope?"

The woman leaned in across the table, her eyes darting to the door and back, "I do."

"OK, so what is it? Who's behind the disappearances?"

The woman crossed her arms nervously. "Not who, what."

Hal coughed back a laugh, bowing his head quickly to suppress further giggles. Beside him, Bobbi deflated in her chair, only barely managing to retain a professional tone as she spoke. "Ah, and what might that be?"

The woman's eyes continued to dart about the room, piercing each crack and corner as one of her fingers tapped quickly on her own plump bicep. "You won't believe me."

Hal, unable to help himself, replied, "Probably not."

Bobbi shot him a sour look. "Ignore my chaperone, what won't we believe?"

The woman held her breath for a moment, a vein throbbing in her neck uncomfortably before she finally spoke. "It's not a person. It's a bug."

Hal groaned. "Jesus, Bobbi, my friend is missing and you make me listen to this."

The woman continued. "No, it is. It lives in the woods. It watches everything." She turned to face the cracked window. "It's probably listening to us right now."

"Look, Bobbi, I don't want to be rude but—"

"Then don't be."

Hal shrugged and slipped one of the joints into his mouth.

Bobbi still clutched her notepad but her pen remained limp between her fingers. "Please keep going. What's probably watching?"

The woman nodded, her leg trembling. "Well not watching exactly—but listening. It can hear thoughts. I know it can."

"So, this bug. It's telepathic?"

"Yes, it must be. I remember when it spoke to me. Oh god, it took my son."

A thin stream of smoke had begun to pour out of Hal's mouth. Bobbi waved some away offhandedly. "I see, and where did this telepathic bug come from."

The woman froze. Sweat began to stream down her temple and over the glasses pressed against her face. Through clenched teeth she spoke. "I shouldn't have come, oh god, I can hear it, I shouldn't have come." Tears started to drip from the woman's face, mixing with the goblets of sweat falling gently on the wooden table. "I just wanted people to know. They should know."

Hal tapped some of the ash from his joint onto the table and looked at Bobbi. "Well this is unsettling."

Bobbi remained fixated on the woman. "What should they know?"

The woman let out a scream. It caused Bobbi to jump back in surprise. Hal merely continued smoking. "It's still speaking." She buried her face in her hands, the rest of her words spluttered out in choked sobs. "It says my son was a good plaything but now it wants daughters."

Hal took a deep breath. "This is ridiculous." He stood up. His chair, now bereft of its occupant it finally fell to the floor. "Bobbi, let's go."

His cousin's voice quivered as she spoke. "It wants what?"

Hal put an arm on her shoulder. "Bobbi, she's obviously off her rocker. Let's stop making it worse."

Bobbi ignored Hal and asked again, her voice a near whisper in the cabin. "It wants what?"

"Daughters." The woman started to wail and rock back and forth in her chair. "Oh God, I shouldn't have come back. I shouldn't have come back. I just want my son back."

Hal pulled his cousin up. "Bobbi, she's sick," he whispered softly. "Let's give her some space."

Bobbi mumbled an acquiescence Hal couldn't hear over the woman's now hysterical crying. Her fingers dug madly into her knotted hair as she started to teeter back and forth. "It's coming for me. Oh God, it's coming for all of us."

Hal and Bobbi slowly backed away from the woman. Hal's grip, the guiding force for his increasingly distant cousin.

"It says I'll be its food." The woman looked up from the cradle of her hands, her eyes landing directly on Bobbi. "And food for its family." They let what was left of the cabin's door swing shut behind them as the screaming continued. "I just wanted my son back."

Neither spoke as they drove off. Hal fiddled with the radio dials from the passenger seat. He wanted the rock channel but all that came through was a gravely sermon from the local Bible station. Hal left it on to fill the silence.

The words of Genesis drifted out of the speakers as they wound their way along the dirt roads back to town. They were halfway home when the pastor reached what must have been the climax of his lecture.

"I am with you and will watch over you wherever you go. Remember this, children. He is always watching."

Bobbi switched off the radio with a brusque flip of the dial. Hal didn't bother asking why.

Interlude
Present Day

She didn't bother leaving the cabin. She wasn't too old to run, simply too tired. The voice had left her mind after the reporter and her cousin had left. She killed the silence with sips from a plastic vodka bottle.

The drink calmed her, her legs stopped shaking while the scorching tears slowed their pace. She smiled weakly. The drink had always been a friend to her, even before her family fell apart.

She didn't have enough to knock herself out on, but at least her mind would be dull before the end. That was all she wanted, a little distance from reality. It burned sweetly as it slipped down her throat, lighting a fire in her belly that sent smoke into her brain.

She'd nearly finished the bottle when the door opened. She didn't look up immediately, dreading the sight awaiting her. It took his voice to force her glossy eyes from the splintering table to the open doorway.

"Hello, Mother."

He looked how she'd always hoped he would grow up to be. Tall, handsome, strong. His stance was proud, arms crossed and back straight, staring down at her with a look others might mistake for pity.

Despite the soothing of the vodka, the tears returned. They weren't blinding like before, this time they slid gently down her face, warming her as they went. "Oh, my son."

"I thought we told you never to come back here."

She swayed in her chair a little, her eyes losing focus momentarily. As she regained her balance her eyes rested on her son's shoes. They were made of brown leather and fashionable like the rest of his dress. She was unable to look up and meet his gaze again. "Oh, son. It's killing people now. It's killing people."

Her son let out a sharp laugh. "We're killing people, Mother. We're killing people, not that they matter."

She sobbed. "Oh, my boy. What did I do wrong?" Her voice grew more distant. "I loved you, didn't I?"

The man strode from the doorway to her, stilling her swaying body. Her head rested against his chest. She continued murmuring. "I tried to be a good mommy, I did. It was just so hard." She let out a hiccup. "And your father was always working and you and your brother were so hard to understand."

She felt hands brushing her hair, gentle fingers combing each frayed strand. A soft voice whispered into her ear. "Now, now, mother. It's quite alright."

Her voice was little more than a whimper now. "Why did you let it take your brother? The rest I can understand, but he was your brother."

"Shush, Mother, shush. Don't worry about that now."

She felt his fingers slide down her head, wrapping themselves around her throat. She didn't resist the pressure, only closed her eyes to offer a feeble prayer.

In her last moments there were no angelic voices or divine imagery. Jesus Christ did not come down to soothe her suffering, instead the voice of a far crueler god pierced her skull. It filled every eddy of her mind as the last specters of life drained from her.

We told you to stay away.

Ken

Ken had parents growing up, just not good ones. If he'd wanted, he could have easily blamed it on the drinking; Mommy and Daddy got loaded which made them scream and hit each other, but the truth was they were awful people.

His father was a lout, drifting from job to job between bouts of alcoholism and depression, making it two months past Ken's twelfth birthday before succumbing to the barrel of his own hunting rifle.

His mother had often acted superior to his father, as if managing to hold down a part time job at the local convenience store between the hours she spent with a needle thrust in her veins was an Olympic accomplishment. In reality, she was also a disappointment, stealing from her work and dying from an overdose while Ken was on deployment.

Ken despised his parents, but he wouldn't say it had impacted his childhood negatively, if anything it made him stronger. Most children were swaddled and treated like fine china, making them into pitiful human beings. Weak, emotional, unprepared for the adversity of life. Not Ken though, his childhood had made him into a warrior.

He interviewed for the army at seventeen. He made his recruiter laugh when he admitted he didn't fear much, his honesty mistaken for youthful naiveite.

It was hard to recoil from a blustering drill sergeant when you'd seen your own father threaten worse to his bleeding spouse. It was difficult to worry about sleeping on rocks or in the cold when you'd never had a bed growing up. It was even hard to fear the soft touch of death when you knew all it brought is relief from this world and its pathetic people.

He rose fast and friendless through the military, spending so many years soaking blood into the sand of foreign countries that he nearly lost all purpose other than bringing death to the feeble and the stupid. Until they found him.

The Agency.

His messiah in the desert, offering him a glimpse of a world better than his. One where the strong led and the weak obeyed. A world he could help shape.

He joined without question.

The Organization was everything he believed in. A society where the most talented led while the weak and inferior were fixed or removed. No distinctions were made between race, nationality, gender, or sex, only those who would do what needed to be done and those who would find new jobs (or simply fill pine boxes.)

Joining this beautiful society had ignited his passion, causing him to double his effort in proving his superiority to mankind, but it had also ignited something alien to him: fear.

He now feared failure, he now feared being told he was weak or incompetent, he feared losing the rank and honour he had earned through work most men were incapable of. It was this fear he felt gnawing as the laptop screen went dark and his most recent Command briefing ended.

He clicked his earpiece and spoke coolly into it. "Has the autopsy on subject nine finished?"

He'd been up for twenty hours now, a fact he reflected on as he turned on the coffee machine. In his ear the details of the recent dissection were quickly being listed.

"I see, and what did our expert have to say about it?"

He stood motionless as he listened, the only movement in the room the dripping of an overused Keurig. "Well he's the expert and Command thinks the same… no you can't apply for transfer now. Jesus Christ."

He clicked off his earpiece and pulled his cup from the machine. Coffee continued to drip from the spout, each black blob making a sizzle as it landed below.

The first sip was gratifying, the sweet smell of caffeine wafting up his nostrils to slap his brain awake.

He could hear the commotion begin in the building. Men and women pacing through each floor and setting up a command post, his newly granted reinforcements. Some would be wearing suits, others would be wearing military fatigues. A few would look like actual police officers.

The only civilian left (a night receptionist unaware of her colleagues ulterior loyalties) was being gently coerced to leave, told she would have a paid vacation to make room for the special investigation unit. Not the most elegant lie but in Hope it didn't take much to convince someone to take a vacation.

The coffee machine switched off, which Ken took as his cue to finish his cup, relishing it in the calm darkness of the room. His eyes began to widen, and his heart began to pulse a little quicker. He was ready. This was what he was made for.

He greeted the most important of the new arrivals in his office. Three men and four women, all with short hair and neat black suits. They each nodded curtly as he entered. Ken felt a quick surge of pride, he'd been given some of the best. "Command wants this thing and its children captured. Let's not disappoint."

Interlude
1997

The kids were at school, leaving her only the noise of the television for company. She'd cleaned the house from corner to corner, scrubbing the windows, vacuuming the carpets, shining the toilets, and putting each left-out toy back in its proper place. The house was spotless, and it was only one o'clock.

The children wouldn't be home for another three hours and she'd be lucky if her husband would be back in seven.

She opened a bottle of wine. It was a shiraz from the local liquor store. They could afford expensive wine, but she never bothered—it wasn't like she had anyone to impress with refined wine tastes out here in the woods.

In the past, she'd drank to feel less alone, an attempt to numb some of the brain cells constantly complaining about her mundane life so far from the big city of her youth, now she drank to still the fear of her house being less empty than it seemed.

She'd told her husband about her fear, said she felt like something else shared the big house with her, maybe a stalker or a ghost. Her worries made him laugh. He rubbed his temples and pushed his thick glasses up against tired eyes before delving into a dry monologue about cabin fever and the dangers of loneliness on the human psyche.

It had ended with him suggesting she join spin class to make friends.

Her husband was a smart man, she loved him for it, but sometimes his ignorance hurt.

She finished half the bottle by two. She normally restrained herself until the kids were home and supper was made, but that was getting harder and harder.

The sound of birds chirping played over an ad for hunting equipment on the nearby television. She listened with longing, it was a familiar sound but one she hadn't heard in a while.

She'd asked her husband if he thought it strange there were no birds in their yard anymore, but he told her she must be imagining things. He came home too tired and slept too deeply to notice the disappearance of bird songs.

They were gone though, she was sure of it. It had been weeks since she'd heard the droll cry of a pigeon or the happy shriek of a jay. Even the humming bird feeder they kept expectantly on their deck remained devoid of life, the ample birdseed inside going untouched as the spring faded.

Yes, the birds were gone, leaving only silence and the paranoid sense of being watched in her massive house. A house which, no matter how hard she cleaned, always seemed to have a few more cobwebs than it should, especially considering she never found the spiders that made them.

Hal

Hope had three bars, four if you counted the one at the motocross track that opened from June to August. They all turned a profit despite the slumping economy and high competition. The fact that a town with barely six thousand people needed four bars (and seven liquor stores) worried no one but the local doctors.

Of the four bars, Hal enjoyed two. The first was a bowling alley that somehow managed to get a liquor license despite the government of Canada doing its best to prohibit such establishments, the second was a relatively clean alcohol dispenser known as the Chalice. No one knew why it was called the Chalice, the name was much too extravagant for Hope, but no one really cared.

The reason Hal enjoyed the bowling alley and the Chalice was that he hated drinking over the noise of motorbikes in the summer and he'd been banned for life from Hope's only other year-round bar, a shack on the outskirts of town known as The Lounge. He'd earned his entry prohibition by puking on the owner's daughter. In Hal's defense, it had been his first date since his wife left him and any man might have turned to liquor to calm their nerves, if anything the owner should have been pleased he had a daughter capable of inducing such anxiety.

He now took precautions to avoid being banned from further bars, which was too say he didn't hit on the wait staff or their relatives. It was difficult, but he persevered.

Hal was currently in the Chalice. His booth was occupied by two other patrons seated on faded black leather.

One was Sammy, a part-time welder and fulltime barfly. He sipped on a Corona mixed with Clamato juice when his lips weren't weaving tales of bullshit and comedy. He was nearing fifty with grey hair and course skin, sitting on his head was a black cap with the words VIP stitched in white onto it. He'd "won" the hat in a fistfight during his last boss' wedding and never went in public without it.

The other member of the party was Dolores, a sixty year old Hope resident who normally reserved her visits to the Chalice for weekends. Her hair still had the odd blotch of brown mixed with the silver, but her skin was worn and leathery. Her laugh lines were deep and currently extending as Sammy finished a wonderful story about leaving an ex-girlfriend at the bottom of a large hill because Sammy's Moped was struggling to carry both of them.

Sammy chortled as red tinged beer sloshed from his mug. "So I left her. So I left her, because she was too fat." Dolores' face turned bright red with mirth. "And my Moped almost made it, I almost made it, but fuck me if the thing didn't run out of gas before I hit the top."

Hal was laughing too. He'd never met a man with so little shame, and Hal looked in the mirror every morning.

"So I get off, and I start pushing, and it's hard and slow, but what do I get for motivation? I look back and there she is, running up the hill, looked like a bull who'd seen red."

Laughter erupted from a nearby table. "Jesus Christ, Sammy, you need help," someone called out. It wasn't uncommon for people to listen in on Sammy's stories.

"And she's gaining too, she's not much of an athlete but my god, she's getting close."

Dolores began to slap Sammy's shoulder. "Sammy Dewitt, I swear, your mother..." She didn't finish the sentence because she'd begun to snort uncontrollably.

"I could hear her screaming too, *Sammy I'll fucking kill you!* So I got scared, I did, I got scared. Started to figure that maybe visiting my cabin isn't worth it."

Hal tipped the rest of his beer back into his mouth, relaxing into the worn booth.

"So I turned the moped around and hopped back on. You should have seen the look on her face when I whizzed past her." He made a strangling motion with his hands. "She even tried to grab me, but I was too quick." He giggled. "I was too quick for her."

Dolores wheezed out a statement between deep breaths. "Oh Lord, Sammy, you're one of the good ones." She raised her margarita to clink it with Sammy's orange tinged mug. "Even if you are a complete asshat."

"Thank you, my lady, thank you. What's a matter, Hal? Too good to join our toast?"

Hal let out a theatrical sigh. "Alas, my cup runneth empty."

Dolores waved an arm at the bartender, a bored college student more interested in her phone than the sad excuse for humanity that she fed beer. Hal couldn't quite remember her name—Kelly or Shelly or something similar—but he knew she didn't like her job. He didn't blame her, not many big tippers lived in Hope. She'd be gone in a few months, back to college or literally anywhere else, and Hal would miss her because she always laughed at his jokes and was talented at pouring beer from the Chalice's old pipes.

Pulling herself slowly from her phone, Shelly—or Kelly—walked over. "What can I get you guys?" Her voice was sweet, but her eyes didn't light up.

"Hello, dear. Well I would love another margarita, and can you get a beer for my friend, Hal, here?"

"Sure thing, miss."

Sammy was fumbling in his pants for a pack of smokes hiding in his shirt pocket. "Why, Dolores, you charmer, you even got a smile out of the girl."

Hal smiled at them both. "Thanks, Dolores, this doesn't mean I'll sleep with you."

Sammy let out a roar of laughter while Dolores' wrinkled skin turned beat red. "Why I never."

Finally moving his hands up to his chest Sammy rose from the table. "If you'll excuse me I need a smoke." He winked as he moved off. "Don't get too frisky while I'm gone."

Dolores shook her head while Hal saluted. The bartender brought them over their drinks and then some. "You get free shots if your tab pushes one hundred."

Hal was delighted, but Dolores was in shock. "Oh, honey I haven't had tequila since college."

The bartender shrugged. "I'm sure Hal will drink it if you don't."

Hal laughed. "Thanks, Kelly."

Judging by the girl's smile, he had said the right name, or close enough.

"Come on, Dolores. You're on vacation, just have a sip."

Dolores wrinkled her nose. "Surprise tequila for a surprise vacation."

"Who knew the government could be so generous?"

Dolores raised her tumbler and took an inquisitive sniff. "I don't know if it's generosity. I think they just wanted an old bag like me out of the way."

"Nonsense, you're being rewarded for all your years helping the Hope PD."

"Maybe—I doubt it—but maybe." When her words ended, Dolores tipped back her shot. Hal barely had time to follow suit.

When they'd both choked down the liquor, Hal had a smile on his face, but Dolores didn't. "You must have been trouble in college, barely a cough out of you from that," He teased.

Dolores' smile was warm, but her eyes were distant. Hal hoped she wasn't going to pass out. "Oh I had my moments." She leaned back into the leather booth and sighed.

"Seriously, Hal, we have a real police force now."

"Dolores, are you implying Benz, Jeb, and Doctor Freeze aren't a real police force?"

"You know I love Jeb and Benz, but Hope only has three police officers—not exactly the pinnacle of crime fighting. Last night, the detachment was full, and I mean full. Christ, there were even men in suits." She began to stir the thick green slush constituting her margarita. "They were almost like soldiers."

Hal shrugged. "The RCMP is paramilitary."

"That's not what I meant."

"I know, also you didn't say what you thought of Hope's third officer."

Hal might have gotten an answer that made him laugh were it not for the fact he was interrupted—as was quickly becoming common—by his cousin.

"Harold."

"Bobbi, how goes it?" Hal pushed the tequila shot left for the absent Sammy forward. "Drink?"

Bobbi wrinkled her nose and scrunched her face, the beanie she was wearing covered her eyebrows, but Hal was sure they were furrowed. "You've been ignoring my calls."

"Too busy celebrating, Dolores has some good news."

Dolores waved to Bobbi, it was followed by a happy burp. "Unexpected vacation, curtesy of the government."

Bobbi regarded Dolores for an instant, her eyes sweeping her up and down. "You're not working at the cop shop any more, Dolores?"

"Three week holiday—paid—don't want the local dregs messing with their big city investigation."

Bobbi frowned. "Aren't you upset they think you're dead weight?"

Dolores looked puzzled. "Upset? Lord, no child, I'm hoping they take their time solving it so I can get more reading done." She blushed, "Of course I don't actually want them to take long, it's just been so long since I've had…"

Her rambling was interrupted by the elated voice of Sammy cascading across the bar. "Bobbi, Bobbi, Bobbi." The old boozehound thread himself through the empty tables to the booth. "What brings you here, love? I thought you quit drinking."

Hal laughed. "After the night with the piñata?"

Bobbi's face remained stern in spite the gaiety around her. "Harold, I need your help."

Sammy clutched his heart, sinking a knee to the floor. "Not even a hello from the young lady, oh my pride."

Harold still held an outstretched tequila shot. "Bobbi, there's an entire army in the police detachment trying to solve the murders, what more can we do?" Sammy sunk himself into the booth and began to talk animatedly to Dolores.

"I have a lead."

Hal gave up on feeding Bobbi the liquor and drank it himself. "Oh lord, another lead?"

"A good one."

"What is it?"

Bobbi's eyes shifted to Sammy and Dolores who were engaged in a fierce arm wrestling match, one Sammy was losing despite his broad arms. "Not here."

Hal's exasperation was palpable. "Okay, Scully."

Hal's excuse for leaving was barely noted by Sammy and Dolores, who had broken into an animated discussion on the merits of mouth guards in the NHL.

Hal and Bobbi slunk out of the bar, slipping around the side of its worn exterior into a tiny patio sequestered between the kitchen entrance and a storage shed. A cook was finishing a cigarette which he gently stubbed into a dirty ash tray as they approached, waving a friendly hello before stepping back into the noisy galley.

Hal waved back, "Hey Dave… you know, Bobbi, if you want privacy we can head to my cabin. I have tinfoil we can make hats from and I'm sure the only bugs around are mosquitos."

"I'm serious, Harold, I found something," she said with excitement, eyes spread as wide as the pale moon rising behind her. "Even if it doesn't amount to much I could get it published on the story alone."

"I thought you said fiction was the enemy of journalism."

"It's not fiction if someone else tells it to you."

"Right."

"Right, now look at this." Bobbi pushed her cellphone into Hal's face, the white screen a shock to his eyes after spending the last three hours in the dim lights of the Chalice.

"GPS coordinates?"

Bobbi nodded. "Remember when we were kids, there was that forest fire?"

Hal scratched his head. His memory was poor and grew blurrier the farther back it went. It didn't help that forest fires were as common as the flu in the vast swaths of wilderness surrounding Hope. "You're going to have to be more specific."

"The chemical lab that burnt down, the one the government ran. Remember? It spread all around it and they had to close the roads down."

"The one near Inkawathia Lake?" He grasped at the tangled edges of the memory, trying to drag it to the front of his ragged brain. "I remember. The feds came in. They were worried something harmful might have leaked into the air."

"Yes, that's the one. They set up road blocks and we we're excited because we got to see men in those white hazmat suits like on TV."

Hal grinned, "You thought they were aliens. You kept asking me where their spaceship was."

Bobbi let out a rare smile. "I wouldn't have thought they were spacemen if you didn't keep telling me they were." She pushed a strand of loose brown hair out of her face and continued. "Maybe you were right."

Hal hummed the X-Files intro. In a mock news anchor's voice, he followed with "They walk among usss ooooooo." The smile remained on Bobbi's lips, but it didn't widen at Hal's antics. "And who is it that sent you these mysterious coordinates?"

She shifted from foot to foot, slapping a mosquito from her bare shoulder. "You remember the woman we met the other day?"

"As if I could forget, you get used to crazy in Hope, but she was something else."

"Yeah well she sent me this right before she disappeared off the Earth."

Hal whistled. "You can't find the insane drifter who only meets reporters in shady cabins on the outskirts of town? Shocking."

Bobbi shook her head. "She's not a drifter, her name is Jane Howards and she used to be a Hope local."

"Being a Hope local doesn't exactly make her more credible."

"For someone who's lived here his whole life, you sure have a low opinion of your neighbours."

Hal waved his hands over himself, his white shirt was beer stained and his blue jeans still had oil on them from working on his truck earlier. "I didn't say I was better."

"Anyway, she moved away a few years ago but she came back, right when people started going missing."

"So, maybe she's the killer."

"No, she got here a week after Lucy Anne disappeared. I checked with the motel." Gary Anderson who ran Lucky's Motel would sell his own sister for a six pack so getting customer information from him wasn't exactly difficult if you had twenty dollars in your wallet.

Hal rubbed his temples, he could hear shouting from the kitchen, it was likely Jules berating some poor dishwasher for misplacing a knife or pot he needed. "But how do you know she's missing?"

"I was trying to convince her to meet again, maybe get a coherent story out of her but she hasn't answered a call or text."

"Insane woman doesn't want to meet overzealous local reporter, again I think you're grasping at straws, Bobbi."

"I contacted her sister in Toronto. She hasn't heard from her in days."

"Did her sister say this was unusual?"

Bobbi's expression curdled. "Look, Harold, psychotic or not, the poor woman is missing."

"Allegedly missing."

"She hasn't checked into her motel in days."

Hal sighed. "And you want to go looking for her?"

Bobbi shook her head, her short hair tangling as it slid back and forth across her face. "No, I want to go to the chemical lab. It was the last message she sent me."

Hal was tempted, if only because it had been ages since he'd visited Inkawathia, but he also didn't like the idea of his cousin following the directions of a crazed woman and (for all he knew) possible serial killer.

Bobbi flicked a piece of dirt off the corner of Hal's t-shirt. "Please, Hal?"

"Calling me Hal and not Harold? Jesus, you are desperate." Bobbi blushed, it made him think of the little cousin he used to take fishing and tell ghost stories to. "Fine but only if we camp over at Inkawathia after, fishing season is starting and the lake there is amazing."

Her voice grew chipper. "There's the Harold I know."

"Oh so it's Harold now that—" he stopped to look at the passing police car, it's lights shifting over the bar as it cruised slowly by. "They've sure stepped up the patrols since the big wigs rolled in."

Bobbi stared intently at the car as it continued down the dark road into the nearby subdivision. "Suppose it should make me feel safer."

"Some of the local boys would disagree, they're all terrified their "farms" will be compromised with all the extra law enforcement."

"I doubt it, I think these cops are more concerned with catching serial killers than curbing our dope growing problem."

Hal moved away from the kitchen door as a young man walked out screaming over his shoulder. "Problem? Who said it was a problem?"

The young man ignored them as he sat down and lit his cigarette, leaning back and coughing out a cloud of smoke between curses directed under his breath at a "facist fucking fry chef."

Bobbi's gaze continued trailing the fading taillights of the cop cruiser as it disappeared down the road. "At least I hope they're concerned with catching serial killers."

Hal shook his head and turned to the fuming young man. "Jules in a mood, Tom?"

The young man kept his eyes fixed on the ceiling, smoke pouring out of his nostrils like an angry dragon. "Some people shouldn't be given an ounce of power, Hal, not an ounce."

"Isn't that the truth, buddy?"

Without looking, the young man pulled out one of the chairs circling the table. "Pull up a seat, Hal, stop lurking like a fucking crackhead." He glanced over at Bobbi who was still fixated on the dark night. "You too, Bobbi, I haven't seen you since high school."

Hal sunk into the chair with easy acceptance. Bobbi joined him after a brief moment of hesitation. "How you been, Tom?"

Tom stubbed his first cigarette and pulled another one from his pack. Putting it between his lips he let out a wan smile. "Can't complain, Bobbi, can't complain."

Laura

She never saw the fangs coming, only felt them sink into her shoulder. They burrowed deep into her spine, cracking the bone and gushing a warm liquid. A tingling filled her body as the teeth retracted, accompanied by a soft voice.

Daughter...

A strange calm washed over her, she found herself incapable of remembering why she'd been so frightened a moment ago.

We... love you.

The man walked out of the darkness, hunting knife in hand. She didn't flinch as he thrust the blade into the web sac holding her. With a grunt he cut her down, spilling her weak body to the floor.

She didn't cry as her head struck stone, a dark fluid filling her mouth but not words. The man hauled her to her feet where she stood dazed.

"Is it working?" said the man to the writhing shadow behind him.

We... love you,

Laura frowned. Who loved her? Where was she? Her mind struggled to remember the English language. "I'm... what?"

The man tenderly stroked her shoulder. Don't worry, child." he murmured as he slid his hand down her arm.

Laura. Mother loves you.

"M-m-mother?" The word felt foreign on her tongue.

"Yes, girl, we both love you."

Her mind reeled. Mother, of course, mother. "I… love Mother."

Make Mother proud.

Laura nodded slowly. The man's breath was hot on her face. "Proud? I… make… mother proud?"

Mother wants children, Laura. Lots of children.

Dark fluid seeped from her lips as she smiled. Of course, make mother proud. She loved mother. She wanted to please Mother.

She would give Mother children.

Blake

Working at Dairy Queen wasn't bad. It was mind numbing and occasionally demeaning, but it wasn't bad. If the worst thing Blake ever did in his life was deal with a woman screaming because she received a chocolate dipped ice cream cone instead of a chocolate flavoured one, he would count himself lucky.

This wasn't to say he enjoyed being screamed at, quite the contrary. His sister was watching, and he hated for her to have to see such stupidity in a woman who could have been her own mother.

"This happens every time, every time I come to this shithole I ask for a chocolate ice cream cone." Blake peered past the woman to Sarah. She was seated in one of the bright red plastic chairs with her eyes glued to the restaurant's TV. The sound was on, but not so loud as to drift over to the bustling workers behind the counter. "Not chocolate dipped, just chocolate."

Blake nodded his head. "Sorry, ma'am, I'll get you a new one."

The woman scrunched her nose, her blonde highlights shifting as she did. "I don't want a new one, think how wasteful that would be. When you're older you'll understand not to waste things other people don't have."

"Like time, miss?"

Blake bit his tongue, he'd been doing so well.

The woman's face puffed red as her eyes began to bulge from her skull. "What did you just fucking say?" she hissed through clenched teeth. The faint scent of mint drifted from her mouth.

Blake was saved from the impending lecture by a call from behind him. "Hey, Blake, can you help unload the stock truck? I'll help the customer." Dusty, the manager, walked in from out back where he'd been smoking. His lips were pursed but his eyes were alive with mirth.

"Ah, Miss Daniels. Let me guess—wrong ice cream?"

"Oh, Dusty, I swear the kids get dumber and dumber each year. Heaven knows what they teach them in school."

Blake bowed his head in appreciation as he slid past Dusty. The stock truck wasn't due until tomorrow morning. He strolled past the cooks and grilles into the break room. Setting himself down in the comfiest chair, he leaned back to stare at a poster of Taylor Swift hanging from the ceiling. He wasn't a fan, but there were worse things to look at.

"I didn't take you for a Swift fan, Blake."

Wobbling dangerously back and forth in the chair from the surprise, he only narrowly avoided tipping out of it. "Jesus, Michelle, what are you doing here?"

Michelle pulled up a seat beside him, the smell of tobacco and liquor wafting from her. "Party got broken up by the cops, so I came to see how my brother was doing."

"Probably not so good now. He's dealing with Mrs. Daniels."

Michelle snorted. "That bag? You know Russel purposely ruins her order every time? He thinks if it happens enough it will make her stop coming here."

Blake let out a heavy sigh. "I know he does. If he had to deal with her he might not do it."

"Oh, he deals with her plenty. She lives in the apartment across from him."

They both laughed—Michelle's raspier than Blake's but as full of life. "I didn't know. I thought I had it bad having to see her once a week."

Michelle pushed a knuckle into her eye and leaned forward. Blake could smell her perfume over the tobacco. When she spoke, her breath pushed against his face. It was sweet but tinged with the harsh scent of liquor. "Blake, I'm sorry I was a bitch the other day."

Blake's understanding of healthy relationships began and ended with his little sister. It felt strange to receive an apology, even if it was one he deserved. "Don't worry about it—I should have told you I was going to work tonight."

Michelle continued as if he hadn't spoke. "No seriously, you were only thinking of your sister and I was being silly."

Michelle leaned in close, pink strands of hair draping onto his shoulder while her lips hovered beside his ear.

"Ok?"

"Ok, now listen—tomorrow night, let's go out. I still have a bottle of wine left and we can have a picnic." She finished by tilting her head and kissing him on the lips.

Blake coughed uncomfortably. "Michelle, I, uh, don't find you attractive."

He didn't see the slap coming but he felt it, burning against his skin as he hastily tried to rephrase his sentence.

"I mean, of course I find you attractive, you're gorgeous."

"What the fuck, Blake, you know how hard it is to express yourself to a guy?" Her voice trembled as she continued. "I had to drink half a bottle of wine to get the fucking courage to do it."

Blake bit his lip. "Fuck."

"Fuck you," she sobbed. "Fuck."

Blake exhaled slowly. "It's not your fault."

The second slap stung slightly less but still left a red print glowering on Blake's face. "What the fuck, Blake, learn when to stop talking."

"It's not your fault," Blake continued, patience dwindling, "That I don't like women."

Michelle hiccupped, eyes turning downcast in dim surprise. "Oh."

■■

When his shift ended, Sarah was asleep. She'd curled up in one of the booths cradling a colouring book between one arm and a kid's meal toy between the other. She didn't wake as he lifted her and trudged wearily out of the restaurant.

The lights remained on behind him but the restaurant's only occupants were Dusty, nursing a nightcap of whiskey and his little sister sleeping off a bottle of wine and the pain of rejection.

Dusty had been amicable about the situation, shrugging his shoulders and promising his "secret" was safe with him, as if it was something Blake should be ashamed of.

Michelle was understanding in her own way, tears smearing her makeup as she told him it was just her luck that the only nice guy she met didn't like women. Blake was tempted to remind her that at least she could meet men in Hope. Blake didn't know a single queer man in the entire town. He kept his mouth shut though, the poor girl looked so wretched then that criticizing her would have felt akin to kicking a puppy.

Blake told her the things you were meant to tell a broken-hearted teenager; there would be other men, she was a brave intelligent woman, all she had to do was be patient.

It had done little good. It took the soothing words of her brother and a tirade of text messages from her "best friend since, like, grade kindergarten" to coax her into a state of borderline calm.

Sarah burped as an unseen pothole caused him to bounce her in his arms. Pushing back a wave of fatigue he reminded himself to make sure she brushed her teeth tonight, even if he had to do it while she was sleeping.

The jingle of his cellphone echoed across the empty streets. Fumbling, he pulled his phone from his pants' pocket. When he flipped it open he was greeted with the raucous sound of rock music and high-pitched laughter. Sarah mumbled something in her sleep while he pushed the mobile against his ear.

"Blake, hon. Hi."

Blake remained silent. He was surprised the phone hadn't rung earlier.

"Listen, hon. It's—like—super busy." More laughter was followed by a piercing shriek. "Oh, my god. I'm on the phone, Kyle, Jesus."

Blake wished he'd brought a coat as he passed beneath the waning light of a streetlamp. The days were warm, but night still had some bite.

"So anyway, I'm going to have to stay late tonight." Blake started to speak but he was cut off. "Remember to tuck your sister in. Goodnight."

With an electronic click, the phone was silent. Blake grumbled to himself, "As if I'd forget to tuck in Sarah." His pace slowed, the soft sound of snoring carried up to his ears. Sarah was resting her head in the nook of his shoulder. Blake wondered how she could stand the smell of him after he'd spent the last hour mixing milkshakes and comforting drunks.

It was noisy in the trailer park when he arrived but that was usual for a Friday night. Leroy Smith was having a party that had spilled out onto his lawn. Beer bottles littered the grass and more than a little puke coated the rusted Ford sitting in the driveway. A crowd had gathered around two bikers who were either ready to fight or make love—Blake couldn't tell which as their shouts were swallowed up by the laughs and jeers of the surrounding crowd.

In the trailer over from Leroy's, Ms. Brightly was passed out in her rocking chair. Her lights were on and screen door wide open. Her thin body was uncovered and it looked like she'd vomited on her shirt. Blake, who generally did his best not to get emotional about his neighbours, felt a fierce pang of pity. The woman had always been a drunk but at least she'd been able to function before Laura went missing.

Pushing open the unlocked door to their own trailer, Blake was greeted by the smell of beer and a barely dispersed haze of pot and tobacco. His aunt worked with another Hope local, a high school friend name Charlene. The two occasionally (always) got "socially lubricated" before driving to the bar they waitressed at.

Leaving the door open, Blake carried his sister to her room. It was little bigger than a closet and littered with pictures and drawings. Most of them were of pop singers and movie stars ripped from magazine pages but a few were cartoon characters from a Japanese anime she liked. Between the rows of cartoon and celebrity faces, hung a few snapshots of Blake and Sarah.

In one, they were fishing. Blake was holding a massive bass while Sarah stood underneath it waving at the camera. In another, they were dressed for Halloween; Blake, a dashing knight, Sarah, a living pumpkin. Pinned in the honorary spot above her pillow was a picture of Blake, Sarah, and their deceased sister, Linda. It was a faded picture—Blake wasn't sure where it had come from. In it, Sarah wore diapers, her little face alight as she bounced on Linda's lap. Blake was sitting beside her gazing eagerly at a toy car Linda had bought him. He still had the car. It didn't make him smile anymore.

There were no photos of their parents.

With his sister in bed, he checked the fridge. It was devoid of food but contained a glorious supply of beer. He cracked one as he marched to the front door. The smell of pot had dissipated, but the stink of cigarettes clung to the trailer. He sighed. Was it so hard to smoke outside?

Across the lane, Ms. Brightly shifted in her chair, leaning over to wretch onto her lawn. "Well at least this time she didn't get it on herself." Blake bowed his head. Ms. Brightly had always been nice to him and Sarah in her own dysfunctional way, and while it might be warm enough to smoke outside it wasn't warm enough to sleep.

Shaking his head, he walked back inside. He grabbed Sarah's toothbrush and coated the bristles with a tiny goblet of toothpaste. He filled up a glass of water and walked into her room. She was fast asleep, but she woke long enough to brush her teeth, spitting out the thick paste into the cup she before whispering a sleepy goodnight to Blake.

With one child dealt with, Blake walked back to the trailer's doorway and eyed the other. Somehow she'd managed to tip her rocker and was crawling in her own vomit. Blake waited a minute, hoping one of the twenty partiers on the lawn beside her would bother to do something, but the ones who noticed Ms. Brightly's predicament merely pointed and laughed.

Blake had learnt one fundamental lesson in his short time alive: life didn't pull its punches. He shut the trailer door, remembering to lock it—unlike his aunt—and marched across the road. He gave a curt nod to a classmate who waved from a circle of smokers, but didn't bother to call out to him or any of the other familiar faces among the drunken revelers.

He brought his beer with him, finishing it by the time he reached the collapsed body of Ms. Brightly. He tossed the bottle into the woman's formidable pile of empties.

"Alright, Ms. Brightly, let's get you to bed." With a groan he heaved the woman's limp body from the grass, ignoring the foul liquid dripping from her mouth and onto his work uniform. "It seems all I do lately is deal with drunks and assholes."

He shouldered his way into her trailer. Bottles filled it wall to wall, the sight was unpleasant but the stench worse. The saddest sight was the bed—unmade and covered in beer bottles and photo albums. Most of the albums were open, the smiling faces gazing out of them at odds with the derelict house surrounding them.

Gently placing Ms. Brightly in the bed, he did his best to make some space, pushing the beer bottles to the floor with little care and making sure to neatly stack the albums on a nearby table.

He had little curiosity about the photo albums—there was only one person Ms. Brightly would bother photographing and she'd been missing for the better part of a month. The intriguing part to him was how she'd managed to amass such a collection of photos. He'd always figured the woman drank too much to have time for homely activities like scrapbooking.

Placing a wool blanket on the woman, Blake moved to leave when he was pulled back by a weak grip on his arm. "Please."

Her eyes were glassy and drool was dribbling down her mouth. Blake was reminded of helping Dr. Nand and Gale with Ms. McCormack in the Ainsfield Hotel weeks earlier. Ms. Brightly and Ms. McCormack had the same hollow look, as if they'd already died and been left here only to suffer.

"It's alright, Ms. Brightly. Go to bed."

He felt the grip tighten around his wrist. "I can hear it, I can hear it."

Blake pulled his arm back lightly, but the woman kept a frail grip on him. "Go to sleep, Ms. Brightly, you'll feel better in the morning."

"At night, before I sleep. At the edge." She stared up at him pleadingly. "You know, before the dreams."

"Yes, now goodnight." He forcefully pulled his arm back and the poor woman's hand fell to her chest, nearly hitting her own face on its downward arc.

Her eyes remained on him—milky and distant but fixed on his face. "I can hear it talking about my daughter."

Blake winced and took a tentative step backwards. "Your daughter is fine, Ms. Brightly, now go to sleep."

The woman frowned. "Don't you see? It has her, you know." She twisted violently in her bed, knocking a beer bottle Blake hadn't removed onto the floor, shattering it. Her face contorted, and her lips pursed. "It says I wasn't a good mother, it says it will do better."

When Blake left she was curled in her bed whimpering. On his way through her yard he grabbed an unopened Budweiser left beside her chair. He sucked it down quickly with little regard for the taste.

The crowd on Leroy's lawn had changed from a wild throng of bodies into a well-organized circle. The two bikers stood in the center of it, their shouting match now transformed into a fistfight. Blake ignored them as he passed, opening his trailer door with shaking hands.

"From now on no more helping crack heads," he whispered to himself.

He slept in Sarah's room that night, curled up on her floor with only a pillow and a thin blanket, while a picture of a Disney Channel star gazed down at him from above. Sarah's soft breathing eased his mind, but sleep was tough to come by.

He wondered if he'd ever be able to afford therapy when he was older—missing parents, strange neighbours, and discovering dead bodies—he was pretty sure he'd benefit from a few sessions with a shrink.

It was only in the early hours of the morning that sleep finally came to him, heavy and dreamless it washed his worries away.

His sister slept soundly beside him, her dreams filled with images of her mother. She was smiling and beckoning Sarah to join her as they walked to the park. It was a happy dream and Sarah felt safe. Sarah had had the dream many times before, save for one difference—a spider now sat on her mother's shoulder, it's many eyes peering at Sarah in interest as its crooked legs dug into her mother's flesh.

Hal

Normally not one to rise before the crack of eleven, Hal found himself happy to be cruising along the highway in the early morning light. The trees lining the road blurred into an endless stream of greens and brown, interspersed with the occasional break in the tree line that afforded a view of the surrounding mountains. There were no cars on the road this early in the morning and it was likely they would see more than the odd trucker passing on this distant offshoot from civilization.

They were in Bobbi's car. The back half of it was filled with two tents, a large weather beaten cooler, and (at Hal's insistence) two fishing rods.

Bobbi sat behind the wheel, her fingers gripping it loosely as they flew up and down the many hills leading to Inkawathia. Her iPod was plugged into the cars radio—blasting out some airy pop music from a band Hal didn't know.

"Is this what the kids are into these days?"

Bobbi didn't take her eyes off the seemingly endless road in front them as she replied, "If you did more than drink and feel sorry for yourself you might know a bit more about the current music scene."

Their cellphones no longer had service and Hal didn't know why anyone bothered buying one in this province, but the GPS he'd "borrowed" from work told them they were on the right track.

"Good lord, and I thought I hated mornings." From the corner of his eye he could see his cousin's lips purse. "Right up here by the way."

Bobbi didn't slam on the breaks, exactly, but she did slow a bit quicker than Hal would have liked. He felt his fishing rod crash into the back of his seat and as the camping supplies sequestered in the back rattled violently.

His cousin gritted her teeth as she turned the wheel sharply, pulling the car from the smooth pavement of the highway and onto a rough dirt road. "Harold, next time a little warning might be nice."

Hal let out the breath he'd been clenching since he'd told her to turn. "Next time turning slower might be nice." Bobbi scrunched her nose but didn't respond.

They continued on the dirt road, winding their way deeper into the woods that so abundantly covered British Columbia. Eventually the pop album gave way to some rap music, songs about the inner city and "hoes" Hal had trouble relating to. It made him sad, he was getting old.

The road was bumpy but free of fallen foliage—a cloud of dust trailed them as they went. The sun shone bright above them, even as the tree line grew thicker and thicker around them.

There were no signs left but as they made their way closer to the GPS coordinates, Hal began to make out the remnants of the facility that had once stood there. They passed patches of metal fencing engulfed by blackberry bushes and concrete barriers barely visible under masses of moss and other growth. He whistled in wonder at the sight of what might have once been a guard shack, now sitting with its roof caved in by the collapsing of a nearby tree.

Hal was prepared for the overgrown look of the site, expected it, what he hadn't prepared for was someone bothering to lock it up.

"Shit." Bobbi's words were quiet and did nothing to prepare him for the harsh screeching of brakes or the accompanying lurching of his stomach. He felt the seatbelt dig into his flesh, cutting as his body tried to force its way into the windshield. When the car finally slid to a stop, he snapped back into his seat with a jarring thud.

Hal massaged his neck while his eyes drifted to Bobbi. She sat upright with her fingers clenched white against the wheel. When he spoke, it was with leveled annoyance, "Who'd have thought the gate would still be up?"

Bobbi's shoulders began to wilt but her fingers remained wrapped around the steering wheel. "Yeah, that was a surprise."

His seatbelt hissed as he pressed the release button, the polyester band snapping from his body with angry haste. The car was still running when his boots crunched onto the gravel outside.

It was a simple gate composed of a long metal bar that ran from one pole to another. The bar itself hung clumsily, made crooked by more than a few bends in the twisted metal. It had been blue once, probably, but had suffered under the tireless pummeling of the elements. Most of it was covered in moss and what little lay still exposed to the air was marred by rust.

The gate itself was a weary thing, indicative of a something long forgotten, the padlock hanging from it was not. It seemed to flash in the bright light of the sun, shining out to Hal from where he stood. He approached it with wry unease, muttering to himself as he did.

"Who has the time to come out here." With a calm hand but a beating heart he lifted the padlock. "Brand new." He shook his head and spit. "What kind of idiot would lock this place up? It's public land."

"You sure about that, cousin?" Bobbi had pulled herself out from her seat to stand by the car while casting accusing looks over to Hal.

"If there's a fishing spot involved, I can tell you what is and isn't public land in every direction a hundred miles from Hope."

Bobbi raised her iPhone and snapped a few pictures of Hal and the gate. "We're a little farther than a hundred miles from Hope."

"You know what I meant." Aggravated by the surprise and the questioning he marched over to the gate and took a forceful step over it. "If some moron wants to play jokes and lock up the road, we'll see how they like the ticket I write."

Bobbi laughed as the camera continued to flutter. "Aren't we a little out of your jurisdiction, Mr. Forest Ranger?"

Hal shook his head gravely. "Justice knows no bounds," he said with a wave of an imaginary cape. "Come citizen, there's evil afoot."

Bobbi giggled and followed him. The stress that had been welled up behind her face since the early morning was fading ever so lightly as she did.

It was a slow trek, the sun beating down on them despite it barely being past nine. The road continued to wind erratically but, like it had been before the gate, remained free of debris. Occasionally Hal would spot the faint indent of tire marks—little ruts in the stream of orange coloured gravel—no doubt left by the same person or persons who had put a lock on the gate.

Hal could think of many reasons one might bother coming here often, and most of them were illegal. He tilted his head to Bobbi as they marched. "Reckon we'll find a dope farm?"

Bobbi had put down her digital camera and had taken out her cellphone to take photos. "Oh, this will look great on Instagram once I find service."

Hal sighed and turned his eyes back to the walk. It was beautiful out here, in the sun with the trees for company, but he'd be dead before he started taking photos for Instagram. After a little while he tried again.

"So, which do you think we'll find, a grow op or a meth lab?"

Bobbi chewed her lip before answering, "Neither."

Hal groaned. "Come on—lock on the gate, tire marks, crazed drug addict tells you the GPS coordinates—gotta be one or the other." He hoped it was a pot farm. Most times the marijuana farmers weren't crazy enough to try killing you if you caught them, he'd found enough as a park ranger to know.

"Harold, do you really think I'd drag you all the way out here for a drug bust? Barely makes third page news these days."

This was true, the days of Reefer Madness were dissipating. Hal liked to attribute it to the advance of public education and science, but it was more likely because the economy was in a slump and legal drugs were a billion dollar (highly) taxable industry. It didn't change the fact that all he expected to find at the end of the road was a barely coherent hippy growing God's green glory out of a cargo container.

"My bets on weed farm. The dope fiends are trying to get their money's worth before the government cashes in."

Bobbi sniffed. Hal doubted it was due to her hay fever. "You're a man of culture, Harold."

"First time I've heard you be so condescending about smoking."

"Well it's just my opinion that we shouldn't be so casual about the drug war. It's a huge waste of tax payer money used to oppress most disenfranchised segments of society. It's the result racist laws passed…"

Hal tuned out his cousin's droning voice and let his mind wander. This truly was a nice spot for hiking. Maybe he would take his son here when he was older. It would be a good bonding experience, assuming Gloria ever let the boy visit.

They would drive up and park near the gate, regardless of whether it was locked or not. They could haul their gear down the road, sweating and cursing the way Hal and his father had when they went fishing during his own childhood. At night they would build a fire and Hal would tell ghost stories. They could fall asleep looking at the stars shimmering above and the horrendous remains of the building that had once occupied the land.

Hal wasn't crazy about the last part but the image slipped into his mind as they turned a bend and found themselves facing the skeletal remains of the former laboratory.

It was bigger than he expected, three stories still partially standing. The third floor was mostly exposed to the sky with dark scorch marks of fire embedded in its concrete supports. A few windows remined intact on the second floor but the others had been shattered long ago. The front door, a sturdy sheet of pale metal, lay propped up against the wall to the entrance.

Hal whistled while Bobbi snapped photos beside him, her rant on mass incarceration stifled by the view of the laboratory. He voiced the obvious observation for both of them— 'still standing.'

Bobbi walked to the entrance and peered in. "Not even burn marks down here." She raised her camera again to capture the insides of the building.

"Probably got it before it spread. Must have been contained to the third floor."

"I don't know how it could have spread." Hal joined her as she gazed into the complex. The entrance led into a single hallway. Concrete floors and walls lined it with the barest intrusion of greenery from the outside world. "Place is built like a prison."

Hal rapped his fingers gently against the wall, sending a jarring echo down the hall. "Chemical fire. Must have been bad to melt through this stuff."

Bobbi pulled a flashlight from her backpack and pressed it into Hal's hand. "You light the way and I'll snap the photos."

Hal walked in with a casual ease in his step but not in his mind. "Well this should be good for your Instagram." Bobbi ignored him, too busy scanning the dark hallway with keen interest.

As they went deeper into the building, the sunlight disappeared behind them until all that was left was the humble glow of their flashlight.

As they progressed, the walls remained the same, faded concrete devoid of any markings, interrupted only by the occasional door. Most of the doors they passed were locked or blocked from the inside but the few they managed to force open only led into long vacant office rooms filled with old wooden desks and rusted metal filing cabinets.

At first Bobbi had been excited, rushing to one of the cabinets and opening it. She was rewarded with a cloud of dust and little else for her efforts. She continued searching cabinets they found for a while but gave up after finding the shriveled corpse of a dead rat in one.

Their path was a simple one and eventually led to a stairwell. Bright yellow paint was still visible on the wall before it, an arrow pointing up with the number 2 and an arrow pointing down with the letter B.

"I don't think we need a map." Hal chuckled as he let the flashlight waver over the simple guide.

They went upstairs first, the stone steps ending in what had evidently been the primary source of the building's destruction. A few walls still stood, but far more lay in charred ruin, black stone sitting like discarded bones.

The floor was grand, but Hal could see all the way across it to where the walls and roof gave way completely to showcase the surrounding trees.

Kicking his feet gingerly through the rubble, Hal moved away from Bobbi who no longer needed one with the sun blazing above.

This place had likely been like the floor below, rows and rows of offices. What they had done in those rooms Hal hadn't the faintest clue but clearly someone had been working on something flammable.

The fire must have started in the center of the floor, the dark burn marks outlining its spread across the walls and floor.

Bobbi joined him and snapped a few pictures, though her camera was snapping slower than when they had started. "Just a fire."

Hal nodded. "Wasn't even that bad."

Bobbi shrugged and moved to the open end of the floor, standing on the edge of the building looking out onto the world. Hal joined her. It was a good view. He could follow the gentle rises and dips of the forest all the way to the nearby mountain, getting lost in the swirls of green and brown. He inhaled deeply, the fresh scent of the forest only slightly tinged by the dusty smell of the old building.

His cousin didn't take a photo of the landscape, but she did stare for a good long while. When she turned away, her step was lighter over the rubble filled floor. "Shall we check the basement? Not much of the third floor to stand on."

Hal forced his eyes from the woods with a note of resignation, it was looking like an excellent day for fishing. "Sure thing."

Their feet dragged as they made their way down the stairs. Hal was already over the thrill of exploring an abandoned building and daydreaming of reeling and trout while Bobbi was lost in her own train of thought.

It was not until they had passed the first floor in their descent that Hal noticed the noise. It was coming from below, so distant that were it not for the eerie silence of the lab he would have missed it.

He put an arm out to catch Bobbi, who was beside him. As he flashed the light over her face her expression told him she heard it too.

"Wha—" he started but was cut off by a glare and a single finger raised to Bobbi's lips. She nodded her head downward and continued to descend, taking care to tread silently along the concrete stairs.

As Hal followed, the noise grew. Still dampened by the thick walls but near enough to be slightly distinguished. It was talking, or something close, high pitched and too fast to be discernable.

He kept the flashlight pointed at the ground, giving them only enough light to see the steps in front them.

Eventually the stairs leveled into a hallway that was as unlit and barren as the ones above. Hal still couldn't tell where the speaking was coming from, the tight hallway bouncing the voice every which way around, though he could now make out the words.

"And then I stick this here and you tell me if it gives you a shock." A giggle followed. "A curled leg, really? How about if I poke it here?"

Hal searched the darkness for Bobbi's eye, trying to motion that they should turn back, but it was too late. She was ahead of him pressed against the wall with her focus on a dim glimmer of light escaping the bottom of a door deeper down the corridor.

"Don't worry, your friends will be next," another nervous giggle filled Hal's ears. "And then it's nighty night."

Hal waved the flashlight cautiously, trying to both capture Bobbi's attention and avoid shinning it further down the hall. Bobbi waved an angry arm back at him, not bothering to turn as she slithered further along the wall with her iPhone raised.

Hal ground his teeth and turned off the flashlight. After a moment of internal cussing he followed his cousin along the wall, his fingertips tracing dust lines until he joined her at a metal door.

Hal could still hear the voice, but it had shifted to a quieter tone, unintelligible except for a sudden outburst of "Stabby, stabby." His fingers found Bobbi's arm, tightening around them as she raised her iPhone. His lips were dry and voice a weak whisper. "This doesn't sound good."

Bobbi's whisper was harsher. "It sounds like a serial killer."

Hal had never spent much time thinking about what serial killers sounded like, but he had to admit his cousin was likely right. "So, let's call the cops."

Bobbi's voice wavered dangerously as her indignant reply came. "And miss the chance of catching him? Think of all the missing women."

Think of your career, more like. Hal didn't say that though. There was already a possible killer in the next room—he didn't need two.

Breathing in deeply, Bobbi looked at him, her eyes small glints in the black around them. "Ready?"

Hal shook his head. "No."

He felt Bobbi's hair rustle the air near his face as she nodded. "Ready."

She turned and pulled open the door with a loud creak. The light inside streamed out nearly blinding Hal where he stood in the former darkness. No doubt as blind as him, Bobbi raised her camera and began to snap away.

From within the center of the room Hal noticed a small lab, his eyes slowly adjusting. A figure turned to them and a voice called out in surprise, "Who is this?"

Hal raised a hand to shield his eyes from the intense light above, peering towards the person. "Uh, hello." Bobbi didn't bother to speak, her attention still focused on the clicking of her camera.

The figure remained where it was, offering up a hopeful question. "Come to talk to them too?"

Hal coughed uncomfortably. The whole of the room was slowly coming into view and he was only slightly relieved to see it was not lined with dead bodies.

It was a large room, but bare—filled only with what appeared to be necessities. On one side of the room sat a wooden desk, covered with papers and a MacBook with spreadsheets open. Beside the desk sat a large steel filing cabinet, much like the ones they'd seen above.

In the middle of the room was a large metal table, glinting off from the high intensity lights above. Some surgical equipment lay about it; shining metal tweezers, knives, and saws left in careless abandon.

The man—and it was a man—stood over the metal table, his hands hovering over what looked to Hal like a hamster cage. He was bald save for the few long strands of grey hair poking out from behind his ears. His face was pale and his eyes, even so far away, seemed too wide for the harsh brightness of the room. A lab coat covered his body and his hands bore a faint covering of what might have been blood.

Finally, the sound of Bobbi's camera stopped. The man eyed them intently for a second then sighed and turned his gaze back to the glass box before him. His words were barely a mutter as he reached his arms into the top of the box. "It's just I get so few visitors."

Hal stepped forward to get a better look, stopped only by Bobbi's loud gasp. He flicked his eyes towards her. She stood petrified with one hand clasped around her mouth and another pointed at the far wall.

The wall was darker than the rest of the room, spared the blinding light illuminating the rest of it. Hal had barely registered it before but now his eyes raked over what it held. Glass boxes, like the one sitting before the strange man, lined the wall from top to bottom.

Hal had to squint to make out what was inside them. "That can't be…"

At first he thought it was only the shadow playing tricks, but the longer he stared the more it came into view. Each box contained a spider, a very large spider.

They were all moving. Crawling, sliding up and down their cage walls, or spinning in circles from strands hanging from the ceiling of their cages. To Hal it almost seemed they were trying to fight the boredom of their captivity. He noted, to his horror, one near the top of the stacks was too plump for its cage, only capable of lazily tapping a long leg against the glass.

A squelching sound from the center of the room brought Hal's attention back to the odd man. He was smiling now, something thick and hairy raised proudly in his hand. It took Hal a moment to realize it was a leg. "That'll teach you to try flunking the intelligence test." He bashed the leg proudly against the table, it made a hollow thud as it connected. "I know you understand me, you bastards."

Bobbi had turned green, looking as if she might expel her healthy breakfast of oatmeal and strawberries. Hal didn't feel sick, he was merely dazed by the absurd sight before him. "Bobbi, spiders don't grow that big. They don't grow that big."

What sounded to Hal like the whistling of a tea kettle drifted from the table. The strange man stopped wiping his hands on a dirty rag to lean into the box and spit. "Oh quit your whining, you don't need eight anyway."

Bobbi began to wretch on the floor. The man looked up from his work with glazed amusement. "I hope you're not my new intern. The last one only lasted a week but even he didn't puke 'til the third day." The weird hissing noise emanated from the box again. "Oh do be quiet."

Hal tried to speak. It had been easier to form words the previous week when he'd found a literal mass murder. "What… what's going on here?"

The man gave him a puzzled look. "You're not with the Agency?" His wrinkles creased deeply as he did, making the man look somewhat like a corpse.

"No, what's the—" his question was cut off by a furry spider leg striking out from the box. It waved in the air briefly before latching clumsily onto the edge of the cage. The man gave him an honest shrug before turning to the cage. Slowly a rounded back of a spider emerged from the cage, rolling over the side and landing on the table with an audible thud.

The man shook his head and pulled a large hammer from within his coat. "Now, now. You," with a wide arch of his arm he brought the hammer down on the fleshy mass. It made a sickening squelch as it dug into the creatures back. "Know." He continued to hit the animal with the same force, contorting the oval spider into a bloody wreck. "The." He stopped and panted for breath before bringing the hammer down in a final violent swing. "Rules."

Bobbi was kneeling in a pile of her own vomit, her face stark white. When she looked over and saw the spider corpse she continued to add to the puddle surrounding her.

The man dropped the hammer onto the table, letting it spill spider's blood over the plethora of shining instruments on it. He was breathing heavily and beads of sweat dotted his bald head, a thin smile playing across his face.

He grabbed one of the limp legs of the dead spider and lifted it from the ground. It swung back and forth in his grip for a second before he hurled against the glass cages. Turning to them, he started to speak, his voice high pitched and angry. "This is what happens, when you try to keep quiet." He wiped his head and added more softly, "I just want us to be friends."

Bobbi had finished her retching and was slowly rising from the floor. Hal barely noticed. His eyes were fixed on the glass cages while his feet took tentative steps backwards.

The spiders stopped their movement, every single one standing motionless with their unblinking eyes striking out from the darkness.

The man remained facing the cages, wiping sweat from his brow with the back of his hand. He sounded like he was addressing a child when he spoke. "Now I have your attention. Who wants to go next? There's an extra rat for a good volunteer."

The spiders stood still for another heartbeat before emitting a loud screech. It was piercing, digging through Hal's ears and into his brain. For a moment he thought he could hear them speaking inside his skull, a single foreign word pushing itself into his mind: *die.*

The spiders started attacking the thick glass, hurling their bodies against it with menace. The cages began to shake violently and few let out a soft crackling sound.

The man seemed undisturbed by the rebellion. "Cranky children get nap time," he said shaking his head. His withered fingers flourished a remote from within his white coat, his thumb descending upon its single button with zeal.

Gas hissed into the containers, green clouds enveloping the hairy spiders until their tiny heads drooped, and many legs curled. After a minute they were all still save for the largest one. It continued to beat its single leg against the glass, eyes glowering through the haze around it.

The man walked forward and pressed his head against the glass containing the behemoth arachnid. Disappointment was clinging to his words. "Oh, Clarence. You've always been such a good boy. It's why I let you grow so big, why do you insist on acting up now?"

The spider continued beating its leg against the glass, each tap coming slower than the last until finally it too stood still.

Shaking his head, the man turned around. "It's hard work raising children." He turned his head to his feet and let out a nervous giggle. "I should know."

Bobbi crawled towards Hal, placing an arm on his leg to stop herself from swaying. Her voice was hoarse as she spoke. "It had to be spiders, Hal."

Hal was lost for words, only capable of staring forward, dumbfounded.

Bobbi giggled weakly. "And you thought we'd find a meth lab."

Hal remained mute, bending down to help his cousin to her shaking feet.

The man looked up, distress spreading across his face. "Don't go," he pleaded. "They get so few chances to meet other people." His smile was broad, the surgical lights showcasing the scattered remnants of his teeth. "It's good for them to meet new people."

Hal swallowed. "We're, uh, good."

The man shook his head anxiously. "No really, I swear they're normally well behaved." He glanced back behind him quickly. "Just a few with rebellious spirits." He shrugged, "You know how teenagers are."

Hal had dealt with more than a few teenagers in his life. Thankfully, most of them only had two legs and two eyes. "Yes."

They made their way into the hallway where, without consulting each other, they broke out into a fast run. The man's voice chased them as they went, carried along by the stone hallway.

"They just need a few friends."

Bobbi

It had to be spiders. Fucking spiders. Her whole life she'd avoided the creepy bastards and the only story she'd ever uncovered that might make national news involved overgrown arachnids.

Her breath reeked, and her jeans were caked with filth. She doubted she'd ever wear them again regardless of how well her washing machine worked. Tears blurred her eyes and she nearly tripped twice running through the pitch-black hallways, her idiot cousin not bothering to light the flashlight as they went.

In her mind she pictured more spiders crawling above them, weaving webs in the stairwell to catch them as they ran by. It made her shudder as her feet pounded on the concrete steps.

When she'd been little she hadn't been scared of spiders. They were gross but not something to lose sleep over. That had changed during Christmas when she was thirteen.

Her aunt had come down from Toronto. They had a small house, so Bobbi, being the good niece she was, offered up her bed. She would sleep on the couch that night—it wasn't a problem. They didn't have many extra blankets but they had a nice sleeping bag in the attic that her cousin had left last time he'd visited.

They had a wonderful dinner after which they stayed up late playing cards and talking—

everyone laughing and happy. In the late hours of the night Bobbi finally pulled the sleeping bag down from the attic, dragging it to the couch and climbing in with barely open eyes.

She drifted off quickly, her belly full and her spirit high. It was only when she woke that she noticed something was wrong.

The noise caught her attention first, an odd crunching and humming accompanying her movement that was at odds with the soft leather fabric of the couch. Groggy in the six AM light she didn't understand until the rest of her body began to awaken.

As feeling drifted into her extremities, she started to feel them crawling on her. Insects, lots of them. Hundreds of legs pinpricking the skin along her body from her neck to her toes.

Her first scream dislodged a moth crawling onto her face. It flew away angrily while she thrashed inside the bag. Each twisting of her body crunching another noisy insect as she tried to rip the cloth away from her body.

Her screaming woke the whole house before she'd managed to escape her sleeping bag. She stood in the living room raking her hands over her body, flicking insects of all shapes and sizes onto their salmon coloured carpet where they quickly fled into dark corners of the room.

When she'd thought she'd removed them all from her body she stood crying in the middle of the living room, tears burning down a face made red from the exertion. It was only after blowing her nose on her pajama shirt that she felt it climbing through her hair.

She shook her head and danced, wailing as she whipped her hands through her thick strands of hair. Whatever was crawling there wouldn't come out. It took her father, who'd rushed into the room shouting about intruders and waving a baseball bat, to untangle the beast from her hair.

He grimaced as he did so, whispering soothing words about it 'being more afraid of you' as he did. When the spider came free from her hair it fell to the carpet with a soft thud, quickly scuttling across the floor, never to be seen again save for in her recurrent nightmares.

Her parents had got a laugh out of it all, wondering how she had managed to fall asleep without noticing all the bugs. Bobbi didn't though, she spent the next month spraying every square inch of their house with spider repellent.

She spent the next twelve years avoiding spiders, getting boyfriends or landlords to squish them when they wound up in her apartment and bringing out the insect repellent at the first sign of a cobweb.

She'd only recently got to the point where she could handle seeing them outside. They weren't so bad when she found them hiding in trees and shrubs when she went hiking. She doubted she'd be ok with them now.

They'd made it to the first floor and were sprinting to the light of the outdoor world. When they burst free from the strange building she let out a ragged scream. Her cry contained more anger than fright and scared away a nearby flock of birds.

She had to cough before speaking, a splutter clearing the last chunk of vomit stuck beneath her tongue. "Hal, spiders don't grow that big."

Hal was pale and shaking, hands clenched deeply into his khakis as he tried to wheeze a response. "I know. I know." His face twisted into a petrified frown. "Bobbi."

"Yes?"

"What if your friend was right?"

Bobbi stared at her shoes. Her words were hollow when they came. "Did you hear them too?"

Hal's reply was stopped by an authoritative growl. "Freeze."

Bobbi looked up from her sneakers to find the speaker. It was a police officer, badge gleaming and pistol raised. He spoke again, the barrel of his gun twitching with each word. "I said freeze."

Hal whistled. "What is going on here?"

The man took a forceful step forward, he was massive with sunglasses and a thick beard darkening his face. "This is private property, what are you doing here?"

An ounce of calm returned to Hal, the sarcasm that made him so loved in the town creeping into his voice. "My cousin and I wanted to do some fishing."

The police officer continued as if he hadn't heard. "You're trespassing, I'm afraid you'll have to come with me."

Hal stood straighter before replying, the sun seeming to rejuvenate his sardonic self. "Look, I'm actually a park ranger. I'm sure this is all just a big misunderstanding."

"If you take one step you're a dead man."

Hal fumbled his following words. "I'm a park range— wait what?"

The man now stood directly before them. He was almost as wide as he was tall. Bobbi's gaping face reflected in a pair of silver aviators covering his features. He had a standard police uniform, blue shirt with a Kevlar vest. His badge was pinned neatly against his chest. An intimidating figure, made doubly so by the pistol raised to Hal's head.

"Sure man, sure."

"On the ground, both of you."

Bobbi knelt quickly, her mouth dry and eyes still stinging.

Her already dirty knees had barely sunk into the dirt when she felt the hard click of the cuffs around her wrists. The speed of the man's movements were at odds with his size. She heard a similar click over her shoulder.

Hal piped up as the man dragged him to his feet. "Can I see your ID, officer?"

With a sigh the cop reached into his vest and withdrew a small leather wallet. He flipped it open to his identification and pressed it into Hal's face. "Good?"

"Nice to meet you, Officer Goodman," Hal spat.

Gravel crunched as the hot breath of the police officer brushed against her neck. "Up," he said, his words as coarse as the hands dragging her to her feet.

Hal was standing beside her. She looked to him with disbelief. His arms were also locked behind his back. "We didn't know this was private property, man," he said sourly.

The police officer grunted, and nudged Bobbi forward. Hal joined in step beside her. They followed the road they'd came in on for a short while before arriving at the man's truck. It was a newer model, white but covered in mud. An RCMP logo peeked out from behind the layer of grime. There were lights mounted on the top, not the normal cop lights but rather a massive floodlight.

It was only a two seater but the truck bed had been converted into a makeshift cage. It was made from a metal mesh extending in height a foot above the truck cabin's roof. Hal eyed it incredulously as the police officer lowered the tailgate and began unlocking the padlock holding closed the metal door. With a click the padlock came loose and the cage doors sprang open.

Hal, as ever, was ready to voice the concerns for both of them. "That's not safe."

The officer only spit and placed a thick hand on his belt. Bobbi went first, jumping up awkwardly and hitting her head on the roof when she first stood up. "Are we going to jail? This seems a little excessive."

Hal jumped in beside her, staying on his back as he called out indignantly, "This is fucking bullshit, man."

The officer ignored them, burly hands busy clicking a heavy padlock into place. He gave the cage door a testing shake before walking to the driver's side door.

"Mind watching for potholes? There's no seatbelts back here," Hal yelled at the man before the door slammed. The truck roared to live with a heavy splutter. Hal crawled over to Bobbi, nearly screaming to be heard over the sound of the truck's engine.

"What the hell is going on here, Bobbi?" he continued, more to himself than her. "I'm going to die in a cage."

She leaned against the side of the truck bed, the cold rubber siding uncomfortably against her back. She took a deep breath, it was time to stop acting like a scared child. "I don't know, Harold."

The truck was now roaring along the road, going much faster than Bobbi would have liked even if she had been in the front wearing a seatbelt as opposed to handcuffed in the back.

"He was going to shoot us, I swear to God. He was going to." Hal had pushed himself up beside her, his neck twisting awkwardly so they could speak. "If we ran away he would have killed us. It was in his eyes"

"This isn't right."

Hal beat his head backwards against the metal bars. "No shit, cops don't throw people in a metal cage... Christ, I can't die in a cage, Bobbi, I can't."

A large bump shifted her weight uncomfortably, her arms descending a little lower than her shoulder sockets usually permitted.

They sped past her parked SUV and onto the highway, the sound of the open air was near deafening. Hal tried to shout something, but it was stolen by the wind. They endured this for near ten minutes before the truck pulled off onto an exit ramp and entered another swath of forest road.

The thought was in both their minds, but it took a little courage for her to voice it. Her words shook as she spoke. "What if we found our serial killer?"

Hal groaned and shuffled awkwardly to the back of the truck, proceeding to kick at the padlock holding the cage shut, lying on his back to stabilize himself while he did. Between angry puffs he continued talking.

"We." Kick. "Deserve." Kick. "To be." Kick. "Murdered." His final kick missed the padlock, leaving his foot stuck between two of the thick bars encasing them. "Fuck."

Bobbi waddled over to join him, kicking at the lock while Hal violently tried to shake his foot free from the bars, his effort accompanied by a slew of curses Bobbi would have found impressive were it not for their current circumstances.

"Hal, I'm sorry." Laying this close to her cousin she could see the flecks of grey starting to fill his hair, oddly suiting him. "For everything really, I should have helped you more with the divorce."

With a feral cry Hal pulled his foot from the cage, leaving his shoe encased between the bars and forcing him to use his other leg to continue kicking the lock. After a particularly spiteful blow to the lock, he panted a thin acknowledgment of her apology. "It's alright, Bobbi. I won't have to worry about the divorce much longer, thanks to you."

Interlude
Present Day

Bernard watched the two through the rearview mirror. He admired their tenacity, but it didn't worry him. It would take a sledgehammer to dislodge the military grade lock their feet were smashing. It would take even more to rend the bars trapping them. The cage had been built for fiercer prisoners than hikers.

With the flip of a dash button he opened a link to the operation base. "This is Surveillance One, I've picked up two civilians trespassing on Site D."

A crisp voice came through the truck's speakers. "Roger, Surveillance One, patching you through to Agent Dawson."

Ken Dawson's icy voice filled the truck cab. "What is the status of the civilians?"

Bernard smiled. He'd landed this patrol route after dispelling his dinner in the presence of Dawson. This was his chance to escape it. It was difficult to keep the pride out of his voice as he responded. "Restrained but conscious in the cage, I'm enroute to Field Base One."

Field Base One was little more than a canvas tent the forest surveillance teams took turns sleeping in, but it was well hidden and had coffee to replace the thermos he'd drank today.

"Negative, Surveillance One, the trespassers could endanger mission objectives. Please dispose."

Bernard sighed. "Roger, Agent Dawson."

"And S1?"

"Yes?"

"Best to bury them deep, I hear the smell of corpses attracts it."

"Roger."

With a click the channel died. Bernard didn't bother to turn on the radio to cover the silence it left. There had been no note of pleasure in Ken's voice, but Bernard was sure he had earned back some respect. In another week or two he'd be allowed back into the command center where he could work on more important functions surrounded by many, many more guns.

He felt sorry for the two in the back, it was bad business killing civilians. He disliked it, but not enough to disobey his commands. Especially since he wanted off this patrol route. Bad.

He'd followed unpleasant orders before, interrogations involving towels and buckets of water and bombings that left as many children dead as it did terrorists. He hadn't enjoyed it, but he also hadn't felt unsettled while he worked. Here it was different. Here each day left his nerves more racked than the last.

Patrols were creepy, but the worst part came at night, after shift when he snuck into the tent for a few hours respite. Forced to curl up in his sleeping bag with only his ears to scout around him, every inch of him tense for the smallest snapping twig or an unnatural rustling in the surrounding bush.

Each night he fell asleep to the sound of a perfectly normal forest. There was no unnatural squealing of birds or deafening crashing of trees. No horror-stricken cries from his still working comrades. No strange growls permeating the air. Nothing.

And yet he knew, as made evident by the corpses regularly left for them, it was watching.

He constantly imagined it, whatever it was, pacing through the foliage. Its long legs carrying it from tree trunk to tree trunk with barely the shifting of a leaf. Walking silently above them looking to pounce on the man who looked most appetizing.

Each night he fell asleep knowing it could be dangling above him, contemplating if he would make a good meal.

He patted the sleeping pills tucked into his pants' pocket, the only thing helping him get through the nights.

The logging road he'd turned on was part of his patrol. It led away from frequented spots of their target and hadn't seen a vehicle other than Bernard's in a long time. The road was bumpy, he was amazed to see the two in the back were still trying to knock the lock off. They aimed twisting kicks as their bodies bounced up and down in the truck bed. Bernard noted the man had managed to lose one of his boots, its heel lodged proudly between the metal bars of the cage.

He whistled to himself. "Props for tenacity." He didn't want to kill them, he wasn't a monster, but he would. "Sorry, folks, it's for a better tomorrow."

Hopefully a better tomorrow which would involve Bernard returning to his previous position in the Agency.

Interlude
1999

The boy was eleven when the spider decided it was time to rid themselves of the little brother. The brother was a whiny creature that, while still providing plenty of amusement to the boy, had grown into quite the nuisance.

It had started when the brother saw her for the second time. The mother had passed out from her wine and the boy had thought it would be funny to lock the brother in the cellar the spider was sleeping in.

The brother was much too small to harm her, but his screaming had brought far too much attention to her nest. Only the mother's disregard for the wailing boy's story had stopped the cellar being searched and herself uprooted.

It was the first and only time she felt rage at the boy.

She encouraged the boy's games, but only so much as they never endangered them. Those had been the rules. A rule she reiterated by dragging the boy from his warm bed under the dark shadow of midnight. She hung him from a tree where he cried and wet himself, only releasing him in the morning when the rest of the household was near to waking.

The boy did not anger her again after that night, but his brother continually did.

The brother didn't do it overtly. He pointedly refused to bring up the spider in the cellar, letting it be forgotten as a story of boyhood fancy. He continued to play along with his brother's games and pranks and endured the tortures of being the smallest. Outwardly it appeared nothing had changed.

It was only in the small cavern of the boy's mind the spider sensed trouble. The brother would often think of the cellar, a certainty remaining in his memory even as years passed. On more than one occasion she caught the brother scheming to follow the boy and see where he was hiding the "monstrosity."

Her apprentice, as he would often call himself at that age, was quick to agree to her suggestion of removing the brother.

They went into the brother's room late one Tuesday night, the boy there not to help but to watch. They could have done it without waking the small child but the spider wanted to. She enjoyed the taste of the horror blossoming in the brother's mind as he awoke to her inquiring eyes.

She'd tested her venom on a few animals, deer and rodents snared in her webs, the results had been mixed. Most simply died, skin bubbling before their brains exploded from their skull prisons. Others were turned dumb, brains melting away until only a soulless husk remained. A few, usually the healthier deer or occasional dog, retained an ounce of intelligence. It was only the ones who retained a portion of their minds she could control, easily enshrouding their fogged consciousnesses in her own powerful mind.

It was the boy who had first suggested they try the process on a human. His brother would be their first experiment, a grand step even if made from necessity. She felt a flush of pride when the boy commented on how well it worked.

They walked with the brother out of the house, the "apprentice" making little noise as she had taught him while his brother marched heavily on little feet. The rest of the house was silent as they pulled back the glass door to the patio, the children's parents adrift in dreams too deep for even the spider to discern.

They slunk through dew soaked grass to the properties edge. The woods here were thick, unpierced even by the strongest ray of moonlight. The spider and the boy stopped while the brother continued his forward march.

The child's feet were bare, blood quickly drawn from them by a low hanging blackberry vine. His pace remained the same as dark drops of blood trailed him forward, each stride bringing him deeper and deeper into the dark until he was lost from their sight.

She felt many emotions then. Most of them were consistent with her nature such as pride, satisfaction and pleasure. But one was foreign, a strange burning that erupted in her chest when she felt the boy's arm wrap tightly around one of her legs.

It wasn't love, the spider couldn't yet comprehend love, but it was something near. Something that made her feel both closer to and farther from the boy.

That night they slept in the trees together, the boy cradling on her stomach until it was time to return him to his room in the dawn light.

By this point the brother had walked nearly twenty kilometers, his pace uninterrupted since it'd fist begun. By the time his mother awoke and realized her baby boy was missing he'd be thirty kilometers from home, by the time a search was organized for him he'd be a hundred.

The boy was forced to spend all day with people, feigning worry for his missing brother. He did an admirable job. She was pleased.

Blake

"Higher, Blakey, higher." The excited squeals of his sister grew with each heave of his body, her tiny feet pumping hard to add inches to the height of each swing. "Weeeeeeeeeee."

Satisfied with his performance, Blake sunk into the soft sawdust below the swing, breathing heavily as his sister giggled. A soft breeze blew through, doing little to alleviate the midday heat. He brushed some sweat from his brow and leaned back to stare at the cloudless sky.

"Blakey, why'd you stop?"

He heard the crunching of the metal chain holding the swing as his sister turned in her seat to look at him. She was still darting up and down, but her arc was skewed and her momentum was lost.

"I was so high."

Blake let out a tired groan. "Blakey is a little tired now."

His sister's feet plopped into the sawdust below her as she dismounted the barely moving swing. "But you promised we'd play today." He'd closed his eyes, gasping when her little body landed on him. "Remember, Blakey."

"Easy there, kid, I've had a busy week."

His sister's tongue was out and wagging near his nose. "Blakey is getting old. Old, old, old."

With another groan he lifted her up, barely managing to hold her above his body while she stretched out her arms and laughed. "You are too, you've nearly outgrown these pants."

"I've grown a full inch this month," she said proudly.

"Good lord." He dropped her, letting her land on him with a shriek. "We'll have to cut off your feet so you can keep using these pants." He followed the words by grabbing one of her legs and yanking it playfully.

His sister shook her head, her brown hair tangling itself as she did. "Nu uh, we're going to get me new pants. Pretty one's like Jessica has."

Blake crinkled his nose and pushed his forehead against his sister's. "And who's going to pay for these pants, Miss Moneybags?"

Sarah used her sweet voice, the one reserved for begging for presents and ice cream, in her answer. "I thought you were, Blakey."

Blake smiled. "Fine, but only because you've been such—"

The words caught in his throat as a harsh shrieking of tiers on asphalt rang out. Barely audible over the roar of a heavy engine, a deep voice shouted. "There's the fag!"

His sister kept looking at him, oblivious to nearby noise. It was only when Blake turned his head to look at the newcomer that she pried her eyes away from her brother.

Jarret Folger was five foot six with a grizzled beard and a steroid problem. His bare arms were covered in tattoos that, if they hadn't been stretched by his addiction to gaining body mass, would have been censored on television. The one that people laughed at the most, usually behind Jarret's back, was what had once been a cross now so bloated and twisted by his weight gain it could easily be mistaken for a swastika.

The consensus was the swastika suited Jarret much more than the cross ever had.

Blake didn't live his life in fear of the more ignorant individuals in Hope but he also didn't pretend they were nonexistent. He knew who Jarret was and he knew any conversation starting with the phrase "there's the fag" was not likely going to be a pleasant one.

He was on his feet by the time Jarret had set foot on the sawdust and running by the time he'd made it within a meter of the swing. He'd struggled to lift Sarah earlier but now he barely noticed the weight of her little body wrapped around his torso.

The park they'd been playing in bordered a small stretch of woods nestled between a street of sleepy houses and a highway. Their best bet would have been the road where the sound of his beating might awaken some of the neighbours but it was impossible he'd make it there. More men, most of them as burly as Jarret and sporting equally atrocious beards, poured into the park from the surrounding sidewalk.

Sarah started to ask questions as he pushed his way into the woods, the crashing of the bushes around them nearly drowning out her whimper. "Why are we running, Blakey?" He didn't respond, instead focusing on navigating the winding labyrinth of trunks and vines before him.

Over the terror, he felt a bolt of annoyance at himself. He'd been the one who had insisted to his aunt he didn't need to bring his cellphone. "It's Blake and Sarah time, no interruptions," he'd said, leaving the woman curled on the couch nursing chicken broth and a hangover.

Harsh laughter reverberated behind him, it was followed by a deep voice calling out, "Try and run pussy."

His breathing grew more ragged as they pushed deeper into the tree line. There were no set trails but still space to walk. He tried to remember if he'd ever cut through this part of the woods but fear and adrenaline clouded his mind. The hard pumping of his legs left deep tracks in the dirt below them. He was only slowed by a wail from his sister. "Blakey, STOP."

Her mouth was so close to his ear it left it ringing. He stopped, more from reflex to the tone of her voice than her actual words. It took him a moment to discern what had made his sister scream, his head whirling around to check behind them before examining their front.

"Web, Blakey."

He could hear the distant laughter of Jarret and his friends, they group evidently taking a more leisure pace than Blake.

He started to walk forward again but the shrill voice of his sister cried out once more. "Blakey, web."

He tilted his head to follow Sarah's eyes, amazed she had even caught it.

"That's…"

"I don't like spiders, Blakey."

His heart beat hard in his chest, sweat pouring from his brow. He wanted to keep running but something about the strangeness of the sight kept him rooted in place.

The longer he stared the more webs he made out. Long, thick strands shimmering in the downcast rays of the sun. They were everywhere, crisscrossing from tree trunk to tree trunk in cold elegance.

Blake hadn't been snarled in the web, but he felt like his eyes had, his gaze trapped in the vast array of spider silk glistening before him. It took the nearby snapping of twigs and accompanying hollering to drag his conscience from the silver strands.

"We'll have to go around." He'd whispered it to himself, but his sister replied.

"Just as long as we stay away from the spiders. I don't like spiders." She buried her head in his shoulder as he turned to walk adjacent to the sticky mess.

He slowed to a walk, finding it more and more difficult to avoid the thick lines as he went further along.

"Blakey?"

"Yes, Sarah."

"What kind of spider makes webs like this?"

Blake was unsure if he wanted to know the answer to her question.

Hal

He was going to die in a cage. He'd never expected his life to amount to much, but he'd hoped his death would involve more dignity than this. He'd always imagined it would be something common like a heart attack or pneumonia, suffered in the confines of an old folks' home and barely acknowledged by the local populace.

He wanted his death to be unremarkable, mentioned only in passing conversation at the grocery store or deli. "Did you hear old Harold copped it? Yeah, he went to bed last night and didn't wake up. We'll miss him, by the way do you want to get a beer later tonight? The wife is out of town."

Instead his death was going to be the talk of the town. "You hear about Hal and Bobbi? Yeah, killer got them. Cops say he kept him in a cage before he strung them up. Awful stuff." He could almost hear the local gossips feigning pity. "So horrible and leaving his poor child behind. How does a boy grow up right knowing something like that happened to his father?"

Of course, in this scenario he was imagining someone even caught the killer. It was highly probable his body would be left rotting in the woods while he went on to be known as a man who'd simply disappeared. "Did you hear what Hal did? Just upped and left. No goodbye, no new mailing address, just vanished. Sure, he and Gloria had their problems but that's no reason to disappear. Imagine his poor son growing up without a daddy?"

Bobbi's voice called out thinly between heavy draws of breath. "Come on, Hal." She kicked again. "Don't give up."

Hal was still stretched out in the truck bed with his feet towards the lock but they were no longer pounding against the steel. "We're going to die, Bobbi. He's going to hang us from the pine trees."

Bobbi's foot slipped, clanging against the metal bars. "Maybe we can rush him when he stops."

Hal closed his eyes. The truck had slowed as it made its way down the logging roads making the wind gentler against his face. The sun was still gleaming above them and the warm rays were pleasant on his skin. "At least it's a nice day for it."

Bobbi kicked the lock one last time, letting out a fierce curse. She shuffled her body to be closer to her cousin, twisting her neck to put the side of her head against his. She didn't speak until her breathing had slowed and a modicum of calm had entered her voice. "Do you think it will hurt?"

Hal thought of all the dead hikers he had helped the local search and rescue recover from the mountains. Most of them were long gone when Hal and his friends arrived, smelling bad and rigor mortis locked, but a few were (as the highly professional SAR termed them) "still fresh."

Excluding the more tragic accidents, mutilations involving falls leaving facial expressions undiscernible, the recently deceased had always looked rather content to Hal. As huge a nonbeliever in the afterlife as he was, he'd found this a mild, albeit morbid, comfort.

"I don't think it's too bad."

Eventually the truck rolled to a stop and the heavy hum of the engine died. Hal opened his eyes and took one last look at the great sea of blue above him.

The road here was narrow, bordered on all edges by pines extending deep into the sky. The only sounds the soft humming of the forest and Bobbi's sobs.

Hal inhaled deeply, trying to focus his thoughts on his little boy. God, he wished he'd been there for him, wished he hadn't been such a fuck up.

"Hal?"

"Yeah."

"I really am sorry."

Hal wondered what his son would grow up to be. A doctor, a lawyer, a deadbeat like his father? The possibilities were endless. He didn't want to pray, he'd made it this far into life without doing so, but he tried it now. Better than me, he thought, let him be better than me.

"Stop apologizing, Bobbi." He let out a hollow laugh. "It's not like I was going to last long anyway."

He felt Bobbi's warm breath brush against his face. "Hal, I'm so scared."

"Me too."

The truck door opened with a click and the weight of the vehicle shifted as their captor stepped out from the cab. Hal whistled, the sound ringing through the trees. "Big bastard, isn't he."

"Yep."

They listened as the man's footsteps traced their way to the back of the truck. Bobbi sat up when the lock clicked, but Hal didn't bother.

"Out," chimed guttural voice of their captor.

Hal felt Bobbi's weight shift beside him but nothing more. Her voice wavered as she spoke, but she managed to push the words out. "What are you going to do to us?"

The large man's voice remained threatening. "I said out."

Hal slowly rose to a sitting position. The officer stood in front of the cage, sunglasses still covering his face and a pistol pointed towards them. "Fuck you, buddy," said Hal, determined to be true to himself in his final moments.

A hint of humanity crept into the man's voice. "We all gotta go. Wouldn't you rather die standing, than in a cage?"

"So caring," said Bobbi bitterly.

The man shifted, hesitating, from one foot to another, the pistol unwavering in his thick hand. "Look, it's for a better tomorrow."

Hal groaned. "Jesus Christ, what cult does he belong to?"

Bobbi snorted, a hint of mirth sinking back into her shaking voice. "He'd fit right in at the Flint Street Church."

Tears started in Hal's eyes as forced laughter shook his body. "Nah, they take drug addicts not serial killers."

The man's aviators hid his expression. "I'm not a serial killer, now out." He bashed the side of the cage with his pistol, the metallic ring echoing in the truck bed. "Out, I don't have all day."

Hal found it hard to push his words out between his sobbing laughter. "We do."

Bobbi let out a snicker beside him. The man shook his head. "Fine, I tried to be decent to you, now I gotta—" The man's words twisted into a terrified shriek as a blob blurred Hal's vision. In a flash the dark mass sailed back into the sky, taking their captor with it.

Bobbi screeched. Hal let out a long stream of curses mostly starting with the letter c. After a minute they stopped hollering, the silence around them was interrupted only by their heavy breathing.

Hal twisted his head about, scanning the trees for whatever had pounced on their captor. His gaze met only brown bark and twisting branches. Beside him Bobbi made a soft croak before dripping some vomit onto the dark truck bed.

"Jesus, Bobbi, Jesus."

Hal continued flailing his head while Bobbi started to blubber beside him. "What the fuck, Hal." She blew her nose loudly, snot sprinkling onto Hal's legs. "I just wanted to get a fucking story." She sniffed again. "I'm sick of reporting in Hope."

Hal nodded, adrenaline electrifying every vein of his body.

Bobbi leaned forward to place her head between her knees, her sobs continuing. "What the fuck is wrong with this place? What the fuck?"

Hal remained unable to muster more than a curse word from his lips. He could feel a pressure forming in his head making it hard to think. It was most likely his sanity snapping.

Bobbi's voice grew softer. "Why spiders? Why spiders, Hal?"

Hal licked his lips, his mouth tried desperately to remember how to form coherent sentences. He wanted to refute Bobbi's statement, tell her something else had ripped the officer into the sky, something other than a giant spider. He'd almost thought of a reply when the laughter interrupted his thoughts.

It was cool and predatory, echoing through his mind and causing his entire being to shrink in terror. The clicking chuckle grated painfully against the inside of his skull until it was replaced by a soft whisper in the deepest crevice of his own conscious.

You're welcome.

Hal looked up, finally laying eyes on their savior dangling from the branch of a large elm.

"Oh fuck."

Blake

Blake's hand was clasped over his sister's mouth. She'd started crying and hadn't been able to stop. Slobber was dripping from his palm and down Sarah's chin but most of the sound was muffled. He whispered soothing words into her ear but didn't lessen his grip.

They were huddled under a tree, a large elm with drooping arms. Jarret and his friends were nearby, he could hear them trying to navigate the same maze of spider silk he and Sarah had been waylaid by.

One of Jarret's friends, Blake thought it might be Mikey who worked at the gas station, was growing more and more vocal about his distaste for the situation. "Come on, Jarret, this place is creepy. Let's just leave it."

Scared of homosexuals and the woods, Blake thought bitterly.

"No, we're not leaving 'til we beat some manners into this kid."

The crack of foliage snapping came from the other side of their hiding spot. Blake held his breath while his sister slowed her struggling. For a second he worried he'd suffocated her until he felt one of her tiny hands reach up and cling to his wrist.

Mikey continued. "Look man I'm bored," he laughed nervously. "Nothing out here but trees and spiders."

Another voice cut in, a few feet away from the other two. "Lots of spiders, judging by these webs. I haven't seen webs this big since I was tree planting up North." The sound of a lighter clicking was followed by the faint smell of tobacco. "I remember walking into one of those bastards once."

"And then what?" asked Mikey tentatively.

"I brushed it off and kept working, what the fuck do you think?"

"Oh."

"Anyway, Jarret, I'm sorry this guy broke your cousin's heart, but I got shit to do today." The speaker paused, likely blowing out a stream of smoke. "I'm going home."

Jarret growled a reply, but it was too low for Blake to hear.

"Suit yourself man, you coming, Michael?"

"I told you, I hate being called Michael."

"Whatever, dude."

Blake listened to the man's footsteps recede into the forest, followed by Jarret's annoyed voice. "What a fucking flake, probably sucks dick himself."

"We should leave soon too, it really is getting dar—ouch, what was that for?"

"You really are stupid, Mikey."

"Well?"

"Well what? Did we not agree we wouldn't rest until we taught the fag some manners?"

"I'm all for teaching fags manners, Jarret, it's just it's getting late and you know I've never been a big fan of nighttime in the woods." He continued sheepishly, "Besides, I got Church tomorrow morning and I gotta be up early."

Blake and Jarret groaned, one out loud and the other in the recess of his mind.

"What did I tell you about Flint Street?"

"They're nice people, Jarret."

"They're fucking insane."

"Father Joseph says that Satan will always try to belittle the church."

"Father Joseph uses more smack than most of the junkies in the Ainsfield."

"I know, it's good shit."

Jarret let out a heavy sigh. "Jesus Christ, Mikey, you can get drugs anywhere. Church is where you go to find the Lord."

"Well, I don't know, Jarret, we weren't all raised with good Christian grandmas like you."

Blake could hear the defeat in Jarret's voice. "Look, you're right, let's go."

"Finally. I told you, it's creepy out here."

They kept talking as they left, voices lost to the thicket around them. Blake let go of his sister's mouth, hugging her tightly as he relaxed against the tree trunk. He let his chest unwind, feeling the sweet rush of air as his breathing resumed its normal pace.

He was almost ready to stand up and walk out when he heard them. Mikey screamed first, his high pitch wail sending birds scattering above their heads.

"Oh god, it's all around me."

Jarret's voice followed in equal distress. "What the fuck, Mikey? I told you to watch out for that one."

"Oh god, get it off. Get it off!"

"I can't, oh, it's on my hands!"

"What the fuck made this? I can barely move! Christ!"

Sarah started to cry again but Blake didn't bother to stop her. "Blakey, I don't like spiders."

Mikey wailed again. This time there were no more birds left to scare away. "What is that?"

"What is what?"

"That."

A pitched squeal was followed by a tree shaking roar. Sarah buried her head into Blake's shoulder, quickly dampening it with tears. Blake stood motionless, ears pricked to follow the commotion.

A harsh snapping sound, as if a tree had been broken in half, came, followed by another terrified shriek.

"Oh Christ, oh Christ. Mikey."

Over Jarret's whimpers, Blake could make out a crunching noise. Tt was grating and interrupted by soft gurgles.

"Oh Lord Jesus, save me, oh Lord Jesus, save me."

A sound rose that twisted Blake's stomach until it threatened to upend his lunch. It reminded him of a Christmas cracker, the cheap ones his sister used to buy for the Holidays. The ones that made a short pop before dripping their candy onto the kitchen table.

The popping noise was followed by gurgling laughter. Laughter that made Blake think of a drowning man with his head half under the ocean.

"Hue… hue…. hue…"

He could hear someone stumbling toward them, making a faltering path through the ferns and blackberry bushes.

Blake wanted to run too but his feet stood rooted to the spot. Sarah was now crying so hard she'd begun choking on her own sobs, her little mouth twisted in a search for air that refused to come.

With a cry, Jarret bolted past them. His face was wild, eyes wide with a snarl peeking out from his beard. His arms were bloodied, some of the blackberry vines still hung around them. He barely glanced at them as he passed, his narrow pupils only twisting the slightest as he continued to ramble into the forest.

A thick slurping sound trailed them, followed by a gleeful voice. "Food, mommy says food. I get food."

Blake managed to push his right leg forward, shakily inching it away from the tree. He could feel Sarah's fingers digging into his back, her body now wrapped around his in a grip so tight it threatened to squeeze the breath out of him.

He took a tentative step, then another. Going in the same direction Jarret had disappeared into.

The voice behind them rang out again. "Smell. Smell. More food. More food." A giddy excitement creeped into the voice. "Mommy food, mommy food."

Blake walked faster, his breath starting to speed again.

Another gleeful laugh rang out. "Fooooooooooood."

Blake ran, headlong into the mass of trees. He didn't care he was without water or a phone, or that he was following the same path as an admitted gay basher, his only focus was being away from that voice. Away from the voice chasing him as he ran.

"I'm coming, food."

Hal

It didn't speak again, that Hal could hear, only stared. Its eight eyes beating down on them with keen interest. He'd was tempted to throw something at it, his eyes greedily scanning the ample supply of pebbles sitting in the truck bed, but his arms were still clasped uncomfortably behind his back.

It had been an hour since they'd watched it "eat" the police officer/serial killer. Holding his limp body delicately with two hairy legs while its fangs sunk smoothly into his neck. When it finished it had left him dangling from a tree branch, his body moving only with the occasional breeze.

"I don't like how it sits over the body, like it's proud of itself."

Bobbi's eyes stayed downcast, her knees were tucked against her chest and her face was still pale. She'd managed to contort her body enough to sneak her hands from behind her back to the front of her body, though they were still bound in shiny iron. Her fingers were busy tying and untying one of her shoelaces. "There's a lot of things I don't like about it, Hal."

"You heard it too, right?"

"The voice?"

"What else?"

Bobbi continued to play with her laces.

Hal was sitting cross-legged, his arms still locked behind his back and head cocked to one side. His cousin had been kind enough to slip the only joint to survive the day's ordeals into his mouth.

Hal coughed out a cloud of smoke. "So, uh, should we do something?"

His cousin's gaze remained downward.

"Bobbi, there's a giant spider dangling a corpse above us."

"I know."

"Are we going to do something about it?"

Her voice shook as she spoke, her fingers pulling her shoelaces especially tight. "Like what, Hal? Like what?" She stopped speaking as a stream of tears started to fall from her eyes. After a thick sob she pushed out the rest of her sentence with venom. "This was my idea and now we're going to be eaten by a giant fucking spider."

Hal leaned backwards. Wishing he'd gone with Gloria to the yoga practice she'd kept inviting him to before she left, he pushed his arms downward, sneaking them under his legs with a heavy groan. After a little bending and cursing he could look down at his own hands.

Using his elbow to wipe the fresh perspiration from his brow he smiled at Bobbi. "Look, we can't both be pessimists."

Bobbi looked up to meet his gaze, her eyes were red, but a thin smile slowly formed upon her face. "You dropped your smoke."

Hal grinned wider. "If I smoke more, I'll start seeing giant snakes as well."

Bobbi let out a choked laugh, blowing her nose as she did so. "No wonder Gloria left you."

Hal stood up, gripping the bars above him and looking up. "There's the Bobbi we love."

She sniffed again. "Okay, Harold. We're going to find a way out of here." She twisted her torso awkwardly to reach for the iPhone hidden in her jean pockets. "But first, some pictures for National Geographic."

Hal snorted. "The National Inquirer more like."

The lecturelike tone had returned to her voice. "Harold we're going to be famous for this, I mean it's an undiscovered species. Even if it is disgusting."

Hal lifted his knees and hung from the bars above. "Ah yes, every park ranger's dream: discovering an undocumented monster." He met the beast's eyes as spoke, shuddering as they stopped blinking to glare at him. "Maybe monster isn't the right word."

"Harold, do you think there's more?"

Hal dropped from the ceiling and turned to face the truck cabin. He bet that with enough patience they could break the back window. "Lord, I hope not. Bad enough finding the little ones in the bathroom."

His cousin seemed emboldened by his words, her voice perking as she spoke. "They're not so scary, I don't know why I was so terrified to begin wi—"

The truck rocked as the spider landed on it. Bobbi fell forward, her head colliding savagely with iron bar. Hal tipped backwards, landing on his back with his eyes gazing upwards.

The fall knocked most of the air from Hal's lungs, but he still managed to scream at the sight above. Its bulbous body blocked out the sun above, four legs clamped over each side of the cage with its head pushed as close to them as the bars would allow.

Hal could make out seven of its eight eyes, one being obstructed by the thick metal of the cage. They blinked but not in unison. Its mouth was clamping on the bars, a deep hole dominated by two brown fangs. A foul black goop dripped from one fang, splattering Hal's shirt and making his eyes burn.

Bobbi joined in the screaming behind him, shrieking as she tried to press her body through the part of the cage their captor had unlocked.

Hal reached his arms back and caught her around a flailing ankle. "Bobbi, no." She thrashed, but his pull stopped her from escaping the cage. "We're safer in here."

The spider flexed its legs, the cage's metal shrieking as it folded inwards.

Hal closed his eyes, keeping his grip on Bobbi's legs. A small part of him, a part he didn't like much, wondered if it would be better to let her run. It would certainly give him a chance of escaping.

After a seemingly endless minute the metal stopped howling as Hal began to feel the hot gust of the creature's breath beat down on him. A grating noise came from above, "tch tch tch."

Bobbi stopped squirming and Hal opened one eyelid. The spider's face was still pressed towards his while its legs slinked up the bars to pull in around its body.

Bobbi was the first to speak. "Is it laughing?"

As if in answer, four of the spider's eyes blinked at once.

Slowly, one of the spider's legs dipped into the cage. Slenderly passing through the bars until Hal felt its hairy weight on his chest. It dragged slowly across his chest and over his face until it caught the edge of Bobbi's squirming feet. The limb gave a single playful tug at Bobbi's sneakers before withdrawing gracefully from the cage.

Soon, it whispered in their minds as it used all eight legs to eject itself from the truck. The vehicle rocked side to side, each side lifting progressively higher and higher into the air until the pull of gravity brought it down on the driver's side.

Hal and Bobbi landed painfully against cage bars and dirt road. Their legs and arms crossed in a twisted heap, resembling the horror scampering away from them over the treetops.

Hal coughed dirt, blinking to clear the dust and tears accumulated during the fall. "I miss Hope," he moaned as he untangled himself from his cousin. When he stood he felt the contents of his stomach battling to return to their proper place. It was less than pleasant.

Bobbi staggered past him, neck bent to avoid her head scraping the cage roof. "Hal, the window broke."

"Not like we can drive this thing. It's on its side."

Bobbi gingerly poked her head into the driver's cab, taking care not to cut herself on the jagged bits of glass which had miraculously survived the fall. "Hal," she said excitedly. "There's a radio."

"What?"

Her voice rose higher. "There's a radio."

Hal tried to shake the stars from his vision, barely able to hear his own voice over the ringing in his ears. "An actual radio?"

Bobbi reached a hand back to pull him to her, grabbing his head and tilting it towards the beautiful contents of the cab. "Oh, thank Christ."

Bobbi used her elbow to knock the rest of the glass out, her teeth gritted into a wan smile. "Who should we call? Shit, we don't even know where we are."

Hal climbed into the cab, standing on the door so he could look up and examine the radio. He let out a low whistle. "Looks like it still works."

"Any chance you see a GPS in there?"

Hal craned his neck to examine the whole cab. "Pretty fancy set up buddy had going on. There might actually be one."

"Good, you radio the police and while I search for one."

Hal lifted the radio's mouthpiece from its cradle with a small surge of relief seeping into his bones. "On it."

The radio was battery powered and of higher quality than anything Hal had used in his life. The frequency it was set to didn't match any police or ambulance channel he knew of, his mind barely registering the strange setting as he started to skip between channels.

The police channel was technically not for civilians but he reasoned they would look past that when they heard his story. His thumb pressed down on the talk button, a static click rose from the console but before he could speak Bobbi put a hand over the mouth piece.

"Yes, Bobbi?"

"Harold."

He didn't need to look to know she was biting her lip. "Yes?"

"This is a real cop car."

"Well technically it's a cop truck."

"And that was a real giant spider."

Hal lowered the radio. "It was real. I really, really, wish it wasn't."

"So?"

"So what?"

A hint of annoyance crept into her voice. "Do I have to spell it out for you, Harold?"

Hal rolled his eyes. What he wouldn't give for a beer. "I don't think good like you cousin, I only got to the twelfth grade."

"Well, what if the two are connected."

"That's…" Hal sighed. Sometimes he was the idiot people thought he was. "That's, that's a good point."

He turned his eyes to his boot, wondering if he even wanted to find its twin in the mess of steel and dirt behind them. His next words were slow, exhaustion slipping into his voice. "So, who do we call?"

Bobbi shrugged. "You think of someone. I'm looking for the GPS, remember?"

Hal threw his hands up. "Helpful as ever, Bobbi, I should have let the spider get you."

He could feel his cousin's glare needling into the back of his head. "You thought about it, didn't you?"

Hal dropped his head, letting out a heavy sigh. "I did. I really did."

Blake

It hurt to breathe, the fire in his lungs spreading with each labored breath. His heart beat like an angry neighbour against his chest cavity. Sarah had gone limp in his arms, eyes open but her brain somewhere far from the forest they were crashing through.

His jeans were covered in mud with more than a few fresh holes torn in them by spiteful blackberry vines. One of his shoes had been left to drown in a gulch of mud after he'd carelessly dipped his foot in.

"Fu—" he started as he sprinted around the trail's corner, coming face to face with Jarret. The short man was fighting with a tangle of thick webs, wrapping himself deeper into the strands with each twist of his body.

"Fuck," said Blake, quieter than he'd begun, slowing to edge around the thrashing man.

Jarret swore as he tried to pull an arm free, spinning himself around so his back became entrenched in the webbing. Part of his beard ripped out from the motion, hanging like a bird's nest before Blake's eyes.

"You?" said Jarret, eyes widening in recognition. "Fuck, help me."

Blake slowed, tentatively examining the nearly paralyzed man. The web he'd been trapped in hung nearly all the way across the trail, situated on a bend. Blake counted himself lucky he and his sister weren't the one's currently battling the trap.

"Please," moaned Jarret. "Christ, I'm sorry." His face crunched, the missing half of his beard would have made the expression comical were it not for the dire situation it was present in.

"I'm—"

A deep roar from behind him stopped his sentence.

"FOOD."

Blake bit his tongue. Jarret had started to cry. He put his sister down and edged closer to the man, carefully placing an arm on a shoulder that hadn't been touched with webbing. "Hold still."

He pulled with as much might as he could muster, the electric adrenaline filling his body proving no match for the deceptively strong webbing.

"I said stay sill," Blake hissed through his teeth, annoyed as another twitch from Jarret pulled him deeper into the web.

"Fuck, you faggot. Get me out of here."

Blake stopped tugging and glared at the man.

"Fuck, please?" he moaned.

Blake took a deep breath and doubled his effort, labouring to pull the man free. Sweat beaded his head as the pounding footsteps drew closer.

With a curse, Blake let go. "I can't get you out," he said quietly, wiping sweat from his brow.

"Fuck you, try harder."

Twigs snapped behind them. Blake turned sharply in his surprise, nearly entangling himself in the same trap that had snared Jarret.

"MOMMY, FOOD."

Hope secondary's janitor, Mr. Rutgers, stood swaying before them. He still wore the pale blue uniform Blake had last seen him in, only now dark grime and splotches of blood stained the fabric. His mouth was larger than any human's, a bleeding arm clenched between razorlike teeth.

The man chewed absentmindedly on the arm, like a baby with a pacifier. "So much food," he said between slurps of the flesh.

Blake turned to Jarret, meeting the man's terrified eyes. "I'm sorry," he croaked, bending down to pick up his sister. "I'm so sorry."

"Fuck you faggot, get me out of here. FUCK,"

Mr. Rutgers edged closer, the arm dropping with a thud from his mouth. Drool dripped from his lips as his jaw began to descend even lower. "Mommy says eat," he said, his long mouth twisting into a smile more fitting of a funhouse mirror than a man.

"Oh Christ," sobbed Jarret, now so wrapped in the webbing he could only move his eyes and mouth. "Save me," he moaned, eyes turned pleadingly to Blake as he snaked himself around the webbing.

"I... HUNGRY," bellowed Mr. Rutgers, sprinting forward with lopsided steps.

"Mommy, Christ, Mommy," wailed Jarret as the janitor's massive jaws wrapped around his head.

Mr. Rutgers' jaws snapped shut with a sickening crunch. "mmMMMmm," gurgled the man, slurping blood about as he swallowed Jarret's head.

"Holy shit," croaked Blake, trying to navigate the intricate maze of webbing.

Mr. Rutgers pulled his head backwards, tearing out part of Jarret's spine with the motion. The gore ridden bone hung from his mouth like a lollipop for a moment before he sucked it down. Looking up, he let out a satisfied burp.

"Good food," he cried, still swaying side to side, "but Mommy says eat more."

His crazed eyes pierced through the web to Blake who was currently stepping over the last shining line of web.

"Mommy says eat *Blakey*," said the man, elongated jaw drooping lower as a guttural laugh bellowed from his bloodied lips.

"Shit," moaned Blake, sprinting forward as the man darted off the path into the woods.

"Shit, shit, shit."

Interlude
2004

The boy was nearly a man now, on the cusp of assuming the strength and intelligence that would make them unstoppable. He'd grown tall, strong and, according to the thoughts of the girls at his school, handsome.

It had been seven years since they'd sent the boy's brother off into the woods. It had gone well.

The boy's mother drank constantly now, leaving them to do as they liked in the vast woodlands around their estate. The boy's father was equally absent, choosing to numb his mind with work instead of alcohol. The few hours he was home, each spent staring at his son with accusing eyes.

At first she'd been alarmed that the man suspected his own son but as time passed she considered it a blessing. It was proof the boy's bloodline was strong, likely filled with many intelligent people like the boy and his father.

The spider now lived exclusively in the woods, far too large to remain unseen in even the darkest parts of the basement. She spent her days and nights roaming far and wide, learning every inch of the land surrounding the boy's home.

For pleasure and sustenance, she would hunt. Now far too large to be satiated by birds and squirrels, she preyed on deer and elk. Spinning webs so beautiful it was almost a shame to have them ruined by the struggling of snagged beasts.

Occasionally she would steal a child, pulling them gently from a tent they were sleeping or silently snatching them up when they left their families and camp grounds to play in the surrounding forest. These brought the spider the most pleasure. Their blood was sweet, easily sucked from their bodies. A delicacy in comparison to the thick filth she drained from other mammals.

It was only the cautioning of the boy which prevented her from feasting entirely on the campers littering her woods. The boy intelligently explained how a certain number of missing children were expected within a given year and how they could avoid raising attention by not greatly increasing this number.

They could now contact each other over great distances with a bit of effort. The past Christmas, when the boy went to visit his grandparents on the other end of the country, his voice had rung as clear in her mind as if he was in the same room as her. It pleased her greatly.

For most of her days, she was happy. Content to hunt the lands while teaching the boy all she knew. Occasionally she worried about the facility that made her, but it appeared they were content to simply watch her, barely rebuilding their operation after the day of her escape.

It was only in the twilight hours, when the boy and the forest slept and she stood awake with her eight eyes gazing at the pale moon, that she felt discontent. A longing for something that was both alien to her mind and deeply encoded in her DNA: motherhood.

She often watched the other animals give birth, listening to the screams in their mind as the pain of expelling their children nearly killed them, feeling the waves of warm emotions that followed as they felt their ilk's warm bodies against their own. A few of the mothers even had a mate with them to share these happy emotions.

It seemed *pleasant*.

She was the only one of her kind, but that hadn't stopped her from trying to create a "family." So far it consisted of the boy and his brother.

Her venom had stripped the brother of most of his ability to think, but the process was improving. Occasionally, she tested it on the children she stole, forsaking a delicious snack for the chance to fill the hidden ache in her heart.

Most of them died outright, their blood turning green as their body rebelled against the spider's mind and DNA, but a few survived. Some of them could even talk after. She'd cried the first time one had called her "mommy."

She ate the ones who survived. It wasn't yet time to start a family, but in the future she would protect them. In the future she would take vengeance on any who harmed her young.

In the future she would have a family. It would be large.

Blake

The janitor was mere meters from them, sprinting through the thicket with the same speed Blake mustered on the dirt trail.

"FOOD," the man hollered as he tumbled onto the path, long jaw snapping at Blake's heels.

"Run, Blakey," squealed Sara, no longer content to hide in the nook of his shoulder. "Run faster, Blakey."

Blake no longer felt a burn in his muscles or lungs, a trance like state overtaking him with each stride.

"Eat, eat, eat," cried Mr. Rutgers as he jumped forward, Hal felt his slobber slosh across his back as the man's jaw closed over empty air. "Want, tasty," gurgled the man.

The din of the highway almost overpowered Mr. Rutgers' screeches. Blake was close, so tantalizingly close.

"Faster, Blakey, faster," said Sarah, her hair flying over his face as she twisted to follow the janitor. "He's getting closer, Blakey."

Blake felt a rush of relief as he burst onto the freeway side. Semis and campervans skid by him, unaware of his plight. The roar of the motorway drowned out all the other noises, the sound amplified by the surrounding mountains it cut through.

He didn't slow as he came onto the concrete, narrowly avoiding being struck by a honking Ford swerving by him. Midway onto the lines he glanced back to see Mr. Rutgers continuing his lopsided sprint onto the highway.

His tongue hung from his mouth, it was nearly as long as a snake and covered in thin spindles. "Food," he roared over the howl of the freeway, "Mommy, I EAT."

The spikey tongue shot out, wrapping painfully around his leg. He staggered, nearly dropping his sister, as the man arched his neck back in attempt to drag him towards his foaming mouth.

"I love you, Sarah," Blake called, kissing his sister's terrified face before hurling her to the other side of the road.

Mr. Rutgers gurgled as his hands found his tongue, he proceeded to tug it towards him like a rope, his fingers ripping open upon the spindles shooting out from its pink flesh. "MmMmfood," he called.

Blake thrashed on the concrete, skinning his arms against the concrete and yelping as he felt the barbed tongue rip flesh from his shin.

"MmmnoMommy," Mr. Rutgers coughed, the motion causing Blake to shriek in pain as he felt more skin tear from his leg. "Can't move… food."

Blake struggled to free himself, managing to get to his feet but unable to unwrap the fleshy tongue encircling his leg.

"What," slurped Mr. Rutgers, "Truck, Mommy?"

Blake looked up in horror, only now noticing the oncoming semi's wailing horn.

The truck was sliding about the road, tires screeching as they burned into the asphalt. Blake raised his arms to his head, too shocked to even consider another course of action. In the brief second before the truck struck he heard a voice screech in his head.

Look what you've done.

Hal

He was still pissed Glen refused to give him an IV pump, he wasn't a doctor, but he knew enough about being lost in the woods to know the dangers of dehydration.

"God dammit, Hal, just drink the fucking water! Fuck, if I knew you were going to complain I would have left you there." Glen looked like an angel, but his vocabulary was more fitting of someone with nautical experience. "Radio me halfcocked from the middle of nowhere." After a brief pause for breath he added, "I mean really?"

The stretcher Hal was sitting on was strapped in, but it still wiggled annoyingly with each turn in the road. "All I'm saying is that I can feel a headache coming on."

Glen pressed harder on the gas pedal, unafraid to pass a cop car patrolling the highway. "You're giving me a headache. First Keith phones in sick and then I have to waste my morning grabbing your lost ass."

Bobbi sat in the front, peering at Glen with interest. He'd always been so polite the few times she'd met him, acting every bit like the angel he appeared to be. Her cousin had a talent for bringing out the worst in people.

Hal started to fiddle with one of the straps tethering the stretcher to the ambulance wall. It was unclear if he was trying to tighten or loosen it. "Glen, whatever happened to you today, I guarantee I had it worse."

"Haha, Hal, yeah let's play a prank on the lonely paramedic. Convince him a giant spider lives in the woods." He jerked the wheel violently to overtake a struggling semi. "You of all people should know better than to get lost in these parts."

"We almost got murdered."

"You still might."

"Is that why you're driving like this? Want to finish the job?"

Glen didn't reply, only shifted the ambulance to sink its right wheel into an oncoming pothole. The vehicle bucked like a mad bull and Hal, for his part, was thrown from the saddle, connecting his head to the roof before the downward pull of gravity pushed his ass into the floor.

He sat there groaning for a minute before returning to their conversation. "I'm telling you, Glen, we know who's behind the missing people."

"Giant spider, got it."

Bobbi poked her head over her seat, meeting Hal's eyes. "Told you no one would believe you."

"Us, Bobbi, us."

Unlike Bobbi and Hal, Glen didn't nearly miss the turn to the abandoned lab, rolling in smoothly when Bobbi pointed towards it. Bobbi's car was still parked near the side. In the morning it had been in the shade, but the shifting angles of the sun had left it blistering in the midday heat.

Glen made a mock bow. "Here we are, my lady."

Bobbi smiled weakly. "Such a gentleman."

Glen winked before turning back at Hal. "As for you, Hal, I expect a large payment of beer and cigarettes."

Hal sat rubbing his head, pausing only to give Glen a lewd hand gesture.

As Bobbi stepped down from the old ambulance she found her eyes raking the trees, searching for any sign of a black mass running atop their massive trunks. She found nothing but sprinted to her car nonetheless.

Hal had made his way out of the back, eyeing the trees with the same caution Bobbi had before making his way to Glen's window. "Are you sure you don't want to come look inside? We really did see something…" He struggled for a moment, searching for the right phrase. "Something fucked."

The calm smile in Glen's eyes flickered for a moment, replaced by a piercing look. "I know you saw something strange, Hal, you're not the type to waste EMT hours for a prank." He let out a sigh. "I just think you might be off about the giant spider thing."

"No seriously, come look."

Glen furrowed his brow, wrinkles eviscerating his angelic skin. "Fine, I'll come explore the creepy laboratory."

He'd pulled his key from the ignition and had a hand on the door handle when the screech of the radio started. "Unit 1, we have a motor vehicle accident on the 52 South, please respond."

Glen groaned and pressed the walkie taped to his chest. "This is unit one, what happened, Linda?"

"Two pedestrians struck by a motor vehicle, walked into oncoming traffic."

Glen shook his head and twisted the key back into the ignition. "I swear, it's like people in this town go out of their way to be stupid." He stuffed a cigarette into his mouth with his left hand while cranking the stick into reverse. "And I'm out here in the middle of nowhere. Later, Hal."

Hal saluted as Glen pulled away, the ambulance kicking up a dust storm as it twisted to face the exit. The old automobile returned his gesture with a cough of thick, black smoke.

Bobbi wrinkled her nose as black plumes seeped through her open window. "Hope really needs a new ambulance."

Hal walked over and jumped into the passenger seat. "There's a lot of things Hope needs right now."

Bobbi's voice lowered, her head rotating slowly to take a final look around them. "Like a spider exterminator?"

The elation at avoiding death at the hands of a giant spider and deranged serial killer was slowly fading. "Bobbi, what are we going to do?"

She started the car, motoring it slowly through the haze of dust. "We're going to tell people."

"Like who?"

"Everyone. I'll write an article and post the photos online."

"You know no one will believe us. Look how Glen acted."

Bobbi's voice hardened. "Well then we'll find a way to make them believe us."

"You know, it might be safer to just leave."

Bobbi's eyes drifted from the road to her cousin. "Would you leave if there's a chance that thing has Laura?"

"No. No I wouldn't. But you could."

Bobbi let out a heavy breath, an undercurrent of melancholy accompanying her voice. "Hope is my home. People here deserve better than being spider food."

Hal's thoughts drifted to Laura. Her sweet smile, the way her eyes were always sparkling whether she was out in the trees and the dirt or confined to their office doing paperwork. He thought of how she used to bring him a healthy smoothie to work on Saturday's, worrying about how much he'd drank the night before. He thought of how that sweet girl had offered to go search Baker's Ridge alone because it was going to be a wild goose chase and Hal had spent the previous night drinking until he forgot what his soon to be ex-wife looked like. "Some of them do."

Blake

Blake woke to the sight of Dr. Nand's large brown eyes peering at him. The man gave him a warm smile, placing a plastic gloved hand on his shoulder while raising a penlight with his other arm.

"Look who's joined the living." Said Dr. Nand before letting out a deep belly laugh. "Gave us quite a fright, Mr. Turner."

Blake pushed himself up in his bed, the whole world to flicker as he did. His skull pounded as an awful taste bloomed in his mouth. He must have hit the pavement a little harder than he'd thought when he fell.

Dr. Nand eyes narrowed, giant brown saucers snapping shut into tiny slits behind his thick lenses. "No concussion but you'll have a headache."

The words grated like sandpaper against his throat as he pushed them out. "Where's Sarah?"

The doctor pushed the penlight into Blakes left, the blinding beam making him blink uncontrollably. "Not to worry, young mister, she's just outside. I'll bring her soon as we're done." He shifted the penlight to his right eye for a second, stroking his chin while he examined the boy. To Blake's comfort, he finally lowered the penlight, twisted his thick neck towards the door with a sigh. Blake was too tired to bother following his gaze.

When Dr. Nand's head snapped back his eyes were thin again. "You know, people have questions. Do you feel up to answering a few?"

The throbbing in Blake's head was picking up pace. He tried to put an order to the events before he blacked out, but the memories remained a jumbled mess. He remembered the janitor, running with a severed limb in his mouth and screaming about… Mommies? And there'd been the redneck gay bashers, chasing Blake from the school. There'd also been spider webs but that couldn't be right because in his memories the strands were as thick as Sarah's arms.

He scrunched his face and stuttered a response. "Zombies."

Dr. Nand chuckled, a soft smile on his lips. "Maybe I was wrong about the concussion, son. Either way you should get your facts sorted before the police interview. Officer Dawson is a wry one."

Blake muttered "Huh?" but it was drowned by an excited shriek from behind the large doctor.

"Blakey, Blakey!"

Unwilling to skirt around Dr. Nand's towering form, she made her way between his tree trunk-like legs, head barely reaching the man's knees as she danced through.

"Blakey is alright."

Her eyes were red, and hair was tangled, she wore new clothes, but a faint patch marked her left cheek.

"Hello, Sarah."

Dr. Nand bowed his head, brilliant white teeth flashing as he did. "I'll leave you with the little missus. Your aunt was here earlier but she told us she couldn't miss another shift at work."

Blake grumbled something uncouth, struggling to lift his hand and stroke his sister's tangled hair. Dr. Nand raised an eyebrow but didn't reply.

"Language, Blakey," giggled Sarah.

With a curt nod of his head the massive man disappeared through a nearby door, leaving Blake and Sarah alone in the tiny hospital room.

Sarah's arms clamped around her brother, her little head wriggling into his chest. It was a pleasant moment only ruined by a shadow sweeping across them from the doorway.

Officer Dawson stood tall with his thick arms crossed, his aviator sunglasses dangled from the open collar of his shirt. The chill in his voice seemed to have only deepened since the last time they'd met. "Mr. Turner. I have some questions."

Blake placed a weak arm around Sarah's shoulder, keeping her facing him as he looked up at the officer. "Ok."

Dawson didn't bother to move from the doorway, his head cocked with an almost bored interest. "Any reason you why you were running from your school janitor?"

Blake swallowed. "Mr. Rutgers... he was crazy."

Dawson's pale blue eyes sparked at his words, like someone had brought a pickaxe to the ice that made up his pupils. "How so?"

"Foaming at the mouth, like rabies. He attacked someone else in the forest." Names escaped him, every time he tried to picture who it was that had been there he found himself confronting the wild face of Mr. Rutgers, blood still dripping from his lips while his eyes twitched about. "You must have seen the bodies."

Dawson shook his head. "No bodies in the forest. Maybe the assault, if you actually saw one, wasn't so bad."

Screams flashed through his mind, followed by the image of the janitor with a spinal cord dangling from his elongated jaw. Blake shuddered as he remembered the man's tongue snapping out at him, its daggerlike points digging into the flesh of his calf and shin.

"I'm serious."

Dawson put an arm on his hip, his hand was covered by his bulk, but Blake could tell his fingers were twitching from the shadow playing across the floor. "Listen, son, Hope has a lot of degenerates. Looks like Mr. Rutgers got a little too loose with his medicine and went off on you and your sister."

Blake blinked. "I saw him eating a human being."

Dawson sighed and rubbed his forehead with the back of his arm. "You know, kids in this town, they got a real problem with telling stories." His arm draped back down to his side where it rested on his gun. "Real hard to believe them, especially the ones I continue to find in the vicinity of corpses."

Blake felt his brain begin to itch, anger bloomed through the soft fog of narcotics and headaches. "I'm not telling a joke. Someone died out there and me and my sister nearly died out there."

Dawson shook his head. "It's horrible, the tales kids come up with. My advice? Keep them to yourself." He tilted his head towards Sarah. "Better for everyone's peace of mind," he said as he disappeared through the door, leaving Blake speechless and Sarah still afraid to turn around.

"He scares me, Blakey. He talked to auntie Lucy and he scared her too."

Blake could only agree.

A minute after Dawson had left, a nurse came in, bringing more painkillers and a colouring book for Sarah. He tried to refuse the drugs but the man ignored his pleas, hooking the bag onto the IV with a well-practiced efficiency. The dark edges of sleep started to wash over him almost instantaneously. As his vision faded he tried to make a garbled plea for someone to watch Sarah but only managed to expel some drool for the nurse to wipe away with a lazy flick.

Later in the night Sarah grew bored of her colouring books and climbed into the small cot with her brother, listening to his heavy heartbeat while she closed her eyes and tried not to think of the scary man who had chased them. Eventually sleep would come but it was filled with flashes of a tall shadow lumbering towards her through a forest of flame red trees.

Neither Blake nor Sarah woke to see the three eyes pressed against the window to the hospital room. They were each the size of a basketball and nearly as dark as the surrounding night.

Dr. Nand

Drinks with the EMTs weren't something he made a habit of. He was forty with a child and a busy medical practice, his miniscule free time was often far too precious to spend boozing with the depressed alcoholics who made up the local ambulance crew.

They'd finally finished bitching about their pay, an overused but justified gripe, and had moved onto the topic of the day's events.

Johnson had a thin circle of red hair remaining on his crown and a twisted smile. The center piece of his appearance was a thick mustache which had grown in dark brown rather than red like the thin hair on his head. A lifetime of stress and the drink made his eyes droop, with only one of them opening more than halfway at any given moment. "Never figured ol' Rutgers would turn to the drugs. He always seemed like one of the good ones."

Brian, a twentysomething man with black hair and ever increasing gut, chimed in, "he worked at my daughter's school, scary to think a man like that was let near kids."

Johnson let out a belly laugh, sloshing a fair amount of beer from his mug in the process. "You don't know enough about public schools if that's what worries you, Brian."

Dr. Nand joined the laughter, adding his own voice to discussion. "Brian's still young, maybe next year someone will tell him about the birds and the bees." The following laughter was induced more by the paramedics' state of inebriation than his joke.

Johnson finished chortling, pointing a large finger towards the two seated at the end of the bar. "What are those to love birds doing?" Adding louder, "Hey, Glen, you done flirting with the newbie?"

Glen raised a shining pint of beer and winked at Johnson. "Just filling him in on the history of our noble town."

Johnson shook his head. "Well make sure he sticks to coffee. He said he'd drive us home and I don't want to walk."

Glen's nod was accompanied by a sparkling smile. "I would never let our rookie fall into the depths of debauchery you fiends inhabit."

Johnson shook his head again and turned back to his beer. "Fucking talking like that, needs a girlfriend, Glen does." He took a long gulp, pausing to wipe his bristling mustache before placing the mug back on dark bar countertop. "And the new guy needs to talk more. Barely got a word out of him after shift, just wanted to stand around the hospital and think before we left."

Dr. Nand nodded. "Ah yes, thinking. Terrible habit."

"Fuck you, Armand. You know what I meant."

Dr. Nand hoisted his own mug, savouring the overpriced lager as it trickled down his throat. "Give him time, you used to bitch about Brian when he first came here," he paused to reflect on the past few years. "And Dewey."

Johnson puffed a burst of air through his nose, rustling his fine mustache. "Yeah well, they weren't teetotalers, the new guy doesn't drink. Imagine that, Armand, a paramedic who doesn't drink."

Dr. Nand swished the remnants of his lager. "Alcoholism is the binding force of the world." He leaned back in his chair to survey the bar. It was half full, which in Hope constituted a slow night. "You know... the only one you never bitched about was Glen."

Johnson grimaced. "You know I wanted to."

"But?"

"But what? He's a local, and damn good at his job."

"Well, you're not wrong."

"Nope. Wish he looked less like a fucking angel though."

Dr. Nand glanced at the blond haired man talking animatedly to the meek boy sitting beside him. He did have a certain heavenly glow in the bar light. "How's a man like that stay single?"

Johnson waved at the bartender to refill his glass. When the woman placed the foaming mug of ale in front of him he regarded it with eyes so tender they'd make his wife jealous. "He beats them off with a stick, I don't know where he finds the stamina."

"Gay?"

"Maybe, I don't know. Or care. Sometimes he talks about a girl he loved, can never tell what happened, had a rough childhood, that one, so we don't like to press it."

Dr. Nand nodded. "And what about the new guy?"

"Says he's got some girl out in the mountains, sees her on his days off. I don't think it will last."

"Well," Dr. Nand said, raising his near empty mug to meet Johnson's. "Here's hoping it does."

The glasses met with a cheerful clink. It appeared merriment was poised to finally enter their conversation but the crash of the entrance door opening interrupted. Johnson's mustache twisted jovially as he rose to his swaying feet. "I'll be, Hope's number one corpse finder."

Hal greeted them with an outstretched middle finger. "Been finding more than corpses today," he said as he stumbled over a chair sticking out from a nearby table. Pinwheeling his arms, he hopped from unsteady leg to unsteady leg before lurching into his favourite booth.

Johnson's nose flared. "Too proud to come say hello, Harold?"

The rest of the paramedics laughed. "Too drunk more like," said Brian.

Dr. Nand rose, "Well when the real regulars come in I know it's time for me to go home." The wink following his words brought a grin to Johnson's rosy cheeks.

"See you, doc."

His departure was met with equal cheers and boos from the other paramedics. He gave them a warm wave and strolled towards the door. Harold gave him a friendly but glazed smile as he passed. Dr. Nand wondered if he should suggest a psychiatrist to Harold, the divorce must be taking a heavy toll if this is how he was looking on Sunday nights.

Harold's cousin emerged into the bar, he gave her a nod and hello as they passed. She seemed as beat as her cousin but far less drunk. She managed a cordial "hey" before slinking to the booth cradling Hal. Dr. Nand sighed, rough times for both it seemed.

He whistled as he made his way outside. The parking lot was filled with more cars now than when he'd arrived. The single streetlamp made a pitiful attempt to illuminate them all, forcing him to squint into the darkness for a minute to distinguish his car from the crowd of vehicles

Ending his warm tune, he scratched his throat and fought the urge to light a cigarette. He'd been doing well, if he kept up the reduction schedule he was on now he'd be cigarette free by the end of the month, a fact that did little to alleviate the cravings plaguing him.

It was only the thought of his son smiling in bed on the rare night he got to read him bedtime stories that kept his fingers from darting to the shirt pocket holding his e-cigarette.

With a cough, he forced his hand downward into his pants pocket where his meaty fingers wrapped around his keychain. It was a heavy keychain, filled with house keys, ambulance keys, hospital keys, and some keys that he couldn't even remember the purpose for. He even had his own master key to the

Ainsfield hotel. Technically he'd stolen it, but it didn't weigh on his conscience much, he saved more lives there than he did in the hospital.

He wiped a bead of sweat from his brow, grateful the nights were still cool. Most of Hope's locals didn't believe in climate change—the earth had been around too long to be bothered by silly things like people—but he bet this summer might make a few reconsider. Or it might just bring larger crowds to the Flint Street Church when they claimed high temperatures were proof hell had opened and the end times begun.

He found his car, a remnant of a discontinued line of Pontiac convertibles and one of the few luxuries he'd bought solely for himself and not his family. He'd put the top up when he'd arrived, his stereo would be missing if he hadn't, but he opened it for the drive home.

His house was outside of Hope. His wife insisted they live in the city over so they're son could attend a "more progressive school" than Hope Elementary. Dr. Nand thought a little adversity would be good for the child who, as the daughter of a lawyer and ER doctor, would grow up far more privileged than most Canadians. His argument that it would "build character" hadn't persuaded his wife and they now lived in a refurbished farm house on the outskirts of Chilliwack.

He'd thought the commute would drag on him, but he quickly found he enjoyed the twisting highway home, his little convertible cutting a path through mountains people from other parts of the world paid exorbitant airfare prices to see.

The commute had devolved into his own form of after work therapy—one far less harmful than the cigarettes and liqour favoured by so many other medical professionals.

Tonight's drive was meant to be more soothing than the three beers he'd had earlier but it was ruined by a peculiar sight as he edged the automobile through the clusters of cars, most of which were parked at odd angles and over multiple lines, towards the street.

"What… was…" he gaped as he jerked the steering wheel to avoid a large Ford truck.

There were two parts to Dr. Nand's mind. One he referred to as The Surgeon, not because it contained a repository of surgical knowledge, but because it cut away all the useless information, leaving only the bare facts.

The Surgeon was what he used at work. When people were screaming in pain and covered in blood it was the part of his mind that ignored the horrors of the situation and gave him the base facts so he could act. This man let his diabetes get away from him, schedule an amputation quickly. This woman had an overdose, give her the Naxolone or you're wheeling a corpse home. It was cold, calculating, and necessary to his job.

The other part of his mind he simply thought of as Me. The real Me. It was who he was, emotional, caring, willing to experience the full joy and pain of being a human being.

This is what made him bring flowers to his wife when she sounded sad on the phone at lunch and go out of his way to volunteer with the EMTs when their funding got slashed in the last election.

Part of what made Dr. Nand, in his humble opinion, such a gifted doctor was that The Surgeon and Me worked perfectly in sync. He never felt conflicted about the steps needed to alleviate a patient's problems because The Surgeon knew how Dr. Nand could help and Me knew why he should.

This was the first time in years he experienced a disconnect between the two, each confusing the other.

The Surgeon told Dr. Nand he couldn't possibly be intoxicated, he weighed nearly two-hundred and thirty pounds and had only drank three beers in the last four hours. He hadn't taken any narcotics and didn't feel any of the side effects associated with being drugged.

Me told Dr. Nand that he must be loaded because a giant spider had just scuttled overtop the roof of the pub.

The night air had gone from refreshing to chilling. His hands grew clammy on the wheel, the rapid beat of rock music coming from the car's speakers barely matching the rhythm of his own heart.

"That was... strange."

He continued towards the exit, eyes drifting from the road to the roof.

The Surgeon told him he was crazy. He wasn't drunk and he should focus more on his driving than things he'd thought he'd glimpsed out of the corner of his eye. The human brain was laughably easy to trick, and a shadow had played a mean one on him.

Me disagreed, it continued to scream in his head that he was drunk and hallucinating a giant spider crawling across the Chalice's roof. If he squinted right, he could almost make out the long hairy leg sitting on the angled roof. Or maybe it was only an outstretched branch from a nearby tree, its gnarled shadow slithering like a snake over the bar.

Listening, as he wished more people would, to the logical side of his mind, he eased the car out of the parking lot and onto the road. He sped quickly through the dark Hope streets and was almost at the turnoff to the highway when he came across the cruiser.

It was parked on the side of the road. The headlights were lit but the large bar of lights on the cruiser's roof were dimmed. Two officers were standing in front of it with guns raised, there stances rigid in the filmy haze of the headlight.

His eyelids felt baggy and he'd just hallucinated a giant spider. He knew he should keep driving but, unfortunately for himself, Dr. Nand felt an obligation to stop and help, especially if there was the potential of someone being shot.

He pulled off down a side street, parking his car in front of a pretty box house with a dying lawn. He kicked his large legs out of the vehicle with a tired sigh and raised his cellphone to his ear.

Glen answered on the second ring, even when he was drunk he was more reliable than most of the people in this town.

"Howdy, Doctor, please tell me you're phoning because you'd rather meet up with us for beers than spend time with your wife."

"Unfortunately not, Glen, listen I just passed two cops who looked ready to open fire. Do you know who's working the graveyard on the ambulance?"

He heard the cracking of a door and softening of music and laughter as a more serious Glenn answered. "Sorry, I'm moving outside so I can hear. Possible shooting you say?"

"Yes, down Lindal Ave. Could be nothing. I haven't had a look ye—" Five, no six, cracks broke the night air. "Shit yeah, they're shooting."

A dog started to howl and a few window lights turned on. "Jesus, yeah it's Eddie and Tombs working. I'll let them know you're on scene."

"I'm not on, on scene, I know better than to get close to two cops with their guns out." More gunfire cracked the night. "Jesus, they're really letting loose."

"Alright, Doc, keep your head down. I'll phone Eddie and get you updated. They likely already have the police prepping them, having a trauma doctor on hand might not be bad though."

Another volley of shots escaped into the night. He heard the sound of a window shattering and a wild howl of anger. A car alarm started at the end of the street he was parked on. "Oh fuck they're coming my way."

"What?"

Dr. Nand jumped into his car. His middle-aged body, unaccustomed to effort more strenuous than walking hotel stairs, screamed in pain. He dragged the sunroof forward, cursing violently as it jammed on the way.

"Follow the fucking thing, if it gets away it's our heads," called a stern voice from the mouth of the cul-de-sac.

When he finally managed to get the roof up he sunk into his seat searching for where he'd dropped his phone in the panic.

"This way, it's wounded! Come on," yelled another voice.

The phone was on the floor below the brake pedal. He snatched it up hastily, keeping his weight leaned forward as he did. With the phone pressed against his head he peeked out over his small convertible's window to catch the sight of the two cops sprinting into the cul-de-sac. The thing they were chasing was low to the ground. Dr. Nand almost missed it.

It was a person. It was on its hands and toes, scuttling about the pavement like a displaced crab. It took Dr. Nand a moment to notice it had four extra arms.

It had been a man once. It had a clean-shaven face with a friendly neighbour smile. Only the head had twisted the wrong direction with the chin tilting towards the stars while the thing's chest hugged the pavement. It's back was ripped up, wiry bones extending from it in a fashion he could only describe as *spindly*.

No breath escaped Dr. Nand's mouth. He could hear Glen's voice growing more and more concerned over the phone.

The policemen fired round after round into the thing, tearing apart both its legs and three of its arms. The thing continued to drag itself across the blood-soaked concrete, its weight supported gracelessly by its three remaining arms.

"Fuck these things, fuck them." One of the police officers was now in the middle of the street, standing calmly with his pistol raised while the other walked cautiously down the sidewalk across the way.

The thing, Dr. Nand—for all his knowledge of biological science—couldn't think of what else to call it, turned to look at the man. It let out a big smile, only it was upside down and to Dr. Nand appeared like the raising of a violent arch.

"Mommy. Haha. Mommy," it giggled as a bullet tore through its chin. Blood started dripping from the hole, its voice slurring as it continued. "Moomee.. hehehe… moomee eeeeeaaatt youuuu… he… he.." The next bullet went through the thing's head and its laughter turned to a gurgle as what had been its brains splattered across the floor below it.

The policeman in the middle of the street lowered his gun and wiped his brow. "Man, it creeps me out how they talk."

The other man joined him, pistol pointed downwards but still gripped in his hand. "If that scares you, you'd best hope you never meet *Mommy.*"

"Fuck man, you know I hate that."

"Ooh rah, buddy."

A screech came from their walkies but Dr. Nand couldn't make it out from his hiding place.

The two men nodded to each other and marched towards the beast, each grabbing a leg and arm closest to its shoulder. They heaved it up and stood still until a van with windows tinted far beyond the legal limit came barreling down the road. A door slid open and the two police officers hoisted the thing into the van, grunting from the effort. They gave a brief salute before the van was sped back into the darkness it had emerged from.

One of the cops—Dr. Nand labeled him in his mind as the rookie—lit a cigarette while the one with the drill sergeant voice put his gun away. "That was a nice shot, by the way."

"Thanks, I practice."

"Well don't let it go to your head."

"Wouldn't work here if I did." He barely finished a third of his cigarette before he crushed it beneath his boot. "So now my celebratory is over, what do we tell the civilians?"

More and more lights were flashing on in the onlooking houses. A few of the braver locals had even poked their heads out their doors.

The gruff voiced man chuckled. "Tell them the truth. We had a dangerous suspect who didn't want to come in and now his brains are sitting on their quaint street."

"And what about the ones who think they saw a man-spider crabwalk up the avenue?"

The deep voice lost its casual tone. "Orders are, no one saw."

The younger man sighed, shaking his head and casting a sad look at a nearby house with a trampoline in the yard. "Hopefully I won't need to enforce those orders." He pulled out another cigarette. "I'm going to need a full one of these if that's the plan."

The older man nodded. "Suit yourself, I got the left."

He marched across the road, stepping over the small picket fence and avoiding the toys strewn about the path leading to the door. When he knocked the door opened quickly and Dr. Nand could hear his friendly, "Evening folks," from across the way.

The younger man only shook his head and finished his cigarette. "Fucking psychopath," he muttered as he walked past Dr. Nand's car and onto the grass of the first house on the block. He'd barely made it up the stairs when a door opened and a worried woman called out, "What was all that noise?"

The young man's voice was as warm as his partner across the way. "Nothing to worry about, ma'am. We had an unfortunate incident out here but it's all settled now."

They went house to house with a casual efficiency, only stopping long enough to change the tired faces greeting them from worried to relieved. They met at the end of the cul-de-sac, knocking on the maroon door to the last house together.

It took them about twenty minutes, a time Dr. Nand spent cowering in his convertible. When the last house occupant—a grouchy looking old man with a raised cane—finally slammed his door shut the men marched towards the lane exit.

With his knees tucked into his chest and his face pushed into the car's pleather, Dr. Nand held his breath until he saw them turn out onto the main road and continue their stroll towards their parked patrol car.

As the beating of his heart began to abate he became aware of Glen's worried voice still chattering in his ear. "What's going on, Doc? Eddie says they didn't get a call, but I swear I could hear gunshots from outside the bar."

Dr. Nand's left hand was back on the steering wheel, his grip so tight his brown skinned hand had been stretched milky white. "Yeah."

"Yeah? Look I'll come get you."

The upturned face of the creature he'd just seen flashed through his mind. For an instant he felt as if its hot breath was grazing against his face. He imagined those six *arms* hugging him, crushing the life out of him so the creature could have its food.

He squeezed his eyes shut and forced his tongue to move. "No, it's fine."

"Fine? You hang up on me after claiming to see a shootout and then say it's fine?"

"Well not fine but, you know."

"Yeah well, I don't know." A muffled curse gave way to the crackling of gravel. "No, I won't ask him."

Dr. Nand perked up. "Ask what?"

"Two Hope locals have had too much to drink and want to bother a respected Doctor over the phone."

"About what?"

Glen started to speak but his voice was overpowered by Harold's slurred speech. "Did you see," he stopped to hiccup, "see the spider?"

Dr. Nand's brow furrowed as he put the car in drive. "I might join you three for a beer," he said as he cruised back towards the bar, thankful he didn't pass any police cars on the way.

Interlude

Present day.

The bar roof was damp, it had been built lopsided and rather than slipping off onto the pavement below, the raindrops pooled up in little puddles, quivering before what, to them, must seem a great abyss.

The thoughts permeating the walls below her were hazy. Sliding awkwardly in directions unintended, much like the water droplets pooling in the roof. She'd never understood the humans' penchant for alcohol. A numb mind was a weak mind. What silly animal would make itself weak?

The boy told her they drank to feel good. She found this ridiculous. If pleasure was what they sought why not go hunting, stalk prey, maybe have sex after if one had a mate? They could even try falling in *love*.

There were far better things than swimming in whiskey dreams until your insides fought their way up your own throat.

While she did not comprehend the human necessity for intoxication she used it greatly to her advantage. How easy it was to stride over a tent of drunks, too busy screaming over guitar twangs to notice her shadow. How simple it was to slip her legs over some brute stumbling through the dark trails to empty his bladder away from his fellow campmates.

If sober individuals could barely notice her what chance did drunks have?

Even here she was certain the clouds of alcohol drifting about below did more to hide her than the looming pine trees ever could. She knew even if a drunk saw her they wouldn't believe their own eyes, shaking their heads and taking a few deep breaths before trying to look again, finding the place she'd been empty.

Then again, sometimes intoxication wasn't even necessary to make people chalk sightings of her up to an illusion of the brain. The large doctor had done so earlier tonight, as had a logger walking through her forest the previous morning.

So simple, these creatures. So certain of their reality and so defenseless to things unconforming to it. In a way it made her sad, seeing something so evolved nearly incapable of defending itself against a real threat. It was part of why she'd decided to start a family, so she could leave something better for the world.

Something more like her.

Hal

"No, Glen, I'm telling you something is going seriously wrong in this town."

"Hal, you've had six shots in the last twenty minutes, the only thing wrong is your alcoholism."

Bobbi's voice rose up, words wavering on her tongue, "That was unnecessary, Glen, he's not trying to be funny."

Hal leaned forward, head dipping so his forehead grazed the table as one of his hands searched blindly for a nearly empty pint of beer. "Glen, we have pictures." He'd pronounced pictures as *picherz* but the general meaning was conveyed.

Glen gave him the sympathetic look he'd perfected over his lifetime working in ambulances. "Hal, you have a hazy picture of a cloud and parts of a tree, you can barely even tell it's outside from the swaying."

"Fuck you, Glen, what about the crashed police truck?"

"Hal, I told you, Dusty checked it out and found nothing."

"Dusty," Hal paused to burp, "isn't exactly Columbo."

"Look, Hal, I think it's time we get you looked at in the hospital. Drinking like you do isn't exactly conducive to good mental health."

Hal shot up, steadying himself by slamming his tanned hands onto the table. Glowering, he prepared to unleash a stream of insults directed at Glen and his mother when the man's cellphone beeped.

"It's Andy probably begging me to come in on my time off." Glen said with a sigh, glancing through the nearby window to the crowd of paramedics giggling in the cloud of pot smoke slowly engulfing the patio. "He's lucky I don't party as hard as those degenerates."

"Yeah?" said Hal, already forgetting the curses he'd prepared.

Glen's hand reached out to steady his swaying friend. "Look, whatever is going on we'll get it sorted tomorrow. Talk to Dr. Nand when he gets here, he'll have a hundred reasons for what you saw, or better yet go cheer up your cousin. I haven't seen her this sad since Julius Brentwood dumped her in the tenth grade."

Hal rolled his eyes. "Whatever, Glen, be safe out there."

Hal sunk back into his seat, crossing his arms and sinking into the table in the same position as his cousin. The two of them were easily the most depressed looking in the bar and far at odds with the raucous laughter and music surrounding them.

The Doctor didn't announce himself, merely stood looming over them until Hal took notice. His large frame was shaking and his skin, usually dark as the expensive import he drank, seemed oddly pale. Only his eyes were the same, large and inquisitive as if they'd been hand crafted to dig into your soul.

Hal eyed him wearily. "You saw it."

Dr. Nand's lip twitched. "Maybe. Glen told me you've been hallucinating."

Hal waved his hand over at his cousin. "We have a group hysteria here." He slapped a palm on the table to jolt Bobbi upright. "Doctor."

"Evening, Doctor," mumbled Bobbi.

"Hello, Bobbi, having a rough day?"

Bobbi snorted, returning her head to the cradle of her vibrating hands.

"Hal, what's wrong with you two?"

"Glen's medical opinion is that we've both suffered a psychiatric break, probably triggered by being lost in the wilderness."

Dr. Nand nodded politely. "And your opinion?"

"There's a giant fucking spider eating the good people of Hope, British Columbia."

"Ahh."

Hal flicked a peanut at his cousin. "She said you'd believe us but that was a bottle of wine ago."

"I am a man of science."

"I'm an atheist if that helps."

Dr. Nand relaxed his shoulders and even let out a quick breath of air that might have been a giggle. "Some people think of science as its own religion." He placed a meaty hand on the table, fingers digging into it as if to stop him being blown away by some unseen gale. "And part of the religion is a certain level of skepticism. Skepticism about things like giant monsters and, uh, zombies."

"Zombies?"

Bobbi cocked her head up, glazed eyes sliding over the large Doctor. "What now?"

Dr. Nand shrugged, keys rattling in his hand. "I think there's someone we should go see." His big brown eyes rested on the empty beer pitchers. "I'll drive."

Blake

Being awake hurt, but it was preferable to the drug induced dreams. For the past few hours he'd been stuck in a continuous loop of horrors.

They always started mostly sane, if a little morbid. He was reliving his sister's funeral, her pale face staring up at him from a coffin they'd got on discount because it had a large crack near the bottom of the lid.

Music played during his nightmare. Unlike the real funeral, they'd been able to afford an orchestra. They scratched out a somber funeral march that grew louder with each passing second until the inevitable shriek of a violin string snapping caused his sister's eyes to snap open from her casket. She smiled and asked him to join her, pulling him into the coffin with an icy grip he couldn't fend off.

The music sped to a manic pace, each instrument scratching with ear bleeding quality as the funeral attendees started to do a mad jig in their seats. The devilish music continued to speed up until it reached its deafening peak, every instrument joining in a final cacophonic cry before vanishing almost instantly.

When the eerie silence overtook the room, someone came to pull the coffin lid over them. Sometimes it was his mother, glaring at him with sulky eyes. Sometimes it was the priest, giving a sad shrug and a mournful look. Most times it was his little sister, tears dribbling down into the coffin as she screamed.

"You said you wouldn't leave me, Blakey!"

Then came the cold and darkness, him and his sister pressed together in cotton lined boxes with only the sound of his own ragged breathing to fill it.

His sister was freezing to the touch. He couldn't hear her heart or feel her breath in the coffin, but he did feel her tongue in his ear. Digging in like a snake intent on tunneling to his brain.

He squirmed and writhed, trying to escape it until she stopped and started to laugh. It wasn't the sparkling laugh he remembered but a high pitched cackle he found far more terrifying than her cold tongue digging into his ear canal.

If he was lucky he woke up for a brief moment, eyes burning from the sight of the hospital lights that—while dimmed for the night, were far too bright—before falling back into his dreams and restarting the funeral procession again.

More often than not, he didn't wake up. Instead he would remain cramped in the coffin with his sister's hysterical laughter until she calmed enough to speak. She would press her lips against his ear, their damp flesh causing his skin to prickle as her soft voice leaked into his skull.

"Mother wants you, Blake. She wants you very much."

She would resume laughing as the spiders entered. They always appeared in the same way, pouring through the crack in the wood that had made the coffin so cheap.

At first he tried to crush them, flailing his body about in frenzied protest to end their miserable lives, but it was never enough. No matter how many he smothered there were always more streaming through the hole until the entire coffin was filled with their writhing mass.

This was the worst part, struggling to breathe and realizing he was going to drown in spiders. Somehow his sister's laughter continued, growing harsher and harsher as her throat filled with eight legged creatures.

Eventually they started to dig into him, gnawing at his clothes and pushing themselves into him. He felt them tunnel into his ear and try to poke themselves up through his nose.

Mercifully, the dream ended when they made their way into his throat. Forcing their way past his gnashing teeth until they clogged his lungs and he woke in his hospital bed fighting for air.

It was well past midnight now and he'd managed to remain conscious for nearly a half-hour. The hospital wing he'd been sequestered in was quiet, the only noise coming from the soft hum of the machines left to measure the vital signs of the room's other occupant, an elderly heart attack hidden behind a thin curtain a meter to Blake's left.

His aunt had arrived to take his sister home while he was still riding the Novocain express.

With black humour, he wondered to himself how much a traumatic event like they'd just experience could set his sister's diet back. Lord knows his aunt wouldn't try to cook anything healthy, if she even cooked at all while he was stuck in hospital.

He chastised himself as he tried to rise from bed. Was he really worrying about his sister's nutrition after he'd just seen a grown man try to eat her? In his defense, worrying about diets was a lot easier than trying to comprehend what exactly had been chasing him and Sarah.

If he let his mind wander, even for a second, Mr. Rutgers' face popped into his mind, the blood dripping from his mouth as he lurched wildly after them.

He'd walked like a man on drugs, that was for sure, and there were certainly some drugs floating around Hope that might induce insanity and cannibalism, but it didn't wholly explain his behavior. Christ, his mouth had enveloped a man's entire head.

And there'd been the voice too. The one screaming inside his head right before the truck hit them.

He grimaced as he put his shirt on, pain springing from both the effort and the memory. Next, he slid his legs, one heavily stitched around the calf, into the pair of jeans his aunt had bothered to drop off. One of his shoes had gone missing in the accident, forcing him to slip into an ill-fitting pair of hospital flip flops.

Still groggy from the drugs and nightmares he made his way to the room door, opening it gently to let his disheveled self out into the public space beyond.

In the soft orange light of the hallway he was surprised to find himself facing Dr. Nand.

"Blake?"

Blake blinked in surprise. "Yes?"

"You're up?"

Behind Dr. Nand's broad shoulders he could make out two swaying figures. For a brief second, Blake thought it was Mr. Rutgers back to finish the job, his fear only dissipating when one of the figure's let out a loud hiccup that made the other giggle.

"Is that…?"

Dr. Nand removed his glasses and started to polish them, his voice slightly apologetic as he spoke. "I believe you know Harold and his cousin Bobbi?"

"Him and I found some sick shit up in Ladner."

"Language, Blakey," Hal said, inducing another round of giggling between him and his cousin.

"Jesus, are they shitfaced?"

Dr. Nand let out a deep breath, his voice a mix of mirth and exasperation. "They're feeling pretty good."

"Why are you wandering around with a bunch of drunks at three in the morning?" He shook his head and started to press past the group to continue down the hallway. "Forget it, I don't care."

Dr. Nand opened his mouth to speak when Hal blurted out, "We saw what strung those people up."

Blake paused in his step, his gaze focused on Hal. The man's coarse whiskers glowed in the dim orange of the hospital's nighttime lights, his face had grown gaunter in the few weeks since they'd last seen each other.

Bobbi stood beside him with her eyes downcast, her short hair so tangled that it had transformed into a tiny afro.

"We saw it, kid," Hal continued.

Blake's throat was dry, he wondered if his aunt had left him any beer in the fridge. He wouldn't mind being in Hal's condition once he was sure his sister was safe. With an air of defeat he let himself be rung into the conversation. "What did you see?"

"It's a giant spider."

Bobbi let out a sob and Dr. Nand flinched. Hal merely continued swaying on the spot.

"I see," said Blake as he started down the hallway, three started after him.

"Blake, I saw something strange today… OK, something completely fucked up, and we're just trying to get a grip on what's going on," said Dr. Nand, huffing to keep up with the teen.

Blake sped up, flip flops smacking heavily against the smooth hospital tile. The others followed pace, the smell of liquor radiating from them.

Bobbi spoke for the first time. "You saw it too, didn't you?"

Blake shook his head as he opened a door into a concrete stairwell. It reeked of cigarettes, likely from a nurse or doctor too lazy to brave the dark night. "I didn't see a giant spider."

He felt Dr. Nand's large hand on his shoulder. "You saw one of those things though, the things that used to be people?"

Blake stopped, surprised by the fear in the man's voice.

"Yeah. I saw one of those."

Blake was unsure if it was relief or terror at the words that was filling Dr. Nand's face. The trio of adults crowded together to confer while he started his trek down the poorly lit stairwell.

Hal's voice was the loudest. Blake wondered if the man was capable of whispers. "See, told you we're not going crazy, Doctor."

"I know, I know. It's just… it's just, this is fucking mad."

"I'd watch it," said Bobbi. "The kid doesn't like swearing."

Blake was nearly a floor lower when Dr. Nand's voice echoed down from above. "Mr. Turner, please wait up."

The Doctor caught up to him with surprising speed, his long legs stretching down four steps at a time with a nimbleness not fitting his girth. "Blake, there's something wrong with this town—why are you in such a hurry to go into it? You shouldn't even be out of your bed in my professional opinion."

Blake was too sore and tired to be exasperated. Instead he pressed his lips into the simplest explanation he could. "Sister."

From the corner of his eye he saw the realization seep into Dr. Nand's face. "Shit." The large man twisted his thick neck to holler back up the stairs. "Hurry up you two, we have to go pick up Blake's sister."

Reaching the first floor, Blake pushed through one of the three doors available, remembering the way from the multiple times his mother had stayed in the hospital following an overdose.

Racing past waiting chairs and posters requesting patients please refrain from assaulting hospital staff, he soon found himself in the parking lot. He was quickly joined by Bobbi, Dr. Nand, and Hal. Hal was panting for breath but the other two were quiet, their bodies tense in the moonlight.

Dr. Nand waved towards a silver convertible parked auspiciously close to the door. "It's cramped but we'll fit."

As they rushed forward, a puzzle voice rang out.

"Dr. Nand?"

Glen walked out from behind an ambulance. He was wearing his paramedic scrubs and had a large paper cup of coffee clenched in his hand. "What are you doing here so late?" He laughed when he saw Bobbi and Hal. "And why did you bring those drunkards?"

Dr. Nand paused but the others didn't, opening the doors and planting themselves into the leather seats of the convertible. Blake sat with a particularly impatient air, arms crossed and eyes digging into the Doctor.

"Glen, I'm sorry, I'll explain soon." He hurried to the car and pulled the door open. "We're in a bit of a rush."

Glen whistled and walked out into the parking lot. "Jesus, Doc, you guys look rough. Sure everything is okay?"

"It's alright, Glen, we don't..." Dr. Nand's throat went dry as his eyes caught the dark glimmer three stories up. Perched on the thick brick hospital walls was a massive spider. It sat patiently, eyes fluttering in amusement as they met Dr. Nand's. "Oh shit, oh shit, Glen."

Glen frowned, spinning around to see what had caught the Doctor's attention. Finding nothing, he squinted at Doctor Nand in puzzlement. "What's wrong, Doctor?"

"Run, Glen, fucking run!"

Glen's golden face twisted into outright confusion, the hand not holding his coffee reaching up to run through his golden hair. "What's wro—"

Dr. Nand didn't see the spider leave its perch, only caught its eight legs landing around Glen. It scooped him up with the front two, the man's face flickering from surprise to terror in the brief moment before the spider launched back into the night above.

Hal was the first to say something, careening his neck in attempt to find where the creature had gone. "Jesus fuck, fuck, fuck, fuck."

Bobbi started to scream while Dr. Nand stood rooted in the spot, arms resting on the open car door while his eyes lingered over the patch of cement his friend had been standing on mere seconds ago. He might have stood there until the spider came back were it not for Blake's forceful hands pushing him into the car, snatching the keys from him as he toppled into the back seat where he landed on a still screaming Bobbi.

Blake drove fast, a lot faster than he'd ever driven in Hope before, thankful the howl of the engine could drown out the gale-force current of his mind.

A giant spider.

He passed a squad car as he barreled round the corner onto the next street but its lights remained off—likely Dusty sleeping on shift again..

A giant fucking spider.

Dust flicked up into the open cab as he ripped towards his trailer. In the back, Dr. Nand regained enough composure to move off Bobbi and into the middle seat, scrunched like a massive child between Bobbi and Hal.

The street was empty save for Ms. Brightly who was slumped in her lawn chair cradling an empty six-pack of Smrinoff. His aunt's car was parked out front, which was a good sign.

The car was barely stopped when he was already vaulting up the steps into the trailer, crashing through the door with enough force to rock the tiny domicile.

Fumbling for the lights with sweating hands he started to plead in his mind.

Please god, please god, please god.

The kitchen bulb flickered on, his eyes scanned over the trailer's contents. It was trashed. Beer bottles, clothes, and what he hoped was food, littered the floor. His aunt was lying in her usual spot on the couch between the arms of a paper-thin man with a snake tattoo covering his neck.

The man's eyes didn't flutter at his entrance but his aunt's did. She groaned and rolled over in the couch, causing a half empty bottle of cider to fall and start leaking on the floor.

He ripped the door to his sister's room open, snapping one of the hinges as he did. The crack it made caused his aunt to groan again. "Go to sleep, Sarah…. Late…"

The room was dark, his aunt hadn't bothered to turn on the night light his sister used to fend off nightmares. He flicked it on, let out a heavy sigh of relief at the sight of her snoring in the arms of a ragged teddy bear.

She didn't wake as he sat on the bed with her, only her feet twitched as they moved ever so slightly away from his weight.

"Thank god. Thank god."

A shadow crossed over him and he looked up to see Dr. Nand. "She's alright?"

Blake stroked his sister's hair that needed washing. "Yes."

"Is that your, um.."

"It's my aunt."

"Ah."

Blake stood up and walked out of the room with the Doctor. Hal and Bobbi were in the kitchen, Hal helping himself to a beer. Blake gave him a dirty look before proceeding to pull his own from the tiny refrigerator.

He'd nearly finished it before someone spoke.

"Not exactly a homemaker," muttered Bobbi.

Hal put a hand on her shoulder. "It's hard work being a parent, Bobbi."

The hard look on her face remained. "Like you would know, Harold."

Hal frowned and took another gulp from his beer bottle. "That was uncalled for." A flicker of shame crossed Bobbi's face, but she didn't apologize.

Dr. Nand took a seat at the picnic table they'd managed to jam into the kitchen, one meaty arm resting over a string of curse words the table's former owners had carved into it. "Do you think," he frowned. "Do you think Glen is okay?"

Hal put his back against the fridge and slid down it to the floor. "Okay?" He leaned forward so he could open it and withdraw another beer, a feat requiring him to twist his body with more elegance than Blake thought the man capable of. "Okay?"

Bobbi stood standing, arms crossed and eyes darting about the room. "I don't think he's okay."

Blake remained silent in the doorway to his sister's room, glancing back every few seconds at Sarah's little frame.

Dr. Nand coughed and looked down at his shoes. "I mean."

Hal snorted. "You mean? What? Christ, you didn't see what we just saw?"

Dr. Nand shook his head and continued to speak to the floor. "I mean that, spiders don't exactly..." he grimaced as if it brought him physical pain to finish the sentence. Hal's eyes widened in recognition. Dr. Nand pushed the last words out quickly. "Spiders don't exactly eat their prey right away."

Blake shuddered. The Doctor continued. "There might be time to, erm, rescue him."

Bobbi laughed. Blake expected Hal to join her, but he didn't. Her voice cracked as she spoke. "Yeah, let's just go out and fight the giant fucking spider roaming the streets. Maybe we don't even need to do it ourselves, I know a great exterminator."

Hal gave his cousin a pained look. "Bobbi..."

She continued, her voice speeding up with harsh edge. "Great guy, got rid of the ants in my apartment like that," she snapped her fingers loudly. "Even gave me his number, said I'd get a discount next time if we went on a date first." Her shoulders started to shake. "His van had a nice slogan, 'We bug bugs.' Bet he could really show that giant fucking spider whose boss."

Hal's voice was shallow. "Bobbi, I know you don't like spiders."

She let out a hoarse laugh. "You think?"

Dr. Nand stretched out a long arm and placed it on Bobbi's crossed elbow. She flinched but let it stay.

Hal swallowed before he spoke. "Do you think... do you think it has Laura?"

Bobbi's mouth dropped and Dr. Nand winced.

"I mean. Her body wasn't with the ones me and the kid found..."

A long silence followed, each person's mind unraveling the implications of a giant spider hunting their fellow citizens.

Blake had a bitter taste in his mouth. There were some dots he'd refused to connect until they'd been made blatantly obvious for him. "I think I know where my mother's gone."

The looks of pity from the three adults was too much and he turned his back to them, letting his focus turn to his sister.

Hal broke the ensuing silence with a long whistle. "Jesus, kid."

Blake's fist clenched, his voice remaining flat as he spoke. "So, are we going to do something about it?" The others shifted uncomfortably under his stare. "Well?"

Dr. Nand tapped his fingers on the picnic table, the meaty digits pounding out an anxious beat. "Glen might still be alive."

"So might my mother."

"Yes, if the…" Dr. Nand bit his tongue before pushing the rest of his words out. "If the creature even has her."

"It must."

"It might."

Blake's arm started to throb. It would be satisfying to plant his knuckles into something. He was sick of adults giving him reasons not to find his Mom. "Well, let's look," he said in a slightly more agreeable tone. "We can at least tell the cops what we saw."

Hal snorted while Dr. Nand returned his gaze to the floor. When the large man spoke, his words were strained. "I don't think so."

"Why not?"

Bobbi threw her phone to Blake, he barely caught it in the dim light of the kitchen. "I took that photo from the back of a police truck."

"Is that the spider?"

"Can't you tell?"

Blake tossed the phone back. "It's blurry."

Bobbi spit on the floor, shoving the phone back in her pocket with a curse. "Well, you could see the bars, right?"

"Yes."

"Me and Harold were locked in there, like animals."

"Did you do something wrong?"

Hal snorted. "Jesus, kid, you're not getting it. We were arrested for trying to learn about what's going on." A soft hiss filled the kitchen as he opened another beer. "I swear to God, the guy was going to shoot us."

Blake was ready to dispute this claim, but his mind was already reliving the interrogation he'd endured weeks ago. The thought of Ken Dawson's threats lingered in his thoughts, but it still seemed ludicrous the police couldn't be trusted.

"What made you think—?"

Dr. Nand interjected before he could finish. "Blake, I also saw some evidence we can't trust the police." He frowned, his bushy eyebrows disappearing behind the frames of his glasses. "Or heard I guess, I was kind of hiding at the time."

Blake waved a hand towards his sister. "Well, what do we do then? She wants her mother." Pride kept him from adding *so do I.*

His tone weakened as he relented. "No cops, okay, but what about Sarah?"

Dr. Nand raised a tentative hand.

"Yes, doctor?"

"She can stay at my place." His head swiveled at the exhausted group surrounding him. "You all can."

Hal eyed the couple on the couch, still passed out despite the conversation happening feet away from them. "What about them?"

His question went unanswered as Blake had already gone into Sarah's room and started pulling clothes from dressers and shoving them into a backpack.

"What about them?" Hal repeated as Blake disappeared into the bathroom.

Emerging with a toiletry bag, Blake started marching for the door, stopped only by Hal's arm shooting out to latch onto the boy's leg. The boy glowered. Hal smiled thinly and tilted his head towards the snoring couple. "What about them?"

Blake didn't follow Hal's gaze. "What about them?"

"Well, are we going to wake them?"

"And tell them what?"

"You know…" Hal looked to Bobbi for help, finding her making a pointed effort to avoid his gaze.

"I don't know," said Blake.

Dr. Nand stood up, his weight making the trailer shift slightly. "Blake, you should at least leave a note."

A brief flash of anger spread across Blake's face, his hands clenching into a fist before he muttered a sullen "fine." Hal mouthed a thank you to the good doctor, relief washing over him.

Five minutes later they were cruising away from Hope, a sleepy Sarah cradled in the middle of the back seat between a snoring Harold and her somber brother.

Dr. Nand was driving, happy for the brief distraction it provided. No one spoke, the radio was off. His high beams were on, the halogen lights bouncing off the mountains surrounding them. They were bright and did a great job of illuminating the sneaking bends of the highway but did little to alleviate his fears.

Would the harsh light even reflect on the milky silk of a spider web? If they did would it matter? It was easy to imagine how each new turn could end in a giant web, a mass of cords appearing so abruptly out of the darkness that he'd have little chance of avoiding them even if he did see them.

Driving through the darkness with the mountain railing on one side of the car and the looming, evidently spider infested forest on the other, Dr. Nand shivered. Not large shuddering motions like Bobbi beside him, but a small nervous twitch.

Looking in his rearview mirror he couldn't help but envy Hal's self-induced numbness, it was sure better than worrying about what was out *there*.

Part 4: Hunting

Interlude
2008

When the boy—now almost a man—left for school, it was most painful thing she ever endured. The distance was so great between them that even after years of practice they were only strong enough to talk for minutes a day, screaming across the country with their minds until their brains shook in agony.

She had never felt pain like this, the assault on her emotions crippling her for months. It became hard to hunt, too tired to bother with anything but the weakest of prey. Her rare meals consisted of easy kills; injured deer, elderly cougars, the young of any species.

The days fluttered away. She cocooned herself in the *home* the boy had found for her the previous summer, webbing over the entrances and unused passages until only the most enterprising strands of light could slip in.

As the time the boy was away grew, so did her sadness. Emotional weakness growing into physical weakness as her poor diet began to shrivel her once strong body.

For a few brief moments she hated the boy, despised him for leaving her, for making her *lonely*. She wondered if she'd made a mistake bonding with him, wondered if he might be a competing predator instead of the life mate she'd believed him to be.

In these grueling years she almost died, asphyxiated by something as base as *emotion*.

Wasting away of sadness would have been a pathetic end to something as magnificent as herself, an end she surely would have succumbed to if not for her love's return.

He arrived without warning, walking proudly into the deep recess of her home to hug her and nuzzle his head against hers so their thoughts could boom into each other's skulls.

He took in the disarray of their *home*, worry seeping into him at the sight of her malnourished frame.

For him, the past years had been good, his body had grown stronger and he'd earned a *job* he told her, that would let him continue to go unnoticed in the strange world of humans. He'd also had the thrill of his first solo hunt, a kill he believed would have made her proud.

He had not known of her great sadness, it filled him with remorse.

He knelt to rest his hand on her front leg, his soft hands scratching the coarse hairs. Gazing deeply into her largest two eyes, he made a promise. With thoughts as solid as iron he told her he would never leave her, that she would *never be alone* again.

She felt the burn of love reignite in her heart, its powerful energy spreading through her weak husk. She quivered as he nuzzled her jaw.

She couldn't imagine experiencing more pleasure, not if she was drinking the sweetest blood or weaving the most exquisite web. She was the happiest she had ever been. Then, somehow, her love made it even better.

He planted a wet kiss on her forehead, a smile lighting his face. "I'm ready," he whispered. "Ready to start a family."

Ken

He didn't let the anger reach his mind. He pushed it down into his stomach where it could boil, fueling his body with an electric energy far more useful than blind rage.

No, anger had no part in his mind right now.

Later, when the bug had been caught and he'd put a bullet in the skull of every mouth breather who'd so much as looked at him funny in the last year, then he would feel anger. He would lock himself in his apartment and use his hunting knife to cut through every iota of emotion he'd repressed for this assignment.

He'd done it plenty in the past. Emerging days or even weeks later from his home, leaving every inch of it slashed to bits. Often his own body was as patchwork as his apartment—arms and chest slashed open like his bedsheets and pillows. He wondered how badly he'd scar himself the next time, he'd certainly repressed enough rage to make it memorable.

His fury sprung from the operations failures. In the month since they'd started hunting the creature, the casualty list had grown while their intel stagnated. It was toying with him, he saw that now, dismantling his operation—agent by screaming agent—through the long hours of the night. The prowess it assaulted them proof he'd underestimated it.

It was a mistake, but only partially his own, their intel had never suggested the creature had such developed intelligence.

To think, the creature was capable of advanced reasoning. It was a prospect both terrifying and exhilarating. It also meant Ken's reward for capturing it would be great. His mind reveled at the thought of promotion and prestige.

No more postings in influenza riddled shitholes. No more exchanging gunfire with sixteen-year-old militants over a few kilometers of sand. No more dealing with hillbillies in British fucking Columbia.

His anger would come later, but so would his rewards.

"Has the doctor been moved yet?"

His new assistant was twenty-nine, dark hair in a tight ponytail with glasses covering most of her face. He'd smirked during her arrival, certain she'd last half the time his previous underling had.

He'd been pleasantly surprised.

"He's been evacuated from site; test subjects have been euthanized and bagged. Research facility is being cleaned as we speak," she said mechanically.

Ken frowned. Staring out his office window he swore he could still spot the blood stains from where Officer Benz had met her demise. He'd have to have it scrubbed again.

"I ordered the research to be kept intact."

"Report says that the test subjects took the opportunity of being moved to, um, rebel."

"Rebel?"

The woman tapped on her tablet, voice continuing with dry efficiency. "We lost six agents. Commander on site ordered full extermination."

Ken glanced over at the woman, her eyes were fixed expectantly on him.

"He can keep his command, but put out a base alert, from now on we consider anything genetically related to the creature to have higher level intelligence."

The woman's fingers danced over her tablet, nails making a soft click as they connected with the screen. "Understood."

"And I want the research facility and all the land within three kilometers burned." On the off chance one escaped, there was no need to let a second one of those *things* grow up in the woods here.

His assistant frowned.

"What?"

Her eyes were locked on her tablet screen, her pink tongue sticking out through artificially white teeth. "We might lack the resources to do so promptly."

Ken sighed, pausing to purge the anger welling in his mind. "Update command about the change in intelligence evaluation of the creature, they'll send more troops after."

She snapped her head forward. "Yes, sir."

"That's all."

The woman gave a curt nod and headed for the door, her dark suit disappearing into the bright hallway. As the door drifted shut behind her the din of the operation fled into the room, inundating Ken with flurry of voices, radio squawks, and other chatters involved in running the command post, the noise a sweet symphony to his ears.

He cracked his neck and took a sip of cold coffee from a nearby mug. He turned to the window. His gaze pored over dirty brick buildings and cracked concrete roads, piercing the night for a hopeful glimpse of the eight-legged monstrosity.

They'd had reports earlier of a sighting at the hospital, the surveillance van glimpsing it briefly as it scurried down the side of the pediatric wing. More interesting to Ken was the following report of a convertible speeding from the hospital.

People didn't drive the speed limit in Hope, particularly late at night when they believed the cops to be asleep, but it was also possible the vehicle's occupants had been alarmed by something big and hairy with too many legs.

Ken wouldn't be surprised if they had to silence the whole town at the end of the operation. Ken licked his lips at the prospect.

It had been done before by the organization, more than he'd have expected when he first joined. It was messy work and keeping the media attention down was hard, even in an overlooked shithole such as this.

Still, considering the magnitude of their find, it was worth it.

He tapped a button on his watch, a commlink between his assistant opening instantly. Her voice rang in his right ear as if she had her lips pressed against it, a feeling Ken still found uncomfortable despite his years of experience.

"Sir?"

"Add a follow up report, request resources be made available for possible neutralization of the town."

"Of course, sir."

As the line went dead, Ken's thoughts drifting to all the civilians he'd been forced to deal with over the last year. Meth heads, drunks, soccer moms. He hated them all. They were weak, their insignificant lives a cancer to society.

Taking another sip of cold coffee, he focused his anger at these people away, letting it fade into hope. Hope he'd be allowed to eliminate them all.

Hal

The Nand's had a beautiful house. Modern, six bedrooms, three and a half bathrooms, and one of the biggest kitchens Hal had ever seen. The location was great too, an acreage on the outskirts of Chilliwack with lush green mountains to its back and corn fields on its sides.

Hal hadn't done well in school, believing the whole process to be little more than poorly orchestrated brainwashing, looking at homes like this was one of the few times he regretted his lack of effort.

Sophia, the Doctor's wife, made them breakfast. Humming along to the radio as eggs and bacon crackled on her stove top.

She was thin, like a flag pole, with long dark hair and a ruby red mouth that seemed to always be inching towards a frown. She had a pretty face but her real beauty came from her eyes, the way they sparkled when they rested on her husband.

She hadn't questioned why four strangers were sleeping in her house, only put on a coffee pot and brought another pillow for Sarah who she thought looked uncomfortable tangled in the pink sheets of one of the spare beds.

Hal had been given a bed himself, but he'd moved to a couch in the early morning, preferring the cold leather to the unnatural homeliness of the bedroom. The couch was where he belonged, and it was where he slept until dawn began seeping through the curtains of the living room.

First thing he did was check the kitchen fridge for a beer, finding only thirty dollar quinoa and sparkling water.

It didn't surprise him. He'd always pictured the Doctor as the type of man to have special beer fridge, an ornate box sequestered in some rec room or man cave elsewhere in the house. He was about to go searching for it when the sight of Dr. Nand's wife shambling sleepily into the kitchen made him pause.

He'd never met the woman and a small voice in the back of his head whispered that it might be nice to know one person who didn't think of him singularly as a drunk.

This thought collided with an image of what he'd seen at the hospital the night before fluttering through his mind, easily overpowering his care of what others thought of him indulging in nice breakfast beverage.

The house didn't have a rec room and the garage lacked a refrigerator but he did find a little cooler in the reading room, nestled in between shelves of large, rather intimidating, books. He opened it up like it was a treasure chest freshly dug from the sand and with crossed fingers he peered into it.

Gold.

The good doctor had expensive taste in beer and a healthy supply. He'd finished two before the man himself walked into the kitchen, a sleeping boy nestled between his great arms. The man's brown eyes fell over the empty bottles at Hal's feet, but he did little else to acknowledge the situation.

"This is Julius," he said with a yawn. "He wanted to sleep with us when I got home."

Hal tugged at his beer bottle label. "It's tough work, parenting."

Sophia walked over to the table they were sitting at, dropping a plate of bacon and eggs in front of them. Her gaze lingered on Hal's beer for a moment before she turned around to grab the coffee that had just finished brewing.

The child rolled in his father's arms, nudging his face into the man's elbow crevice where he would be shielded from the morning light. "It's tougher work not to, I think," said Dr. Nand, smiling down at his boy.

Hal tucked a fork into one of his eggs. "Yeah, maybe."

Blake entered the kitchen, sleep still written across his features. He slumped into a chair and snatched the mug of coffee Sophia had placed before Hal.

Hal chuckled. "Not a morning person, kid?"

Dr. Nand passed his own mug to Hal. "You can go back to bed if you want, Mr. Turner. The food in our house won't run away."

Blake sucked back the coffee, grimacing from the heat. "I don't want to sleep."

"Come now," yawned the doctor. "Sleep is important for a boy your age. You're safe here, don't worry."

Annoyance flickered across Blake's face. "Am I?" he mouthed.

Hal finished his beer. He started reaching for another, but Sophia's glare induced him to lift a coffee mug instead.

Bobbi was the last adult to rise, walking into the kitchen wearing a turquoise bathrobe she'd found in her room. She was the only one who appeared refreshed.

"Good morning," she said pleasantly.

Hal passed her the rest of his coffee. "At least one of us is chipper."

Bobbi ran a hand through her short blonde hair, a thin smile playing on her lips. "Best sleep I've had in weeks." She glanced over to Dr. Nand. "Feels good to be away from Hope."

"Fucking fantastic," said Hal.

Blake and Dr. Nand spoke at the same time, the latter cupping his hands over Julius' ears.

"Language."

Hal rolled his eyes. "So. Are we going to talk about it more yet?"

Dr. Nand sighed and eyed the plateful of bacon in front him. His wife had brought him a second helping. Hal was starting to understand why the man was so large. "Let's eat first," he turned to catch his wife's eye. "And then maybe Sophia could take Julius to the park and give us some privacy?"

Sophia cast a puzzled look over the table and shrugged as she took the sleeping boy from Dr. Nand. "I need the exercise anyway."

Dr. Nand flourished a brilliant smile, the one reserved for the love of his life. "Thank you, dear."

The woman's nostrils flared. "Just don't let that one make a mess." She didn't have to point for them to know she was talking about Hal.

When they heard the front door slam, Dr. Nand leaned back in his chair and patted his belly, giving a content and rather undoctorly burp. "I love her so much."

Bobbi pushed away the plate she'd been given, the bacon the only part remaining. "She seemed lovely."

Blake refilled his coffee cup from the pot, casting a hateful look at the sunlight pouring through the kitchen window. "So, what now?"

Hal had hoped he'd have an answer to that question by the time the sun came up. "I don't know."

"Well we need to stop it, obviously," said Bobbi.

Hal glanced at her, alarmed by the sincerity in her words. "Says the girl who pukes at the sight of spiders."

Bobbi shifted uncomfortably in her chair. "Well, I thought about it, and that thing is killing people. People who can't defend themselves. Women, the disenfranchised, children." Her eyes fell on her plate and her voice dropped a little. "The kind of people I always wanted to help."

"It's why you went into journalism—I know, cousin—but how are *we*," he waved around the room for emphasis, "Going to stop whatever that thing is." He bit his lip. "We shouldn't even be the ones to do it, it's why we have police and the army," he added dejectedly.

Bobbi's voice quavered but her resolve remained. "And what if those people won't help?"

"Surely someone will believe us."

"And what if they don't? Or worse, what if they're like the cop we ran into yesterday?" She leaned forward and continued, "I was thinking about it and..."

"And?"

"And what if the truck cage wasn't meant for people?"

Hal was silent for a second, his cracked brain feebly trying to recall the details of their one-time prison. "It did seem a little much for keeping people in."

"The bars were nearly a foot thick, Harold."

Hal shrugged looking to Dr. Nand and Blake for their opinion.

Dr. Nand spoke first. "I think the police in Hope aren't to be trusted." He paused to stroke his chin. "At least the newest arrivals."

Bobbi's brow crinkled. "Yeah what's up with that? I checked the internet today, not a single report of a task force being organized to investigate whatever happened up at Ladner."

Hal sat upright, a smile rolling onto his face sparked equally by both his morning beers and flash of insight. "Let's talk to Dusty."

Bobbi sniffed. "I think Dr. Nand is right, I don't trust the police of Hope. Especially since yesterday."

"But, Bobbi, Dusty is barely a cop." Hal's grin widened. "Remember that time he held a door open for the guy who robbed Dairy Queen?" He met Bobbi's reproachful stare. "Besides, I saw him at the bar last week. He was all bummed out because he didn't get to be on the special investigation crew. They have him out busting speeders. Alone too, Benz had to rush out east for a family emergency."

"Well," said Bobbi tentatively. "It is always nice to have an inside source."

"Lord knows Dusty can't keep a secret."

Blake guzzled the remnants of his coffee before slamming the mug onto the table. "Let's get on with it then."

Dr. Nand turned to the boy, jawline drawn and brow creased. "Blake," he said carefully, "I think this is something for the adults to worry about." He winced as the boy's mouth pursed. "You've already done more than enough for a kid your age."

Blake waved to Bobbi and Hal. "He's half drunk, she pukes at the sight of spiders, and I'm the one you're trying to stop from helping?" His voice lowered. "I'm the one whose lost the most."

"Blake," said Dr. Nand gently. "We don't know if whatever that thing is has your mother."

Blake snorted, condescension filling his words. "Sure, I bet she just got lost in the woods and wasn't abducted by the giant spider roaming the streets of our hometown."

Dr. Nand thought about voicing his real concern, that Blake's mother was dead (or worse one of those things he'd seen the police shoot) but it was a little too early in the morning to crush the boy's hopes entirely.

"I'm helping or I'm going out to look for her alone." The boy crossed his arms and glared defiantly across the table. "You guys can choose which."

Hal threw his arms up. "Oh, for fuck's sake, Armand, let the kid help. He's one of the only people who actually knows about whatever is going on."

"Language," muttered Dr. Nand.

"Fuck you."

Dr. Nand massaged his temples. "Fine."

A silence settled over the room, no one willing to continue the conversation. It was only broken when Sarah marched sleepily through the door, chubby hand rubbing sleep from her eyes. "Blakey, is there breakfast?"

Blake gave a weary smile. Hal looked guiltily at the remnants of his own breakfast—he might have thought of the girl before taking seconds.

"Why don't I cook you some pancakes," said Blake.

"Just how Mommy makes them?"

"Of course," said the teenager as he raided the fridge for eggs. "Just how Mommy makes them."

Dusty

Cigarette packs littered his car floor. It was a filthy habit and one he'd thought he'd kicked the previous summer after a cancer scare. He sighed as he lit one now.

Smoke filled the car, pushing up against the windows in a weak attempt at escape. His hand twitched towards the window crank—god he wished he'd paid the extra thousand for automatics—but he stopped himself from unwinding it.

He'd rather sit in the smoke-filled cabin of his Honda than unnecessarily expose a single inch of himself to Hope's air.

There had to be something in it. Some carcinogen proliferating endlessly through the lungs of the unaware townsfolks. Some yet unheard-of molecule that turned people mad, making insanity as contagious as sneezing. It was the only explanation for what was happening.

Hope had always been a little off kilter, he'd dealt with more than a few drugged up locals in his work, but none of them had been like *that*.

The fucking guy had bit him, his neck stretching and jaws thrashing out through the car window while Dusty was looking at his license. It had hurt too, blood spraying in a way he'd only seen in the movies while the guy panted like a dog. All over a simple breathalyzer stop because the guy was staggering in the middle of the road.

Backup came when he asked, faster than he would have thought, but they were surprisingly nonchalant about the situation. One of the officers, Dusty didn't know their names because he'd done nothing but road duty since the task force arrived, told him he should go get his bite looked at.

Bleeding in his squad car, he'd radioed Dawson who told him to go see a nurse and stop wasting his time. At least Benz would have asked if he was okay. She might have laughed about him being crackhead food but she would have made sure he was alright.

So he'd left the officers with the would be cannibal and gone home. He locked every door and window to his apartment so he could feel safe while putting tiny, grey Band-Aids over a wound most likely needing stitches.

When his phone rang, he jumped in fear.

It was Harold. He wasn't drunk, as far as Dusty could tell, and wanted something other than help with a speeding ticket. He asked Dusty if anything felt strange in the town lately, if he might want to talk about it.

Strange? Strange like seven dead bodies hanging from trees taller than most rock walls? Strange like the fact there were thirty new officers crammed into the station and he knew the names of two? Strange like his partner taking a mystery vacation without saying a word to anyone? Strange like a literal cannibal trying to eat him during a routine road stop at seven thirty in the morning?

Dusty itched to tell Hal everything but his police instincts got the better of him.

Even if things were strange you didn't discuss official police business with civilians. You didn't talk to the cousin of the town's would be investigative reporter about confidential matters of law. You didn't spill your guts about what was worrying you to some washed-up park ranger you had beers with on Tuesdays.

At least you didn't do it over the phone. So here he was, parked at Hal's ranger station with a cigarette shaking in his hand and sweat beading down his back.

The heat was thick in the air and the wonderful view of the valley below was distorted by summer haze. The houses far below seemed to shimmer through the glare while the river's white currents transformed into crowding phantoms. Only the Ainsfield Hotel seamed unaffected by the haze, it's pale walls gloating over the town.

Lord, he wished the town would condemn that shithole.

Focusing on the ugliness of the Ainsfield made his recent fears vacate to the back of his mind, replaced by mundane worries of meth epidemics and the rise of petty theft. It was almost relaxing.

The tap on his car window made him drop his cigarette. It landed on his jeans and smoked a little hole to the left of his fly. Cursing, he wriggled in his seat and let it fall onto the floor where he crushed it with a dirty boot.

With blood rushing into his flabby cheeks, he unwound the window to the half grinning face of Hal.

"Jesus, Harold, don't be sneaking up on a man like that."

Hal gave his usual *it's not my fault* shrug and languidly pulled a cigarette pack from his blue jean pockets. With apologizingly slightly glazed eyes, he passed it through the open window. "Sorry, Dusty. Here, I know you always feel guilty about buying these, so I saved you the trouble."

Dusty started to push the pack away. He met little resistance from Hal's lanky arms, but his fingers snatched greedily at the pack before it withdrew through the window. With forced composure, he removed one pale stick and thrust it between his gums. Hal's tired gaze made him fidget in his seat. "Well, Hal?"

Hal frowned and shook his head. "Of course, will you come into my office?"

Dusty shook his head. "I'm not getting out of this car."

Hal nodded. if he thought Dusty's request was strange he didn't show it. "Okay, boss." He flicked his head back and called out, "Everyone into the car!" He walked around to sit in the passenger seat while three others flung the back door open and pressed themselves inside.

First was Dr. Nand, his thick legs barely nestling into the space between Hal's seat and his own. Beside him sat Bobbi, a serious look on her small face despite the fact her knees were tucked into her chest to make space. She wrinkled her nose at the car's smell but didn't open her mouth to discuss it.

Last was a kid, his lips drawn into a scowl and his eyes gravitating to Dusty's in the mirror with almost open hostility.

Dusty swallowed. "Is that the kid who found the…" He looked over at Hal. "Found the bodies with you?"

Hal was lighting a joint, some of the ash falling on his already dirty white t-shirt. Through puckered lips he replied, "The one and only."

Dusty bit the inside of his cheek. "You didn't tell me you were bringing friends."

Hal met his worried gaze. "I think we got more important things to worry about, Dusty."

"Like what?"

Bobbi tilted her head forward, her bony neck jutting into the front. "Like what's going on with the police force, for starters."

Dusty turned to look at her, only an inch from the gaze of her wide, inquisitive eyes. "Is this off the record?"

"If you want."

Dusty let out a sigh. It would have made him feel better if it had only been Hal. Not that it mattered he supposed, telling Hal something was as good as telling his cousin for the amount they gossiped together.

"I don't know exactly, but something's not right."

Hal let out a smoke filled laugh while the kid in the backseat rolled his eyes. Bobbi continued to stare at him, her expression unchanging. "How so, Dusty?"

"Well, uh, someone bit me today."

Hal cast him a weary glance while Bobbi frowned. "And then what?"

"And then nothing. New cops took over." He looked around, unsure of what else to say. "They told me to go home."

Dr. Nand spoke up from the backseat. "Are you alright?"

Dusty rubbed his neck, it was still tender, but the bleeding hadn't returned. "Physically you mean?"

The teenager cut in, a hard edge in his voice. "Can we hurry up?"

Hal glared over his shoulder before flashing an apologetic smile to Dusty. "Teenagers, man, so what did they do with the person who bit you?"

"I don't know, probably hauled him off to the station."

Bobbi's voice cut in. "They're still using the station?"

"Yeah, filled it up with a whole new crew. Sent everyone else on traffic patrol or vacation."

The three adults frowned while the kid's face split into a grim smile. "Do you still have a keycard?" he asked.

Dusty let out a weak laugh. "Actually, we use keys to get in, the station is pretty old. Only real security is in the cells."

Hal scrunched his face. "Jesus."

"I can't give you a key, if that's what you're asking," said Dusty, shying away from the teenager's icy glare. "I'd lose my job."

The kid brushed a hand through his brown hair, letting out a bitter laugh. "He'd lose his job—how terrible."

Hal's voice was more sympathetic. "Listen, Dusty, we think there's a bit more at stake here."

"Like what?" His thoughts flickered to the mad face of the man who'd bit him, the dark spit dribbling on his lips as they twisted into a mad smile. "Like what, Hal?"

The four gave each other conspiratorial looks. Hal smiled delicately. "Have you seen any spider webs about town recently?"

Michelle

She almost lost her nerve walking through the trailer park, scared first by a barking dog tugging at a chain that seemed much too long and second by a disheveled drunk offering her twenty dollars and a case of beer for a little "good fun." It was only the sight of Blake's aluminum home that kept her from turning around.

Now, walking up its creaking wooden steps, she considered leaving. It was quieter in this part of the park. The only nearby resident was a hollow faced old woman asleep in a lawn chair across the road. No one would know if she left, if she went home to her warm bed and pretended she hadn't come down to see the Turners in their quaint abode.

Her hand hovered over the cracked door frame, her aunt's distraught features flashing through her mind. The woman had been a wreck, staying with Michelle and her mother for the past day. Barely able to get out more than a few words before sobs overtook her.

"He wasn't a good boy," she wailed as Michelle passed her a tissue. "He wasn't a good boy, but..." Her face crinkled as a wet cough escaped her throat. "But... but... he was mine."

It was hard to find sympathy for her aunt. Her cousin had never been a *good boy*, the whole family thought it a miracle his stints in juvie had never graduated into full prison terms.

Racist, homophobic, and too big a fan of country music to fit in with the rest of the family, he was tolerated only at the most important of family events. And even then he was often told to go home early for voicing his incredibly uninformed opinions on race mixing and Jews.

Michelle remembered a Thanksgiving when Jarret had needed stitches after getting into a fight with another cousin over his Korean wife. Michelle was the only one who hadn't openly called for Jarret's ass to be whipped and had been tasked with accompanying him to the hospital. It was a labour she'd regretted ever since.

Not only had Jarret refused to be treated by the brown ER doctor available, causing him to lose significantly more blood than he would've if he hadn't been a complete moron, he had taken Michelle's presence as a sign of affection.

From that night on he—quite wrongly—believed Michelle was one of the few members of their family who truly loved and cared for him, even if most of their conversations ended with her calling him a fucking idiot and asking him to kill himself.

How he came to hear that one Blake Turner had broken her heart was beyond her, where he'd disappeared to after leaving to defend his cousin's honour (likely through slur filled violence) was an even greater mystery.

Her first assumption was Blake had put her cousin in the hospital. Jarret's view of gays was limited at best, believing them all to be tiny little boys whose only interest in physical activity was dancing to Madonna. She was sure, doubly so after seeing the trailer park, Blake would inflict more than a little damage on her cousin if backed into a corner.

Everyone in her high school still remembered the time Blake got in a fist with a kid on the Chilliwack soccer team over a kick delivered quite intentionally to the head of Hope's goalie.

The Chilliwack player had been two feet taller than Blake with far larger arms, but Blake left him with a broken nose and a concussion before a group of players managed to tear him away from the crying boy.

She checked the hospital first, learning from one of the older and more gossip prone nurses, her cousin wasn't present—but Blake Turner was. Blake's name had drawn the blood from her face, fear Jarret had managed to seriously hurt him welling in her stomach.

The nurse caught her expression and elaborated further. Blake had only been grazed by a passing truck on the highway while an older gentleman had taken the full blow. The nurse couldn't explain what exactly Blake had been doing on the highway, but she could assure Michelle the older gentleman hadn't been her cousin. The nurse told her she would recognize Jarret instantly because of the multiple times she'd stitched him up after bar fights.

Michelle asked to see Blake, but the nurse simply ruffled her face and said he'd run out in the night. She'd wanted to go to Blake's house right then. Only a phone call from a friend claiming they saw her cousin's truck, "the white one with the big confederate flag on the back right?" parked in some lot at the edge of town stopping her.

Michelle went to the park, finding her cousin's truck sitting with its rebel flag waving proud. She scoured the park and some of the surrounding woods but found nothing. She'd considered delving farther into the green, but the strange quiet and setting sun held her back.

Sitting on the cracked seat of a seesaw, she dialed the Hope RCMP number. They listened patiently, promising to organize a search when it was brighter. Michelle was puzzled by their reluctance to start the search tonight, but she figured her cousin's long list of misdemeanors and open hostility to law enforcement probably influenced their reluctance in finding him.

So, at a loss as to where her cousin could possibly be, and her aunt's voice still ringing fresh in her ears, she'd found herself cutting a twisting path through the town to Blake's house. She'd never been there in person, but another friend knew the address from when her and Blake had worked on a group project after school. Michelle suspected this girl had also had a crush on Blake in the past.

If she saw Blake she could ask about her cousin's whereabouts but, more importantly, she could apologize for the last Friday. God, she'd been drunk and crying in the Dairy

Queen break room. It hadn't been her greatest moment.

She silently rehearsed her apology as her fist struck the door, the cracking of her pale knuckles causing the trailer's metal siding to shake. Her hand swung back to prepare for another rap, but the door opened before it could descend.

She took a deep breath and let the words rush out of her.

"Blake, I am so, so, sorry about the other day. God, I was too drunk, and it was so embarrassing. Like, Jesus, my brother still hasn't stopped talking about it and—"

She blew a strand of pink hair out of her eye as she tilted her head to look at the man standing in the doorway.

He cracked an easy grin and let out a small laugh. "Lordy, child."

Michelle's cheeks flushed. "Oh my god." She swallowed hard and bit down on her lip. "I'm so sorry."

The man shrugged, the sweet scent of cigarettes drifting from him. "Not a problem."

Michelle peered past the man's torso, trying to make out the poorly lit interior. "Is Blake home?"

The man shook his head, his lips thinned but the warmth stayed in his eyes. "'Fraid not, missy. You'll have to come back another time."

"Oh, do you know when he'll be back?"

The man tilted his head and put a hand on his chin. "Gosh, should be tomorrow. He wasn't very specific in his note."

"Note?"

The man gave another sharp grin, this one with teeth. They were nice teeth, bright and straight, but a little too sharp in Michelle's mind. "Yep, took his sister and left a note. God, his aunt was furious."

Michelle shifted her weight onto one leg, her hands digging unconsciously into her jeans. "Are you his uncle?"

Another sparkling laugh curved the man's features. When his mouth opened, Michelle could make out the splotches of his throat, a darker shade of the same tar colouring she was starting to develop from her bootlegged cigarettes. "No, just a friend."

"Oh." Michelle took a step back and waved halfheartedly. "Well if you see him, tell him Michelle will see him soon."

The man raised a hand to his head in mock salute, his weight staying in the doorframe while his eyes trailed her down the steps. "I'm sure you will."

She heard the door slam as she made her way down the road, but the feeling of the eyes on her back never left. Even as she rounded the corner and made it well out of sight of Blake's trailer she couldn't help but feel them pressing against her back. She twisted her head about as she walked, but all she caught sight of were cracked windows and rusted fences.

Unnerved by the strange quiet of the neighbourhood she sped her steps and stuck two headphones into her ears, letting a screaming boy band accompany her home.

Along the way she felt a strand of spider silk brush against her shoulder. She pushed it away with disinterest, letting it float away with a passing gust of wind. As the cobweb spiraled through the air, she wondered if she should have stayed home today. After all, she didn't care about her cousin.

In the back of her mind a soft voice started to whisper. The words were difficult to make out, like remembering a dream, but one sang clear in her mind.

Tasty.

Interlude
Present Day

Her love referred to this room as the playhouse. She approved of the term.

In the colder seasons she would spend weeks cooped up in here, snacking on the treats she'd stowed away for the winter while practicing her voices. She'd even started trying to make her dolls dance. At first this often led to her dropping them where they'd splatter on the floor, but now she'd grown quite adept at making them "do the jig" as her lover said.

In years past, when the snow was too thick for her love to visit and the old feeling of loneliness crept in, she'd started to imagine her playhouse was a real town. A place of homes and roads, not falling steel walls and dangling chains. To fight the boredom she invented lives for her dolls, let them fight and fall in love as she moved their dangling bodies about the room through deft tugs of her web.

As months past, her interest in her dolls' lives increased and she found herself spending more and more time with them, even going as far as to stage a wedding for the two campers she'd collected the past spring.

In the far back of her mind, a part not even her love could touch, she imagined it was a wedding not for her dolls but herself.

Her favourite was the girl. Tiny with slender little arms and a cute dress. She'd even been able to make the girl smile, an effect that went great with the squealing little voice she was close to perfecting.

She'd asked her love to pick up some new clothes for the girl, her dress had been ripped the last time she took her out to play, but he'd refused. He said it was too odd for him to be seen buying children's clothes. Secretly she thought it was because he didn't like her doll games.

This was one of the only cracks in their relationship, from what she understood of humans—it was a great sign. So many of the minds she read were utterly filled with worries and complaints about love.

Fear, distrust, and anger permeated their skulls while their lovers sat not a foot away. She was thankful her love was not like that; above the base human passions, he gave her romance that was strong, faithful, and most of all, unwavering.

Even today he was out, doing what was needed to keep her safe while she hid herself away from the dark suited men and their annoying rifles.

At first she'd hunted them herself, snapping one up for every one of her children they took. Sucking their blood and leaving their corpses for their friends to find as they prowled the thick forests in search of her.

It was the second time she was shot that her love declared he would exterminate them himself, a rage boiling in his mind and spilling frighteningly into her own.

When they'd been younger he'd read her a story of a knight slaying a dragon. She'd been unimpressed at the time, not understanding how a silly human with a big knife could possibly take down the creature the boy described, but now she understood. The story wasn't about the how but they why.

The knight killed the dragon for his love and now her knight was setting out to do the same. An idea making her heart burn with joy as hidden dreams of marriage twisted feverishly across her imagination.

Sliding a leg slowly across a thick strand, she made one of the campers dip his head forward, his rotting crown brushing against the bloodied flesh of his bride. She concentrated on making his voice appear. It was gruff, and rose too much at the end, but the words were what she wanted. "I do."

With two of her hind legs she made the bride and the little girl start to jump in joy, mustering her will to make a happy voice come from little girl's pale lips.

"It's love, love, love."

The voice bounced off the rusted steel walls of the building, echoing down until the last little "love" died far below.

Bobbi

Dusty's car was dirty. It reeked of cigarettes and fast food with more than a few stains of both patching the grey seats.

Dusty wasn't looking much better than his car.

Never a peak physical specimen, he could easily be mistaken for someone who worked in what the elderly of Hope referred to as "the computer industry." Thick glasses and drooping cheeks topped by a bald spot that had started developing when the man was twenty-three.

Today he looked downright sick. His flabby cheeks had sunk inwards, their rose tinge transformed into a splotchy merlot. When he blushed, as he frequently did, it marked his face like a pox. His eyes were unable to remain fixed on the same spot for more than a few seconds, constantly rolling about their sockets to take in every inch of his surroundings.

From what Bobbi could tell, he hadn't showered in a while either but that was really none of her business.

From the back of the car Hal's soft whispering competed with the pop song on the radio. "I know you live in Kamloops now. What I'm saying is don't bother coming to Hope anytime soon."

Her cousin's brow was clenched with his eyes trying their best to roll into the back of his skull. His well-known smile had been replaced by a small frown which grew deeper with each word he spoke into the phone.

"I don't care what your mother thinks, it's not safe to come here right now." Unconsciously, Bobbi hoped, her cousin pushed a fist into the seat in front of him, twisting it to massage Bobbi's back in a less than pleasant manner. "No, I'm not coming to Kamloops this week."

The fist pulled back only to again thrust into the upholstery, making Bobbi give an audible gasp. Hal met her glower through the mirror and pulled his arm back, moving his hand to his knee. An expression of apology briefly filled his face before it reverted to its state of anger.

"What? I sent you five hundred last weekend. Jesus Christ. No." His knuckles turned white digging into his knee. "Fine, whatever. Tell your mother she's a bitch and remember not to come to Hope 'til I tell you it's safe."

Hal let out a sigh, swallowing before he continued. "And tell my son I love—" He paused, taking the cellphone away from his ear to confirm from the glowing screen the call had, in fact, been terminated. "Motherfucker."

Bobbi reached an arm into the back to rub her cousin's knee but he brushed it away tersely. "Don't get married, Bobbi, don't do it."

She gave a thin smile. "Hippies don't get married, Harold."

The approval Hal appeared ready to give was cut short by Dusty's voice ringing nervously through the automobile. "We're here."

Their plan wasn't great. Hackneyed was the term Bobbi would have used if she was still in journalism school. Unoriginal and relying far too heavily on Hal's knowledge of eighties' action movies. It was a miracle they'd coerced Dusty into taking part in the hairbrained scheme.

In the poor light of the car, Bobbi noted the first glaring problem; Dusty's uniform was dirty with a large blood stain near his collar. Dusty himself seemed less than ready to start, his hands shaking as they gripped his steering wheel.

Hal, for his part, was ready to play his role of town drunk. Likely already more than a little buzzed before phoning his ex, he was now ingesting the contents of a bottle of tequila with speed that would impress even the most Olympic drinker.

The tension in Dusty's voice was thick, words dripping weakly from his mouth. "You think you've had enough, Hal?"

Hal raised the middle finger in his free hand, making Dusty shake his head and curse under his breath.

Bobbi was more forceful. "Jesus, Harold, we need you to be able to speak when we're in there."

Hal burped and let the bottle fall to his feet where the meagre remainder of the tequila spilled onto a pile of empty fast food bags. "Fuck you."

Bobbi rolled her eyes. Even in situations like this Hal had to insist on retaining his immaturity. "Fine, let's go."

Dusty grabbed her arm, a sweaty palm pressing into her bare flesh. "Are you sure we should do this?"

A pang of sympathy ran through her spine. Dusty was a good man, known for being fair with even the vilest louts he dealt with while patrolling the streets of Hope. However, he wasn't a man prepared for the danger they seemed to have found themselves in. Bobbi could relate and it took a fair bit of effort to stop her voice from shaking as she replied.

"Dusty, why did you become a cop?"

His eyes fell guiltily to the floor. "I wanted to help people."

Bobbi squeezed his shaking hand. "And people need help. This thing, whatever it is, isn't going away anytime soon."

Dusty let out a bitter laugh. "I also thought the job would help me get laid more."

This made Hal giggle, but Bobbi continued to grip Dusty's clammy hand, her voice retaining its serious tone as she spoke. "Baby steps, Dusty. Today you help us find out what's going on, tomorrow we help you find the girl of your dreams."

For a moment Dusty almost looked like his old self, his regular red tinge filling his cheeks ever so slightly. "Ok, Bobbi." He turned his head to the ceiling, a white knuckle pushing into his mouth. "Lord, help me."

Hal's voice started to slur, the stench of alcohol overwhelming in the small confines of the car. "Atta boy, Dusty. Brave little trooper."

Dusty pushed the door open. "Piss off, Hal—then come here so I can cuff you."

Blake

They'd followed Dusty's car but not into the police compound itself, opting to park under the shade of a large tree. Blake used an expensive set of binoculars, leftovers from Dr. Nand's onetime love affair with birdwatching, to follow Hal, Dusty, and Bobbi as they made their way to the entrance of the police department.

Hal played the drunk convincingly, his stuttering stride forcing Dusty to continually propel the man forward with thick shoves. Bobbi stood a few feet away shaking her head and making pleading motions at her cousin.

Only Dusty, the one with an actual reason to enter the building, seemed out of place. His steps too small and shoulders too hunched to convince anyone he'd come into work for legitimate purposes.

A cloud of smoke from Dr. Nand's e-cigarette drifted in front of the lenses, making Blake take the binoculars away from his eyes to polish them furiously. "Can you blow that out the window?"

Dr. Nand's meek reply was accompanied by the sound of a window unwinding. "Sorry, Mr. Turner."

Blake let out a growl and leaned back in his chair, letting his head rest against the leather headrest and his eyes rest on the ceiling. "We're so fucked."

Dr. Nand pushed a heavy cloud of smoke out of the window before turning his round face to Blake's. "Yes."

"You'd think a cop could be a little more brave."

"Most men aren't as fearless as you, Mr. Turner."

Blake crossed his arms. "Cops should be."

"He agreed to help us, didn't he?"

Blake chewed on his cheeks before lifting the binoculars again, catching the group's backs as they disappeared into the swinging door of the police detachment. "I guess he did."

Bobbi

A single person sat in the foyer—a young man in a black suit sequestered behind a desk too tiny for his large body. He raised his head in cool interest as they entered, his gaze inspecting Bobbi and Dusty before settling flatly on Hal's wobbling frame.

Dusty gave a nervous smile, his yellow teeth drawn too wide to look normal. He pushed Hal towards the detachment's stairwell, but stopped when the young man gave them a commanding wave.

"Drunk tanks full," called the young man, notes of boredom permeating his words.

Dusty twisted his head to Bobbi and she bit her lip looking at the floor. The idiot, why was he looking at her? "Oh?" he finally said.

"Send him to the ER." The man leaned back in his leather office chair that creaked under his weight. "Or drop him on the street, I don't care."

Hal started to giggle. "Just my luck."

Dusty didn't speak, only looked on dumbfounded. Bobbi shook her head and channeled years of cousinly bickering to keep up the charade. "Just *your* luck Harold, I told you not to drink the whole tequila bottle."

Dusty darted his gaze from the receptionist to Hal to Bobbi and back again. His lower lip had started to twitch. "I really think he should go in the drunk tank," he said dully.

The young man stiffened in his chair, jaw clenching as his eyes burrowed into Dusty. "I told you it's full, get the fuck out of here." Under his breath he added something about local cops and sheep fornicating, but Bobbi didn't quite catch it all.

Dusty shrugged his shoulders and shot Bobbi a look half apologetic and half relieved. "I suppose you're right and Hal doesn't need to go in the drunk tank." He stood a little taller, a touch of firmness entering his voice. "As long as he's learned his lesson."

Hal leaned forward, his head dipping over the desk, only Dusty's shaking grip on his back and arms kept him from colliding onto the increasingly annoyed receptionist. "I learned… learned…. learned?" A mighty hiccup escaped from his mouth, causing the receptionist to wrinkle his nose in quiet distaste. "Learned you're a little bitch, Dusty."

The receptionist glared at Hal. "Get this man out of the fucking station or I'll have you sent to the coldest fucking part of—"

Bobbi would have liked to know where this young receptionist could have Dusty—and possibly her cousin—sent but his final words were interrupted by a heavy spew of vomit from Hal. It was horrible to watch, smelling worse. The receptionist caught most of it with his suit.

For a brief moment the young man's hand twitched towards the pistol on his, now puke soaked, belt but thankfully it remained holstered.

A blue vein bulged from the man's forehead and a stream of curses emanated from his mouth. From what Bobbi gathered he hadn't spent six years in the marines to deal with *this*.

Rising from his dripping chair, Hal had managed to expel more than she'd have thought possible, he walked towards the washroom, pausing at its entrance to look back at them and say in a deceptively pleasant voice, "It might be best if you left now," before disappearing through the swinging door.

Hal coughed out a few more bits of his insides before a hoarse giggle overtook him. "Learned him, didn't I?"

"You're disgusting, Harold," whispered Bobbi.

Hal spit, wiping his chin awkwardly on his shoulder, his hands still bound behind his back. "Worked, didn't it?"

Dusty stood transfixed by the puke, no doubt wondering what his career was coming to.

"Dusty, where now?" asked Bobbi, rolling her eyes as the man appeared deaf to her question.

Hal sighed and stepped down harshly on Dusty's left foot. "Dusty, we don't have much time."

The man lurched back. Broken from his trance, he turned—wide eyed—to Hal. "You guys are insane."

Hal nodded while Bobbi pointed towards the stairwell entrance. "Is it this way? We have to be quick."

Dusty swallowed, his entire flabby face bouncing with the effort. "We should go downstairs first." He looked over at the closed bathroom door, the sound of running water and cursing seeping out from under its frame. "I didn't think we'd get this far."

Hal groaned as his stomach made a squelching sound. "Think or want to?"

Ken

He'd switched from coffee to the stimulants days ago. They were given in generous allowanceess from the onsite doctors and kept him alert as the operation dragged on. He couldn't recall the last time he'd slept, only aware he was far too high on adrenaline and narcotics to succumb to fatigue anytime soon.

He'd allowed his assistant a nap earlier, three hours on the couch in his office before a bloody contact with the creature had made him call for her.

She looked like shit, the rims of her eyes as dark as the frames of her glasses and a vein had popped in her left knuckle. The look he caught from her as she walked in told him he looked much worse.

"We lost it."

"What, sir?"

Ken coughed, feeling a clenching in his lungs that would no doubt hurt much more when his drugs wore off.

"I said it's gone, and I don't know where."

They'd been baiting it with the creatures they'd captured prowling the streets of Hope, tying her beloved *children* to street lamps and shooting off their legs for fun. It had worked better than Ken would have hoped. He lost two men through the night, but they'd been rewarded with a confirmed hit on the target and a trail of warm blood to follow into a nearby patch of trees.

The only problem was it was no longer coming to the aid of its family, no matter what Ken ordered done to the things they'd captured. He'd been quite creative with his attempts to motivate it out of hiding but all it amounted too was a lot of screaming that left his men soaked in blood and other bodily fluids.

His assistant tried to stifle a yawn as it came out but only got half way, her eyes meeting Ken's ashamedly as it finished. "I'm sorry, sir."

He felt his foot twitch. "You're second in command."

She looked about the room, no doubt imagining what her predecessor had thought when he'd stood with Ken in this spot. "Technically, sir."

"The target's gone, we've lost more men than I could have imagined." His voice lowered. "We finally managed to land a shot on the creature and it runs and hides."

"Yes, sir."

He slapped her, his palm cracking her jawbone. It surprised him just as much as her.

She didn't cry out. Fear and anger welled in her eyes as a trickle of blood dripped from the corner of her mouth. "I'm sorry, sir?" she said through gritted teeth.

Ken gripped her shoulders and started to shake her. "What would you do, you're second in command and your senior is out of ideas." He let out a bitter laugh. If they survived the week he wouldn't be her senior for long. His first time in command and he'd been outwitted by a fucking spider in the asshole of Canada.

"I'd look for it, sir." He raised his hand again, the woman reaching out to stop it. "And I'd stop acting like a child." Her eyes met his, flaring behind their lenses. "Sir."

Ken gritted his teeth and nodded, he could feel her blood pooling on the ends of his fingers. Shaking, he tried to bottle the rage flowing from him—it was unprofessional. "Where should we look?" he seethed.

She furrowed her brow, sinking an incisor into her lip. "The scientist told us he doesn't know where it makes its nest."

Ken narrowed his gaze on the woman's tiny face. "Yes."

"But he's been here since the thing was born."

Ken's lips started to vibrate and he was unsure if they were trying to smile or frown. "Yes."

"And in his dossier, it says he lost a child in the forest around his home."

"So?"

The woman's brow furrowed as a flicker of annoyance crossed it. "So, if you helped engineer that monstrosity, and knew it was loose in your neighbourhood, the same place your child just happened to go missing, would you not at least look for its home?" She raised an arm as if to rattle the inside of Ken's thick skull. "Would you not at least have some theories on where the creature you created would live?"

Ken blinked. "Why haven't you told anyone this before?"

"What?" She hissed a curse before continuing. "I have sir, the problem is this organization is more concerned with active intel than theories."

"Ah?"

"Especially when the theories come from someone with as little field experience as I have."

"Ah."

It was true the girl had little field experience, Ken himself had objected to her presence when he'd read her file. Still, she might be onto something.

He laughed in the back of his increasingly foggy brain. No, he was on to something. After all, as his future reports would indicate, he'd long suspected their chief researcher on the subject was less than honest in his findings.

He smiled at the girl. She shuddered, involuntarily he hoped. "Good work."

She wiped her mouth with the back of her hand, eyes still fixed on Ken's. "Thank you, sir."

His other foot started to twitch, this one he could feel. "Let's pay a visit to the good doctor."

"Excellent idea, sir."

Hal

They met no one on the way downstairs. Dusty left the handcuffs on but no longer kept an arm on Hal's shoulder. When he missed a step and nearly careened down the steep passage it was his cousin who struck out a palm and caught him. Meeting her gaze, she gave him a weak smile before continuing forward with him in tow.

The doors to the basement were locked by a keypad that chimed happily as Dusty input a six-digit code, the doors opening to yet another long, concrete hallway.

The police detachment had originally been an accounting firm. When it crashed in the 2008 recession, the RCMP saw a good opportunity to upgrade from the single story building they'd been using since the twenties. The basement of the firm had housed the vast catalogues of financial papers amassed through the years. With cement floors and few windows, it hadn't been hard for the police to convert it into the jail portion of their building.

The basement was lit but devoid of the sound of police officers. There were no boots clanging along the floor or voices murmuring about upcoming court cases, only the slight hum from the energy efficient lights above.

Dusty led the way hesitantly, his head continually twisting to look at the door they'd came through. "The cells are just around the corner."

Bobbi had her phone raised, and Hal caught the dim red glare coming from its front. "You really want video evidence of this, Bobbi?"

Bobbi's voice was low and fierce. "Remember how Glen didn't believe our photos?"

Hal sighed and continued forward. His head was starting to pound—he was unsure if it was the liquor or the stress. "Poor bastard."

Bobbi winced. "We couldn't do anything."

As they progressed, the hallway twisted to bring them to the cells. There were sixteen of them, far more than Hope would ever need despite its colourful reputation. Only a single cell had light streaming through its window.

"Not exactly full."

Bobbi raised a finger to her lips while Dusty pressed himself against the hallway wall. "I'll, uh, keep watch," he said.

Hal stared at the man in disbelief, twisting his back so his wrists were exposed. "Well, at least take these off if you're going to be our noble look out."

A heavy click sounded as the cuffs fell, crashing loudly into the floor. Bobbi shook her head and Hal winced. "Jesus, Dusty."

Dusty's reply was overpowered by screaming from the nearest cell, a guttural voice accompanied by a heavy pounding on the walls. Bobbi and Hal looked at each other before walking forward, Hal massaging his wrists as he did.

Arriving at the cell the voice remained undiscernible, whatever speech it was making garbled by the sound of the door rattling from its blows. Bobbi raised her phone and placed it against the small window to the room, the red light from her recording flickering back on them in the reflection.

Removing the camera, she waved Hal forward. He shook his head and mouthed some unpleasantries at her until she rolled her eyes and placed her own face against the small window.

"Jesus Christ."

"Yes, my daughter?"

Her fist caught him in his gut, nearly making him vomit again. With a stone face she backed away from the door and pushed him towards it. Swallowing hard, Hal placed his own face against the thick glass.

"That's… unpleasant."

The arm Bobbi was using to hold her camera began to shake, she bit her lips and placed her other hand on it to steady it. "People shouldn't have that many legs, Harold."

"Jesus, I can see parts of the rib sticking out from where—" Bobbi's revolted gaze stopped him. "You know, Bobbi, I'm proud of you for doing this."

His recovery earned him another eye roll. "Let's check out the next one."

The second cell housed one of the local mechanics, Hal remembered he'd fixed his truck's gear belt the last summer. He was lying on the floor in a pile of what was either his own blood or piss. Bobbi pressed her phone against the window, only letting it linger for a few seconds. Hal could have sworn he heard her whispering a prayer as she removed it.

Hal pointed towards the lit cell, drawn to it like a moth. "Let's check that one next." They slunk down the hallway, this time Hal pressed his face against the glass first. "It's the guy from Inkawathia," he whispered.

"What guy?"

Hal groaned. "You know, the man who was busy tearing apart the spid—" Bobbi shoved him aside to press her own face into the window.

"What's he doing here?" she said as she pulled back from the window.

Hal restrained himself from answering what was clearly rhetorical. "How do we open this thing? Jesus, why does Dusty have to be such a pussy?"

Bobbi tapped on her phone screen before raising it to her head. "You know I don't like that word, Hal."

Hal rolled his eyes and pulled at the door handle. "Sorry, optimal word would be coward."

Bobbi shushed him with an icy glare before speaking into her handset. "Dusty, how do we open these doors?" Bobbi's foot started to tap as she stared back into the cell. "Fifteen sixty-three. All of them? The same code?"

Hal started to tap on the keypad but stopped when Bobbi put a hand on his shoulder. "Dusty says someone's coming."

Hal looked down the hall, he could see Dusty waving his hands frantically and pointing towards a nearby cell. He looked at his cousin. "Do these things open from the inside?"

"Dusty says he'll let us out after."

"Where's he going to hide?"

Bobbi brushed past him and hit the keycode of the cell across from their spider dissecting friend. "Janitor's closet."

Hal crossed his arms and followed her in. "We got farther than I thought."

His cousin pulled the door shut, the electronic click of the lock confirming their imprisonment.

Interlude
Present Day

It had taken some time for her love to convince her this was the only solution, she was unwilling to let her children face unnecessary harm and even more unwilling to let him, yet in the end his cool logic had prevailed. Nothing short of destroying these enemies would stop them from hunting her, a destruction her love promised to ensure.

Still, following his and her children's movements from the comfort of her playhouse weighed her down with guilt. She should be there with her love, inhaling the fear of these would be hunters as they spent their last moments in terror as her fangs descended on them. More importantly she would be protecting her love. The one who had helped her catch their surrogates, the one who was keeping up his promise of providing her *real* children.

It was only the cool certainty she felt in her love's mind preventing her from abandoning her play to accompany him on his task. She felt him watching the police department with quiet pleasure.

While winding the limp body that would serve as her lunch up to her perch, she struck her thoughts out hard, forcing them into his mind. *I love you.* She shuddered with pleasure when his own thoughts replied, their warm taste rebounding off her brain. *I love you, too.*

The man she ate was old, his blood too stale to offer any real delight, but she was happy nonetheless. So happy.

Ken

The withered scientist rose violently from his cot when they entered. "What have you done with my research subjects?"

Ken raised an arm to make the man sit back down, his wiry frame looking uncertainly about the room. "I told you, Doctor, they've been transferred to your next facility."

The man tugged at loose strands of grey hair. "Alive?"

"Unfortunately, no. It seems you've been raising some rather hostile pets."

The old man snarled, his bony features twisting in rage. "They took me years to engineer, I was close, close." His features softened as he raised his knees to his chest on the cot. "I was so close."

Ken glanced at his assistant. She stood upright by the door, arms crossed and a calculatingly looking shining behind her glasses. Her cheek had swollen significantly in the last twenty minutes, making her appearance surprisingly intimidating. When she spoke, the Doctor started to whimper. "Close to what, Doctor?"

The man's eyes closed, pain spreading over his face. "Close to curing it. Close to making it stop."

Ken frowned. They paid the man to research the spider not to fix it. "Curing the spider?"

The doctor snapped his teeth, spit flying from his gums and striking Ken's chests. "Curing its children."

"Those things out there can be cured?" asked his assistant.

The Doctor shook his head violently. His voice plunging into a whisper. "Not yet."

"Pardon?"

The Doctor leaned forward, eyes glaring. "I said not yet, you dumb bitch." At the sound of his own words he jumped and shuffled back to his cot. "I'm sorry, it's not well for me to be kept here."

His assistant didn't respond, only continued to stare coolly as Ken took a step forward. "Now, Doctor, I've come to think you haven't been completely honest with us."

The Doctor shrunk further into the cot. "No, I always submitted my research. I was told I could study anything on the subject as long as I shared my research."

The man started to shake and Ken put a hand on his knee. Their faces only an inch apart, he let the doctor continue his rambling.

"Year after year I've worked there, always submitting results. Sending blood vials, answering questions, I even went to Ottawa last year for that silly conference." His face grimaced.

Ken's smile grew wider as his fingers dug into the man's kneecap, twisting in the fleshy divide between his muscle and bone.

"Oh, God. Ouch. I did everything for you. Everything. Wife's gone, sons are gone. All I have is this work." He looked pleadingly about the room. "What more do you want from me?"

Ken released the man's knee. "We just want to know where it lives," he said sweetly.

"Where it lives? I couldn't possibly know where it lives. Far too many places for it to nest." He looked past Ken to the assistant who remained unmoving by the door. His voice rose as he continued. "We live in the Pacific Northwest, I heard in grad school you're never more than a meter from a spider in this part of the world. They live everywhere here, so many places for them to thrive, they love the weather and—"

Ken felt a flood of relief as his fist connected with the man's throat. This, this was what he was made for. Making a difference.

"Now, Doctor. I think you might be lying to me."

The man whimpered something about his son and Ken responded by sinking a fist into his gut. The man's spectacles fell to the floor as he hunched over wheezing.

Ken leaned in, lips pressing against the old man's ear. "Please," he whispered. "Please take your time in telling us where it lives."

Blake

Dr. Nand looked tired and unsettled but not bored. Blake envied him. Never one for simply sitting around, waiting outside the police station while Bobbi, Gutless, and The Drunk (trademarks pending) continued the investigation alone, proved an excruciating exercise.

He'd phoned Sarah twice, happy to hear she was having a great time staying with the lovely Mrs. Nand, even if "the food she makes is hot. Too hot, Blakey."

Her voice numbed his agitation at being cooped in the car and it was only a respect for her looming bedtime, no later than 10 PM he'd insisted before leaving the Nand's house that morning, that made him refrain from phoning a third time that night.

Dr. Nand and Blake hadn't had to voice their agreement that Sarah and Mrs. Nand didn't need to know the specifics of their business in Hope, but it was there. When leaving the house Dr. Nand had told his wife he was helping Blake find his mother after she relapsed, conveniently leaving out the part with giant arachnids and literal zombies. Blake had told his sister even less, preferring a lie about having to work too much to look after her in the next few days instead of giving her hope mommy might be returning.

Blake drummed his fingers on the dash, tapping out the rhythm of the love song playing quietly over the radio. "Do you think their done yet?"

Dr. Nand sighed, "Blake, I know as much as you."

"Well. What do you think they could find in there?"

Dr. Nand had been busying himself with a crossword, using the light from his phone to illuminate it as they'd agreed turning on the interior lights was too obvious, even if they were parked far from the sight of the police department. "Hopefully, they find out something useful." He bit his lip and scratched out the word he'd just filled in.

Blake stared at the man, his brow narrowing. "You don't say."

"Mhmm."

Blake thought silently for a second, his vision sweeping over the dark street they'd parked near. "Hal and Bobbi said they think it came from the chemical plant that burnt down in the nineties."

"Yes."

"What kind of research do you think they were doing to make something like that? Like it can turn people into,"—a lot of words flickered through his mind to describe the janitor that had tried to eat him and Sarah, it was hard to settle on one—"those things." He coughed uncomfortably. "I've never even heard of something like that outside of movies."

Dr. Nand put his pen down, turning to look at Blake. "Mr. Turner, I assure you whatever research they were conducting far exceeds my knowledge of scientific literature." He frowned, crumpling up his crossword and threw it in the backseat. "I think it exceeds most of my peers' knowledge as well."

Blake looked at the discarded crossword that Dr. Nand was only halfway through. "I thought doctors were supposed to know things."

Dr. Nand let out a dry laugh and started to rub his temple. "It's a very narrow field of knowledge. Unfortunately, they don't prepare us for stuff like this in medical school."

Blake let out a small grin. "What's the point then, I mean really?"

Mirth flashed in Dr. Nand's tired face. "Was that a joke, Mr. Turner? I didn't know you made those."

Blake sighed and started to drum his fingers again. "I'm bored."

"And worried, I assume."

"Yes."

Dr. Nand nodded. "I am too, if it makes you feel better."

Blake shook his head. "It doesn't… Jesus, change the station. This song is terrible."

Dr. Nand gave him a puzzled look, his ears perking at the noise. "I don't think—"

Blake twisted the nob on the radio but found dialing back the sound didn't stop the wailing he'd mistaken for modern music.

"What?"

The howling grew, piercing their ears even as they sat in the confines of the car. Dr. Nand twisted about, trying to see where it was coming from in the darkness. Eventually he spotted something and settled looking to his far left, motioning for Blake to do the same.

Blake's breath stopped. "Oh no."

Dr. Nand continued to look wide eyed out the window but his hand was busy tapping on his phone, shaking as he raised it to his ear. "Fuck."

There came a point when the caterwauling was loudest and even in the dim light Blake could see every detail of the horde as they passed by the car.

Their gait was skewed like the janitor's had been but they were moving quickly, running in a strange lopsided fashion that made it seem like the entire procession was only one slipped foot away from crashing down.

Most of them retained a human appearance, though a few had extra arms and legs jutting out awkwardly from their hips and ribs. Some only held the slightest remnants of their former humanity, faces and torsos connecting to bodies that scuttled along the pavement with too many limbs to count.

Dr. Nand cursed and looked at Blake. "They're not answering."

Blake was mesmerized by the procession. It felt like he could almost make out a chant from the incessant screaming.

"There's so many…"

Dr. Nand hit redial on his cell, raising a big fist to bite down on while it rung.

A man in a shabby suit with a pastor's collar looked at them as he passed, his glazed expression unchanging as it fell over the car. His left foot kept walking forward but his right turned towards them, making him split as he tried to walk two directions at once.

Blake tapped Dr. Nand's shoulder slowly. "I don't think we should move."

Dr. Nand's eyes twisted to look at the pastor while his frame went still. "Blake."

Blake spoke through clenched teeth, hoping the tree they'd parked under was enshrouding them in enough darkness to keep the interested creature from coming any nearer. "Yes, doctor?"

"I think I know where these people came from."

"Hmmm?"

"It's a congregation."

The pastor's body twisted so that he fully continued lurching towards the car. He slipped halfway and fell flailing on the pavement. His limbs lacked the coordination to push him to his feet and it looked like he would stay there permanently until a third arm pushed its way out of his chest to help him to his feet.

The extra limb was green and dripping a strange pus onto the pavement, it lacked human fingers and instead had a sort of claw.

Blake swallowed. "From Flint Street?"

The pastor spun around in a circle before settling on the direction of the police station. His jagged legs started to twist as he began a half run, his third arm outstretching towards the station as its claw started to curl.

"Yes." Free from the sight of the pastor, Dr. Nand shook his head, phone still ringing in one hand. "They're attacking the police department."

Blake's eyes widened as the creatures flooded over the drab office building, some crashing through the entrance door while others rammed their heads against the sides of the building. A few of the smaller, many legged creatures started to climb the building, their whirling limbs helping them scurry up the brick walls.

"They're organized," Dr. Nand murmured in amazement.

"Yep."

A mechanical voice from the cellphone informed Dr. Nand the caller he was trying to reach was unavailable. He swore and hit redial for a third time, his finger making the screen bend slightly from the force he hit it with.

"It can control them," said Dr. Nand.

"Would explain why the guy who chased me kept going on about his mother."

Blake started to catch sight of the organization stemming from the seeming chaos of the creatures' attack. Even the ones who had initially ran right into the walls of the building were now backing up and attempting to walk into the front door or climb through some of the lower windows.

Dr. Nand had started to sweat profusely. "It's smart," he croaked.

"What?"

"The spider, it's intelligent."

A touch of disbelief entered Blake's voice. "You thought it wasn't?"

"I thought it was just a big spider." A scream carried from the police department as a man was thrown through a window, the mass of creatures below quickly swarming him. "But it's not, this is a targeted attack."

Blake raised the binoculars to his eyes, shuddering as he saw one of the fallen man's arms fly through the air.

Dr. Nand continued, more to himself than Blake. "It can make actionable plans, it sees a threat and is trying to remove it." His weight shifted in his seat, body drawing in on itself. "It has goals."

Blake put the binoculars down, self-aware enough to know he would save money on future therapy if he stopped watching now. "What type of goals do you think something like that has?"

Once more the voice from the Doctor's cellphone told him the customer he was trying to reach was unavailable. He flung the phone down and leaned forward on his steering wheel. "Same goals we all have. Finding sustenance, shelter, a good mate, and reproducing." He looked at Blake with wide eyes.

"Wouldn't a spider do that regardless of how smart it was?"

Dr. Nand nodded. "Yes," he said softly. "But if it's intelligent it might actually succeed."

Interlude

He watched the boy and the doctor from the shade of a nearby tree, a dwindling cigarette clinging to his lips. He had to hand it to them, they were brave. Nearby, glass shattered as another wailing man was thrown from the building. He smiled, today was going perfectly.

In another few hours their enemies would be dead, and his love would be gushing over the sweet present he brought her. Chewing on his cigarette, he rummaged in his pocket and pulled out the note he'd liberated from the Turner's apartment. The rust coloured stains on the paper indicated it had pressed up against his knife, but the writing remained legible.

Dr. Nand and his wife will be looking after Sarah for the next few days. They're clearly more capable than you.

P.S. Stop bringing meth heads home from the bar.

It was a shame he had to drive all the way to the Nand's tonight—he wanted to continue watching the carnage—but his present was too important. For months he'd been searching for a perfect replacement for his love's doll. The little McCormack girl had been worn to her bone and Ken was sick of the smell.

His feet crunched on the gravel as he turned away from the bloodshed, leaving to go collect his gift.

Hal

It was Bobbi who noticed the room wasn't empty, letting out a small shriek before clasping a hand over her own mouth. Backing against the now shut door, she pointed into the dark corner of the cell.

Most of its body was on the cot save for a leg drooping onto the floor. Its lower jaw was missing, but long, needle-like, teeth stood in its place. Hal counted six appendages that might be mistaken for arms on top of its two human shaped legs.

The smell was atrocious. Hal wondered if there was anything left in his stomach to expel.

He kept his voice low as he spoke. "Is it alive?"

Bobbi shrugged beside him, her phone raised in attempt to record despite the darkness. "I don't know, Harold. Why don't you poke it?"

The cell was too dark for his cousin to get a good shot of whatever the thing was, but not so much to hide the face Hal pulled.

"I think its chest is ris—" The heavy clatter of boots on the stone floors of the hallway stopped him from finishing.

Hal locked eyes with Bobbi, she nodded and they both pressed their ears against the door. The steps grew louder and Hal's heart started to beat faster as the walker neared their cell. A shadow flickered over the cell window as the walkers stopped. Hal held his breath, freezing in his place.

He recognized Ken Dawson's voice immediately, smug asshole was unmissable, but he couldn't identify the other speaker. "Have Edwards prep a strike team. If we find where it lives I want to be able to go immediately."

"Yes, sir."

"And have a medical team on standby. I don't want us losing our chief researcher if our discussion gets out of hand."

"Of course, sir."

"And, Johnson?"

"Yes, sir?"

"Put some ice on your face after, you look terrible."

A beep of the keypad was followed by the hissing of the cell door across from theirs opening. Unlike Bobbi and Hal, Ken and whoever he was with opted to keep their door open.

Hal couldn't make out the conversation following but he did hear the screams of pain rising from the old man. They were shrill and mixed with pleas for mercy. Hal broke into a cold sweat before they finished. Bobbi opened her eyes briefly to position her phone against the cell window, careful to ensure the red light from its camera was blocked by the stone wall.

When the screaming finally stopped, Hal let out a deep breath, thankful for the momentary peace. He heard Ken and his companion return to the hallway, slamming the cell door behind them. "Looks like your prediction was correct, Johnson," said Dawson smugly.

"Yes, sir."

"Let the strike team know we have a location. I'll be joining them in twenty for the operation."

The other speaker's voice was curt. "Sir."

"I'd say you'd earned the chance at some field experience, you can join us if you—"

An alarm started to blare from a speaker in the corner of the room and Hal covered his ears as the creature in the cot spasmed at the noise. Bobbi's eyes flicked to the creature in horror. "Shit."

Dawson let out a similar curse, it was followed by the sound of boots pounding towards the stairwell. The alarm continued blaring above.

The creature twisted in its bed, its pointed teeth snapping into the spindles growing from the area that had once held a jaw. The cellphone in Bobbi's hand shook, causing the creature to cock its head towards them. Bobbi deftly moved her hand to cover the red light of the phone, too late to stope creature's interest from piquing.

Its teeth stopped thrashing as a long tongue poked out of its broken mouth to wiggle about the air. The motion was accompanied by a slur of speech as jagged as the creature's teeth. "Brothers. Sisters. Here." The tongue bent awkwardly to lick the thing's remaining lips. "Feed time."

Hal rose slowly, putting an arm on the door handle and pulling it. He could feel his phone vibrating in his jean pockets but ignored it to pull harder on the door, finding the sturdy quality of the Hope jail cells growing more unamusing with each tug.

The creature pushed itself out of the cot. It crunched as it landed on the floor, two of its arms bending unnaturally under its own weight.

Bobbi banged wildly on the door, most of the noise she made covered by the wailing of the alarm above. Hal started to ram the metal barrier with his shoulder, screaming between each impact. "Dusty, we need a little help."

The creatures tongue pointed towards them, rising up and down in the air with anticipation. "Feed. Mommy wants feed."

Bobbi added her own voice to Hal's. "For fuck's sake, Dusty, let us out."

The creature's torso twisted completely around, its legs bending at impossible angles as it propped itself up on the floor. Its forehead dragged across the floor while its teeth gnashed. A clump of spittle flew from the area a jaw should have been. Hal felt its damp warmth against the side of his cheek.

"Dusty."

Bobbi put her camera down and pulled the knife from her pocket. Hal did the same. The knives were far smaller than they'd wanted, made for cutting fishing lines and tangled snares, not combat, but it was all they'd felt safe smuggling into the police detachment. A machete, which Hal would have loved right now, might have garnered a little more attention than they'd wanted.

"Watch the teeth, Bobbi."

Bobbi snarled as the creature clawed itself forward. "Great advice, Harold. Don't let it bite me. Noted." She kicked the door with the back of her foot. "Dusty, let us out."

The creature jumped. Hal would have thought this physically impossible from the shape of its body, but its legs and arms contorted, accompanied by the horrendous crackle of bones breaking, to allow it to push itself upwards. It let out a guttural growl as it crashed into Hal, one of its dagger-like teeth digging into his shoulder.

The knife he'd raised sunk into the creatures' torso, digging inward until it struck thick bone. The creature seemed undisturbed by the penetration, its mouth biting down harder as its limbs began wrapping around his body. Bobbi plunged her own knife into the creature's neck, ripping it out upwardly with a spray of green fluid.

The creature's hug grew tighter. Hal heard the cracking of its bones as arms and legs bent the wrong direction to encircle him. With his breath shortening, Hal tried wiggling the knife. He was rewarded by the damp spray of more blood, but the creature remained unperturbed.

He screamed as he felt the creature's tongue press into the hole in his flesh, digging inward towards the tendons of his shoulder. Bobbi cried as she struck out once more, this time pushing her knife into the contorted mess of the creature's skull.

Hal gasped in relief as the tongue slowed its tunneling into his flesh, sliding from his body like a wet noodle. The creature's grip remained suffocating, making each lungful smaller than the last.

Sensing the success of her blow, Bobbi pulled the knife out and prepared another strike. Her thin arm darted out again but caught only air as the door Hal was pushed against opened. He fell cursing into the hallway, the creature using the fall to further tighten its hold.

Through blood pooling over his eyes, Hal caught sight of Dusty looking down in terror at Hal and the creature.

"Fucking, help me Dusty," Hal croaked, following his plead with a scream as what felt like needles shot out from the creature's chest into his own, puncturing and squirming into him the same way the things' tongue had.

Bobbi rushed from the cell, kneeling beside him with eyes locked on the creature. She raised the knife again, this time pausing to confirm the trajectory of the blow.

Hal felt the needles start to dig deeper into his chest, one of them managing to tear into an abdominal muscle. "Do it, Bobbi," he moaned. "Christ."

She struck out hard and once more the knife pierced the creature's skull, jamming so deep the first quarter of the knife's handle disappeared in the mass of blood and bone. To Hal's sweet relief he felt the creature go limp, the needles no longer edging deeper into his flesh as the dead weight of the creature fell limp on him.

"Pull it off me." Tears of pain welled in his eyes and he was desperate for a drink. "Please."

Bobbi ripped the creature from his body, eyes widening at the squelching sound it made. Hal clutched his chest, blood leaking through the hundred pinpricks marking his shirt. He shuddered at the sight of the fleshy spikes protruding from the limp body before him.

Bobbi helped him unsteadily to his feet, her voice difficult to hear over the shrieking alarm. "We should get out of here."

Hal nodded, flinching from the discomfort brought by his first step. "We should," he bit his lip in pain, able only to tilt his head towards the old man's cell.

Bobbi nodded and ran to punch the door code in. "Of course," she said before disappearing into the cell, reemerging thirty seconds later with a small frame leaning heavily on her body.

The old man's glasses were cracked and a bloody rash marked the spot on his scalp where some of his wild grey hair had been ripped from him. His small eyes didn't look up as he staggered over with Bobbi, but a steady stream of murmuring escaped his mouth.

"Told them. I shouldn't have told them," he sobbed. "Son. Son, why did I tell them? They wouldn't have known if I didn't tell them." The old man's voice sped up, spittle falling as he spoke. "Told them. But only a theory. Never actually tested."

"Tested what?" said Bobbi gently, her hand massaging the battered man's shoulder.

The man looked up with dazed eyes. "Tested? No, I never tested it." He bit his lips, turning his eyes back to the floor. "Only theorized, thought it would be a good place to hide."

Hal spit blood before speaking. "Where is a good place to hide?"

The man whimpered, shying away from Hal's gaze. "The mines. God. I told them the mines. They're secluded, hard to get to, tunnels would be warm in the winter, lots of room for—nesting," he licked his lips.

Dusty let out a pitched laugh, his voice shaking as he spoke. "What the fuck did you get me into, Hal?"

Hal shrugged, his shoulder screaming in pain from the motion. "I don't know, Dusty, I don't know."

Ken

He'd killed six of the things before they made it to the second floor. Between the roaring gunfire and screaming beasts, Ken was certain he'd have permanent hearing damage if he survived the night.

The comm chatter was frantic, calls for reinforcements and target sightings ending in garbled screams. Ken had removed his earbud halfway upstairs, finding the screaming distracting to his brain's attempts to form a plan.

Clearing a path to his office had been bloody work. Bodies, human and otherwise, littered the offices and hallways on their path. His assistant had surprised him by killing two of the things herself, ending their lives with rounds placed perfectly into their foreheads. Ken chuckled beneath his breath—she'd wanted field experience.

His office, despite being on the top floor, had not survived the brunt of the assault. Wind blew freely through shattered windows while the floor was so sticky with blood it felt like walking on glue. The bullet ridden corpses of a few Hope locals lay bleeding on the floor around the half devoured body of a black suited agent.

He stepped over the chaos to his laptop, brushing the gore from its screen as he opened a line to command. He didn't have to start with an update, his assistant had already sent a message off with the pertinent details. The video conference was reserved for requests agents had deemed to be of the upmost priority.

"Agent?" came the brusque voice.

The video screen was black on Ken's end but the glowing blue light atop the laptop informed him his superiors were watching. "Sir. Requesting immediate access to additional troops. The target's location is known and we have reason to believe it can be apprehended immediately."

"Request denied. New orders incoming." His assistant's pocket gave an electronic ping but she didn't lower her pistol to check it.

"Command, be advised that as the commanding officer I highly recommend we make use of this intel."

His assistant's pocket chimed again.

"Agent, be advised that upon review of on-site data we have decided to shift operational command." The screen flickered as a picture of his assistant's dour face appeared over her new rank. "Agent Johnson will now be acting head of this mission."

Ken froze, heart stopping in his chest. His assistant continued to swivel the room with her gun, but her eyes had locked onto the portrait staring blankly from the computer screen. Rage seeped into his voice when he finally spoke.

"Command, be advised I doubt Johnson's leadership capability."

The computer screen flickered to a table of mission statistics. Columns detailing money spent, man hours, and casualties sprawled about. The drawl of his superior's voice continued, "Command doubts Agent Johnson's leadership would result in the continued misuse of Organization funds and life, Agent Dawson will comply or face retiremen—"

Ken spit on the computer screen before slamming it down. Clearly there had been a mistake in the relay of operational knowledge. Command would no doubt correct themselves upon further evaluation.

"Johnson, contact the surviving members of the prep team. We depart in ten."

A cold smile played across the woman's face, her gun no longer wavering about the room but pointed directly at him. "Agent Dawson, you are aware with our organizations policy on non-compliance?"

"Agent Johnson, you will lower your weapon and alert the assault crew. We will be acting upon our fresh intel immediately."

The woman laughed, smile widening. "You know, I heard you were quick to rush in, but even I didn't think you'd fuck up the operation this colossally."

"Agent," Ken hissed. "You must have misheard my request—contact the assault team immediately."

The woman used her unoccupied hand to rub her puffy cheek. "Nearly ninety-five percent casualties on your first mission in command, Jesus." She let out another mocking laugh. "Lucky I sent command an update detailing my doubt of your methods, might have taken them a little longer to clue in that you're absolutely useless."

"Command," Ken said darkly. "Will soon see the error of their ways."

"You really think that, don't you? Can't accept that maybe, just maybe, you're not a superior specimen of the human race?"

"I am," he said flatly.

His assistant chuckled again, eyes flickering in disbelief. "You should know, I'd be killing you even if you had complied to orders. It's a service to our organization."

It was this little gloat that gave Ken his opportunity, the slight shifting in her pistol grip as the pleasure of her situation overtook her concentration.

His muscular arm shot out with a primal anger, connecting with the woman's shoulder as her finger managed to slam down on the pistol's trigger. The bullet ripped through his gut, but he barely felt it, his other arm slamming into the woman's head. They tumbled onto the floor where the gun went off again, leaving a smoking hole in the foot of his desk.

She gurgled as his hands found their way to her throat, tightening around her thin frame. He leaned in closer, so his lips were nearly on hers, and whispered, "Crossing me was a mistake."

Fear flooded the woman's face, but it was soon replaced by the dim gaze of death, her eyes going limp as drool began to drip from her mouth and onto Ken's hands. He took great pleasure at the sight.

He wiped his hands on her suit before rising. Outside his office the sounds of battle continued, screaming and gunfire roared from all parts of the building. In the distance he even heard the crack of what might have been a grenade exploding.

It seemed unlikely many of his fellow agents would survive, and even then, the low numbers and refusal of reinforcements were less than ideal for the capturing of the creature Ken had planned.

Still, as the dead body at his feet could attest to, Ken was used to dealing with things himself. Command might be angry now, but they would certainly change their tune if he brought them something to make the operation worthwhile, something like a hulking spider carcass.

Ken nudged the woman's body with his foot, bending over to remove the cellphone that had been vibrating in her pocket, relishing the sound of it cracking under his boot.

Even if command didn't return his rank after his capture of the creature, would it even matter? He would have proven them weak, cowards who fled just as their prey was in sight. More importantly, Ken would have proven himself superior to them. And in the end, that was all he wanted.

Bobbi

Even in the bunker like basement, they could hear the gunfire. Loud cracks shook dust from the ceiling while hoarse cries and inhuman roars sent shivers down their spines. The wailing alarm had finally subsided, but the moment of clear-headedness this brought Bobbi was extinguished by a quick downpour from the overhead sprinklers. The unexpected drenching had made Harold laugh and Dusty scream.

Hal raised his arms and basked in the water, letting it rinse away some of the blood and bile coating him. His face turned sullen when the downpour stopped a mere thirty seconds later. He stared accusingly at Dusty who only shrugged and said, "Someone must have overridden the fire alarm."

Bobbi had feared the only way out would be through the upstairs, forcing them to either hide in the monster filled basement or go upstairs into whatever battle was raging there. To her sweet relief, Dusty informed her the building was built on a modest incline, leaving some of the windows in the basement opening onto the ground floor.

She stood with the old man while Harold and Dusty tried to pull out the rusty latch on a long-shuttered window. The two tried for a minute before they agreed in panting breaths to simply smash it. Harold had been keen to point out no one would hear it over the racket, as if they'd suddenly forgot about the horrific noise above.

The old man had a strange odour that made Bobbi's nose wrinkle, a mix of simple mustiness and some chemicals she couldn't quite put her finger on. It reminded her of chemistry class in the tenth grade. Back then Hope Secondary had a less than stellar science teacher who'd only asked they not light their eyebrows on fire while he snuck off for a cigarette. One time, Patty Deschenes got drenched in formaldehyde during a prank and the room had reeked of the substance for months after.

The man didn't stop chattering save for when they came across a rat in the hallway— the little creature making him squeal as it darted past. "I don't like those. I don't like those at all." Bobbi, who had memories of him pulling the legs off a football sized spider, was at a loss for words.

"Presto." Hal grinned as he wiped the shards of glass from the former window. He was standing on filing cabinets pushed on its side and already looking better than he had walking towards the unused office.

"Very good, Harold." Her voice was dry but her lips twitched into a smile.

Hal pushed himself through the newly made hole, grunting savagely as he did. For a brief moment he disappeared from view, only to quickly reemerge and lend a helping hand to a struggling Dusty.

Getting the old man out was difficult. He protested loudly, giving a speech in equal parts about the need to care for his joints and the need to remain so he could continue his research. It had taken Bobbi's soft words to finally coax him into the frame, assuring him she would help him continue whatever research he was doing once they'd escaped.

They'd come out on the side of the building, crawling through the dirt of a small garden. Bobbi cursed when she caught her foot on a blackberry vine. They grew abundantly in Hope and were, in her mind, little more than a nuisance.

In the fresh air, the sound of the fighting was deafening. Glass shattered, guns cracked, and people screamed. At one point something was thrown from a window above, crashing through the glass to land with a splash a few meters away from them. Bobbi was curious as to what had fallen, but thankful it was too dark to see—she'd seen enough stomach-turning images in the last few days.

The police detachment bordered a small thicket of trees. They looked less than inviting, but given what was happening behind them, Bobbi realized they didn't have much of a choice. Dusty finally pulled his gun from his belt while Hal raised his bloody hunting knife— Bobbi had left her own knife embedded in the skull of whatever had been trying to eat her cousin and opted to simply continue helping the old man.

The trees weren't dense the dark made it difficult to find their way. Bobbi stubbed her toe twice before painfully catching her head on a particularly thick branch. It was only passing through a soft patch of spiderwebs that made her scream, dropping the old man to cover her face in expectation of the worst.

Dusty had looked at her in confusion while Hal walked over and helped the old man up, turning to drop the knife at her feet. "It's alright, Bobbi, why don't you carry that for a bit? Might make you feel better."

Bobbi took a deep breath, pressing the knife to her chest. God, she hated spiders.

Eventually they made their way out of the woods, slipping into a cul-de-sac that let them (by sneaking through someone's backyard) set foot on the road their car was parked on.

They found Dr. Nand and Blake crouched down in their seats, lights off and binoculars raised. They screamed when Hal knocked on the window. Two doors burst open as the teenager and doctor started to babble. Bobbi missed what they said, her attention stolen by her first full view of the police detachment.

Bodies littered the parking lot, not a single window remained intact, and a fire had started on the top floor. A few creatures, not unlike the one that had attacked Hal, were crawling over the building's walls.

Only the old man's voice broke her reverie, his speech more lucid than it had been in the last hour. "Fascinating. I always wondered if her children could climb like her." He adjusted his cracked glasses before continuing. "The neurotoxin she injects makes incredible changes to the internal structures of the body." Hal tugged her arm but she ignored him. "Eventually it erases everything but bits of the central nervous system, chunks of the brain left to rot in a body not their own."

Hal pulled her more forcefully and she got into the backseat, the elderly scientist squeezing in beside her. His eyes didn't leave the building, the slight frown forming on his face reminded Bobbi of a confused toddler. "Terribly difficult to make a cure for. Been trying for years."

The engine roared to life and Bobbi missed what he said next, catching only the end of his sentence, "—for my son, you see." The old man gurgled as tears flooded his eyes. "So many years, could never get it right."

Bobbi held the man awkwardly while the car made a right turn onto the highway, speeding once again along the narrow river valley towards Dr. Nand's house.

Interlude
Present Day

Sophia Nand had never wanted children. Her law practice had kept her fulfilled enough with what little free time she had being far too precious to trade for diaper changing. Her pregnancy had been a surprise, her husband attributed it equally to divine intervention and a failure in her birth control regiment during their holiday in Barbados.

Armand had a difficult job convincing her to keep the baby, resorting to wild promises of reduced shifts in the ER and agreements to her continued law practice. In the end she'd agreed and, to her husband's credit, found he kept his promise of doing more than his fair share of the child rearing. Four year later she couldn't be happier with their little family.

Julius, named for Sophia's favourite uncle, grew quickly in body and mind. Already a master of the alphabet, he'd progressed to simple children's books. She knew every mother thought their child was special, but she held strong to the belief Julius would be as exceptional as his father.

Dr. Nand thought Julius was special too, but he also held firm to the belief everyone was special given the chance. It was one of, to Sophia's more cynical mind, Armand's only faults. Her husband never ceased in his effort to help people, all of which he believed equally deserving of his care. She'd often joke with her girlfriends that her husband would light himself on fire to warm a cold friend.

This incessant altruism often strained their domestic life, despite Dr. Nand's best efforts. Whether it was by blowing off date night so he could volunteer after work or by, as was the case this morning, filling their house with a bunch of desperate strangers.

It was true Dr. Nand's good nature might occasionally inconvenience her, but Sophia wouldn't have her husband any other way. She still remembered when she'd first met him, running into the rain to bring her the coat she'd forgotten in an overpriced Vancouver.

She couldn't resist gifting him a smile, those big brown eyes and earnest expression digging through the metal plating of her lawyer heart. It was nice to meet someone who was genuinely kind in the rather aristocratic part of the city she frequented. He didn't even mention he was a doctor until the third date, brushing off his work as something in the medical field (Sophia had guessed x-ray technician).

Sophia reminisced over their early romance as she put a plate of grilled cheese affront the child she'd been left to care for. The curry she'd made, despite her best efforts, was too spicy for the little girl, eliciting a stream of tears from her eyes and a stammering plea for water. Julius had liked the curry but also received his own grilled cheese, incessant he should eat whatever his new "frand," (the word friend still eluded his little tongue) had for dinner.

With the children served, Sophia started to chew her own meal, enjoying the vibrant taste of the sopping red chicken.

"Thank you, Mrs. Nand, this is very nice."

Sophia nodded to the girl. To her husband's (and whoever had raised the child's) credit, she was easy to babysit. Content to play with Julius when he was awake and watch TV quietly when he napped. Not once did she hear a word of complaint from her save for when she talked to her brother over the phone, alerting Sophia who hadn't even considered that her food might be too spicy for the little girl's taste buds.

Pausing to sip some wine, a wonderful shiraz from the Okanogan, she leafed through a divorce settlement she was helping with. Seeing what her client stood to lose regardless of how well she lawyered made her thankful of her own prenup. She'd worried Armand would have been offended by the suggestion of getting one but to her relief he agreed with the good grace he exhibited in every other aspect of his life.

She nearly choked on her wine as she flipped the page and saw what her client's wife was asking for alimony. She reached for her ever-present cell phone, intent on calling whichever lawyer had erected the document. While conducting business during dinner hours might be considered rude, it paled to this insult of an alimony request.

Her fingers dialed the number listed on the documents, hoping the lawyer wouldn't ignore her call. It was always better to express your anger directly than through a voicemail. She hit the last number and flipped her finger to call right as the doorbell rang.

Shaking her head, she put the phone down and rose from her seat at the kitchen table. "God, who could that be?"

Pausing at the edge of the room she looked back at Julius and Sarah. The alimony figures running through her mind dissipated for an instance and were instead replaced by the glowing image of her little boy smiling at his new "frand." His small face glowing with joy as Sarah offered him the rest of her sandwich.

This, often far too rare moment of maternal pride was ruined by another shriek of the doorbell. She closed her eyes and turned away, calling down the long hallway as she went. "I'm coming, hold your horses!"

She looked through the eyehole before opening it, even in the countryside there were "ne'er-do-wells" as her Grandfather would say. Just last week the farm across the road woke to find the contents of their toolshed missing, a fact Sophia was keen to remember.

Relieved by the sight of her husband's colleague she opened the door. She couldn't remember his name, only that he'd sat with her and Armand last year at the Hospital's Christmas banquet.

He gave her a charming smile as she inched the door open. "Hello, Sophia, is Armand home?"

"Sorry, he's gone to Hope," she scratched her head. "I can't remember if it was to volunteer or work."

The man nodded. The friendly smile remained but for a brief second Sophia caught something dark slip through his merry expression. "Is it just you?" His eyes darted past her shoulder.

Unconsciously her hand reached to the closet at her side. They kept an old wooden baseball bat in it, the only real tool of violence in an otherwise peaceful house. The man followed her grasping with his narrow eyes, his tongue emerging to lick his lips like a wolf before eating.

"I'm sure Armand will be back soon," she said as her hand continued searching for the bat.

Warmth fled the man's eyes, replaced by an iciness that dug into Sophia's quivering frame. "Well, Mrs. Nand, it looks like I've come just in time."

She thought of her son as the man's fist lashed out, terror filling her mind as she realized her beautiful little boy was defenseless only a room over.

Sophia put up a fight, even managing to pull the bat from the wall and connect it weakly with the man's back, but she was quickly overpowered. He leapt on her with a surgical precision, his strong hands quickly driving consciousness from her body.

He left her in a heap at the entrance, blood pooling around her as her breathing turned to ragged gasps, pausing only to wipe his hands on her blouse before proceeding into the hallway.

Hal

Hal was the first one to notice the door was ajar. Blake and Bobbi were behind him helping the old man climb the driveway while Dr. Nand stood beside his car, busy explaining his inability to come in that evening despite an apparent staff shortage. Hal nudged the door open slowly, cautiously poking his head inside while his fingers curled around the hunting knife in his pocket.

The sight of Sophia Nand's body made his heart skip, but he restrained himself from screaming. Knife raised, he edged forward, checking the small entrance room for any signs of the freak creatures that had assailed the police station. Finding the room empty he knelt down and checked the woman's pulse. From deeper in the house the thick sobs of a child rang out.

Blake shouldered his way through the door behind him, the decrepit old man leaning heavily on his shoulder. "Could you give me a hand? Bobbi had to take a phone call from her editor and…" his words trailed off as his eyes fell across the floor.

Hal rose and met Blake's eye. "It's alright, she's alive." The boy nodded slowly, helping his ward take a seat at a wooden bench adorned with a quilt saying "WELCOME." The old man sat wearily, continuing to speak as he had the entire drive from Hope. His voice was low and manic while his eyes barely took in the violence around him.

"I got into the work for the thrill of it at first, no one really believed in telepathy back then. The idea of studying senses we couldn't identify materially yet was too enticing for me to turn down."

Hal handed Blake a baseball bat that had been lying by the poor woman, tilting his head in the direction of the house as he did. "Whoever did this might still be here."

Blake flexed the wood handle in his hand. "I hear Julius." His eyes narrowed as he started to the door. "But not my sister."

They crept into the hallway connecting the entrance to the rest of the house, the old man's words following them out. "Pay was good too—I have no idea what branch of the military these people were from, but the contracts were unbelievable...."

A harsh sob echoed from the kitchen down the hall and Hal flinched from the noise but Blake merely sped up. His shoulders were squared, making him appear much larger than he was, the bat raised in cold fury.

They rounded a corner and found themselves in the kitchen. A chair had been knocked over and a plate thrown against the wall. Hal couldn't spot Julius at first, only heard him crying. It was Blake who, after looking menacingly around the room, pulled the boy out from his hiding place behind a small island.

Julius had a black eye and some snot running down his shirt but appeared mostly intact. Fear was written across his face and he didn't open his eyes at Blake's touch until after the boy assured him he was safe a few times.

Blake carried the boy in his practiced arms while passing the bat to Hal. His voice was gentler than the expression playing on his face. "Julius, what happened?"

The boy buried his head into Blake's shoulders, blowing his nose on the boy's shirt. "Man came. Bad man came."

Blake nodded. "It's ok, Julius, what did the bad man do?"

Julius let out another wild cry, tears streaming down his little brown face in an increased fervor. "He hit me." The boy scrunched his eyes as Blake patted him gently on the back. "He took frand."

Blake nodded and continued to pat the boy's back, his expression darkening with each passing second.

Dr. Nand crashed into the room, his arms raised and expression wild. "Where's my boy?" Upon spotting Blake, he lowered his arms and let out a soft sob, rushing to take the child from him. "Oh, sweet child!" Dr. Nand nuzzled his head against his son, engulfing the boy in his thick arms. "I'm so sorry."

Blake motioned to Hal, taking the baseball bat back from him. "We should check the rest of the house."

They went room by room, finding them all empty. Blake called out his sister's name a few times as they went, the hollow echoes of the home's old walls the only reply.

They finished their search in the entrance, finding Bobbi nursing a dazed Sophia. Hal put a hand on Blake's shoulder, trying to think of a speech that would be even slightly consoling given the circumstances. "Blake, I'm sure—"

The boy cut him off with a growl. "Where are the keys?"

"The keys?"

Blake shook his head and looked about the room, curling his lip as he spotted them lying beside Bobbi's foot.

Hal cleared his throat and continued, "Blake, we need to think about this. Why would someone take Sarah?"

Blake looked at Hal with disgust. "Why would someone take my mother?" He swiped the dropped keys from the floor and shoved past Hal to the door. "Why would someone bother tormenting a town of rednecks and junkies?"

Hal followed the boy out of the house, having to run to keep up with his fast steps. "You're right, but who took your sister?" He thought about the lack of blood in the house and Julius' description of the "bad man." They made it to the car before he finished. "Tt certainly wasn't one of those things," he panted.

Blake opened the door and threw the baseball bat into the backseat. His fiery eyes met Hal as he motioned to the back seat. "Look, Hal, are you coming or not?"

Hal swallowed as he darted around to the passenger's side, barely sliding into the leather seat before the car was pulling out of the driveway. Blake let out a scream as they made for the highway, his anguish barely overpowering the howling of the speeding car's engine.

Blake

It was only the knowledge he couldn't help his sister if he died in a motor accident that kept him from pushing the convertible past one-fifty. The needle on the RPM gauge had been pushed into the red since they turned out of the driveway and Blake had no plans of lowering it until he reached his trailer.

Hal sat silently beside him, for once willing to quit his constant moaning. The man's eyes were heavy, laying downcast on the road before them between the odd glance of pity.

Blake's mind screamed. Terrors and doubts rippled through him, shredding the last edge of calm he'd retained through the trying ordeal that was his life.

Sarah. He'd let Sarah get taken. He'd lost his sister.

His jaw clenched so hard it felt like his teeth would begin to crack, his fingers wrapped around the steering wheel and dug into his own palms until they drew blood.

He'd lost her because he'd been selfish. He'd wanted his mommy back so badly he'd pawned his sister off on some suburbanite with a nice house rather than care for her himself.

Hal let out a strangled yelp as they passed a semi on its right, Blake refusing to slow for a long bend in the road.

God, why had he left her there? Why had he gone looking for his mother instead of taking his sister even farther away from the black hole of disappointment that was Hope?

An angry honk came from a hummer as he sharply cut into the left lane to avoid being stuck behind a smart car struggling with the highway's steep incline. By now Hal's face had turn ash white.

When they reached the turnoff to Hope he twisted the wheel violently, lowering his speed only the tiniest modicum as they descended into the township.

Rage began overpowering his anguish. Mostly it was directed at himself, fuming over his own stupidity, but some was directed at his mother. Even if she had been kidnapped and not simply relapsed, Blake and Sarah only lived in Hope because the stupid woman had spent all their money on heroin.

He sped his way through the town until he reached the road to his trailer, turning violently with an effort that earned him a middle finger from a leather clad biker who'd been in the process of making his own turn.

The sight of his trailer stilled his breath. A pain burned in his chest as a dull throbbing flooded his ears. He left the car idling as he ran into the tiny mobile, forgetting the bat he'd brought to fend off the horrors that might lurk inside.

Hal

He walked into the trailer more cautiously than Blake had. It was dark, the curtains were drawn and the lights didn't turn on when he flipped the nearby switch. He kept the baseball bat he'd pulled from the back of the car raised as he scoured the room.

It appeared the same as it had when Hal had visited days earlier. The kitchen and living room were still covered in beer bottles, the smell of cigarettes still permeated the room, and Blake's aunt was still cuddling her friend on the sofa. Hal's blood chilled at the last sight.

He edged closer, still scanning the room for other occupants. In close proximity the situation was made clear.

The blood spilling from their throats had dried, turning the blanket they were wrapped in a rust colour. The man's eyes were shut but the woman's hung open, staring emptily at the tin ceiling. A cluster of flies covered her mouth, intent on digesting the bright red lipstick she'd been wearing when she died.

Hal took a deep breath before backing away, stifling a cough from the harsh scent of the corpses.

He found Blake in his and his sister's room. He sat at the base of the bed, arms wrapped around his knees with a photo clenched between his hands. His eyes were focused at the glossy picture, but Hal doubted he could see anything through his silent stream of tears.

Hal sat down beside the boy, their shoulders pressing against each other in the narrow confines of the room. Hal waited, taking in the girlish posters and drawings adorning the room. The only sign that Blake even inhabited the bedroom was a pair of soccer cleats discarded in the corner.

Blake's voice was barely audible in the deathly stillness of the trailer. "I was meant to protect her…"

"I know."

"I was all she had."

"I know."

Blake let out a strangled cry and rose to his feet, the photo slipping from his grip and drifting lazily to the floor. Hal's eyes lingered on it for a second, it contained the smiling snapshot of three children at a fair.

"You don't know, you've never lost someone you were meant to protect."

Hal sighed. Laura's cheery smile fluttered through his mind, the smell of the coffee she brought him each morning, the warmth of her hand in his. "I have," he said weakly.

Blake punched a fist into the metal wall, his knuckles cracking as some of his sister's drawings fell from the ceiling. "So, what do you do about it?"

Hal had a hangover the day Laura went missing. She'd been happy to follow his suggestion she go to the fishing hole instead of him, always eager for a nice hike. She gave him a wry grin and peck on the cheek before walking out of their office. Hal was still finalizing the divorce then, but that little moment had made him believe he might be happy in the future.

"Drink mostly," he sighed, answering the boy's question.

Blake leaned his head against the wall, nestling it into a coloured picture of a unicorn with the words "Sarah age 5" below. His tears started to blot the picture, sending bright streams down the white paper and on to the drawings below. "Fuck."

Hal stared at the sobbing boy. "Don't give up, Blake."

They sat there for a while, Hal reclining on the floor while Blake rested his weary head against the wall. When the silence finally broke it was by the vibrating of Hal's cellphone. He opened it unenthusiastically, letting out a tired "yes" as he did.

"Harold? Oh. thank god! Where are you?" cracked Bobbi's worried voice.

"The kid's trailer, his aunt is...." A sharp look from the boy cut him off, he let out a nervous cough. "Is not good, we can't find his sister."

Bobbi sounded unsurprised. "It got her."

"Which it, Bobbi? The police who aren't police, the fucking zombies, the giant spider?" He groaned as he rose from his seat. "Christ, I thought we'd be safe from those things all the way in Chilliwack. Who taught them to drive?"

Bobbi's voice was hurried as she spoke, "No, cousin, no one. Don't you get it? It's the son."

"Come again?"

"The scientist, he's always raving about his son, right?"

"Yes?"

"And the woman, she was talking about how it had her sons, plural."

"Oh?"

"Sophia is awake, she says it was a man who assaulted her. He was white with blond hair."

Hal thought about the woman they'd met in the cocaine cabins, her voice tilting with drink as her faded blond hair brushed the picnic table they were seated around.

"Christ."

Bobbi continued, sounding pleased with herself despite the circumstances. "The spider isn't alone, Harold, it has a friend."

"Blake's aunt," Hal whispered, shying away from Blake's hurt gaze. "She was done in with a knife. It had to be."

Bobbi paused for a moment. Hal could envision her face scrunching as she puzzled over his statement. "Blakes's aunt is dead, not taken?" she finally asked.

"Unfortunately."

"So," she continued in an undertone. "She wasn't ideal for him."

"Ideal? What are you talking about, Bobbi."

"I have a theory, about why the majority of people who went missing were women."

"Go on."

"Well, you know how it's been making those *things*."

"Christ, Bobbi, how could I forget." He closed his eyes, even in a trailer with an emotionally devastated teenager and two corpses he found it hard not to bicker with his cousin. "Get to the point please."

"Well, they're made from a neuro toxin, the old man told me." She paused, taking in a deep breath before letting the rest out. "They're *her* children but they're not true children, slaves more than family."

Hal let the sentence hang in the air before responding.

"So?"

His cousin let out a huff. "Jesus, Harold, think about it. Do those things look like ideal offspring to the creature we saw at the hospital? Think about the creatures we saw storming the police department, mostly men."

"Go on."

"Christ, it probably only saved us from that lunatic cop because it wants me as a surrogate too."

Hal's mind clicked into place, his stomach twisting in revulsion as understanding seeped through him. "Oh God."

"Yes."

"A man couldn't…" The words tasted sour, his mouth turning dry as he tried to continue. "A man couldn't mate with it, but he could with one of those… things. Christ, Bobbi what do we do?"

His cousin's voice took on a granite edge as she spoke. "We're going to kill it, Harold. Tomorrow."

Hal nodded firmly, catching the eyes of Blake who was slowly turning in interest at the conversation. The boy's eyes blazed in the small room, he gave a curt nod of approval at Bobbi's suggestion.

"Ok, we'll be back soon." He clicked the cellphone off, a soothing emptiness washing over him. Languidly he placed the cellphone in his pocket and spoke with an almost relieved calm. "I guess we're ending this."

Tears still glimmered on Blake's cheeks. "Let's go," he said brusquely.

The boy marched from the room, pausing only to let his gaze linger over the bodies lying in the corner of the living room before continuing outside. Hal bent over to pick up the discarded photograph as he followed him.

Hal drove them back to the Nand's, surprised when Blake drifted off in the seat beside him. It was late, but he'd figured sleep would escape the boy. After all, a missing sibling was often inconducive to restful slumber. Hal himself wouldn't sleep tonight, painfully aware that consuming the amount of liquor necessary to help him sleep would leave him utterly useless for the following morning's endeavour.

Little occupied him during the drive, his mind embracing the calm thousands of dollars spent on drugs and liquor had been unable to produce. Tomorrow they would find the thing terrorizing his friends and town, they would kill it along with whatever lowlife was helping it, or they would die. Hal was equally content with both outcomes.

Sarah

When the strange man came she'd been terrified, wetting herself when he struck Julius with his backhand and tumbling to the floor as she tried to back away from him. He'd dragged her from the house screaming. She'd told him her brother would be angry if she went missing but the man had simply ignored her cries, smiling as he forced her into the trunk of his car. Before the lid closed she felt a sharp pinch in her arm before everything had gone dark.

She awoke floating, sure she must be in heaven with Daddy and Sally. Her little feet kicked freely in the air while she drifted about. Her fear was gone, happiness overcoming her like a malaise. Distantly she remembered Blake would be worried about her, but it seemed like such a trivial concern.

Why did she need to fret? She was in heaven, floating about. She was sure she would see Daddy and Sally soon and they would be happy. She even had a new Mommy, one she felt watching over her despite the darkness surrounding her.

She sensed others around her too, floating through the same void with her. Maybe they were angels, maybe her sister and father were with them.

Something tugged at her leg to make it kick as her arms were tugged above her head. She couldn't tell what was making her dance, but when the unseen force made her spin about the darkness she let out a giggle.

This was fun.

Blake

They left at Dawn, slowed only by Dr. Nand who had to fight past his crying wife and child to get in the car. Sophia had a swollen face and a mild concussion, but the pain caused by her leaving husband seemed to far outweigh her injuries.

Her anger erupted in threats of divorce and phone calls to the police, both of which Dr. Nand hurriedly tried to prevent.

"Sophie, you know I have a good reason," he begged.

"Good enough not to tell your wife, the woman who nearly died looking after the child you brought here?" Her voice cracked as she continued. "Christ, what if he'd gotten Julius?"

Dr. Nand nodded morosely and pulled his wife in for a hug. She resisted at first, arms beating on the big man's back before they clamped down to return the embrace. When Dr. Nand finally pulled away, tears marked his face. He bent down and kissed Julius who was sitting at their feet, the boy's somber face brightening as his father's lips brushed his forehead.

Blake had watched them impatiently until the man finally extracted himself from his family and lumbered over to the car. The group had remained silent through the process save for the old man who muttered something about having a family like this once.

It took them two hours to drive to the base of Caroline Mines, Dr. Nand's small sports car barely managing to traverse the narrow dirt roads leading through the mountains to it. They were met by Dusty, his car parked against the cliff face with smoke spilling from its windows.

Of the guns he'd brought, only one was a rifle. After each of them had a turn trying to peg a bottle a few meters away it was determined Dr. Nand was the best shot and so he had the honour of slinging the thing over his back.

Hal, Bobbi, and Blake all received a pistol. Two of them were slim little Glocks, technically property of the Royal Canadian Mountain Police, while the third was a long barreled revolver befitting a Dirty Harry cosplay.

Hal had snickered at the sight of the revolver. "Lordy, Dusty, we're not planning to rob the O.K. Corral."

Dusty shrugged, dim eyes barely rising at the gest. "Grandpa's old pistol. He taught me to shoot with it, but I never liked it. Kickbacks too strong."

Blake had offered to take that one but Bobbi had insisted she do it, her reasoning being that as the second best shot of the lot she should hold the pistol with the least room for error. It was tenuous logic but Blake had to admit he didn't mind holding the pistol that held fifteen bullets as opposed to six.

The final weapons removed from Dusty's trunk were axes, bright red and "borrowed" from the poorly locked Hope Fire Department. They gleamed sharply in the pale morning light. Blake hefted one in interest, surprised by how light the cold metal was. Giving it a few test swings, he imagined the satisfaction sinking one of these into whoever had kidnapped his sister would bring.

"You know, Dusty," said Hal as he shoved the pistol into his belt pocket. "We could always use more help with this—we're not exactly the special forces."

Dusty didn't reply, only slammed the trunk to his car and slunk around to the front seat.

"I mean, you're the one who swore an oath."

"Piss off, Hal," said Dusty as his head disappeared into his car. The old automobile's engine spluttered to life. It started to reverse but stopped, kicking up dust as the window unwound. "For what it's worth, I'm sorry."

"Sorry doesn't help much, Dusty," said Bobbi.

The nervous man dipped his head, shame filling his face. "Well, I tried to warn you."

Hal grinned. "That you did, Dusty. Catch you on the flip side."

Dusty flashed a peace sign before speeding off down the mountain, leaving them alone with the trees and wind.

"Well," said Hal. "I guess it's up to us."

Bobbi let out a nervous laugh. "Hope's heroes."

"Just like Rambo," Hal replied.

The incline leading up to the actual mines was far too steep for the car, forcing them to hike it in the morning heat. Blake had worried the old man, who insisted on joining them, would slow them down but he pushed forward with more vigor than any of them, his stringy legs outpacing them upwards through the towering trees and boulders.

The mine had been abandoned in the mid eighties, the search for gold proving fruitless despite an initially promising evaluation of the mountain. The owners, already deep in debt from a previous costly investment in a casino, had opted to simply abandon the project and flee to Mexico. The mine and surrounding area were consumed in a legal battle between thirty different companies and investors, suspending it indefinitely in a legal limbo unresolved to this day.

For a few years after, the mine itself became a spot for adventure hiking and bush parties, but as time passed the path inward became harder to traverse and interest faded. Occasionally the odd hiker would visit, happy to prowl through the quarries and even climb some of the skeletal structures, but most would leave quickly, finding little but rust and dirt to keep their trouble.

Blake saw the tower first, a four-story obelisk of twisting red metal. A few of its walls had fallen off leaving large sections exposed to the glare of the sun. From the very tip, a thin conveyor belt sprouted, descending away from the building at a steep incline.

As they got closer, the road ended, their path blocked by thickets of trees and blackberry bushes. They found a small trail off to the side, threading its way through the bush. It was blocked by a large spray-painted sign.

KEEP OUT

Hal pulled it away with a groan, tossing it into the nearby woods where it sent a magpie cawing into the air. "This is inviting."

Blake lost sight of the metal tower as they thread their way through the tree line. Struggling through roots and blackberries, they made their way to the edge of the quarry. Through the thick bark of two Elms, Blake surveyed it all for the first time.

The building was larger than he'd though, pillars of metal thrusting into the sky like the bones of a colossal animal. A temple to rust and decay, Blake felt both drawn and repelled by the looming sight.

The quarry was mostly filled with grey rock, slate and boulders riddling ground, pockmarked by the occasional hole. The largest of these holes was beside the tower, the conveyer belt hanging from the building disappearing into its black mouth.

Dr. Nand panted as he unslung the rifle from his back, peering through its scope. "I don't see anything," he whispered.

Hal sat down and unscrewed the cap to his water bottle. "Well," he panted, "it's not like it would be sitting out in the open."

Bobbi sat beside Hal and pulled out her own water bottle. "Do you think it's in the building or the actual mines?"

Dr. Nand bit his lip as he hovered the rifle over the tower shooting up into the sky. "Well..." He steadied the scope on one of the exposed walls. "Wait, I think I see movement in the tower."

Blake sucked his breath in, raising his own pair of binoculars. At first, he couldn't see a thing, but soon his eyes caught a flicker near the third floor. A shadow was moving over the wall, bouncing up and down before disappearing.

Dr. Nand lowered the rifle, letting out a breath of annoyance. "Either way, we'll have to get a little closer if I plan on hitting it with this thing." The rifle hung lamely in his hands, its antagonizing metal at odds with his friendly countenance.

The old man snatched Blake's binoculars, his glasses clacking as they pressed against the lenses. "Oh yes, I must have been right. Perfect spot for it to live."

Hal groaned, tossing his bottle to Blake so he could have a drink. "Why did we bring him?"

Bobbi rose and gently pried the binoculars from the man. "He knows what we're dealing with…" Her voice dipped in volume before continuing. "Besides, he's lost family too."

It was past noon when they walked into the quarry. Dr. Nand and the old man set up camp between two massive boulders. The larger man laying prone with the rifle stretched out before him while the old scientist sat down to chatter beside him.

Grey rocks crunched beneath Hal's boots as he shifted his weight, busy checking his own pistol. "Where'd you learn to shoot, Dr. Nand?"

Dr. Nand didn't look up from his scope as he spoke. "I used to hunt with my father."

Hal nodded, continuing lowly. "You know, everyone thinks I'm a good hunter, because I'm a park ranger."

"Yes?"

Hal looked about guiltily. "I'm not. It kills me."

"Oh," said Dr. Nand flatly. "And… uh…. where did you lot learn to shoot?"

Bobbi and Hal locked eyes before laughter burst from their lips, each quickly raising hands to their mouths to stifle the mirth echoing off the surrounding stone. Hal wiped his brow while a smirking Bobbi answered Dr. Nand's puzzled look. "Sorry, Doc, sometimes we forget you weren't born here." She waved her arms around emphatically. "Everyone in Hope knows how to shoot."

Hal grinned as he patted his pistol. "Miss hippy over there, used to love hunting as a kid."

Laura rolled her eyes. "I didn't know better then, Harold."

"I once saw her peg a deer from a near mile, honest to—"

"Harold."

Blake tightened the straps of his backpack, making sure the fire ax remained in place as his weight shifted in the process. "We ready?" He asked.

The boy's voice had a sobering effect on the group, even the old man stopped his rambling to look up in pondering silence. Dr. Nand nodded, his eyes fixing on the skeletal remains of the mines. "Lure it out and I'll put a bullet in one of its eyes."

Hal and Bobbi nodded in agreement. Blake rose, face grim as he turned to the faded remains of the mining outpost. "I guess we should start with the tower." He looked about, prepared to hear a contrary suggestion but finding only silence in reply.

Swallowing, he took a step forward, praying his sister was still alive.

Ken

If anyone had survived the creature's assault of the police department, Ken didn't see them. Bodies covered the drab carpet with their blood, making his march out a sticky affair.

He caught a bad bite from one of the things hiding behind the entrance desk, barely managing to put a bullet in the creature before it ripped out most of his calf. A few of the creatures lying around him stirred at the noise, but were evidently too wounded or too full to do more than look at him with salivating mouths.

As he limped into the parking lot he became acutely aware of the vibrating of his phone, he didn't need to check the screen to know it was the head office. They were likely pondering the total lack of communication coming from the station.

Ken laughed as he smashed the phone on the hard concrete below him. He'd contact them when he had something worth showing.

One of his agents, well half of one, had fallen onto his windshield. He pulled the man's torso from the squad car with a grunt, leaving the mutilated corpse splayed over a handicap parking mural.

The drive to the mines was a strange one. He used his GPS which seemed to work well enough, but there were odd lapses in time. He didn't remember pulling over and sleeping but he also couldn't account for the sudden changes from dark to light. He'd left the police department near midnight but found himself at the mouth of the mine in the early morning.

He got out of his car in surprise, staring up at the rising sun with incredulity before he blinked again and found himself lying on the gravel road. The sun was harsher now, he could feel his skin burning despite it only being early morning. He blinked a third time and found himself lying in the back of his car.

Fortunately, he'd left the door open, not being locked in like the drunks he preyed on during the week, but he still found the sudden teleportation disconcerting.

Rising unsteadily, he checked his watch. The numbers spun in his vision, only settling into recognizable orders after a minute of heavy concentration.

"What?"

He shook his head and pulled a bottle of amphetamines from his pocket. He hadn't brought water, but it didn't matter, he barely registered their chalky texture on his throat as he swallowed them.

Smiling, he pulled himself from the car. Trees blocked his path forward, but he spotted a small path. He tried to walk to it but fell almost immediately. Rising, he steadied himself on his squad car, wondering if the blood on its hood had come from the conflict at the police department or his drive to the mines.

He shut his eyes, reining his brain in from the realm of fantasy as he did. When he looked up again a modicum of sobriety had returned to him. Scanning the path before him, his eyes stuck onto a tall metal building. It jutted out above the trees blocking his way, like a giant beacon guiding him.

He was distantly aware he'd seen a path earlier but didn't bother looking for it. Instead, he pushed forward into the thicket, fighting his way through blackberry vines and tree arms on a direct path to the building before him.

Vines and twigs bit at him as he went, tearing his clothing and inducing a trail of blood that followed him into the woods. Twice he stumbled and found himself with his head pushed into the dirt below him, but he rose each time, continuing his mad crawl towards the mine.

Interlude
Present Day

Her body quivered in ecstasy from the day, legs furrowing in near uncontrollable spasms while milky tears filled her eyes. Her love had vanquished their foes and returned with a wonderful tribute. How joyously she found herself playing with her new pet, dancing its little body about her doll house where it now presided as an honoured guest.

It was a precious thing, tiny mind easily accepting the love of her and her mate. What few thoughts she mustered for her family were disjointed, doing little to inhibit the games they played.

She started by making the little girl perform a dance recital, ending it with thunderous applause from the other dolls. After they played house. She put the little girl in the care of the mommy and daddy who loved her very much. It was good fun.

Her love had gone into the mines, reminding her not to get too lost in her play before their guests came. She had assured him she wouldn't, letting him kiss her forehead before he plunged into the dark tunnels below.

She was aware the guests were arriving, but took little concern—she still had a few more minutes to play with her dolls. She'd even managed to make the mommy and daddy hold the little girl, their pale arms embracing her in a floating hug brought on by the careful tugging of a great many strings.

Hal

They stared up at the tower. From directly beneath it, its metal body seemed to spiral endlessly into the sky. The quarry was silent save for the odd gust of wind which scraped the metal walls to send shivers down Hal's spine.

To the right of the building was an entrance to the actual mine, the massive conveyor belt disappearing into the ground like a burrowing snake. Hal had looked into the hole with some interest as they approached, craning his neck outward while gripping his pistol tightly. Even with the noontime light his eyes could only follow the conveyor belt a few meters down before it was engulfed by darkness.

Even during such a tense moment, his temptation to spit into the hole was strong.

Bobbi nodded towards the tower door. The top was bent inward, metal crushing down onto itself until it poked out the other side. Somehow, it was still attached to its hinges. Blake opened it with a hoarse screech that echoed through the building.

Hal expected the sound to send birds flying but to his cold discomfort none erupted from the building.

Both he and Bobbi had hand free torches strapped to their chests while Blake had to settle for a clunkier, but brighter, hand held flashlight. With tense fingers they turned on their lights, walking into the building as quietly as possible.

Inside the air was rusty. The sour taste of copper and aluminum permeated his lungs, yet far less dust coated the metal interior than he'd expected. While not exactly spotless, it had a certain wild cleanliness to it, as if the passing wind had tided as much as it tarnished. Hal's discomfort grew as they progressed forward and found the place felt… lived in.

They found themselves in what must once have been a center for processing. Pillars of defunct machinery sat around them, most of it collapsed and twisted. The light from their torches made wild shapes on the walls, bent demons and crooked serpents given life from the shadows.

Hal flinched as Bobbi's torch fell upon a pair of crimson chains dangling from above, his mind initially mistaking them for spider legs.

Blake held up a hand and they stopped. With a tilted head he craned his ears towards the ceiling. Hal stood silently, trying to catch the notes the boy had evidently heard.

His ears were likely far worse than the boy's, damaged by a lifetime affair with rock music and bars, but he still caught the noise: little giggles, rustling down on them from somewhere far above.

What little colour remained fled from Blake's face, blood and emotion draining from his features at the sound. Hal tried to give him a reassuring nod, flinching as the wind made the dangling chains rattle.

They threaded their way through the machinery, making as little noise as they could, stepping upon long rotted boards and shifting metal. Eventually the came to the staircase in the center of the room. They scaled it nervously, streams of rust fluttering downwards with each step on its creaking stairs.

The second floor was filled with troughs and large metal containers, a long defunct center for sorting and purifying ores. The scent of rust was strongest here, nearly every inch of the room painted dark orange by decaying metal.

The giggling was stronger here, unmistakably a child's laugher. Hal grimaced at the thought of what might be causing it.

Bobbi winced at the sound while Blake sped his pace, feet rattling on the metal staircase as he sprinted upwards. Hal sighed and followed, he doubted their stealthy approach had gone unnoticed, but it had made him feel slightly better knowing they'd tried.

The staircase twisted, giving way to a flat stretch before rising upwards to the third floor. It was here they heard the other voice.

"Oh, Christ, oh, God! HELP!"

All three stopped. Hal looked at Bobbi's perspiring face and mouthed: "Glen?" Her eyes widened as she turned to a nearby window. Moving to it she stuck her head outwards, careful not to scrape her neck on the tiny portion of glass still clinging desperately to the frame.

Again, the voice screamed from below, "FUCKING, CHRIST SOMEONE HELP, I HEAR IT COMING!"

Pulling her head back inside, she met Hal's gaze, worry on her face. "Hole," she whispered, the words barely reaching Hal's ears.

Blake fidgeted on the spot, his body tensing towards the third floor while his eyes scraped aggravatedly upon Bobbi and Hal.

Hal took a deep breath and pointed to his chest, motioning downwards slowly. Bobbi shook her head, a worried frown playing across her features. Hal winked in response, a lifetime of bickering condensed into a single eyelid flutter.

He backed away slowly, peeking over his shoulder on his descent to make sure his cousin didn't leave the boy to come follow him. From above, a child's shriek came, followed by some lighter giggles. He strained his ears to catch more, making out only the word 'higher,' before losing the voice.

As he exited the building Glen's voice cried again, clearer now that Hal was in the open air. "FUCK, HELP!" The wailing that followed set Hal's teeth on edge.

He looked down into the hole with his pistol raised, again finding little but darkness. He could still hear Glen's terrified cries, but they grew distant with each passing moment, fading into mere echoes from within the mine.

Hal closed his eyes, willing his body to follow the brave steps he'd proposed in his mind. With shaky legs he stepped onto the conveyor belt, crying sharply as it shifted under his weight. Panting, he took an unsteady step down, one arm gripping the belt's edge while the other raised his pistol.

Glen's last plead drifted like a whisper through the tunnels below Hal. "Please come. Please."

Taking a deep breath, Hal let go of his grip and plunged into the darkness, his body sliding quickly down the rough belt as the light of day disappeared above him.

Ken

When he finally extracted himself from the thick mess of trees into the dull grey quarry, it was with a dazed wonder. Like some ancient pilgrim he had braved the elements and broke through the barrier to a mystical new world. The urge to pray overtook him—not to Gods of any sort, but to his own strength.

Who alone could have done what he'd done? None of his fellow agents would have dared defy the will of their masters, braving punishment of death to complete a mission. As he lurched forward, it was with a reverence to his own strength of will. He would kill this thing and bring its corpse to his agency, and if they were displeased with his actions he would die knowing they were unworthy of his talents.

The last of his amphetamines slid happily down his throat, stirring a small fire in his otherwise numb body. The elation they brought him was instant, a primal power flowing through him as if he'd been possessed by a mad god.

Roaring in challenge he rushed forward into the quarry, eager for the glorious, near mythic, battle awaiting him.

Dr. Nand

The old man kept rambling, but Dr. Nand had tuned him out. While his explanations of the scientific phenomena that had led to the creation of a giant, telepathic, zombie creating spider were fascinating, they were quite distracting to the doctor's goal of killing said spider. Taking on the same meditative air he used in medical emergencies, he channeled out all stimuli save for what was present in his scope.

Blake and Bobbi were on the third floor. He could see them easily as all but a single column of walls on their floor had fallen away. They were proceeding cautiously, guns extended and eyes alert. Hal had left them, descending into the massive hole in the quarry with a bravery that made Dr. Nand both surprised and angry.

They'd agreed the group would stay together, only going so far as to check the tower for the creature and try to draw it out. This break of plans left a sour taste in Dr. Nand's mouth, increasing the perspiration already drenching the collar of his shirt.

Initially, he thought the roar was emanating from the mines, the animal like scream bouncing about the quarry as he frantically tried to focus his scope on its source. Only the heavy sound of feet pounding on gravel alerted him the cry came from behind him, his large frame twisting in surprise to find the approaching figure.

His first thought was of one of the creatures that'd attacked the police department. It was running towards him in the same lurching fashion as the beasts. It wasn't until he came within ten meters that he could spot the spark of human intelligence the creatures lacked.

The old man whimpered beside him. "Officer Dawson?"

The man stopped his charge abruptly, wild eyes bearing down on Dr. Nand as he panted heavily in his place. His clothing was shredded with blood leaking profusely from his exposed flesh. "You," he growled.

Dr. Nand heard dirt scraping as the elderly man pushed himself away from Ken. "Yes… me."

Dawson let out another bellow, his hoarse voice ringing through the quarry and making Dr. Nand tremble. "I should have known I'd find you here," Dawson continued, taking a heavy step towards them. His mouth sprayed blood and spit as he screamed at them. "YOU were hiding IT!" he said, thrusting a finger towards the elderly man scrambling away from him.

"No, no, no. I wasn't," whimpered the old man. "I just wanted my son to be safe. So long missing, no body, must be with it. He has to be with it."

Dr. Nand raised his rifle tentatively, noting the pistol gripped in Dawson's bloody hand. The man's wild eyes flickered over to the doctor, a smile curving on his lips. "A fellow hunter." He waved his arms to the sky, blood and dirt flicking from him with the motion. "This is what we are."

Dr. Nand didn't understand his meaning but he did note the man's incredibly dilated pupils, his eyes appearing like black saucers encased in the tiniest ring of pale ice. He spoke to the shaking man in as gentle a tone as he could muster. "Are you feeling alright, Officer Dawson?"

Dawson laughed harshly. "I'm feeling excellent, doctor. Excellent." His lips curled into a sneer as his gaze shifted to the old man, drugged eyes drilling into the squirming scientist's ever retreating body. "I'm finally what I need to be."

"I see," said Dr. Nand tentatively. "And what might that be?"

Dawson frowned for a second, eyes closing slightly as he swayed on the spot. "Not like you," he murmured.

"Not like me?"

Dawson's crazed smile returned, gun waving wildly in his hands as his eyes snapped open. "Not like any of you. I'm going to be better. A true hunter." He stopped, struggling to point his gun at them. "Strong."

The pistol crack was deafening, echoing off the rocky confines of the quarry and out over the surrounding mountains. The bullet landed at Dr. Nand's feet sending shards of rock flying, their sharp particles cutting his face as they whizzed past.

The second bullet narrowly missed his ear, crashing into one of the boulder's Dr. Nand was scrunched between. He sat up but saw no way of rising to a standing position in time to escape the onslaught. A third bullet sped past him, embedding itself into the old man with a fleshy pop.

Dr. Nand leveled his rifle on Dawson and pulled the trigger. It was awkward in his sitting position, but he still managed to send a shard of the man's shoulder flying. Dawson roared in pain and fired again, this time landing a shot in Dr. Nand's meaty stomach.

The pain was instant. Lurching forward he dropped his rifle, its wood frame erupting a cloud of dust as it landed in the gravel. He let out a cry of agony, only stopping when blood filled his mouth and muted his scream. Behind him the old man let out a howl.

Dawson lowered his pistol and approached them in a near saunter, crazed eyes staring down at them with delight. "I'm better than all of you. You're weak, weak." He passed by Dr. Nand's huddled body to the elderly man, a loud cry of pain elicited from his mouth as Dawson's foot crunched down on his shoulder.

"Weak." He raised his boot and stomped it again. "Weak. Weak. Weak." A loud crack came as his boot connected with the old man's arm.

Dr. Nand clutched his open stomach, blood seeping over his fingers to paint the rocks red beneath him. He tried to tell Dawson to stop, a splutter of blood escaping his mouth instead of words.

Dawson bent over the now limp body of the old man, his forehead pressing against a caved in skull. "I should have done this yesterday." He let out a giggle. "I'm strong, I should have done whatever I wanted."

When the old man spoke, his words garbled by a jaw twisting in the wrong direction. "Su—" Tears blotted his eyes as his body twisted away from Dawson's frame. "Su—"

Dawson sat on the man's chest, his fingers digging into a hole in the man's leg where the bullet had entered. "All for your son, pathetic."

The old man cried under the pressure, tears intensifying on his face, as he tried to look away from Dawson, his unbroken arm grasping at something in the tree line.

"Weak. Families are weak, you are weak, your son was weak. The spider ate him and I'm going to eat the spider." He rose from the old man, flicking his head back to Dr. Nand who watched with gritted teeth. "You're all weak."

Dr. Nand closed his eyes as Dawson's foot descended onto the old man's throat, more from pain than revulsion at the sight. There was so much pain, his insides aflame as every contraction of his stomach muscles brought fresh tears to his eyes.

He heard Dawson walk towards him, his heavy boots crunching rocks in unsteady steps. The first kick nearly erased Dr. Nand's conscious, sending black spirals through a mind otherwise preoccupied with pain.

He opened his eyes to Dawson standing above him, so covered in blood he appeared more a demon than man. "You know," he kicked Dr. Nand again, this time aiming for the exposed flesh of his stomach. "I killed a lot of your kind."

Dr. Nand cried out as the foot connected, screaming pain blotting out what little of his rational mind remained.

"I enjoyed it too. They were weak, I was weeding them from our species." He bent forward and continued, whispering into the Doctor's ear. "My only regret is it took me so long to realize I am stronger than everyone, not just towel heads like you."

Dr. Nand was incapable of understanding Dawson's words, the pain leaving him able to do nothing but sob weakly. Another blow landed on his head, this one coming as a relief. The pain in his stomach numbed slightly, a welcome dark filling his vision.

"You're all weak. All of you. We should be like the thing in there, strong, doing whatever we want because—"

Dr. Nand's vision was gone, engulfed by the beckoning darkness, the pain still remained but it weakened with each passing second. He could still hear Dawson's voice, but it was less captivating than the image of his wife and son now floating through his mind.

"What? Another one? You know how many of you I've killed?"

Dawson's laughter was replaced the sweet voice of Sophia. "You always do what's right, I love you for it," she cooed.

He was holding her, Dawson's voice rippling through his mind in only the most distant echoes. "I'll kill you, then I'll kill your whore moth—" A sharp cry rebounded in Dr. Nand's mind but he paid it no mind. The pain was gone now, replaced by the warm embrace of his wife. He held her as the world faded, descending into the thick blackness with her words again repeating in his mind.

"You always do what's right, I love you for it," she said as he faded from life.

Interlude
Present Day

He'd been her first child, a test of her blooming power. At first, he'd been afraid of her, the legged creature hiding in the basement, but when she bit him that had changed. How silly he'd been, thinking she didn't love him.

When he awoke the world was different. Before it had been confusing, filled with rules to follow and things to do he didn't wholly understand, now it was simple. All that mattered was eating and pleasing mother.

So, he did what she told him to, because he loved her, leaving his silly wooden house and silly wooden life to go into the forest like mother wanted him to. He went long and far, eating when he was hungry and thinking of mother when he was not.

Years passed like this, his little body growing strong on the diet of wild deer and mother's love. He loved her so much and obeyed her, his wild mind doing its best to understand her commands. Yet, sometimes, when mother was in town or he accidentally wandered too far into the mountains, his little brain thought of things other than mother and food.

It tried to grasp at memories from before his change, thoughts of a mommy and daddy who were far different than his current ward. He even remembered a brother, though these thoughts made him shake for a reason he couldn't understand.

They were curious, these thoughts pertaining to things that weren't mother, but he could never fully grasp them, each one twisting away from his unstable mind when he tried to squeeze them for meaning.

Still, in his own way, he was sure he'd been loved like mother loved him but by someone who wasn't mother. He wanted to ask mother about these thoughts but lacked the language, capable now of only making the smallest gurgle of speech.

So far gone was his communicative abilities that even mother, connected to his mind at a level so deep she could command him from nearly a thousand miles away, failed to notice this strange hunger for answers.

Years passed and the questions clung in the back of his corroded brain, rarely raised save for in his deepest moments of solitude.

When mother had called him home he'd complied, racing to their home with blood of his last kill still dripping from his lips and onto his naked body. His only occupation had been pleasing mother. That was, until he saw them.

Food, standing in their home. It surprised him—mother rarely let food get so close to home, preferring to catch it in webs or have him hunt it long before it set foot in the quarry, and yet here they were.

He crept forward slowly, a lifetime of practice helping hide his approach.

The large man held his attention first, a big juicy belly that made his own stomach rumble. Saliva rolled down his split lips at the thought of sinking his teeth into the big, brown flesh.

The other two seemed inconsequential in comparison, one too old to be tasty and the other too lean.

The gunshots scared him. Initially making him jump and retreat into the tree line before his muddled mind pressed him forward with a reminder mother had beckoned him home.

When he returned to the group, the big man's stomach was leaking. The flow of saliva in his mouth increased at the sight, teeth gnashing at the thought of drinking him whole. He crawled on all fours towards them, pace quickening with thoughts of tasty, tasty food.

When he was mere meters away he licked his lips in preparation of feast. He lowered his body to the ground and prepared to spring on the trio, using a pouncing method mother had taught him a decade earlier. His hunger and excitement building at the prospect, soon he would be crunching on human flesh. It would be sweet and tender, not like the filthy caribou he regularly ate.

The prospect of dining on the three men brought him to near ecstasy, yet he found himself incapable of launching, his mangled limbs refusing to jettison him towards his feast. Somewhere in his brain, protest screamed. His grey matter too corroded for the reasoning to be immediately apparent.

It had something to do with the old one, the one who was currently being bludgeoned by the lean one. His brain tickled, fuzzy thoughts overpowering mother's love.

No, he was being silly. Mother told him to eat, so he should eat. He pushed off, again ready to devour the three men, yet found himself only moving a few inches.

The man, the old one who was leaking blood like the big one, had reached a hand towards him, eyes pleading as blood trickled over them. Why did he look so familiar? Food shouldn't be familiar, food should be food.

He shook his head, no longer attempting to launch himself at the men but acquiescing to his brain's strange desires to crawl forward. His interest remained fixated on the old one, by now his features were mangled by the stomping of a boot yet he was still recognizable to him. How? How did he know this food?

By now the lean one had left the old one and turned to the big one, kicking viciously between two boulders.

He crawled further forward, the old one was seizing on the ground, eyes spinning in his head while a white foam filled his mouth. And yet, his hand was still outstretched. Reaching towards…

"What? Another one? You know how many of you I've killed?"

The old man twitched violently one last time and then lay still. His motionless features were easier to examine, his bloodied visage causing a violent uproar in parts of his brain that'd been dormant for the last two decades.

The hunger left him, replaced by something he was unused to. Anger, rage? He didn't have the words to describe it because mother had never taught him, still he felt it.

The burning in his stomach at the sight of this dead… food.

No. Not food.

Father?

Memories scratched his conscious, harder than they had anytime before, trying to break through and illuminate his understanding. He had mother—he loved mother—who did he love more than mother. Mother wouldn't like that, mother would be angry.

Yes, angry. This was the word he'd forgotten. He felt it now. Not hunger or love but anger.

He turned to the one who had killed father. Why did he kill father? He loved father. He didn't know why but he was sure he loved father, and now father was dead. He bared his teeth at the man, limbs twitching again in anticipation of assault.

"I'll kill you and then I'll kill your whore moth—"

He sprung, this time his limbs complying to his demand. Body hurtling forward, he crashed into the man who had killed father, limbs twisting around him in a bone cracking hug as his teeth sunk into the fleshy part of his neck.

He killed father. Why did he kill father?

He tore out a strip of flesh, spitting it away in rage rather than swallowing it as was his normal custom.

Why did he kill father? Why did mother let him kill father? Mother loved him, why did mother let him hurt like this?

He let out a wail, his screeching cry articulating what he was unable to say through speech, as he sunk his teeth into the man, oblivious to the bullets tearing at his own flesh.

He fell backwards, a chunk of the lean man's neck still in his mouth, its sweet blood dripping down his throat. His brain, never truly coherent, had trouble explaining why. He'd bit the man. Normally when he bit a man he kept biting until he was full and mother said he'd done a good job. Still, here he was on the ground, sky turning black despite the sun still being up.

Why did he hurt? Daddy was dead and he hurt. He crawled away from the man as he struggled to stem the spray of blood from his neck. Another crack sparked from the gun in his hand—it was terrifying.

He turned from the Daddy Killer and ran, his shambling stride taking him towards mother.

Why did he hurt? He wanted to be safe, he didn't want to hurt. But he had to hurt—Daddy was dead—it hurt.

He fell, rather than jumped, into the mine shaft. Darkness washing comfortably over him as he sank into the pit. He was safe here. He hurt but he was safe. He would stay here until it was safe and he didn't hurt anymore. He would wait here until Mommy made it better.

Mommy always made things better.

Blake

The gunshots made him freeze, his whole body tense mid step on the rusted metal staircase while his eyes shot towards Bobbi's. She was similarly posed, lips drawn in pale surprise while her hand stood outreached towards the ladder hanging down above her.

Blake took a deep breath. "What was that?"

"Maybe it's outside?"

The two were standing below the narrow portal leading to the final floor, the metal bars of a rusted ladder hanging a few feet above them. The floor they were on was drafty, walls crumbling away years before Blake had been born. They were standing under a ladder near the center of the room.

"Should we check?"

Bobbi shrugged, her hand still reaching tentatively towards the first rusted bar. "Do you want to?"

Blake looked at the dark hole that the ladder before them disappeared into, it was less than inviting in comparison to the fresh sunlight below them. He shook his head. "No, we heard Sarah."

Bobbi winced but nodded in agreement. "We heard someone, at least." With a small grunt she pulled herself upward, Blake following her with the muzzle of his gun.

Their reasoning had been that Bobbi, being older and freer of dependents than Blake, had the least to live for and should climb into the final floor first. As her upward struggle brought a heavy stream of dust down on him, Blake wondered if it had really mattered who went in first. The thing undoubtedly knew they were coming regardless—who went in first would hardly matter if it was waiting for them.

Still, adults liked their rules and he wasn't going to complain if he had a small chance at saving Sarah.

As Bobbi's feet disappeared into the blackness, Blake jumped up and grabbed for the ladder, fingers scrapping across its rusted surface as his legs flailed beneath him. With a heavier grunt than Bobbi, and a larger amount of sweat, he pulled himself up until his feet stood on mostly solid metal.

At first, he tried to climb with the pistol raised but found the ordeal too awkward, leaving him more likely to fall and snap his neck than stop any would be attacker. With gritted teeth he pushed the dark metal into his belt loop and started climbing with two hands.

He could make out Bobbi's frame above him, her long limbs fluidly drawing her up the ladder, as of yet still free of entanglements in webs of any kind. The sight of her made him wonder if Hal, so full of booze and cigarettes, would have been able to pull himself up at all. Lord knew he would have been much noisier.

Blake cursed inwardly at the thought. Even if the man was a little out of shape he should have still been here. Christ, why had they split up? Everyone knew not to split up during something like this yet the first thing the adults did when presented the chance was split up. It was a miracle anything got done in the world.

Bobbi heaved herself through the hole, body disappearing save for one heel extended out over the gap. Blake continued upwards, pulling himself through the portal to join her on musty wood floor.

The room was pitch black, the walls here far more intact than in any other portion of the building. Trying to still his breathing, he pulled his pistol from his belt, holding it tightly in preparation of the slightest sign of movement.

Sarah hadn't made a sound since the gunfire had roared in the quarry, the only noise he could distinguish in the room a soft rustling, like a rope being tightened. He raised his flashlight, preparing to click it on, but Bobbi put up a hand.

"Wait a second," she whispered sharply.

He paused, poised in anticipation. His eyes adjusted slightly the darkness but not enough to make out more than the general lay of the room. It was more open than the other floors, the roof arching higher with less machinery marking the floor. If he had to guess this must have been a simple storage place, ore was sent up here from the mine where it sat until it was ready to begin its arduous journey of purification and shipping.

Above them, something rustled. It reminded him of the willows brushing against each other outside his bedroom window. He craned his neck to search for the source but found only more darkness.

A giggle cracked the dry silence. Blake snapped his head in the direction of its source, his eyes still struggling to penetrate the thick black. "Sarah? Are you there?" Beside him Bobbi recoiled, her head darting about in fear of what might be brought down by his voice.

Blake continued, voice growing stronger with each word. "Sarah, I'm here for you. It's me." His words seemed to die as quickly as they came out, suffocated by the too-quiet air of the room. "I'm sorry I left you, Sarah, I'll never leave you again…" He choked out the last words, remembering how often his sister had made him say them. "I promise."

For a minute, silence filled the room. He crouched with his breath inhaled while Bobbi spun slow circles with an outstretched gun clamped tightly in her hands. When Sarah's light voice called out it made Blake's heart burn and blood chill.

"Blakey? I missed you, Blakey."

"Sarah?" Blake called, voice filling the room as he ignored Bobbi's worried looks. "Honey, where are you? I'm here for you."

His sister's words were slow, as if emanating from a record played at half speed. "Blakey, it's so nice here. I'm playing with Mother." Her stoned speech raised a little in her final sentence, a hint of confusion seeping in. "She even brought Mommy to play with."

Blake swallowed. Bobbi was still spiraling beside him, the gun quivering in her hands. "Mommy?" he croaked.

Another happy giggle floated down, the girlish crescendo that had been one of the best parts of the last six years of his life. "Yes, silly, Mommy didn't leave us. She was just here with Mother."

Blake's breathing was heavy, his heart speeding too fast in his chest. "Where are you, Sarah? Where's Mommy." His words caught in his throat, fighting their ejection from his body so they came out in a hoarse whisper. "Where's Mother?"

A tiny trickle of sweat dripped from the handle of Bobbi's gun, each droplet drank greedily by the thirsty wood boards below. Sarah's voice grew elated, speeding slightly but retaining its dazed edge. "You're silly, Blakey. They're here, can't you see them?"

Blake's pulse beat frenziedly, his breathing out of control while horror constrained his voice to a mere whisper. "Where are they, Sarah?"

"Oh, Blakey, you're silly. Mother says you should play with Mommy more, she says you were a bad son. She says... she says you should play together more, Blakey."

There was a crack, like a rope snapping, seconds before a heavy weight struck him. Bobbi screamed but Blake was unable, his breath knocked from his body as he slammed into the wood floorboards under whatever had been dropped. His stomach twisted, the smell was horrible.

"Jesus Christ. Jesus Christ. Fuck." He closed his mouth and gave a hoarse scream and tried to squirm out from beneath the stinking mass.

He shifted it uncomfortably, crying in horror as his fingers sunk into the flesh of whatever it was. With a squeal he shoved it from his body, letting it land flatly beside him while he panted dusty air. He turned and squinted at what had been dropped, his eyes adjusting painfully slow to the darkness.

Beside him Bobbi stifled a gasp, "Blake, don't…"

But she was too late. Blake found himself staring at the face of his mother's corpse. Her mouth hung open, a cracked tongue poking out from it. Her eyes were open, one looked dully outwards while the other had rolled into the back of her skull.

"Jesus Christ, Jesus Christ." Blake pushed himself away from the corpse, trying to claw himself towards the nearby ladder. "Oh fuck. Oh fuck."

Sarah giggled again, the soft tinkle of her laugh forcing Blake's eyes shut. "Oh, Blakey, you're silly. Mother said she likes you. She likes Mommy too, she says we're family."

Bobbi's voice was low and hoarse. "Fuck this," she muttered before a loud click let Blake know the torch pinned to her breast was lit.

Blake forced himself to sit up, his hand searching the dusty floor for the torch he'd dropped. He gave another cry as his fingers brushed his mother's cold skin, but he didn't stop his inspection. When he finally felt the thick rubber handle, he gave a deep breath and clicked it on, pointing it upwards before opening his own eyes.

The pistol dipped in Bobbi's hands as she slowly spiraled to let her light cascade over the plethora of bodies hanging from the rafters above. "There's so many," she said in stunned amazement.

Blake's own torchlight was drawn to a singular source, the tiny body dancing near the center of the room. Her small legs writhing while her arms contorted about her in some made flamenco dance. Even from far above he recognized his sister.

"Sarah?"

She turned to face the light, body swinging softly from side to side from the effort. "Blakey."

God, she was so high up. What could he do? Christ, where was the fucking spider? "I'm going to get you down Sarah." He tripped over the body of his mother as he tried to move, her corpse causing him to crash in a heap as his sister laughed.

"Oh, Blakey, you're so silly. Isn't it nice to see Mommy again?"

Tears burned his eye as he rose. Careful not to trip, he continued forward. "Where's Mother, Sarah? We need to know where Mother is so I can get you down."

"Get me down?" she said in confusion. "Blakey, we're in heaven. We don't come down from heaven." She giggled again. "Below heaven is earth and below that is the H E double hockey sticks."

Bobbi shuffled over, still scanning her light over the ceiling in search of *Mother*. "What the fuck," she mumbled.

Blake nodded to her and raised his own pistol. "Just… hold on, Sarah…."

"Oh, Blakey. Mother says you're rude… Rude Blakey." His sister giggled again. Her little body twisted about, the movement propelling her into a limp corpse dangling beside her. As her laughter slowed, so did her swing. "You didn't even wave hello, Blakey. Look, everyone else is waving hello."

The thin light of their torches illuminated the jerking hands of the bodies above, all spastically waving like poor marionettes as their feet danced on air.

"What the fuck, Blake," said Bobbi in a shaking voice. "What the fuck?"

One of the corpses, a black suited man with round glasses, lowered suddenly. He fell ten feet before stopping with an audible snap of his spine. Bent forward, his legs kicked out awkwardly before pressing into the wood to help him stand—nearly—erect. A hand rose to his head in a limp military salute.

"That's Mr. Terrance," squealed Sarah. "He's marrying Jean Norrish. Remember them, Blake? I get to go to the wedding. Mother says I'll be a flower girl."

From the corner of the room another corpse dropped. It hit the floor with crack before it was pulled upright. She wore a green dress nearly torn in half on the left side. When Blake swept his light over her it caught the glint of bone near her forehead.

"That's Jean. Mother says she loves Mr. Terrance very much."

On cue the woman started to waltz forward, head dipping up and down to an unheard beat as her legs folded and unfolded against the floor. There was a thick slapping sound as the bodies above began to beat their arms together, limp limbs cracking into each other with poor unison.

Sarah joined in the clapping too, forcing Blake to turn his eyes away in revulsion. "I love it here, Blakey. I never want to leave. Mother says Daddy and Sally are coming here too."

Blake fell to his knees, it was too much. Bobbi crouched beside him, her warm hand gripping his shoulder. "Fuck. Come on. Fuck. We're not going out like this." She heaved him to his feet, finishing her tirade by screaming at the ceiling. "We're not going out like this!"

Blake thought of his sister, dangling above them with nothing but rotting bodies and a psychopathic arachnid for company. Choking a sob, he returned his flashlight to the ceiling, sweeping across it in search of the monster who had done this to his family.

A laugh rang out, not from his sister but from Mr. Terrance's corpse. Bobbi swung about and fired. She hit him, his body swaying slightly from the impact. A shard of bone fell, unaccompanied by blood. Blake's ears cried in pain from the pistol crack, the tight enclosure making it near deafening.

For a moment Blake could hear nothing but the ringing in his ears and Bobbi's heavy breathing, even Sarah had stopped speaking. Then it started, lowly at first but building into a thunder shaking the wooden frames of the room. Laughter. Deep, rasping cackles booming from the mouths of the corpses above them.

Bobbi covered her ears, twisting the hand with the revolver so the base of the wooden handle covered the canal. Blake looked about dumbfounded, unsure if the laughter was truly coming from the bodies above him or emanating from some dark recess of his own mind.

The laughter continued to grow, pushing against the walls of the room like a pot of water boiling over. Bobbi scrunched her face in pain as she twisted about, still scanning the room for the creature.

With a shriek, she stopped in place, the beam of light from her torch pinned against a bulbous mass in a high corner of the room.

It was pressed deep into the crook with its legs sitting on a hundred silver strands. Its legs were darting about, tugging and pushing strings at frenzied speed while its furry palps clicked against each other in an insectile delight. Its shiny black eyes flickered to the source of the light, the largest two squinting as they looked downwards at them.

Blake pulled the trigger, the recoil nearly knocking the pistol from his sweat drenched hands. A loud clang echoed as the bullet struck metal, leaving a fresh hole for light to spill in near the spider's abdomen.

The laughter stopped, replaced by a harsh hiss from the creature. Bobbi raised her own pistol and fired too, clipping one of the creature's hairy legs near its pointed base.

Eyes glaring, the spider jumped forward. Blake and Bobbi struggled to keep it under the beam of their torches as it crawled swiftly across the walls of the room. Above them, Sarah started to scream.

"No, why are you hurting Mother? We love Mother, Blakey."

Blake fired again, sending a shower of blood as the bullet sped past the nimble spider and into the hanging corpse of a hiker.

"Stop, Blakey, stop!" wailed Sarah.

The spider jumped from the wall onto a strand of web holding a man's body, legs curled around his pale head as it swung in place. Reaching down with a single leg it cut at a strand invisible to Blake's eyes. The twang of ropes snapping was followed immediately by the sight of the first body falling.

The floor shook as body after body splattered upon old wooden boards. Most of them were too shrouded in darkness to be made out but the sound of their impacts was enough to make Blake's stomach twist. One crashed through the boards, its downward descent letting in more light from the floor below.

Bobbi pressed up against Blake, the back of his head meeting the back of her neck. "There," she said before firing another ear shattering shot.

Blake had stopped following the spider's scuttle, instead his gaze was fixed on the small frame of his sister. Her body still swinging in the air, face reduced to tears.

The sound of lines snapping increased, an angry hiss building as more and more bodies continued to fall.

"We have to catch Sarah," Blake cried.

Bobbi fired again. "What?" she screamed.

"We have to catch my sister," Blake said, shining his flashlight on Sarah.

Bobbi nodded, her body shifting as they started to shuffle closer to the middle of the room. She fired two more shots before they reached the patch of floorboard directly below Sarah's swinging feet.

Blake called up, vaguely aware of the eight eyes angrily pinned to him from across the room. "Sarah, we're here!"

His sister tried to reply, words garbled by sobs as she kicked her feet about in a tiny fury. "…happy here…. Mother… loved….."

"It's ok, Sarah, I'm here for you."

Her voice erupted in a scream, her tiny lungs filling the room in a high pitched wail. "No, Blakey, no! You RUIN EVERYTHING!"

Blake grimaced as he shone the light upwards. "I know, Sarah, but you still need to come down. Can you come down?"

His sister tried to shrink away from the light, sending herself into an awkward spiral with the action. "I'm staying here. I'm happy here."

Beside him Bobbi cursed as her revolver made a soft clicking sound when she pulled the trigger. A few meters away another web snapped as a woman fell to the floor, smashing in a bloody mess. "Blake, you have to cover me," Bobbi said breathlessly, her hands jamming into her jean pocket in search of bullets.

Blake swung, about to catch the spider in the light of his torch. It still hugged the wall but its long legs had scuttled it closer to the ground in the time he'd been looking at his sister. He fired, the noise of his pistol a tiny spat in comparison to Bobbi's booming revolver.

His first bullet connected with the tail end of the creature, sinking into its abdomen with a meaty splat making it hiss in anger. Its eyes dug into him with rage as he fired again, dark pupils narrowing as the second bullet clipped one of its mandibles.

Bad Blakey.

Blake shuddered as he felt the voice inside his skull, his third shot going wide of the mark to pierce another hole in the tin walls.

"Fucking freak," Bobbi screamed, the revolver cylinder snapping into place. Her gun erupted again, this inducing the spider into movement. The creature's eyes giving an almost gleeful look as it jumped away.

Blake trailed it with his torch, taking the odd shot at it as it scuttled about the wall. He missed it twice before he had the satisfaction of sinking another bullet into its massive hide.

I.... ughhh.... Will drink you dry, boy, it whispered in his mind as another corpse fell from the ceiling, barely missing Bobbi as it splattered them with blood.

And then, your sister and I will.... play....

Blake roared and fired again, missing the spider as it ducked downwards, one long leg reaching out from the wall to snap a final line of webbing. Above him Sarah screamed, her shrill voice falling through the air with her body.

Bobbi barely noticed, her head only twitching slightly towards the sound while she kept her pistol trained on the speeding body of the spider, but Blake reacted. He threw his pistol and torch to the floor, spreading his arms and legs as wide as he could to catch her.

Her tiny body hit him like a bag of bricks, sending them both to the floor, which creaked ominously in protest of their weight.

The breath was knocked from him, a thick patch of stars bursting into the peripherals of his vision. Her body was cold but her breath on his face was hot. Even in the daze of the impact, his arms instinctively wrapped around her, pulling her sobbing body to his for a hug.

"Blakey.... Why is everything ruined, Blakey?"

Bobbi called out, words drowned by another crack of her revolver.

Blake held his sister tight as he rose, her head burrowing deeper into his chest. "Blakey, I'm scared. Where did Mommy go? Where's Mother?"

Blake patted his sister's head and started to tell her it would be alright, his words cut off by Bobbi's angry voice. "Blake, grab your fucking gun!"

He blinked. What was he doing? Christ. He knelt and searched for his gun, unable to see it in the dim light of his discarded torch. "Fuck. Fuck." He picked up the flashlight, using it to scan floorboards. He spotted it, merely a few feet away, but the clicking sound of Bobbi's revolver gave him pause.

She looked at him, eyes wide with fear. "Shit."

Blake gulped. "What do we do?"

The spider was perched on the wall in front of them, body inflating and deflating heavily with laboured breath. One of its legs tapped lightly on the metal wall, beating out a clocklike rhythm.

Tap. Tap. Tap.

Blake stepped slowly backwards, the spider's eyes darting to him as the rhythm it was tapping quickened.

Tap-tap. Tap-tap. Tap-tap.

"I'll jump down first, then you drop the girl through. It's only a few meters," Bobbi whispered, revolver still raised towards the creature.

Those few meters had felt rather long when Blake had been climbing the ladder, but it was hard to argue with her plan given their predicament. "Shit. Ok."

The spider's drumming grew to a frenzied pace, the heavy knocks making the entire room shake.

Tap-tap-tap. Tap-tap-tap. Tap-tap-tap.

Bobbi took a shaky breath, body tensing in preparation. "Ok. NOW!"

Her legs were longer than Blake's and she was unencumbered by the body of a child, yet she only made it to the porthole slightly before him, her body disappearing into it in a single fluid movement.

Blake didn't bother to look down before dropping his sister into the hole, her screaming protest going ignored.

He paused for a second, giving Bobbi the slightest moment to catch Sarah if she had even managed to prepare for it, and jumped into the hole himself. For a brief moment he was in freefall, weightless joy overtaking him as he realized he might escape.

His hope crumbled as he felt himself yanked upwards, the harsh jerking motion cracking his neck and making his stomach jump into his throat. Pain screamed in his shoulders as two of the spider's pincer-like feet dug deeper into them.

It raised him close to its face, a hairy mandible reaching out to delicately stroke his cheeks.

Blakey... stays.

She pushed him closer to her face. The proximity allowed him to see the glossiness of her eyes, the two largest peering unblinkingly into his face.

You keep me... company.

Hal

The caves were winding and seemingly endless. Each path he chose only going for a few meters before splitting aggravatingly into two new tunnels, forcing him to constantly decide which one seemed to be leading him closer to Glen's ever softening screams. There was no consistency to the tunnel design either, some halls so wide he could walk upright while others forced him to suck in his gut and squirm through. Most lacked debris but a few were collapsed, leaving him a solitary choice in which direction to continue in.

The farther he went the colder it grew.

"Oh god, the webs. They're everywhere. Christ," echoed Glen's cry.

Hal gritted his teeth and pushed forward. He'd already walked into one of the webs, thankfully stopping quickly enough to leave one arm free to reach for the knife in his pocket. It had been an unpleasant experience.

Edging his way through a particularly thin fissure, Hal grumbled as his boot sunk into ice cold water. The floor here was flooded, rising to the middle of his shins with a chill that passed directly through his jeans and into his bones.

Another wild scream echoed from within the mine. Hal waded forward, sending dark ripples out across the narrow cavern, flinching when a cool water droplet landed on his head from above.

"Glen? Where are you? I'm here." For what felt like the umpteenth time he received no reply, the cavernous silence only interrupted by the odd howl. He waded across the room, thankful when the path rose gently out of the frigid water. "Glen, can you hear me?"

Hal rounded a corner, the rocky walls expanding slightly so he could stand straight as he walked. His torchlight flickered off the dark walls of smooth rock, sometimes arching into strange shapes that gave him pause but mostly it showed him what he expected to see: long, drab, and abandoned tunnels of rock.

"Hal?"

He froze, the voice was dim but clear.

"Hal, is that you? Oh Christ, help me, Hal."

Hal rushed forward, intent to find the source of the voice. "Glen? I'm here! Where are you?"

"Jesus, Hal—this thing—it took me. Oh God. There's other people here, they're… they're hanging and," Hal's foot caught on an abandoned bucket, sending a pile of stone clattering around the dark floor beneath him. He cursed as Glen's voice was drowned out momentarily. "Hal, I don't want to die like this."

"It's going to be alright, Glen. Keep talking, I'm coming."

"Jesus, Hal, what the fuck is going on? The thing that took me… it… it wasn't human."

Hal grimaced. Not human was right. "It's ok, Glen, I'm almost there."

Now Glen's voice was near, ringing from the end of the corridor Hal had found himself sprinting down. "Hurry, Hal, hurry."

The tunnel twisted and Hal burst into a new cavern. It was open and partially flooded, a small trickle of water dripping from a pinprick skylight far above.

"Glen?" He scanned the room, his torch sweeping about and finding nothing. "Jesus Christ, Glen?"

His words echoed hollowly around him, mocking his own ears.

"GLEN," he shouted, anger boiling over his fear. Silence greeted his rage. He took a step forward, water splashing up his back as he did. He'd been so close, he was sure of it. Was he too late? Had he failed his friend? Left him to be food for the revolting creature despite his best efforts?

He waded deeper into the room. The water rose to his waist, numbing everything below his torso.

"Hal?"

He froze, unable to make himself continue through the chilling dark water.

The voice came again. "Hal?" It was quiet and confused, not the harsh shrieks of Glen but a softer, almost forgotten voice.

Hal shivered, still paralyzed by her words. "Laura?" he croaked.

"Is it... Hal?" A dark ripple of water spread out from the corner of the room. Hal inhaled deeply, turning slowly so his light skimmed the water's surface until he found her.

She rose slowly from the pool, the only sound the soft dripping of water from its body, each drop making a tiny plunk as they struck the dark mirror Laura waded through.

Hal swallowed, words catching in his throat. "Is it really you, Laura?" Control was returning to his limbs. He started walking, the harsh waves of his movement colliding with the gentle ripples of her own.

She was barely a meter away, swaying gently in the water, yet her voice barely reached him. "So long since.... Since I saw you."

Hal took another tentative step forward, pistol shaking in his hand. His torch's light spread over her, her frame made dark by sopping clothes and drooping hair.

"I'm here now, Laura. I'm going to take you home," said Hal hoarsely, hand reaching out to her.

Her skin was as pale as the single beam of light trickling into the cave, her lips as dark as the water. Her head tilted as she spoke. "Home?"

Hal shivered, freezing water soaking through his shoes and into his socks. "Yes, home. You're mother's so worried about you. Can barely stay sober... course she always had a little trouble with that." He finished with a hollow laugh, his voice reaching for comfort he didn't feel. "We miss you."

"Mother?" Laura swayed on the spot. Hal was close enough to make out the puzzled expression in her eyes... and the bulge in her stomach. "I'm going to be a mother... make

Mother happy." Her teeth flashed in a drunk smile. "I'm making Mother… happy."

Hal moaned. "No… No…."

Laura's smile widened, the beautiful grin of Hal's memories replaced by knifelike teeth and crazed eyes. "Mother wants children. I make mother happy."

Tears burned Hal's eyes, salty droplets falling heavily into the water. "Christ, Laura. Christ. I'm sorry. I'm so sorry."

Her fingers trailed the water surrounding her dark khakis, the water bottle he'd given her for her birthday still hanging from a loop on her waist. "Sorry?" Now she stood directly in front of him, allowing him to see her eyes, stunning green pupils replaced by a milky cloud. "No…. Happy… Happy for… Mother."

Hal felt as if someone had reached into his chest to strangle his heart. "No," he sobbed. "No. No. No."

From the end of the room another voice shot out, clear and amused. "And what a good Mother she has."

Hal twisted, his light quickly illuminating the speaker where he stood at the edge of the pool.

"Glen?"

Even in the poor light, Hal could make out Glen's wry smile. "Yes, indeed, Hal."

Hal's hand tightened around the pistol, disbelief and anger mixing in his words. "You… You're really helping that… thing?"

Glen gave a light chuckle, the happy laugh Hal had so often heard ringing in the local beer halls. "Oh, Harold, it's not a thing, it's my lover."

"What the fuck, Glen? What the fuck?"

Glen spread out his arms in a theatrical shrug. "What can I say? We keep it pretty quiet. The world's an intolerant place." Hal started to shake as the man went on. "It's hard to build a family when people don't approve of your relationship," Glen licked his lips.

"So you go around murdering with it? Abducting women and…" Hal looked at Laura's round belly, his words tasting acidic as they rose to his throat, "…raping them?"

Glen chuckled again. When he spoke, his voice had lost its friendly charm, dipping in temperature to match the frigid water surrounding Hal. "Surrogates, Hal. And it's not rape." His voice rose, returning to the casual tone Hal was familiar with. "They're more than willing to help my wife and I build a family."

Hal's stomach rebelled as it never had in his long years of drinking, the harsh burn of stomach acid rising to his throat. His whole frame shook in revulsion. "You.. you…." Hal searched for an insult, unable to convey the hatred boiling his blood.

"You what?" mocked Glen. "Come on, use your words, big guy."

The sentence Hal was trying to form twisted into a venom filled scream, culminating with the roaring of his pistol.

Glen lurched forward, arms clenching the hole ripped in his abdomen. "Jesus, Hal," he wheezed. "Why do they even let you people have guns? Can't shoot for shit."

Hal straightened his arm, intent on proving the man wrong. As his finger twitched towards the trigger, a shriek filled his already ringing ears.

"NO!"

Laura tackled him, dragging him into the cool water as her jagged teeth sunk into his neck. The last thing Hal heard before water rushed into his ears was Glen's laughter, icy and contemptuous.

He'd been unprepared for the submersion, instantly gasping for air that wasn't there. Rusty water cascaded down his throat as he struggled to push himself to the surface. Laura's arms wrapped tightly around him, her teeth digging deeper into his flesh. Thankfully, no needles shot out of her body as had happened with the last creature to attack him.

They writhed in the water, dark spots already clouding Hal's vision as he tried to push away Laura's unnaturally strong grip. He'd managed to close his mouth, but he nearly opened it in horror when he felt her belly, pressed against his torso, start to wriggle.

Hal twisted violently. He felt, for the second time in twenty-four hours, a chunk of his neck ripped out. He managed to raise his head above water, gasping a quick breath before Laura dragged him back down. This time her teeth sunk into his chest, scrapping against a rib.

His gun was gone, drowned somewhere in the dark waters and all he had left was his knife. He managed to reach it, numb fingers barely able to grip the handle. Despite the excruciating pain, he paused before pulling it from his belt.

"I'm sorry, Laura," he thought, closing his eyes as the memory of her face pressed against his chest intruded on his mind.

With a feral cry he thrust the knife forward, the blade sliding easily into Laura's soft flesh. Her struggling ceased as her body went limp. He rose weakly from the water, massaging his throat with a pale hand while coughing water from his mouth.

Laura floated backwards, her teeth dislodging from his flesh as she went. "Why.. why…" she gurgled, blood as dark as the water pouring from her mouth.

"Laura, I'm so, so, sor—"

His words were caught off by Laura's shriek, her head twisting back as her stomach thrust towards the ceiling. Her belly was writhing, entire patches of skin shooting out in fleshy spindles before retracting back into the quivering mass. "Oh God. It hurts."

She gave another blubbering cry, this one stopped midway by the mass erupting from her stomach. It flew a meter upwards before falling into the pool, bulbous body quickly sinking beneath the inky surface. Distantly, Hal felt the splatter of gore spray his face.

From his perch Glen called out, joy ringing in his voice. "A child! Finally! A child!"

Hal backed away from Laura's floating body. Her ribs were exposed to the air, and half of her spinal cord poked through her throat. "Oh God," he moaned, fingers still wrapped around his hunting knife.

Glen jumped into the water, lurching quickly to the dark bubbles rising in the center of the room. Without hesitation, he thrust a muscled arm into the water and pulled out his… Hal's mind rebelled against the word, feeling literal pain as it rang out: child.

It squirmed in Glen's hands, thin legs wriggling as it attempted to escape his grip. Glen pulled the black body close to his own, voice reverent as he spoke. "Finally… a child."

Hal shuddered, the reality before him couldn't be real. Too bizarre to be anything but a drunk dream from too much tequila at The Chalice.

Glen held the spider out to Hal. Its legs had stopped squirming as its tiny eyes bore down on Hal with infantile interest. "Hal. You solved it for us. So long I've tried to induce labour, but they kept dying, you see. Fading away before the child popped out." Glen nuzzled the spider's abdomen, angelic blond hair rubbing against its dripping, black frame. "Blake Turner's mother went that way. So did Stacy Adams from the diner."

He started to pet the creature, pleasure filling its eight-eyed face with each heavy stroke.

Hal felt himself going light headed. After everything, this was what proved too much for him.

Glen drawled on, face radiating with joy. "You were the trick to making it hatch… live food. It must have felt you pushing against the womb." He let out a bellowing laugh, the noise of it filling the whole cave. "I can't believe I never thought of it."

"Fuck you, Glen."

Glen glanced over, hand still stroking his child. "How original, Hal. Great insult."

"Yeah… well."

"Well?" sneered Glen.

Fuck you," howled Hal as he rushed forward, his hunting knife still slick with Laura's blood.

"Oh for—"

Glen's sentence was cut off as Hal collided with him, the knife sinking into his ribs where Hal twisted it gleefully.

Glen grunted in pain, struggling to hold onto his child and fend off Hal. "Harold, you… are quite a nuisance," he gave Hal a savage blow to the head, sending him spiraling back into the water.

"Fuck you," spat Hal, tasting both blood and rust in his mouth.

"You know," groaned Glen, limping towards the edge of the pool. "That… that wasn't very nice." He sat wearily on the stone, spider still cradled against his bleeding chest. "But, I think you can make it up to me."

From the cavern behind Glen, bodies started to shuffle in. They bumped against each other with drunk disinterest, a few falling into the water where they splashed about before rising unsteadily.

There were too many to see clearly in the dim sweep of his torch, but Hal still noted a few familiar faces. Sarah Henderson who worked at the bakery and always reeked of cigarettes, Jenna Grandview who used to sit behind Hal in grade ten math, the librarian Linda Howard who always looked stern despite her willingness to shoo away even the most outrageous late fees.

Glen waved a hand towards the crowd of women, each growing a mad grin. "This child is only the first. The first of many." His eyes narrowed, a small smile playing across his face. "All thanks to you, Hal."

Hal was already splashing away as the women piled into the water, floundering bodies pushing each other as they rushed forward.

Their voices trailed him through the tunnels, clouding his brain and making it hard to remember the way to the mine's entrance.

"Make Mother happy. Make Mother happy."

Blake

The end didn't come immediately. Instead of large fangs sinking into his body he felt the warm embrace of webbing, his body twirling as white cocoon enveloped it. He struggled during it, every muscle trying to break free from the creature's embrace, but in the end he found himself dangling in a dark corner of the room, barely able to do more than breathe.

Blake had been afraid—at first—but his tension eased as the spider descended from the ceiling in front of him, hanging upside down with a thin strand of web clutched between its legs and eyes peering intently at Blake. With every passing moment relief flooded him. Bobbi and Sarah got away, that was all that mattered.

Upside down and swinging gently before him, Blake noted how damaged the spider was. Blood dripped from her body in a thick stream, patches of torn flesh pockmarking most of her giant body. One of its legs had been nearly bisected, white bone peeking out from behind dark fur.

"Someone…" Blake paused to cough. Her pincer like feet had bore deep into his shoulders when she snatched him. Even now he could feel his own blood pooling around him and soaking the webbing red. "Someone really did a number on you."

Its eight eyes narrowed, dark head twisting towards him in interest.

You. Amuse me.

Blake shivered. "Jesus."

His hands were pinned near his belt, one of his fingers painfully close to the knife Hal had given him. He inched the finger towards the handle, pushing against the binding encasing him while trying to outwardly hide his struggle.

He tried to relax himself, a weak smile tugging at his lips.

You are happy?

It was an unsettling sound, hearing the creature's voice inside his own mind, but it no longer made him jump. "Yes."

And you think that knife is enough to cut you free?

He froze, the spider's eyes blinked in what might have been mirth.

Amusing.

Blake continued edging his finger towards the hilt, if for no other reason than to spite the thing that had stolen his sister. "Why do you do it?" His finger grazed the thick handle, the blade shifting slightly in the webbing. "Why do you…" He looked at the bodies littering the floor below him. "Abduct people?"

The spider was silent for a moment, bug eyes blinking slowly before him. When it finally spoke, its body deflated with the answer.

Lonely.

"Lonely?" Blake bit his tongue, what could he possibly to say to that?

The creature spun in its place, round body making lazy spirals about the room. When its stomach passed, Blake caught sight of a jagged cut running through the fleshy center.

One friend.... Wanted more. Wanted...

Images of a chubby blond woman playing with two small children flashed through his mind. It was Christmas and they all had Santa hats on. The smallest child was giggling while the bigger one held him down and tickled him. The mother had a wine glass clenched between her fingers and was telling them to stop with a voice implying she didn't truly want them to.

Wanted this.

Blake let out a ragged breath, the knife was in his hands and cutting weakly at the strings around him. "A family?"

Yes.

The spider's mouth opened. Was it... was it smiling?

And now I have one. Children. Living children.

Blood trickled from the creature's mouth, running down its face to join the already thick stream dripping from its body.

A picture of a baby spider, about the size of a cat, splashing in dark water rippled through Blake's mind. He shook his head, but the image lingered, a sense of alien joy accompanying it.

The knife was cutting faster through the webbing, the choking tightness around his chest began to lessen. He felt the spider grow more distracted as another uninvited image of splashing spiders flickered through his brain.

This world. Ours.

She turned her head back to him, gaze focused on Blake who was no longer trying to hide the thrashing of his knife.

You, food for my sweet children.

Blake grimaced at the last words, knife finally breaking through the sack of webbing into the open air. He was still bound but now able to cut more freely at his bonds. The spider rolled its eyes in exasperation.

Pointless, didn't want to.... subdue... you but necessary now. Children should hunt fresh game, but I'll start them off easy.

Blake was nearly free of the binding, body tensing in preparation of the long drop to the floor. The spider reached out a ragged limb, steadying the swinging sac holding Blake.

So much fight. Shame only food. Would add good... genes...

Its face pressing keenly against his, Blake heard rather than saw its mouth open, mandibles stroking his neck and drawing him forward.

Blake thought of his family, his mother was gone, his father was gone, his older sister was gone, his aunt was gone, and soon he would be gone. He'd be gone and Sarah would be left alone. A small twinge of guilt ran through his body at the last thought but it was overridden by his comfort in knowing she would at least survive the day.

Blake closed his eyes. Better to spend his final moments picturing Sally and Sarah, their happy smiles and warm laughs, than gazing into the dark pit of fangs clamping down on him.

What a strange life he'd lived. Short, full of bitterness, but not entirely unhappy. Still, with his eyes gripped shut, waiting for the snapping jaws, he was fine with it ending. He felt a weariness beyond his age and looked forward to its relief. He'd done his best to protect his sister and finally he was being relieved of his struggles.

He didn't fully cognize the gunshot, only noted he was falling.

The floorboards were more welcoming than would be expected, giving a gentle creak as his body flopped onto their worn faces. Blood flooded his mouth but not pain. He heard the spider land beside him, the crack of a bone snapping accompanying its heavy thud.

Lying there on the soft wood, Blake considered keeping his eyes closed. A soft but persuasive voice spoke in his mind, reminding him he didn't have to fight. He felt a warm darkness encircling his mind and the voice lulled him deeper into it. Sleep, rest, freedom from the constant hassles of life, an alluring proposition.

"Blake, what are you doing? Get up."

With slight annoyance, he pushed an eyelid open.

"Jesus, Blake, get moving."

He was facing the spider. Its breathing was heavy, eyes wide in fury as it tried to rise, legs continually slipping inward as if it was standing on a patch of ice. A hole leaked blood into one of the top eyes, causing it to blink spastically as the spider tried to lumber to its feet.

Blake looked past the spider to the figure of Bobbi, her body sticking out of the tiny hole in the floor. She was waving him towards her, the light of her torch spraying about the room from the motion.

Blake grimaced. What was she doing here? She should be getting Sarah away. He spit out blood. It landed on the spider's face, causing it to recoil slightly.

"Blake, COME ON!"

He groaned as he pushed himself up, the spider doing the same. It stood awkwardly on seven legs, one of them hanging limply with a bone poking awkwardly out near one of the joints.

If Bobbi was here, it meant Sarah wasn't safe. He shook his head and took a labouring step forward. He couldn't sleep yet—Sarah wasn't safe.

I'll. Kill.

He started to run, the spider chasing him in an awkward ramble.

Kill.

He watched Bobbi disappear into the hole before him, the light from her torch vanishing to leave Blake near blind in his escape.

Hopping over corpses he neared the porthole, the spider careening wildly behind him.

Kill you. I'll.

He fell, more than jumped, into the hole. Landing at the bottom of the ladder with an impact that caused more blood to spray from his mouth.

Above him the spider screeched, her insectile scream reverberating off the metal machinery and surrounding them. Meters away, Bobbi shuddered before waving him to follow her as she jogged down the stairs.

Blake felt a warm fluid drip onto the top of his head. Looking up he saw the spider trying to squirm its body through the narrow hole, fangs gnashing as a single leg pushed through to claw inches above Blake's head.

"Come on, Blake, we're going," Bobbi called as she descended another flight of rusted stairs.

"But…" murmured Blake, lips trying to articulate the idea his concussed brain had produced. "Why?"

He looked up at the creature, its battered body growing still as it met his gaze. His mind was hazy, clouded with pain and adrenaline, but he realized something Bobbi hadn't. They were winning. It could barely walk, why were they retreating?

From his back he unslung the fire axe, eyes gazing up at the snarling spider.

It blinked in surprise, eyes darting to the shining red axe before it pulled itself from the hole, head vanishing back into the darkness above.

Fine. Sarah then.

Blake took a deep breath and turned to run, calling hoarsely as he did. "Bobbi, where's my sister?"

"I hid her down below. Hurry!"

His leg muscles cramped as he ran, his gait turning lopsided as he descended the rickety metal stairs.

Sarah was on the second floor, sitting against a metal cart filled with dark rocks and dust with her face buried in the top of her knees. When Blake reached her, the spider was already slinking through a missing patch of wall, shaking legs struggling to pull it into the room.

He lifted Sarah, as the spider fully entered the room, a trail of blood staining the walls and floor behind it. One of its eyes was shut, the other seven blinking forebodingly as it tried to steady its shaking body.

Blake ran, the sound of his heavy breathing overtaken by the boom of Bobbi's revolver. She hit the mark, a spray of blood erupting from the spider, but the creature seemed unconcerned. It hunched its legs, mouth clicking in a wheeze of anticipation.

The spider launched ungracefully, its body flying brazenly through the air and crashing into a wall to the right of Bobbi. She fired again, cursing as the pistol once more clicked empty. "Blake," she called. "We gotta go, I don't have more bullets."

The spider wheezed as it rose to unsteady feet.

Sarah's blood.

Blake caught up to Bobbi, pushing his sister into her arms.

Smells...

"Take her."

"Blake, no. We can come back when Sarah's safe."

His blood had started to pump freely again, the little voice encouraging him to sleep was drowning in the torrent of rage filling his mind.

"No, if we don't finish this it might escape."

"Then you take your sister and I'll stay."

"You're terrified of spiders and all we have are axes."

Bobbi bit her lip, eyes flicking to the lumbering arachnid over Blake's shoulder. "Fine," she said flatly.

Blake turned to face the spider, tightening his grip on the cool metal of the axe. The creature rose unsteady, flinching as he took a step forward.

I will drink Sarah. Her tasty blood… …

He struck at its outmost leg, grazing it as the spider retracted it hastily.

You… are… food…. Nothing more.

His second swing caught what might be referred to as a shoulder, digging into the flesh beside the creature's twisting face.

It snarled as he pulled the axe free, a shower of blood spraying out. The creature crouched, eyes ablaze with rage. Blake raised the axe again, poised for the assault.

When it launched, screaming clouded Blake's mind, the sharp metallic of its voice stabbing into his conscious like a knife. There were no words, only a cold hate attempting to smother every inch of his being.

Blake smiled as he swung the axe, the blade dipping into the creature's neck as their bodies collided.

Hal

He was nearing the mineshaft's entrance when the screaming started. The cries of food and loving mother dissolving into one harsh screech of pain and anger. Despite himself, he looked over his shoulder, seeing the mass of bodies following him drop to their knees as they clutched their heads and stomachs.

"What the fuck?" Hal muttered as he sprung onto the metal chute, his wet feet slipping on the slick surface as he attempted to scale upward. The screaming grew ear piercing, drowning out his continuing stream of curses.

The sun was still bright above, its harsh light blinding in comparison to the cool darkness of the mine. As he neared the top, he steadied himself, pausing briefly before jumping off. He collapsed on a bed of shale, finally free from the subterranean labyrinth.

The wailing continued below, dimming slightly as it was funneled through the exit.

Hal took a deep breath, rising with shaking legs. A quick scan of the quarry found it nearly identical to how he had left it, each grey boulder still in place while the surrounding trees continued to sway with leisurely ease. The only difference he could note was where he'd left Dr. Nand and the strange old man. There were now three people instead of two.

He approached cautiously with his knife raised, thankful the caterwauling from the mines grew quieter with each step. As he neared, his eyes adjusted to the unfriendly glare of the summer sun, allowing him to comprehend the scene.

Two lay in the grey dirt, bodies baking in the hot sun. One was slumped forward in a stoic stillness. Hal grimaced as he realized it was Dr. Nand.

He tried to discern what had happen. The old man, recognizable only by the clothes he'd been wearing, had had his face crushed in, checks smothered into the pale gravel beyond recognition.

The body beside him was drenched in blood and wearing clothes so shredded he was practically nude.

"Officer Dawson?" Hal said, jumping back in alarm as the man's eyes shot open.

"Where is it?" croaked Dawson in a voice as ragged as his clothes.

Hal regarded him for a moment before walking over to Dr. Nand, confirming what seemed beyond evident. He dropped his finger from the man's large neck with a sigh, another good citizen of Hope gone.

"I said, where is it," repeated Dawson as he struggled to push himself up, blood dripping from a hundred different gashes.

Hal gave him a piercing look. "Did you do this?"

"Where's is it, you fucking yokel?"

Hal knelt and picked up the rifle Dr. Nand had dropped, still pregnant with the weight of its clip. He squinted through the scope at

Dawson, coolly pulling the bolt back. "I said did you do this?"

Dawson didn't answer, his effort focused on crawling away. His eyes were fixed on the looming mine shaft, fingers making a soft crackle as they clutched and tore at the dirt and rock beneath him.

"I'll kill it," he growled. "I'm… strong."

Hal watched in wonder as the bloodied man pushed himself upwards, part of his shirt falling away to reveal his entire back had been turned into a crisscross of bloody cuts. "I'm…" He gave a strangled cough, bending forward to spit a tooth into the gravel. "I'm the strongest," he continued, wiping his mouth with a bloody arm.

Hal looked down at the slumped body of Dr. Nand, remembering the howls Dawson induce in the basement of the Hope police department. He felt the strong temptation to shoot the man and be done with it.

"Dawson, did you do this?" he called again, voice bouncing off the walls of the quarry.

The man's limp turned into a warbling run, his fists raised as unsteadily before him. "Who is Dawson?" the man laughed. "Oh yes, fake names. How silly. We're strong. Strong shouldn't hide."

Hal frowned. "What are you even talking about, Dawson?"

The man continued lumbering forward, his muscled arms still raised to meet an unseen foe. Hal lowered the rifle, more from contempt than pity.

"Harold?"

Hal's heart leapt as he saw his cousin emerge from the desolate building, a small bundle clutched in her arms. She was sprinting, long legs blurring as they carried her towards him. Hal tried to wave her away from the bodies, but she ignored his gestures and ran directly to him.

"Bobbi, don't... you don't need to see this," he bit his tongue.

Bobbi looked over the corpses with wide eyes, hands rising to push the twisting face of the child in her arms away from the scene. "No...."

Hal sighed, raising the gun so he could peer through the scope at the doorway Bobbi had just exited. "Yes." Finding the entrance empty, he tilted upwards to scan the building but found no other signs of life. "Where's the kid?"

Bobbi was panting, shame tinging her voice as she forced her eyes away from the slouched body of Dr. Nand. "He's still in there. Couldn't." She paused to gulp for air. "Couldn't convince him to follow me."

Hal groaned. After all that, they'd left the teenager alone with it. Very responsible of them.

"Harold?"

"Yes, Bobbi?"

"Who is that?"

Hal didn't need to look to know who she was pointing to.

"Ken Dawson."

Bobbi was silent for a moment. "Did he bring his friends?"

Hal thought back to the crazed look the man had given him when he rose like a vengeful ghost from the pool of blood he'd been sleeping in. "I think he came alone."

"Why so?"

"He doesn't seem…. well."

"Ah."

Dawson had made it to the edge of the pit, shifting his gaze between the hole and the building rising above him.

"In fact, I think he's gone mad."

Sheet metal fell from the building, careening down and nearly slicing Dawson who barely managed to take a step backwards. For a moment he was silent, gazing at his feet before a cry dragged his eyes upwards.

Dawson let out a roar of pleasure as the spider emerged through the newly formed hole, so covered in blood that it slid more than crawled downward from the building.

Hal's voice was incredulous. "It's running away?"

His cousin giggled weakly, her words wavering as she spoke. "Didn't you always tell me they were more afraid of us than we are of them?"

Ken

Finally, his moment of glory. He and the creature would finally meet, both bathed in blood and ready for wonderous battle.

He let out a war cry, a beautiful ode to the strength and glory of his flesh, a testament to his superiority over the feeble creatures of the world. The spider sunk away at his howl, eyes widening in fear of his approach.

Yes, this was his moment, his shining minute of glory when he would truly prove himself as the fittest of god's beings. The apex predator. The man above men. Strong.

Hal

"Jesus Christ, he's running towards it."

Bobbi was rocking Sarah in her arms but stopped to look up. "No."

"Yes."

Through the narrow sight of the scope, Hal could make out the man's facial features as he charged towards the spider, spit spraying from his screaming face. "Jesus Christ."

A choked sob came from the bundle pressed against Bobbi's breast. "Language."

Hal ignored the comment, keeping the scope fixed on Dawson. The creature still had two legs on the wall when the man launched himself at it, arms spread wide as he fell towards the creature's alarmed face.

"Are you going to help him, Harold?"

Hal glanced over at his cousin, her eyes glowering with annoyance. He licked his lips, sure he'd refrained from shooting the man, but was he really obligated to help him now?

Whatever moral debate might have raged in his mind over saving Dawson, the spider ended it before it began. Two massive legs rose to catch the man's leaping body, tossing him into the nearby hole with a flicker of what might have been annoyance.

Hal shrugged. "I guess not, Bobbi."

"What was he even doin— Harold, why aren't you shooting that thing?"

Hal cursed, of course. He pulled the trigger, smoke hissing from the barrel as the bullet rang out across quarry and into the hide of the spider. It was followed by a wail oddly reminiscent of the women's shrieks in the mine.

He pulled the bolt back, a grim smile tugging his lips as he fired again. This would be for Laura.

Ken

The fall didn't kill him, although he wouldn't have been surprised if his afterlife involved being surrounded by women in a dark room.

He'd heard his leg snap from the impact, but he couldn't feel any pain from it. The real injury was to his pride. It was shameful to be pushed away from a fight. What if the cowardly thing ran away before he escaped this pit?

The women had been screaming when he fell in, the howls he'd first noted from above much louder at the bottom of the shaft. They'd shushed now though, spreading out around him in keen interest.

Some of them were naked, most wore ragged clothing. All of them had large bellies and milky white eyes.

The hush continued as he tried to stand, the only noise in the dark hole the panting of his breath and hands scraping on the dark stone beneath him. When he finally managed to rise, leaning heavily on one leg, the whispering started.

It was a low murmur, drifting from deeper down the mines and growing steadily as more and more women added their voices to it.

"Mother says…"

Dawson limped towards the metal chute leading outwards, pushing a tubby blonde woman out of the way to do so. She gave way to the pressure of his hand, but her eyes followed him hungrily as he went.

"Mother says, mother says…" they whispered.

Ken never had nursery rhymes sung to him as a child and his backwards mind imagined they might sound something like this.

"Mother says, mother says."

The whispers grew. Spit struck Ken's face as the women around him pushed the words out. His limp turned into a hop as his broken leg gave out, no longer tolerating even the slightest weight.

"Mother says, mother says," they chanted, voices bellowing about the cavern.

He stopped to leer at the women. Pathetic creatures, pregnant and rotting away in the dark. They would never be strong like him.

"Shut up." He growled the worlds, reaching forward to the metal chute as a stillness overtook the room.

He steadied himself on the railing, praying the spider had not run away in fear of their combat. Soon he would kill it, and then he would know, he would know he was the strongest.

He moved to climb the chute, surprised when a thin hand shot out to stop him. It was chubby, belonging to an equally chubby redhead. "What?" he sneered, icy eyes falling on her dazed face.

"Mother says," she said meekly, pupil-less eyes staring out unblinking.

Dawson laughed and pushed her away, nearly toppling from his one-legged stance with the motion. "Mother says what?"

Another arm reached out to steady him, fingers digging into the exposed flesh of his back. A voice behind him whispered again, "Mother says."

Like a ripple, the words carried out, the surrounding women each repeating the words in their dull, confused voices.

"Mother says..."

"Your mother's a bitch," snapped Dawson. Looking about, it dawned on him for the first time how odd it was that thirty pregnant women were sequestered away in the side of a mountain.

"Mother says... birth... mother says... birth," they chanted.

The arm on his back pulled him backwards, collapsing him on the floor. He let out a cry, more from confusion than fear. The women were pressing forward, crowding around him, their bellies twisting in unnatural directions.

The woman nearest to him–a short girl wearing glasses with no lenses—had a tiny spider leg poking through her stomach. It was cutting at the air, pulling itself towards Ken.

Around him, other legs were appearing, bursting from plump bellies with tiny plops flicking blood and placenta over the room. The women were crowding closer, bending to press their bellies against Ken's shaking body.

No, no. This wasn't right. He should be up there. In the light. Fighting the beast. Showing his dominance.

The popping noises grew louder and more frequent. Football sized spider bodies plunked on Ken's chest and legs, their limbs waving frenziedly from the surprise of their new world.

He could no longer see the light of the sky, his vision clouded by the floundering bodies of women and spiders. He was encased in a mass of them, the cool flesh of the mothers and wet hairy limbs of their children pressed against every inch of his body.

He didn't scream when the first one bit him—tiny teeth tearing into his calf—only shuddered from the thought of his business going unfinished.

Was he destined to die here? Away from the glory of battle, suffocated by lesser beings?

At least the chanting was nice, relaxing him even as he heard part of his throat ripped away.

"Mother says. Mother says."

Ken had never had a mother. At least not one worth the name.

"Mother wants. Mother wants."

He sighed, going limp as the wriggling darkness enveloped him. Maybe it was true some mothers were good, that not all of them were the beacon of inadequacy his own mother had been. This mother was providing for her children, even if it was at the expense of Ken's life.

"Mother says. Mother says."

Blake

The axe shimmered with blood, the metal slippery in Blake's sweaty palms. His breath came in ragged pants, legs aching as he sped towards the exit to the building. The creature had fled, scuttling out down the side of the wall with only his angry curses to chase it.

Frustration flooding his veins at the thought of the thing getting away, going free after what it had done to him, to his mother.

He roared as he burst from the building, the midday sun blinding him as he rushed into the quarry. He could hear the rifle firing, each angry crack followed by a hiss of pain from nearby.

Blake turned to the cry, finding the spider crawling feebly towards the mine entrance. A trail of crimson marked its path through the grey gravel. One of its legs had nearly detached, a single tendon of muscle clinging to an exposed bone.

The rifle discharged again, bullet popping one of its largest eyes like a dart in a balloon. It howled in pain, bloodied mandibles scratching against each other like nails on a chalkboard. Another crack of the rifle made part of its chest explode and splatter Blake with gore and blood as the creature crumpled to the floor.

You... monster...

Blake slowly approached the creature, axe raised.

My children... all for them....

"We're going to kill them next," said Blake, savouring the creature's pained expression.

Feebly, it tried to push itself up, shattered remnants of its jaw gnashing as Blake smiled.

"All of them. Every single one."

The rifle discharged again, bisecting the creature's front leg and causing her chest to slam into the gravel.

My children... Will take revenge... My love... Will raise them.

Blake shook his head. "I already told you, we're not finishing with you."

The spider blinked, eyes shimmering as thick droplets started to fill them.

Please.

Blake, now standing directly affront her, hefted the axe.

Only wanted....

The creature's glistening eyes were covered by his outreaching shadow. "Only wanted what? To kill? To steal?" he said, his own eyes growing wet with each word. "To take my mother?"

Only wanted.... family.

With a snarl, Blake swung the axe down, burying the blade deep into the creature's skull.

Blood and thoughts squirted out from it, both coating Blake. For a moment, the divide between his own mind and the spider's disappeared, their memories intermixing until Blake was unsure where his consciousness started and the hers ended.

Haunting visions of lab coats and cool metallic instruments, of children playing and painful yearning. There were flashes of the man he knew as Glen and the spider knew as her love. The sweet taste of blood filled his mouth while loneliness chilled his heart.

He saw women abducted and raped, only to die in the agony of childbirth, frustration at both the loss of children and the inability to create one permeating his mind. Blake even glimpsed his own mother. Her terror numbing as the spider's sweet venom flooded her body.

The images slowed as the spew of blood from the creature's brain turned into a drizzle. A spatter of foggy half remembrances of childhood play and tiny dolls fading into each other as Blake felt the boundaries of his own mind weakly reform.

Their last shared thought was of family. A foreign concept to both of them, as if they'd pieced together its meaning from a collection of incomplete dictionaries. It was accompanied by longing, an insatiate hunger rotting both of their souls.

I just wanted… family.

Blake was lying on the ground, the swirling images of scientists and webs slowly replaced by the blue sky and glaring sun.

He could hear Hal's worried cries, "Blake? What happened? Are you alright?"

Blake groaned, the weight of the day and his life pushing him down deeper into the sweet embrace of the quarries sun warmed rock bed.

Rocks scattered as Hal skidded to a stop over to Blake, panting with the rifle slung around his shoulder. "What happened? You just collapsed."

Blake scrunched his eyes, trying to order his thoughts and expel the foreign ones. "I'm just… I'm just a little exhausted."

Hal smiled weakly, reaching down to heave Blake to his weary feet. "We should move away from the mine entrance," he said with a bitter laugh. "Wouldn't want to fall in, would we?"

Blake's legs were weak, carrying him like a drunk ghost towards the edge of the quarry. When he finally collapsed against a warm boulder, his sister ran over and hugged him, wordlessly snuggling into the welcome fold of his arms.

He was aware, distantly, of the bodies nearby. Two figures sitting far too still in the midday heat. Blake felt another piece of his heart chip away when he finally forced himself to look closer, eyes only able to linger for a moment over Dr. Nand's still body.

With a sigh, Blake shut his eyes, listening to rushed whispers of Bobbi and Hal.

"I'm telling you, Bobbi, there was at least thirty of them down there."

"And Glen?"

"And Glen. Bastard. But what are we going to do?"

"You said you got him."

"I did get him good, yeah."

"How good?"

Hal sighed. "I saw a lot of blood."

"Enough to be fatal?"

Blake cracked an eyelid to catch Hal's drawn expression. "Enough to be fatal but not enough to be sure," he said after a moment's consideration.

Bobbi went silent, foot tapping as she pushed a dirty hand through her mousy hair. The large revolver poked out from the waist of her dirt spattered jeans.

"We could wait," she said finally.

Hal nodded. "I guess so."

Hal

Day turned to dusk and dusk turned to the thick black of night. They lit up the quarry with a bonfire, kindled from wood Hal chopped from the nearby forest and the body of the spider, its massive carcass dragged over by a groaning Blake and Hal. Bobbi watched over them with the rifle, ready for anything that might erupt from the hole during their labour.

They took turns pretending to sleep during the night, keen gazes falling over the portal to the mine while their ears craned for the slightest hint of a living creature.

They saw and heard nothing.

They'd brought food—survival bars and water—and ate it with quiet acceptance in the morning. Sarah was the only one to speak, finally coming from her dazed shell enough to mutter something about wanting chocolate.

The sun rose, the second day hotter than the first. They scorched in the quiet quarry, unwilling to speak or acknowledge their precarious situation.

No one debated leaving, the only discussion they held over whether they should cover the bodies of Dr. Nand and the elderly scientist. This was followed by an even shorter argument between Bobbi and Hal regarding who would break the news to Sophia.

After this, Hal sunk fuming into the mound of rocks he'd inhabited for the past day. "Fine. I get it. My friend and colleague, not yours."

Night fell over them with a suffocating stillness. The mine as devoid of the nighttime whistles of bats and owls as it was of the daytime songs of birds and squirrels.

They lit another fire, this one made solely from wood, and set about watching the hole again. This night there were no question of taking turns watching, each person keenly aware of their inability to sleep and instead choosing to quietly sit up together with guns and axes clenched. Even Sarah stayed awake, head resting on Blake's lap with little eyelids peeled while her pupils danced in the firelight.

"THERE!"

It was Hal who raised the alarm but they all saw it. With mouths open they watched as the writhing black cloud poured out from the mine.

Bobbi fired indiscriminately into the thick mass, each spider she killed doing little to slow the tangled herd of dark legs. Hal and Blake stood beside her, axes raised menacingly. Sarah hugged her brother's legs, unwilling to look at the swarm.

Bobbi's voice was hoarse over the crack of the rifle. "There's so many."

A few of them broke away from the mob to charge at the group, hissing angrily at the people who had killed their mother, only to be quickly bisected by the swing of Hal's axe.

Bobbi's voice shook, equal parts anger and sorrow. "How many women did he have down there?"

"I told you, it was at least thirty," said Hal tepidly, sweating as he pulled the axe from the body of one of the things.

The rifle clicked, its final bullet spent. Bobbi cursed and lowered it to her knee, watching in horror as the dark blob passed over the quarry sides and into the open embrace of the forest.

Hal whistled. "Shit."

Blake lowered his axe, petting his sister's head. "Language," he murmured, eyes trapped in the twisting shadows of the tree line.

They stayed another day. Each knowing it was unnecessary given the exodus of their prey but enduring it out of a sense of obligation none could vocalize.

They only took Dr. Nand's body with them, leaving the old man to the elements. Hal asked Blake if he wanted to retrieve his mother, but he'd only shaken his head, lips pursing as he tugged his sister towards the quarry's edge.

Hal drove, the body of Dr. Nand bouncing in the trunk with less dignity than the grand man deserved.

Sarah fell asleep first, seatbelt digging into her armpit as she tried to lay on Blake in the cramped confines of the backseat. Bobbi was next, head tilting forward as the drowsiness of two days' wakefulness finally overcame her.

The quiet roads lulled Blake's eyes closed, the soft invite of a deserved sleep washing over his weary mind. It was a peaceful sleep, devoid of any thoughts of whispering spiders, filled only with his family. Sarah, Sally, and his mother laughing at the carnival. They watched a puppet show as Sarah took her first ever bite of cotton candy, eyes widening in delight as her tongue tasted its sugary softness.

It was a pleasant dream but fleeting. Like most happy moments in Blake's life, it was ending before he'd even realized it had begun.

Glen

Glen shivered, as much a result of the blood loss as the chilly air blowing through the dark tunnels. He could no longer walk, collapsing against the jetting side of a tunnel and enshrouded in darkness.

At first his children had comforted him, nuzzling him and warming him as he sobbed and screamed over the death of their mother. It was pleasant to know his children cared for him, a glimmer of pleasure in his grief which only evaporated with the first bite.

They were hungry, Christ he was too, and had already long devoured the bodies of their surrogate mothers. Glen was vaguely aware he shouldn't be angry with them, they were newborns after all. Teething more than anything. Still, he crushed them with impunity, tearing limbs from the squealing body any child that dared to bite its loving father.

Once they realized he was inedible, they left. Eschewing Glen's love for the grander exploration of the outside world.

It wasn't until the third day that he ate one of his own babies. Hunger driving him to sink his teeth into the newborn's bloated body.

It disgusted him, the feeling of eating his own young. Even his children had left the bodies of their siblings, preferring to seek new habitats than eat their own brothers and sisters. Glen choked down his children's raw flesh with seething anger.

He would kill Hal. He would kill him and his wife. After, he would kill Bobbi and the boy, torturing them until he grew bored of their screams and mercifully ended their existences.

Days passed. His diet of spider young ebbed some strength back into him, but he remained unable to rise. He passed the time in mourning, thoughts drifting between desolation at the loss of his love and rage at the thought of the ones who had killed her.

"Brof... fer...."

Glen's eyes snapped open. "Oh, thank Christ." He tried to stretch his mind out, calling to the creature in the way his love had taught him. He found his power to do so had grown weaker in the days since her death, his mental commands only scraping the edge of his brother's tattered mind.

"Get over here, you fucking idiot! Help me up."

"Broffer... where... mommy?"

Glen groaned as his weight shifted to send pain shooting through his body. "She's dead. Come here."

His brother emerged before him. Naked and plastered with filth and blood, what looked like a bullet hole had festered around the boy's emaciated shoulder.

"Dead?" he whimpered.

"Gone, fucking gone," snapped Glen. "Now help me up."

His brother swayed before him, eyes as dull as the rockface behind him. "I want. Mommy."

Glen sighed. They should have killed the boy when he was seven, but instead they'd kept him as a pet. The first true member of their family.

"I want Mommy too. Now help me." He groaned as a stab of pain shot up from his stomach. "The fuck up."

His brother knelt in front of Glen, the unmistakable stench of gangrene wafting from him. "I'm hungry broffer. Where Mommy?" His voice grew louder. "Where Mommy?"

Glen reached out to his brother, hand gripping a clammy shoulder. "Help me out of here."

Glen gasped as the boy shook his head, it was a human movement he hadn't exhibited in years. "Where is…" He scrunched his face as if struggling to find the words, "Mommy?"

"She's dead," answered Glen. "Gone. Forever."

His brother's face contorted, a dizzy anguish playing over his milky white eyes. "Dead? Mommy dead?"

"Yes, now help—"

"Why Mommy dead?"

"What?"

"WHY MOMMY DEAD!"

Glen went still, trying frantically to soothe his brother with his mind, annoyed by the erratic flow of his thoughts and his own severely diminished ability to communicate telepathically.

Years of mother's milk, as Glen called it, should have eradicated his ability to feel rage towards Glen. Numbing his mind into a submissiveness that made him a far more ideal brother than the whining creature he'd been as a child.

"I SAID WHY MOMMY DEAD!"

"She just is, okay? Now help me up. I don't want to bleed out in a fucking hole in the—"

Horror filled him as he watched his brothers jaw descended, falling nearly to his chest as inhuman bones dethatched to allow a long tongue to slither from his mouth.

"BAD BROFFER!"

Glen let out a scream, a harsh shriek quickly lost in the twisting caverns of the mine. With horror he felt his brother's abnormal jaw clamp around his neck. The last sound he heard was the snapping of his own neck.

"BAD BROFFER!"

Epilogue

Winter in Hope meant one thing: rain. Blake, and the site he was working on, were drenched. This particular deluge had started an hour ago and didn't appear to be ending any time soon.

With a sigh, Blake put down his wrench. Wiping beads of water from his eyes, he checked his watch. It was large and electronic, costing more than a month's rent. He'd bought it for himself after finishing his apprenticeship. It served as both a reward for his hard work and as a promise to value his time wisely.

5:01 read its sharp face.

"Hey, Jimmy," he called, making the round contractor look up from the broken pipe he'd been toiling over. "I'm going home."

Jim pushed his yellow hardhat up to scratch his bald spot. He chewed his words before he spoke, his sopping moustache curling when his lips finally parted. "You know," he said slowly. "We need this water main repaired A-S-A-P."

"If people need water, they can look at the sky and open their mouths," said Blake, marching through the mud and puddles to grab his lunchbox.

Jim spat. "Heh, guess you're right, kid. Still, sure you don't want the over time?"

Blake shook his head. "I'm good, sir."

"Sir?" said Jim, eyes rolling. "Christ, been long time since someone called me sir."

"People in this town have bad manners."

"That they do," said Jim as he straightened up. "Is she cute?" he asked, squinting at Blake through the downpour.

Blake grinned. "The cutest."

Jim shook his head and spit again, turning back to his labour. "Well then, get on out of here."

The smile clung to Blake's face the whole drive home. Overpaid and underworked, becoming a plumber was the best decision he'd ever made.

His house was on the outskirts of Hope, four bedrooms and two baths with a large kitchen and even larger yard. A tall willow tree loomed over the driveway, its tendril like branches rippling gently as rain and wind spattered them. The lights were on, glowing against the quickly darkening sky.

Blake whistled as he tread up the steps to his porch. Sarah had recently got into baking and he hoped she'd decided to make some more of the brownies he loved.

"Sarah," he called, ripping off a muddy boot in the entrance hall. "I'm home."

His voice echoed off the walls, carrying through the house unmet with response.

"Sarah?" he called again, sighing as he reached into his pocket for the never absent knife. "Are you here?"

Faintly, in a distant corner of the house, a giggle rang out. Blake sighed and walked toward it.

The door to her room was closed, a boy band poster stapled to the wood frame covered by a smaller sign reading KEEP OUT. Blake pushed his ear against the door, knife gripped firmly in his hand.

He heard something crunching, accompanied by another giggle.

"Yummy, yummy."

Outwardly his sister was fine, at fifteen she was taller than him and a menace on the volleyball court where she spent most of her nights treading. Her friends and teachers adored her, all more than willing to share with Blake their surprise on how a girl without parents could turn out so cheerful.

The crack of a bone snapping rang out, followed by heavy slurping. With a sigh Blake turned from the doorway, replacing the knife in his pocket and walking to the kitchen to fix himself a drink.

His after-work drink of choice was an expensive scotch on the rocks, another luxury of his newfound upper middle-class lifestyle. As he swished the first sip of spirit in his mouth, he mulled over what to do about his sister.

Before Hal had moved to Kamloops to be closer with his son, he'd told Blake to avoid a psychiatrist. Psychiatrists bought questions and questions led to people discovering things better left unknown.

Things like the fact that Hal and Blake had buried the bodies of Blake's aunt and her boyfriend up near Ladner Creek, or that they were the ones who dumped Dr. Nand's corpse in the entrance to the Hope ER ten years ago.

Worse still, the psychiatrist might tell other people about the strange story he'd unearthed, possibly bringing the attention of whatever organization had been trying to capture the creature Blake and Hal only referred to as *her*.

Sure, they appeared to have left Hope, evidenced by a mysterious "electrical fire" burning down the RCMP detachment shortly after *the incident*. But you could never be too safe. For all Blake knew they could still be watching him and his sister, monitoring them for signs of *abnormality*.

Blake drained the rest of his glass, quickly refilling it when he heard the door to his sister's room crack open.

"Blakey," she whimpered from down the hall. "It happened again."

He took another long gulp. Hal was right, better not to get a shrink involved, better to hide their problems like the rest of the world.

He met his sister in the hall, wiping a strand of cat dander from her glistening red lips with his free hand. "It's alright, Sarah, I'm here."

"Why," she moaned, pushing a tangle of blonde hair form her eyes. "Why does this keep happening, Blakey?"

Blake hugged his sister, letting her bury her wet face into his shoulder. "It's alright, Sarah, it's alright."

"It was Ms. Jameson's cat," she whimpered. "Blakey… what are we going to tell her?"

Blake stroked her hair, pausing to take another sip of his scotch before replying. "We'll tell her coyotes must have got it. Now go wash up. I'll make us supper."

"I'm not..." Sarah looked up in shame, lips trembling as she finished. "Okay." With another sigh, she pulled away from her brother, head downcast as she marched to the washroom.

Blake made pasta while she showered, enjoying the patter of rain on the roof as he did so. He didn't hear her emerge from the washroom, only felt her eyes on his back. He turned, finding her fresh faced and wrapped in a white towel.

He shivered at her expression, his hand absently dipping into his pocket for the handle of his knife. He held it tightly until the moment passed, the hungry look on her face replaced by a dazed smile.

She looked about in confusion for a moment, as if only now realizing where she was and shaking her head before disappearing through the swinging door to her room. With a sigh Blake let go of the knife handle, once more reaching for the bottle of scotch.

Everyone has problems, he reminded himself while taking yet another long sip. Christ, Bobbi had to move because every flickering shadow gave her an anxiety attack. His problems were strange but no worse than other people's.

He stirred the pasta, extracting a tiny noodle to taste test as he finished.

His sister remerged from her room, wearing jeans and an old volleyball jersey. "It's almost ready, Sarah," he called.

"Whatever," she said absently, her long frame sinking into a kitchen chair.

Blake ate another noodle, nodding approvingly before removing the pot from the stove top. "It tastes good. Grab a plate."

"I told you," said Sarah in aggravation. "I'm not… I'm full."

Blake set a plate in front of her. "It's okay, Sarah. I'm only asking you to pretend."

"Pretend?" she said dully.

Blake nodded with an encouraging smile. Sarah pretended she wasn't full, he pretended she didn't eat cats and rodents in strange trances—it was how they went about their lives.

"Blakey," she said quietly, eyes plastered to the floor. "You'll lock your door tonight, right?"

Blake reached out to put an arm on her shoulder, rubbing it gently before picking up a fork to eat. "Of course."

He didn't add "I always do," instead he tucked eagerly into his pasta, a smile drawing across his face as he chewed. Even with all the pretending, their life wasn't so bad.

END

About Your Author

Ty Greenwood is a high school English and Psychology teacher based in Melbourne, Australia. When he is not busy grading papers he is writing and reading.

If you wish to learn more about Ty you can follow him on twitter at https://twitter.com/tygreenwood94

Other HellBound Books, Available at: www.hellboundbooks.com

Shopping List 3

By popular demand, the third volume in our bestselling anthology series, twenty-one spine-chilling, terrifyingly creepy tales of terror by a bunch of the best independent horror authors writing today!

Featuring horror stories - and shopping lists - from: Richard Raven, Dhinoj Dings, Jeremy Thompson, Jeremy Wagner, Nick Manzolillo, Steve Stark, Jeff C. Stevenson, Kevin McHugh, James Watts, Don Jones, Nick Swain, Mark Thomas, Brian McGowan, Jason Gelehrt, Mark Deloy, Richard Barber, Sergio Palumbo, Megan E. Morales, Angela Thornton, JN Cameron, and David Simon

The Synagogue Horror

Rabbi Avrum Steinberg is so much more than just a horror movie loving rabbi of a small, run-down synagogue on New York City's Lower East Side - he is also a small time private eye, albeit with cases no more exhilarating than locating debtors and errant, deadbeat husbands. Following the bizarre murder of a young woman in his synagogue, Steinberg begins to suspect that a vampire may be loose in New York, and before long, his suspicions are proven true. It takes the help of Wilomena - a young, mysterious, African-American minister - to help the rabbi hunt down the infamous Count Dracula himself, who is holed up in an abandoned subway tunnel beneath the City's bustling sidewalks. In their perilous and terrifying journey, the rabbi and Wilomina are joined by a band of elderly Kabbalists and Steinberg's son, and along the way the vampire hunters encounter zombies, fallen angels, some familiar vampires, and even a ghost or two. This unique urban vampire story pits the powers of faith against an ancient, dark power of evil - proving once again, that dispatching the master vampire is by far no easy task.

Made in Britain

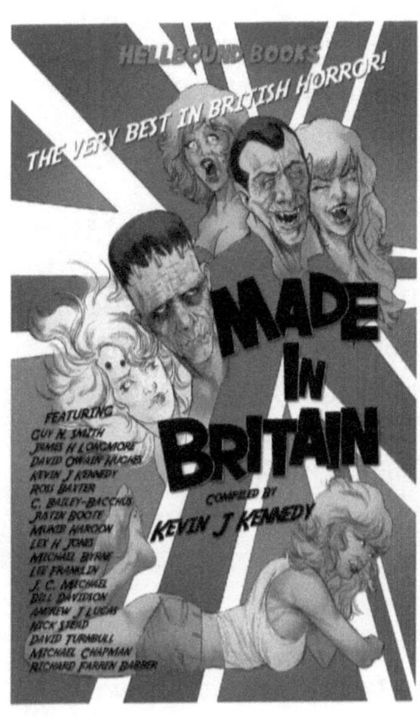

There is something quite special about this fine collection of tales of terror from the Sceptered Isle, each and every one crafted in the dead of the night by twisted, fevered minds, who have brought crawling and slithering to life the darkest denizens of the blackest shadows to terrify those brave souls amongst you who are brave enough to read...

For your delectation, Dear Reader, we have assembled together between these illustrious covers an array of the finest British authors writing today:

Guy N. Smith, James H Longmore, David Owain Hughes, Kevin J Kennedy, Ross Baxter, C. Bailey-Bacchus, Justin Boote, Munib Haroon, Lex H Jones, Michael Byrne, Lee Franklin, J. C. Michael, Bill Davidson, Andrew J Lucas, Nick Stead, David Turnbull, Michael Chapman, Richard Farren Barber

I'll Come Back to Get You

In the midst of a Manhattan heat wave, Adel Daniels' husband doesn't return home from work. A few days later, she receives a Polaroid of him; on the bottom of the photograph are the words I'll Come Back to Get You, on the back is written their six-year-old son's name - is he the ransom, or the kidnapper's next target?

Assistant Chief Detective Steve Willards heads up the task force assigned to the case, along with FBI Profiler Gail Skillman. They quickly learn that every person involved has a secret, and the truth is only as reliable as memory.

A week later, Penny Spencer's husband Graham, doesn't return from work and she receives a Polaroid of her husband - on the bottom of the photo is written, One, Two, Don't Be Blue, I'll Come Back to Get You; their son's name is written on the back.

Before Willards and Skillman can unravel the motivation of the twisted kidnapper, one person is murdered, a third adult is taken, and one of the children is abducted.

But, it isn't until an assault is made on the FBI profiler that the final pieces fall into place; but even then it may be too late for those who have read the words - I'll Come Back to Get You.

Them

Ray Sanders returns home from Florida to bury his mother.

Soon, the supernatural evidence behind his mother's demise begins to surface in the form of dreams and mysterious happenings.

During all of the madness, Sanders must face his destiny and vanquish the generations-old evil that has plagued his family since the 1800's…

In 1854, Louis Sanders, with the help of Elias Atkins, dug a well to provide water to the family farm. What they did not anticipate was the water to be infested with Odomulites - ancient sins. These malevolent beings - were trapped in our world on their way to the spirit world - formed a pact of protection with both Sanders and Atkins; the families would serve as guardians of the Odomulite nests and in return, a blind eye would be cast when the Odomulites took host bodies to inhabit and feed upon. It was this pact, which in 2016 would propel Sanders and Julie Fontaine - a young woman with a special connection to the Spirit World - into the heart of the last active nest to rid the town of its insidious Odomulite population.

A HellBound Books LLC
Publication

http://www.hellboundbookspublishing.com

Printed in the United States of America

www.ingramcontent.com/pod-product-compliance
Lightning Source LLC
Chambersburg PA
CBHW032155180726
48284CB00001B/49